THE SKIN MAP

Other Books by Stephen R. Lawhead

King Raven Trilogy:
Hood
Scarlet
Tuck

Patrick, Son of Ireland

Celtic Crusades:
The Iron Lance
The Black Rood
The Mystic Rose

Byzantium

Song of Albion Trilogy:
The Paradise War
The Silver Hand
The Endless Knot

The Pendragon Cycle:
Taliesin
Merlin
Arthur
Pendragon
Grail
Avalon

Empyrion I: The Search for Fierra
Empyrion II: The Siege of Dome

Dream Thief

The Dragon King Trilogy:
In the Hall of the Dragon King
The Warlords of Nin
The Sword and the Flame

BRIGHT EMPIRES **QUEST THE FIRST:**

THE SKIN MAP

STEPHEN R. LAWHEAD

LION FICTION

To find out more about Stephen R. Lawhead
visit: www.stephenlawhead.com
or: www.facebook.com/StephenRLawhead

Text copyright © Stephen R. Lawhead 2011
This edition © Lion Hudson 2013

The right of Stephen Lawhead to be identified as the
author of this work has been asserted by him in accordance
with the Copyright, Designs and Patents Act 1988.

Published by Lion Fiction
an imprint of
Lion Hudson plc
Wilkinson House, Jordan Hill Road,
Oxford OX2 8DR, England
www.lionhudson.com/fiction

ISBN 978 1 78264 013 4
e-ISBN 978 1 78264 026 4

Acknowledgments
Cover design © 2010 Thomas Nelson, Inc.

A catalogue record for this book is available from the
British Library

Printed and bound in the UK, February 2013, LH26

'Why is the Universe so big?
Because we are here!'

JOHN WHEELER, PHYSICIST

Part I

The Old Straight Track

CHAPTER 1

In Which Old Ghosts Meet

Like most Londoners, Kit endured the daily travails of navigating a city whose complexities were legendary. And, like many of his fellow city dwellers, he did so with a fortitude and resilience the ancient Spartans would have admired. He knew well the dangers even the most inconsequential foray could involve; venturing out into the world beyond his doorstep was the urban equivalent of trial by combat, and he armed himself as best he could.

Kit had long ago learned his small patch of the great metropolitan sprawl; he knew where the things most needful for survival were to be found and how to get to them. He kept a ready-reference library of street maps, bus routes, and time schedules in his head. He had memorized the London Underground tube schematic; he knew the quickest ways to work, and from work to his favourite pubs, the grocer's, the cinema, the park.

Kit prided himself on his ability not only to weather the storms of chaos the Gods of Transport routinely hurled into his path, but to prevail, to conquer in the face of daunting adversity. Sadly, it was pride misplaced. His record of success was not good.

This morning was a perfect example: only minutes before, he had stepped out of the door of his flat in Hackney on a jaunt to accompany his girlfriend on a long-promised shopping trip. Full of optimism and brimming with confidence, he had proceeded to the nearest station, swiped his Oyster card at the turnstile, stormed onto the platform as the train came rattling in, and leaped aboard bare seconds before the doors closed. He counted off his three stops and then switched onto the Victoria line.

'All passengers must disembark,' rasped a voice through crackling loudspeakers. 'This train is terminated.' The line was closed ahead for routine maintenance.

Joining the grumbling pack, Kit was directed once again to street level where a special bus had been provided for Tube users to continue their journey. The fact that it was Sunday – and that Tottenham Hotspur was playing Arsenal – had completely slipped his mind. One look at the queue of Tottenham fans stretching halfway down the street, however, and he quickly came up with a better plan: just nip across the road and take the train one stop further, switch to the Piccadilly Line, then get off at Turnpike Lane; from there it would be a quick bus ride down West Green Road. A brisk walk through Chestnuts Park would bring him to Wilhelmina's place. *Easy peasy*, he thought as he dived back into the station.

Once again, Kit fished his Oyster card from his pocket and flapped it at the turnstile. This time, instead of the green arrow, the light on the pad flashed red. Aware of the foot traffic already piling up behind him, he swiped the travel card again and was awarded with the dreaded 'Seek Assistance' notice. *Terrific*, he sighed inwardly, and began backing through the queue to the scorn and muttered abuse of his fellow travellers, most of whom were dressed in football jerseys of one kind or another. 'Sorry,' he grumbled, fighting his way through the press. 'Excuse me. Terribly sorry.'

He hurried to the nearest ticket window only to find that it was closed; he saw another on the far side of the station and, after negotiating an obstacle course of barriers and hoardings, he arrived to discover there was no one around. He pounded on the window and after a minute or two managed to rouse the attendant.

'My Oyster card needs topping up,' Kit explained.

'You can do it online,' replied the agent.

'But I'm here now,' Kit pointed out, 'in person.'

'It's cheaper online.'

'That is as may be,' Kit agreed. 'But I have to travel now – today. Can't I just pay?'

'You can pay at a ticket window.'

'The ticket window is closed.'

The attendant gazed at him pityingly. 'It's Sunday.'

'What's that got to do with it?' enquired Kit.

'Early closing on Sunday.'

'It's barely nine o'clock in the morning!' cried Kit. 'How early do they close?'

The attendant shrugged. 'There's a ticket machine. You can use that.'

'Okay, okay,' said Kit, accepting this set-back. Down on the platform below, he could hear the train clattering in, and hurried to the ticket machine – which, after repeated attempts, refused to accept his five pound note, spitting it out each time. The next machine along was out of change, and the next was out of service. Kit ran back to the ticket window. 'I don't have any change,' he said, sliding the fiver through the gap in the window. 'And the ticket machine won't take my money.'

The attendant regarded the crumpled note. 'This isn't a ticket window.'

'I know that,' replied Kit. 'I just need change for the machine.'

'We're not allowed to give change.'

'Why not?'

'This is an information window. We only give out information.'

'You're kidding.'

The attendant shrugged. Directing his gaze past Kit, he called, 'Next!' – although there was no one in line.

Admitting temporary defeat, Kit made his way back to the street. There were numerous shops where he might have changed a five pound note – if not for the fact that it was Sunday and all were either observing weekend hours, or closed for the day. 'Typical,' huffed Kit, and decided that it would be easier and no doubt faster just to walk the three miles. With this thought in mind, he sailed off, dodging traffic and Sunday-morning pedestrians in the sincere belief that he could still reach Mina's on time. He proceeded along Grafton Street, mapping out a route in his head as he went. He had gone but half a mile when he hit upon a short-cut that would shave a good twenty minutes off his route. All he had to do was work his way across Islington through the back streets. He turned onto the first street east, tooled along splendidly, quickly reaching the next street north which took him to a main east–west thoroughfare which he followed until he came to an odd little street called Stane Way.

So far, so good, he thought as he charged down the narrow walkway that was really nothing more than an alley providing service access for the shops on the parallel streets. After walking for two minutes, he started looking for the crossing street at the end. Two more minutes passed… he should have reached the end by now, shouldn't he?

Then it started to rain.

Kit picked up his speed as the rain poured into the alley from low, swirling clouds overhead. He hunched his shoulders, put his head down, and ran. A wind rose out of nowhere and whipped down the length of the blank brick canyon, driving the rain into his eyes.

He stopped.

Pulling his phone from his pocket, he flipped open the screen. No signal.

'Bloody useless,' he muttered.

Drenched to the skin, water dripping from the ends of his hair and tip of his nose, he shoved the phone back into his pocket. Enough of this, he decided. Abort mission. He made a swift about-face and, shoes squelching with every step, headed back the way he had come. Good news: the wind ceased almost at once and the rain dwindled away; the storm diminished as quickly as it had arisen.

Dodging one oily puddle after another, he jogged along and had almost regained the alley entrance at Grafton Street when he heard someone calling him – at least, he thought that was what he had heard. But, with the spatter of rain from the eaves of the buildings round about, he could not be sure.

He slowed momentarily and, a few steps later, he heard the call again – unmistakable this time: 'Hello!' came the cry. 'Wait!'

Keep moving, said the voice inside his head. As a general rule it kept him from getting tangled in the craziness of London's vagrant

11

community. He glanced over his shoulder to see a white-haired man stumbling towards him out of the damp urban canyon. Where had he come from? Most likely a drunk who had been sleeping it off in a doorway. Roused by the storm, he had seen Kit and recognized an easy mark. Such was life; he prepared to be accosted.

'Sorry, mate,' Kit called back over his shoulder as he turned away. 'I'm skint.'

'No! Wait!'

'No change. Sorry. Got to run.'

'Cosimo, please.'

That was all the vagrant said, but it welded Kit to the spot.

He turned and looked again at the beggar. Tall, and with a full head of thick silvery hair and a neatly trimmed goatee, he was dressed in charity-shop style: simple white shirt, dark twill trousers, both sturdy, but well worn. The fact that he stuffed the cuffs of his trousers into his high-top shoes, and wore one of those old-timey greatcoats that had a little cape attached to the shoulders made him look like a character out of Sherlock Holmes.

'Look, do I know you?' asked Kit as the fellow hastened nearer.

'I should hope so, my boy,' replied the stranger. 'One would think a fellow would know his own great-grandfather.'

Kit backed away a step.

'Sorry I'm late,' continued the old man. 'I had to make certain I wasn't followed. It took rather longer than I anticipated. I was beginning to fear I'd missed you altogether.'

'Excuse me?'

'So, here we are. All's well that ends well, what?'

'Listen, mate,' protested Kit. 'I think you've got the wrong guy.'

'What a joy it is to meet you at long last, my son,' replied the old gentleman, offering his hand. 'Pure joy. But of course, we haven't properly met. May I introduce myself? I am Cosimo Livingstone.' He made a very slight bow.

'Okay, so what's the joke?' demanded Kit.

'Oh, it is no joke,' the old man assured him. 'It's quite true.'

'No – you're mistaken. *I* am Cosimo Livingstone,' he insisted. 'And anyway, how do you know my name?'

'Would you mind very much if we discussed this walking? We really should be moving along.'

'This is nuts. I'm not going anywhere with you.'

'Ah, well, I think you'll find that you don't have much choice.'

'Not true.'

'Sorry?'

'Listen, mate, I don't know how you got hold of my name, but you must have me mixed up with someone else,' Kit said, hoping to sound far more composed than he actually felt at that moment. 'I don't mean to be rude, but I don't know you and I'm not going anywhere with you.'

'Fair enough,' replied the stranger. 'What would it take to change your mind?'

'Forget it,' said Kit, turning away. 'I'm out of here.'

'What sort of proof would you like? Names, birthdates, family connections – that sort of thing?'

He started off. 'I'm not listening.'

'Your father is John. Your mother is Harriet. You were born in Weston-super-Mare, but your family soon moved to Manchester where your father worked as a managerial something or other in the insurance trade and your mother was a school administrator. When you were twelve your family upped sticks again and resettled in London…'

Kit halted. He stood in the middle of the alley wrestling with the twin sensations of alarm and disbelief. He turned around slowly.

The old man stood smiling at him. 'How am I doing so far?'

Even in the uncertain light of the alley, the family resemblance was unmistakable – the strong nose, the heavy jaw and broad brow, the hair that rippled like waves from the forehead, the broad lips and dark eyes – just like his father and obnoxious Uncle Leonard – it was all of a basic design that Kit had seen repeated with greater or lesser variation in family members all his life.

'Since university – Manchester, Media Studies, whatever *that* is – you have been working here and there, doing nothing of any real value –'

'Who are you?' demanded Kit. 'How do you know these things?'

'But I've already told you,' chuckled the old gentleman. 'I am your great-grandfather.'

'Oh, yeah? Would this be the great-grandfather who went down to the shops for a loaf of bread one morning and never came back? The same one who abandoned a wife and three kids in Marylebone in 1893?'

'Dear me, you know about that, do you? Well, lamentably, yes. But it wasn't a loaf of bread, it was milk and sausages.' The old man's gaze grew keen. 'Tell me, what did *you* go out for this morning?'

Kit's mouth went dry.

'Hmm?' replied the stranger. 'What was it? Tin of beans? Daily paper? This is how it always happens, don't you see?'

'No…' said Kit feeling more unhinged by the second.

'It's a family proclivity, you might say. A talent.' The older man took a step nearer. 'Come with me.'

'Why, in the name of everything that's holy, would I go anywhere with you?'

'Because, my dear boy, you are a lonely 27-year-old bachelor with a worthless education, a boring no-hope job, a stalled love life, and very few prospects for the improvement of your sad lot.'

'How dare you! You don't know anything about me.'

'But I know *everything* about you, old chap.' The old man took another step closer. 'I thought we had already established that.'

'Yeah? What else?'

The elder gentleman sighed. 'I know that you are an overworked drone in a soul-destroying cube farm where you have been passed over for promotion two times in the last nine months. The last time you don't know about, because they didn't even bother telling you.'

'I don't believe this.'

'You spend too much time alone, too much time watching television, and too little time cultivating the inner man. You live in a squalid little flat in what is referred to as a no-go zone from which your friends, of whom you see less and less, have all fled for the suburbs long ago with wives and sprogs in tow. You are exceedingly unlucky in love, having invested years in a romantic relationship

14

which, as you know only too well, is neither romantic nor much of a relationship. In short, you have all the social prospects of a garden gnome.'

Kit gaped in amazement. Except for the low crack about his love life, the old geezer was remarkably close to the mark.

'Is that enough?'

'Who *are* you?'

'I'm the man who has come to rescue you from a life of quiet desperation and regret.' He smiled again. 'Come, my boy, let's sit down over a cup of coffee and discuss the matter like gentlemen. I've gone to a very great deal of trouble to find you. At the very least, you could spare me a few minutes out of your busy life.'

Kit hesitated.

'Cup of coffee – thirty minutes. What could it hurt?'

Trepidation and curiosity wrestled one another for a moment. Curiosity won. 'Okay,' he relented. 'Twenty minutes.'

The two started walking towards the street. 'I've got to call my girlfriend and tell her I'll be a little late,' Kit said, pulling out his phone. He flipped it open and pressed the speed-dial key for Mina's number. When nothing happened, he glanced at the screen to see the 'Network Not Connected' message blinking at him. He waved the phone in the air, then looked again. Still no tiny bars indicating a signal.

'Not working?' asked the older man, watching him with a bemused expression.

'Must be the buildings,' mumbled Kit, indicating the close brick walls on either side. 'Blocking the signal.'

'No doubt.'

They continued on and, upon approaching the end of the alley, Kit thought he heard a sound at once so familiar and yet so strange, it took him a full two seconds to place it. Children laughing? No, not children. Seagulls.

He had little time to wonder about this for, at that moment, they stepped from the dim alleyway and into the most dazzling and unusual landscape Kit had ever seen.

CHAPTER 2

In Which Lines are Drawn, and Crossed

Before his bewildered eyes spread a scene he had only ever glimpsed in movies: a busy wharf with a three-masted schooner moored to the dock and, beyond it, the grand sweep of a sparkling, blue-green bay. The brilliant, sun-washed air was loud with the cackle of seagulls hovering and diving for scraps of fish and refuse as fishermen in the smaller boats hefted wicker baskets full of silver fish to women in blue bonnets and grey shawls over long calico dresses. Broad black headlands rose on either side of the wide scoop of the bay and, between these craggy promontories, a tidy town of small white houses climbed the slopes. Stocky men in short, baggy trousers and droopy shirts, with straw hats on their heads, pushed hand carts and drove mule teams along the seafront, helping to unload hessian-wrapped bundles from the tall ship.

Kit could only stand in stark-staring disbelief while astonishment whelmed over him in great, rolling waves.

Gone were the Islington streets with their office blocks and narrow roads clogged with cars and double-decker buses, the innumerable coffee shops and take-aways, betting shops, and newsagents, the Belgrave Arms, the Post Office, the community college. No more the world-beating urban sprawl of metropolitan London with its dense clusters of neighbourhoods and shopping districts connected with traffic-bound streets and four-lane carriageways.

Everything familiar that Kit had known with the solid certainty of concrete had vanished utterly – and with it his own concrete certainty in bricks-and-mortar reality. It had all been replaced with a seaside vista at once so charming, so evocative, so quaint and winsome it could have been a painting in the National Gallery. And then the stench hit him – a stringent pong of fish guts, rotting vegetables, and tar. He felt woozy and his stomach squirmed with a queasy feeling.

Turning hastily back to the alleyway, he saw that it was still there, still straight and narrow, its length deeply shadowed as if to shield a dreadful secret. 'Where…?' he said, gulping air. 'Where are we?'

'No need to speak until you're ready.'

Kit turned his wondering eyes to the bustling panorama before him – the tall ship, the muscled stevedores, the fishermen in their floppy felt hats, the fishwives in their wooden clogs and headscarves – and tried to make sense of what he was seeing and remain calm in the face of what he considered a shocking dislocation. 'What happened to Islington?'

'All in good time, dear boy. Can you walk? Perhaps we can forget the coffee – have a drink instead. Fancy a pint?' Kit nodded. 'It isn't far,' the old gentleman informed him. 'This way.'

Dragging his rattled self together, Kit followed his guide out onto the waterfront. It felt as if he were walking on borrowed legs. The boardwalk seemed to lurch and shift with every awkward step.

'You are doing marvellously well. When it first happened to me, I couldn't even stand up.'

They passed along a row of tiny shops and boat houses and simple dwellings, Kit's mind reeling as he tried to take in everything at once. Away from the fetid alley, the air was cleaner, though still filled with the scent of the sea: fish and seaweed, wet hemp, salt and rocks.

'In answer to your previous question,' the old man said, 'this place is called Sefton-on-Sea.'

Judging from what he could observe, the town appeared to be one of those forgotten coastal villages that had been frozen in time by a local council intent on capitalizing on the tourist trade; a settlement that time forgot. Sefton-on-Sea was more authentically old-fashioned and picturesque than any West Country fishing village Kit had ever seen. As a re-enactment theme park, the place put all others in the shade.

'Here we are,' said the elder man. 'Come in, we'll have a drink and get to know one another better.'

Kit looked around to see that they were standing at the door of a substantial brick house with a painted wooden sign that said Old Ship Inn. He allowed himself to be led through the door and stepped into a dark room with low ceilings, a few tables and benches, and a tin-topped bar. A few snugs lined the perimeter of the pub which was presided over by a broad-beamed young woman convincingly costumed in a cap of plain linen and long white ale-stained apron. She greeted them with a smile. There was no one else in the place.

'Two pints of your best, Molly,' called the old man, leading his docile companion to a stool in the corner. 'Sit yourself down, my boy. We'll get some ale in you and you'll begin to feel more yourself.'

'You come here often?' Kit asked, trying to force some lightness into his voice.

'Whenever I'm in the neighbourhood, so to speak.'

'Which is where, exactly? Cornwall? Pembrokeshire?'

'So to speak.'

The barmaid appeared bearing two overflowing pewter tankards which she deposited on the table. 'Thank you, Molly,' said the old man. 'Do you have anything to eat? A little bread and cheese perhaps?'

'There's cheese in t'back, an' I can go down t'bakery for a loaf if you like.'

'Would you, please? There will be an extra penny in it for you. There's a good girl.'

The young lady shuffled off, and the white-haired gentleman took up his tankard, saying, 'Here's to dodgy adventures with disreputable relatives!'

Kit failed to see the humour of that sentiment, but was glad for the drink. He took a deep draught, allowing the flowery sweet ale to fill his mouth and slide down his throat. The taste was reassuringly familiar and after another swallow he felt better for it.

'Let's start at the beginning, shall we?' said the old man, putting down his tankard. 'Now then.' He drew an invisible square on the tabletop with his forefingers. 'What do you know about the Old Straight Track?'

'I think I'd know one if I saw one.'

'Good,' replied his great-grandfather. 'Perhaps your education wasn't entirely wasted.' He redrew the square. 'These trackways form what might be called intersections between worlds, and as such –'

'Hold on,' interrupted Kit. 'Intersections between *worlds*... we *are* talking about trains?'

'Trains!' The old man reared back. 'Great heavens, it's nothing to do with *those* smoke-belching monstrosities.'

'Oh.'

'I'm talking about the Old Straight Track – Neolithic pathways. In short, I am talking about ley lines.' He studied the younger man's expression. 'Am I to take it you've never heard of them?'

'Once or twice,' hedged Kit.

'Not even that.'

'No,' he confessed.

'Oh dear. Oh dear.' The old man regarded him with a glance of rank disapproval. 'You really ought to have applied yourself to your studies, young Cosimo.'

Kit drank some more, reviving a little more with every sip. 'So, what are these lay lines, then?'

Into the invisible square the old man drew a straight diagonal line. 'A *ley* line,' he said, speaking slowly – as one might to a dog or dull-witted child, 'is what might be called a field of force, a trail of telluric energy. There are hundreds of them, perhaps thousands, all over Britain, and they've been around since the Stone Age. I thought you might have stumbled across them before.'

Kit shook his head.

'Early man recognized these lines of force, and marked them out on the landscape with, well, any old thing, really – standing stones, ditches, mounds, tumps, sacred wells, and that sort of thing. And, later on, with churches, market crosses, crossroads, and what not.'

'Hey, hold on,' said Kit, breaking in. 'I think I know what you're talking about – New Agers out in Wiltshire on Bank Holidays traipsing around the standing stones with witching sticks and

19

tambourines, chanting to the Earth Goddess and –' he looked at the frown on the old man's face. 'No?'

'Not by a long chalk. Those poor deluded dupes, spouting all that neopagan poppycock, are to be pitied. No,' he shook his head firmly, 'we're not talking New Age nonsense, we're talking *science* – as in "There are more things in heaven and earth than are dreamt of in your philosophy", et cetera.' His eyes took on a slightly manic light. 'Truth, dear boy. Sci-ence!'

'R–right,' said Kit warily. 'I thought you said they were some kind of intersection between worlds.'

'Precisely,' replied his great-grandfather. 'You see, this universe we inhabit is made up of billions of galaxies – literally beyond counting – and this is only one universe.'

'There are others?'

'Oh, yes – possibly. Maybe. We're not sure.'

'We?'

'The Questors – but never mind, I'll come to that later.' The old man brushed the word aside with a stroke of his hand. 'Now then, where were we?'

'Billions of galaxies,' said Kit, staring into his tankard. If he had for a moment allowed himself to feel that sitting in a friendly pub conversing with a genial old man who was, by any reckoning, well over 125 years old might be a reasonable activity… that feeling evaporated, replaced by a steadily mounting anxiety. And it was not only due to the outlandish nature of the old codger's demented ramblings. The thing that had him in a sweat was this: in spite of everything he had a sensation of being told a secret he knew to be true, but which would be far, far easier – and much safer – to ignore; all the more so since he strongly suspected that acknowledging the truth meant his life would change utterly.

Then again what Cosimo had said was true: he *was* nothing but an overworked drone in a cube farm, a minor cog in the dreary machinery of a third-rate mortgage mill, overlooked, unloved, a sidelined player in the big game, and – how did the old man put it? – a lonely bachelor with the love life of garden gnome. What then, really, did he have to lose?

'Look, no offence,' said Kit, rousing himself, 'but if you really *are* my great-grandfather, why aren't you dead?'

'I suppose the simplest explanation is that all the popping back and forth between one world and another does funny things to one's aging mechanism; ley travel seems to inhibit the process in some way.'

'Oh.'

'If we can continue?' The old man dipped his finger in a little puddle of ale and drew a large circle on the tabletop. 'The visible universe with its many galaxies occupies one dimension of our common reality, but there are other dimensions – many of them.'

'How many?'

'Impossible to say. But each dimension has its own worlds and galaxies and so forth. And we know that these dimensions impinge on one another. They touch. They interpenetrate. And where one dimension touches or passes through another, it forms a line of force on the landscape.' He glanced up and saw his explanation was falling short of total comprehension. 'Ever played with soap bubbles in the bath?'

'Maybe.'

'Well, you could think of these different dimensions as clusters of soap bubbles. Where one bubble touches another – or passes through another – it forms a line. It's true. Look the next time.'

'I'll try to remember to do that.'

'Now then, if each bubble were a different dimension you could move from one to the other along that line.'

'A ley line.'

'Precisely,' smiled his great-grandfather. 'I knew you'd understand.'

'I can't say I do.'

'By methods yet to be explained, we have travelled, you and I. Crossed from one world, one dimension, to another via a ley line.'

'Stane Way,' surmised Kit, beginning to grasp the smallest part of what the old fellow was telling him. 'The ley line was the alley?'

'Was and is.' The old man smiled triumphantly. 'Stane – from the old Saxon word for stone – is literally the Stone Way, named after the row of standing stones that in a former age marked out the path.

The stones are gone now, but the ley is still there.'

Kit took another swallow and, fortified by the ale, attempted a rejoinder. 'All right. Assuming for argument's sake that what you're saying is in some cock-eyed way *true*: how is it that such a monumental discovery has gone completely unnoticed by any reputable representatives of the scientific community?'

'But it isn't unnoticed at all,' replied the elder gentleman. 'People have known about this since –'

'The Stone Age, yes, so you said. But if it's been around so long, how has it been kept a secret?'

'It hasn't been kept a secret by anyone. It is so very ancient that man in his headlong rush to modernity and progress has simply forgotten. It passed from science into superstition, you might say, so now it is more a matter of belief. That is to say, some people believe in ley lines, and some don't.'

'I'm thinking most don't.'

'Quite.' The old man glanced up as Molly appeared with a wooden plate heaped with slices of brown bread and a few chunks of pale yellow cheese. 'Thank you, my dear.' He took the plate and offered it to his great-grandson. 'Here, get some of this down you. It will restore the inner man.'

'Ta,' said Kit, taking up a slice of bread and a chunk of crumbly cheese. 'You were saying?'

'Consider the pyramids, Cosimo. Marvellous achievement – one of the most impressive architectural feats in the history of the world. Have you seen them? No? You should one day. Stupendous accomplishment. It would be a heroic undertaking to build such structures with cranes, earth movers, and the kind of industrial hydraulics available today. To contemplate erecting them with the technology available to the ancient Egyptians would be impossible, would it not?'

'I suppose.' Kit shrugged. 'What's the point?'

'The point, dear boy, is that they are *there*! Though no one remembers how they were built, though the methods of their construction, once considered commonplace, have been lost to time, the pyramids exist for all the world to see. It's the same with ley lines – completely dead and forgotten like the people who once marked them and used them – until they were rediscovered in the modern era. Although, strictly speaking, the leys have been rediscovered many times. The latest discoverer was Alfred Watkins.'

'Who?'

'Old Alf was a photographer back in the day – quite a good one, actually. Nice chap. Had an eye for landscape. Travelled around on horseback in the early days of the camera, taking photographs of the brooding moors and misty mountains, that sort of thing. Helped enormously with his discovery,' explained the old man, biting off a bit of cheese. 'He made a detailed survey of ley lines and published a book about them.'

'Okay. Whatever,' said Kit. 'But I fail to see what any of this has to do with me.'

'Ah, yes, I was coming to that, young Cosimo.'

'And that's another thing,' protested the younger man. 'You keep calling me *Cosimo*.'

'Cosimo Christopher Livingstone – isn't that your name?'

'As it happens. But I prefer to go by Kit.'

'Ah, yes, diminutive of Christopher. Of course.'

'I don't know about you, but where I went to school anybody walking around with a name like Cosimo was just asking to get his head dunked in the toilet.'

'Pity,' sniffed the elder gentleman. 'Sad, really. Names are very important.'

'It's merely a matter of taste, surely.'

'Nothing of the sort,' replied the elder Cosimo. 'People get named all sorts of things – *that* I will concede. Whimsy, ignorance, sudden inspiration – all play a part. But if anyone guessed how monumentally important it was, it would all be taken a lot more seriously. Did you know – there are tribes in the jungles of Borneo that refuse to name an infant until he or she is four years old? See, the child must develop enough to demonstrate the attributes they will carry into adulthood. The child is then named after those attributes. It's a way of reinforcing desirable qualities and making sure they don't disappear from the tribe.'

'But… *Cosimo*?'

'A fine name. Nothing wrong with it.' He gave his young relation a glance of stern appraisal. 'Well, I suppose you have a point.'

'I do?'

'We cannot both be called Cosimo, after all. As we will be spending a lot more time together from now on, it would make it far too tedious and confusing.' He tapped the table with his fingertips. 'Very well, then, Kit it shall be.'

Although he was unable to say why, Kit felt a slight uplift of relief at having won the point. 'You still haven't said what any of this has to do with me.'

'It's a family matter, you might say. Here I am, your dear grandpapa,' the old man winked at Kit and flashed a disarming smile, 'and I need your help with a project I've been working on for quite some considerable time. You're all the family I've got.'

Kit considered this, but in spite of everything, he could still scarcely credit that he had any residual familial ties to the relic sitting across the table from him. His expression betrayed his disbelief. The elder man leaned forward and grasped Kit's hands in his own.

Speaking in a hoarse and persistent whisper, he said earnestly, 'See here, young Cosimo – excuse me – *Kit*. It will be the adventure of a lifetime – of several lifetimes. In fact, it will change you forever.' The old gentleman paused, still holding the younger man's hands and fixing him with a mad stare. 'I need you, my boy, and I've gone to a very great deal of trouble to find you. What do you say?'

'No.' Kit shook his head, as if waking from a dream. He pulled his hands free, then ran them through his hair, then clutched his tankard. 'This is crazy. It's some kind of hallucination – that's what it is. Take me back. I want to go home.'

Cosimo the Elder sighed. 'All right,' he agreed, 'if that is what you wish.'

Kit sighed with relief. 'You mean it?'

'Of course, dear boy. I'll take you back.'

'Fine.'

'Only, funny thing – I think you'll find there *is* no going back. Still, if that's what you want. Drink up, and let's be off.'

Kit pushed aside his tankard and stood. 'I'm ready now.'

The old man rose and, digging two coins out of his coat pocket, flipped them to the serving girl and promised to come back next time he was passing through. They walked out onto the dockyards and returned to the narrow alley between two warehouses. 'Here you are. Just continue on the trackway and you'll be home in a trice.'

'Thanks.' Without a moment's hesitation, Kit started down the alley.

As he passed into the shadow between the two buildings, he heard the old gentleman call behind him, 'If you change your mind, you know where to find me.'

Fat chance, thought Kit, hurrying into the shadows. He cast a glance over his shoulder, but already the alleyway entrance was dim and far away. A wind gusted through the alley and the shadows deepened; clouds gathered overhead and it began to rain – sharp, stinging little pellets – and above the sound of the swiftly gathering storm, the clear, distant voice of his great-grandfather shouting, 'Farewell, my son. Until we meet again!'

CHAPTER 3

In Which Wilhelmina Takes Umbrage

Kit emerged from Stane Way soaked to the skin and completely disoriented. He felt as if he'd just taken a trip through an automatic car wash without a car. He staggered forward, dashing water from his eyes – almost colliding with a mum pushing a pram. 'Sorry!' he sputtered. The mother glared at him as she hurried on. Kit gazed around at the street lined with tall buildings and heaving with traffic. He was back.

Relief rippled through him. *It worked*, he thought. *I'm home!*

Then, without warning, he felt a sudden rush of nausea. He clamped a hand over his mouth, lurched to the nearest gutter and threw up.

'Very nice,' muttered a teenage girl passing by just then. She and her friend gave him a wide berth and hurried on. 'Get a life, creep!'

I'm trying, thought Kit. He spat and wiped his mouth with his sleeve. Gradually, the seasick sensation dwindled and he started making his unsteady way back to his flat to change his clothes.

Walking along familiar streets in the sober light of day, it was almost possible to convince himself that the whole impossible series of events owed more to some sort of weird delirium than actual, physical happenstance. Did not the strangeness of the situation have about it the very peculiar quality of a dream? It truly did, he argued. And was it not common knowledge that hallucinations were often extraordinarily vivid? Obviously, the episode was a hallucination brought on by acute unhappiness, triggered by fatigue, and fuelled by frustration. And yet…

And yet, it had none of the surreal hallucinatory quality of a dream. The ground in that place had felt solid beneath his feet, the sun warm on his face, the scent of the air redolent of the sea – all that and more had felt just as real as the waking world he'd always known, just as concrete as the hard-paved London street on which he now stood. What was dreamlike about that?

What else could it be? He had read about alternate worlds and such like. But wasn't that all just the over-inflated musings of theoretical physicists with way too much time and funding on their hands? In any case, people simply did not go popping from one place to another easy as you please and back again. No, it had to be some sort of mental aberration – admittedly of an extremely robust kind. Hysteria, maybe. Or hypnosis. Maybe old Cosimo had hypnotized him, made him fantasize the seaside village and all the rest. As he considered this, another, darker, prospect suggested itself for his consideration: schizophrenia.

While Kit refused to seriously entertain that possibility, he nevertheless was forced to admit that those suffering from that mental aberration often saw and held conversations with people who were not physically present, and had difficulty recognizing their surroundings. And it was true that schizophrenia often manifested itself in young men of his age, striking without warning, and resulting in just the sort of dislocation and disorientation he had experienced.

Whatever the explanation would turn out to be, the less said about his so-called travels the better. Nothing good would come of blabbing about what had happened. That much was clear. He would, he vowed, die on the rack with red hot pokers in his eyes before confessing it to anyone.

Halfway home, he abandoned this plan and headed for Tottenham where Mina was waiting for him; his clothes could dry on the way. He doubled back to the nearest station, swiped his Oyster at the turnstile, and received the dreaded 'Seek Assistance!' sign once again. Rather than repeat his former escapade, he dutifully purchased a ticket from the machine, pushed through the turnstile, and headed down the steps to the platform. When the train came whooshing up, he climbed on, took a seat, and uneventfully travelled the rest of the way to Tottenham, where he proceeded straightaway to Wilhelmina's flat with the firm resolve to forget the whole strange interlude, put it behind him; to never, ever breathe a word about it to another living soul. This resolve carried him all the way to his girlfriend's tower-block apartment building and her front door.

He knocked.

There was a click and the door swung open. 'You're late!'

'What? No kiss? No cheery greeting?'

Wilhelmina frowned, but gave him a quick, dry peck on the cheek. 'You're still late.'

'Yeah, sorry about that. I had this –' He stopped abruptly, and backtracked. 'I mean, my Oyster card was out, so I had to walk.'

'And that took you eight hours?'

'Huh?' he wondered. 'No, really.'

She moved away from the doorway, and he stepped in, kicking off his damp shoes. Her flat was ample by London standards, as clean as a dentist's surgery and nearly as cold. Wilhelmina was nothing if not tidy – perhaps owing to the fact that she had once *been* a dentist's assistant, briefly, before chucking it in – too many people, too many mouths – to become a baker.

She was still stuffing things in people's mouths, albeit in a different and, for her, much more satisfying way.

As Kit watched her slouch back to her big blue sofa, which was her habitual nest, he was once more impressed with the idea that he simply *had* to get a better girlfriend at the first opportunity. Dressed in black jeans and a black turtleneck with the horrible ratty hand-knitted purple scarf she wore everywhere, with her feet stuffed into flat-heeled, sheepskin boots, she was a dead-ringer for the undertaker's anaemic daughter. Why, he wondered, did she have to look so austere? Whatever happened to sugar and spice? When enumerating the qualities he desired in a mate, vim and vigour, a zest for life, and a keenness of mind and intellect came quite near the top of the list. Wilhelmina's idea of excitement was an extra scoop of sultanas in the cinnamon buns.

Her intellect might have been keen enough – if anyone could ever catch her awake long enough to stimulate her into meaningful conversation. Her job at Giovanni's Rustic Italian Bakery – 'Artisan Breads Our Speciality' – meant that she had to rise every weekday morning in the wee hours to be at work by four o'clock to fire up the ovens and mix the first of the day's dough. She finished work just after one in the afternoon, was completely exhausted by six in the evening, and usually sound asleep by eight – all of which meant one hardly ever saw her when she wasn't yawning, stifling a yawn, or having just yawned. If sleep were an Olympic event, Wilhelmina Klug could have slept for Team GB.

Her eyelids drooped, and her shoulders, too. Like many tall girls, she had developed the round-shouldered, hunched over posture which would in time grow into a widow's hump; in Wilhelmina's case, since marriage seemed so very remote, it would be a spinster's hump.

Everything about her was retiring. Even her chin receded.

Her hair was mousy, both in colour and texture: very fine, shiny, and slightly bristly; and she wore it aggressively short. The better to keep it out of the pastry, she claimed, but the style was far from flattering. She had large, dark eyes which might in themselves have been pretty if not for the matching large dark circles beneath them.

Wilhelmina was no catch. As one of Kit's colleagues had put it after spending a rare evening with the unfortunate couple: 'For warmth and affection, mate, you'd be better off with a pair of ferrets and a hot water bottle.'

Kit could not disagree.

But until something better came along she was, for him, it. And, despite her many obvious flaws, and his continually renewed determination to do better in the dating game, he inexplicably turned up time and again outside her door. It was as if his feet had a mind of their own and weren't over fussy about whose table they parked themselves under.

'Well?' she said.

'Sorry? Am I missing something here?'

'You're late, dope. You promised to go and help me pick out curtains for the bathroom this morning.'

'So, here I am. Let's go.'

'Is this your lame idea of a joke?'

'Sunday morning – John Lewis, yeah? So, let's go and pick out some curtains.'

'You're winding me up, right? You know well and good they close at six on Sunday.'

'Wait!' He stepped close. 'What did you say?'

She puffed out her cheeks with exasperation. 'I'm too tired for this.'

'No, really, what time is it?'

'Five-bloody-thirty!' She gave him the full frontal glare of a woman on the edge, and collapsed on the couch. 'Idiot man.'

'It's never half-five.' Pulling his phone from his front pocket, he checked the display. He saw the number five followed by two threes, experienced a twinge of disbelief, and quickly shoved the phone back into his pocket.

'Are you *trying* to pick a fight? You waste the whole day and this is the best excuse you can think up? "Duh, I forgot what time it was…" Pathetic.' She rolled her big brown eyes. 'You can't do better than that?'

'No, really, Mina,' said Kit, suddenly desperate to explain. 'Listen, something's happened –'

'Something's happened all right. I missed my chance to go shopping on the one day of the week I have off and all because of you. Where were you anyway – at some pub? I tried to call you but your phone was off.'

'We'll go next week,' he offered.

'No thanks. I'll do it myself – as usual.'

'No, Mina, listen – I'm trying to tell you the truth.' Even as he spoke he could feel his former resolve evaporating in the heat of her righteous indignation. He slid onto the couch beside her. 'Something's happened. I didn't believe it myself – I'm still not sure I believe it yet – but I can explain. Really.'

'This should be good,' she snipped. Crossing her arms across her chest, she thrust out her chin, daring him. 'Go on then.'

'Okay,' he said, his vow to say nothing about his hallucination effectively dwarfed by the need to make her believe, 'but you can't tell anybody what I'm about to tell you.'

'Yeah, right. As if I would.'

'Well, I was on my way here, but my Oyster was out of money –' She opened her mouth to protest, but he cut her off. 'No, just shut up and listen. The ticket machine wouldn't co-operate, and I couldn't get change, right? So, I decided to walk. Well, I'm walking along and decide to cut through this alley. All of a sudden there's this terrific storm – wind, hail, lightning, the whole works – this is where it gets weird, but you gotta trust me on this – I'm telling the truth, I swear – I met my great-grandfather.'

'Your what?' her voice climbed to another register.

'Great-grandfather, I met him –'

'I didn't know you had a great-grandfather.'

'Neither did I. Turns out his name is Cosimo, too, and he took me to this old-fashioned pub at a place on the coast called Sefton-on-Sea and he –'

'How'd you get there?' Wilhelmina demanded.

'We walked,' he hedged.

'All the way from London?'

'Well, yeah. Sort of.'

Her eyes narrowed. 'Define *sort of*.'

He had hoped to avoid that part of the experience, fearing, and rightly so, that he would not be believed. 'Thing is,' he confessed, 'I'm not exactly sure *what* happened.' Her eyes narrowed further.

'Whatever it was, it happened when we were in the alley – it has to do with ley lines and stuff. See, we started walking and when we got to the end of the alley we were somewhere else.'

'Somewhere else?' Mina's eyes became slits of suspicion. 'Boy, you just don't give up, do you.'

'Cornwall, I think,' said Kit. 'Or Devon.' He saw her face harden in disbelief. 'Possibly Pembrokeshire. Anyway, that's where we found this little old-fashioned fishing village and this pub.'

Mina was shaking her head.

'You don't believe me.'

'Oh, I believe you,' she replied sweetly. Then, marshalling her anger, cried, 'Liar! Why should I believe this load of old rubbish? Give me one good reason.' She glared defiantly. 'Liar!'

Her disbelief angered him; a heat flash of rage seared through him and he was seized by a powerful compulsion to make her understand. In that instant, he realized he simply could not carry the weight of the experience on his own. Nothing else mattered but that she should know he was telling the truth – as if getting another human being to acknowledge what had happened to him would make it more believable to himself.

Gripped by this sudden, irrepressible conviction that someone, anyone, should share in the curious nature of his experience, he leaped to his feet. 'I'll do better than that,' he declared. 'I'll *show* you.'

'Yeah, right.' She yawned. 'Pull the other one – it's got bells on.'

'No, really. I'll show you.' He crossed the room and lifted her green Oxfam jacket from the coat stand. 'Here, take this. It's likely to be raining when we get there.'

'Might as well. The day is shot anyway.' She yawned again, rose lethargically, and padded after him. 'Where are we going again?'

'You'll see.'

A quick Tube journey followed, and soon the two were marching along Grafton Street in search of Stane Way. 'It's just along here,' Kit assured her.

'I can't believe I let you talk me into this,' Mina said. 'As if I didn't have better things to do.'

'You don't, honest,' he said, her reluctance forcing him to become a cheerleader for the expedition. 'This'll be fun, I promise.'

'Quit saying that – because so far it isn't.'

'C'mon, Mina,' he cajoled. 'Just think – you'll get to see some fetching landscape, have a nice cream tea somewhere, and a walk in the fresh sea air. You'll like it. It'll be fun.'

By way of reply she scowled and gave him a smack on the arm.

'Ow! What was that for?'

'I warned you,' she said, shoving her hands deep into the pockets of her jacket. 'Anyway, I don't want to go to the seaside, thanks all the same.'

'You've got to see this.'

'So is he going to be there?'

'Who?'

'The bloody Pope!'

'You mean my great-grandfather?'

'Who else?'

'No.' He shook his head. 'Then again, maybe.' He shrugged. 'I don't know.'

'If I said I believed you,' Mina ventured, 'would we have to go through with this?'

'You make it sound like an ordeal,' he countered. 'This'll be' – He saw her eyes glint dangerously and abruptly changed tack – 'an education.'

They walked on. A few hundred yards later, Kit spied the street sign for Stane Way. 'Look! This is where it happened – or hereabouts.' He stepped to the mouth of the alley and started down the long, shadowed street. 'This way, and don't worry – it's not as bad as it looks.'

They walked a short way, the shadows deepening around them.

'My, this is a lovely spot.' Mina stepped over a plastic carrier bag spilling sandwich boxes and crisp packets onto the pavement. 'Why haven't you brought me here before?'

'Just keep walking.'

'You're gonna make this up to me, boy,' Mina warned. 'And it's gonna take more than a cup of tea and a microwaved scone.'

Kit was striding down the middle of the alleyway with big, exaggerated steps. She followed, imitating his walk – more from boredom than conviction. 'I don't know if it will work,' he called back to her. 'I was closer to the other end when it happened.'

'When *what* happened, exactly?'

'This fierce little storm boiled up out of nowhere, and –'

'What?' she asked, raising her voice to be heard above the sound of the wind just then gusting down the alleyway.

'I said…' he shouted back, 'a storm came along –'

'Like this one, you mean?' she hollered, shouting at the top of her lungs.

He stopped. The storm! Black clouds roiled above them, a wild wind screamed through the gap between the buildings, and it started to rain. 'This way!' he yelled. 'Do you feel it?'

'What?' cried Wilhelmina, trying to hear and be heard above the uncanny shriek of the gale.

'Follow me!' he shouted. 'Stay close! You don't want to get lost.'

He started running to get out of the rain, and felt the ground give beneath him in a fluid, shifty way – like jogging on the floor of a bouncy castle. In the same instant, his vision blurred and he felt himself falling: no great distance, as it turned out, merely the space between a stair tread and the floor.

Dashing water from his eyes with the heels of his hands, he shouted. 'Over here!'

Receiving no reply, he turned to the alley behind him. Wilhelmina was nowhere to be seen.

CHAPTER 4

In Which the Unwanted Attention is Drawn

The storm howled away into the heavens, leaving Kit wet, nauseous, and with a head that felt two sizes too big. He wiped drool from his chin with a sodden sleeve, and waited, listening to the sound of the rapidly diminishing storm.

'Mina!' he called after a moment.

No answer.

He called her name again, and started walking back the way he had come, searching for a doorway, an alcove, any cubby-hole however small where she might have sought shelter. He found nothing but blank brick walls on either side and, upon reaching the end of the alley, was forced to conclude that she was not there.

Of all the things that might have happened, this was one he had not anticipated: that he would make the jump to the other place, as he now thought of it, and she would remain in the real world. The thought of her wending her soggy way home, cursing his name aloud to the four winds, made him frustrated and angry – almost as angry as he had been before, when she didn't believe him.

She believed him now, perhaps. Having seen him vanish before her eyes, what else could she think but that he had been telling the truth all along?

On the other hand, he had abandoned her in a filthy alley in darkest Islington. That could cancel out whatever he might have gained in the truth-telling stakes. Who knew? With Wilhelmina, one could never tell.

But it came to him that the remedy was perfectly obvious: he would go back.

Taking a deep breath, he braced himself and gathered his feet under him for another run. Just as he was about to launch himself into the deep-shadowed darkness of the alley, he heard someone call his name. Turning once more towards the alley entrance, he saw the vaguely familiar figure of the old man who claimed to be his great-grandfather.

'Hello, Kit,' called Cosimo, hastening to meet him. He was dressed, as before, in a long dark coat and a broad-brimmed felt hat pulled low on his head. 'I knew you'd come back,' he said as he came to stand before his great-grandson. 'Am I to take it that you've changed your mind? Settled your affairs, made your farewells, and now you're ready to lend a willing hand to a most vital enterprise that requires your particular good self?'

'Okay, okay,' conceded the younger man. 'Whatever.'

'Stop evading the question. Are you ready to join me?'

'Yeah, well there's a little problem with that. This girl I know – my girlfriend, Mina – is waiting for me back home. In Stane Way, actually. We were supposed to come here together and –'

'You what?'

'I was just going to show her, but she didn't make the jump.'

'Make the jump?' echoed Cosimo, his brows lowering in a scowl. 'What did you do, Kit?'

'Nothing!' protested Kit. 'I was just going to show her – she didn't believe me, so I wanted to show her the ley line, you know. Well, the same thing happened as last time, and I ended up here, but she got left on the other side.'

'Stupid boy!' roared Cosimo. 'How could you do something so utterly asinine?'

'It seemed like a good idea at the time,' replied Kit lamely. 'Anyway, there's no reason to assume the worst. Nothing happened.'

'You'd better hope so.'

'She'll take the Tube home. Big deal. She'll be royally annoyed at me, but she'll be fine.'

'You don't know what you've done, do you? You haven't the foggiest idea how incredibly dangerous this is.'

'No, I –' Kit began, then paused. 'How dangerous?'

'More dangerous than you can possibly imagine.'

'But you said if I changed my mind I was to come back, so –'

'I didn't expect you to try to bring along your paramour. I suppose you told her everything? Why not tell half of London while you're at it – place a notice in *The Times,* broadcast it on the BBC?' The elder fellow shook his head in dismay. 'Well, the churn is upturned. All that remains is to assess the damage. Pray that it is not a complete disaster.'

Kit frowned. 'Okay, okay, I get it. I'm sorry. Let's move on.'

'See here, my boy. Telluric energy is one of the more subtle yet powerful forces in the universe – the least understood and probably the most unpredictable,' explained Cosimo. 'You have travelled through what some are pleased to call a low frequency window – a threshold, if you will, separating dimensions. You have ended up here, as anticipated, but there is no way to tell where your girlfriend has gone.'

'But she didn't go anywhere,' Kit protested. 'She didn't follow me. She stayed on the other side –' One glance at the elder man's face and he lost all confidence in this assertion. He finished weakly, 'Didn't she?'

'It is possible, but not at all certain. You have neither the skill nor the experience to be bringing others with you. In time, should you live long enough, you may develop your talents. But until then, you really must refrain from attempting to drag others along – however good an idea it might seem at the time.'

'Well, I didn't know, did I?' muttered Kit peevishly.

'I suspect your friend travelled, too,' Cosimo continued, 'but inasmuch as she did not arrive here, we must surmise she went somewhere else.'

'Where, then?'

'That's the trouble, you see – the possibilities are endless. Your friend could be anywhere or *anywhen*.'

'Any*when*?'

'Moving from one world or dimension to another, you inevitably travel in time as well. There is no way around it. Believe me, I've tried.'

'Time travel – of course.' Kit realized then why he had arrived back in London eight hours late, and grasped the fact that Sefton-on-Sea was something other than a quaint tourist attraction.

'Stay right here,' commanded the old man. 'Don't move a muscle. Can you do that for two minutes end-to-end?'

'Got it, professor.'

'Good,' said Cosimo, already starting away. He turned back after only a few steps. 'What does this Mina of yours look like?' Kit offered a brief description, including the colour of her jacket and the jeans she was wearing. 'Yes, that's enough,' said the old man. He turned and walked into the shadows. His body grew hazy – as if viewed through the pane of a frosted glass window. There was a sudden gust of wind and he vanished completely.

Kit waited, and wondered how long he would have to stand in the alley. The thought was still bouncing around in his head when he felt the breeze stir and saw Cosimo hurrying out of the shadows once more.

'She's not there.'

'Where?'

'Stane Way.'

'Maybe she went home.'

'No, she should have been exactly where you left her.'

Kit shrugged. 'If you say so.'

Cosimo shook his head slowly. 'You really have no idea what's going on here, do you?'

'If you put it like that,' muttered Kit, 'I guess not.'

'If your friend has travelled to another plane of existence it is a problem – a very *big* problem – and one that must be addressed with all urgency and seriousness of purpose. So come along, my boy,' Cosimo began moving towards the seafront. 'We're going to see an old friend of mine. He's giving a lecture this evening, and I've arranged for us to have dinner afterwards. We'll explain the situation to him. As it happens, he's a colleague and a scientist, and he may be able to help.'

Emerging from the alley, they walked along the quayside. The seafront was quieter, almost deserted now. The large schooner was still there, but the stevedores and fishermen were gone, their boats secured for the night. A sprinkling of early stars was beginning to appear in the eastern sky, and the sun was going down like a molten globe behind the blue-shadowed headland. 'Red sky at night, shepherd's delight…' mused Kit. The sea was calm and taking on a silvery glow.

They soon came to a deeply rutted road, and turned onto it. With the bay at their backs, the two proceeded up a steep slope, climbing through a clutch of low houses to the top of the sheltering hill. Kit was puffing and sweating as they gained the rim, and was allowed to pause and catch his breath. The bay spread out below them in a gleaming arc, bronzed by the light of a setting sun.

'Where are we going?' Kit asked, feeling the air cool the sweat on his skin.

'See that stone?' Cosimo pointed to a finger-thin standing stone beside the road a couple of hundred yards away. 'That marks a ley I have found particularly useful.' He cast a hasty glance at the darkening sky. 'We'd best be getting along.'

They continued on the road at a sprightly pace. The old man seemed to gain vigour with every step and Kit found himself having to scurry time and again to keep up. Upon reaching the standing stone, Kit called, 'Hey! Can we stop a second?'

Cosimo stopped. 'Young people have no endurance.'

'We have other qualities.' Kit stooped, hands on knees, and gulped air.

'Sorry, old chap, but we must push on,' his grandsire said. 'We really cannot dilly-dally any longer.'

He beetled off again, leaving the road and forging out cross-country, striding through long grass towards a broad rise, the first of a bank of hills glowing deep emerald in the dusky twilight. Kit followed, jogging to keep up.

'The leys are mostly time sensitive, you see,' Cosimo informed him. These words were still being spoken when out of nowhere

39

sounded a horrendous, blood-curdling snarl. The sound echoed across the quickly darkening landscape, driving out all lesser sounds.

'What was that?'

'We've been careless,' said Cosimo. 'Now they've found us.'

'Who?' Kit demanded, looking around frantically for the source of the unnerving growl. 'What *was* that?'

'Listen to me,' said Cosimo, desperation edging into his tone. 'Do exactly as I say without hesitation or deviation.'

The snarl erupted again – a vicious, guttural rumble that reverberated in the pit of his stomach.

'Sure,' said Kit, gazing around furiously. 'What do we do?'

Three dark shapes appeared at the spot where they had left the road. They hesitated for a moment, then picked up the trail and came on – two vaguely human shapes either side of a low-slung mass too small for a horse, but too big for a dog.

'Pay attention,' snapped Cosimo. 'That notch –' He pointed to a V-shaped cleft in the crest of the hill directly above them. 'See it?'

Kit nodded.

'Run for it and don't look back.' He gave the young man a slap on the back. 'Go!'

Kit scrambled for the notch, climbing, leaping, flying over the uneven ground. Shouts rang out in the valley below; he ignored them. Upon reaching the curious gap cut in the rim of the hill, he paused and risked a fleeting backward glance. In the fading light he imagined he saw an enormous cat roughly the size of a small pony, tawny brown with a spray of dark spots across its muscular shoulders and back. The creature was straining at a leash made from an iron chain in the grip of a very large man. A second man of similar size carried a torch. Both wore wide-brimmed green hats and long green coats.

Cosimo pounded up behind him. 'Kit! Don't stop. This way.' His grandfather motioned for him to follow. 'Hurry!'

Stretching out across the broad upland expanse, Kit saw a thin trail worn in the grass. He set his feet to it and started running.

'Stay right where you are!' shouted one of the men behind them.

'You know what we want,' came the voice beyond the torchlight.

'Give it to us,' added the voice at the end of the chained cat. 'You can walk free – you and your little friend there. No harm done.'

'I don't have it,' shouted Cosimo, frantically gesturing for Kit to keep moving. 'Now leave us alone… we don't want any trouble.'

'It's time to pay the piper, old man,' said the one restraining the chained beast.

'I may be forced to use violence,' Cosimo called. 'I'm warning you.'

A dry laugh was the only reply he received.

Cosimo moved on down the path with Kit right behind.

'You can't get away!' shouted the man holding the chain. 'Stop, or we'll let Baby gnaw on your leg bones.'

'One last chance,' called the man with the torch. 'Give us the map – and you'll walk away in one piece.'

'I'll count to three,' said his companion, 'and then I'm going to release Baby.'

'You're making a big mistake,' called Cosimo over his shoulder. 'I don't have it.'

'One…'

'A very big mistake indeed.'

'Two…'

'Grab my hand, Kit,' urged Cosimo, his voice a tense whisper. 'Whatever happens, don't let go.'

'Three!'

There was a rattle of chain and the brute shouted, 'Feed, Baby! Kill!'

The huge cat seemed to gather itself, then gave out an ear-shattering roar as it launched itself at them.

Kit, grasping the old man's hand felt himself pulled along with such force it nearly wrenched his arm from the socket. The creature bounded effortlessly up the hill and on to the trail, dragging its over-sized keeper with it. If not for the man hanging on to the end of the chain, the beast would have been on them in an instant. As it was, the human slowed the animal enough for them to stay a step or two ahead of it – until Kit stepped in a hole, stumbled, and went down – inadvertently releasing his grip.

41

He squirmed on the ground and caught a glimpse of a curved tooth and the evil glint of a golden eye. He felt the air vibrate with the creature's roar as it bounded nearer. Hauling himself up, he lurched into flight once more and heard the clatter of the chain and the dreadful rush of great clawed feet slicing through the grass. Somehow, Kit snagged the old man's hand once more and, holding on like grim death, was yanked further along the track. The next thing he knew they were running hard into a rising headwind. He felt drizzle on his face, and he could hear cursing and shouting behind them.

'Don't stop!' cried the old man. 'Keep running.'

Their pursuers' voices seemed to dwindle behind them, growing smaller and further away.

'Hold on!' cried Cosimo. 'Here we go!'

The wild howl of the enraged cat was suddenly swallowed by the shriek of the wind as Kit sprawled headlong into the unknown.

CHAPTER 5

In Which Kit Attends a Lecture at the Royal Society for the Improvement of Natural Knowledge

The next moment was filled with the scream of the wind and blinding rain. It lasted only a second or two and when he could see again Kit found himself on his hands and knees in yet another coal-dark alley – this one stinking of urine and slops. But the storm which had brought them was quickly vanishing. 'Are we…?' he gasped.

'Safe now,' Cosimo reassured him. 'We gave them the slip. As soon as you're ready, we should be getting along.'

Kit spat and raised his head. They were in a space between two timber buildings – so narrow, he could have touched either wall with outstretched hands. The passageway was sunk in the deep gloom of night. He dragged himself together and stood, wiping something unpleasant from his hands onto his trousers. 'Who were those guys?'

'All will be revealed, dear boy,' Cosimo said, 'but not here. Not now. We had best be on our way.' He took off his coat and, handing it to Kit, said, 'Put this on.'

'It's okay. I'm not too wet.'

'It's not for warmth, dear boy. We have to cover your clothes.'

'What's wrong with my clothes?'

'We cannot risk drawing the wrong kind of attention.'

Kit pulled on the coat, and Cosimo led them out of the alley and onto a street lit in a haphazard fashion by the soft glow of lanterns on poles and hanging from the windows of buildings. Most of the structures were wooden: of the old half-timbered variety, black-and-white with steeply pitched roofs, tiny diamond-patterned windows, and deep-set eaves over narrow wooden boardwalks that fronted them. A horse-drawn cart clattered by, disappearing into the night.

Something about the atmosphere of the place felt uncannily familiar. 'Is this London?' Kit asked.

'Well done,' commended Cosimo. He fished an old-fashioned wind-up watch from an inner pocket. 'We're a little late, so we'll have to hurry. This way.' He charged off down the deserted street. 'And do step lively.'

'After you.' Kit followed, and immediately felt his right shoe sink into soft mush; his delicate stomach was instantly assaulted by the sharp tang of fresh, ripe horse manure and too late he understood what his great-grandfather meant. 'Oh, *that* lively,' he said, scraping his foot vigorously against a kerbstone. 'Right.'

They turned onto a larger thoroughfare and strolled along, occasionally passing through banks of wispy fog steeped in coal smoke. Few pedestrians were about, but they were overtaken by the occasional carriage. The comforting clip-clop of horse's hooves made a rhythmic music as they walked along. Kit marvelled at the monumental facades of buildings that, though mostly made of timber, nevertheless seemed vaguely familiar beneath their thick black patina of soot. He marvelled, too, at how wide and open and empty was the avenue they walked along: absent the customary clutter and congestion of the overcrowded modern city. While there might have been heaps of rubbish in the gutters and small printed flyers pasted at eye-level on posts and walls all around, still there was no glare of electric advertising, no garish shopfronts, no rampant tangle of power lines and telephone wires, no thrusting television aerials and satellite dishes. As with the little fishing village, no taxis, buses, cars, scooters, or other motorized vehicles plied the roads – all of which made for a quieter, more tranquil city, to be sure, but also a much darker one.

This was, Kit decided, how the old dame had appeared once upon a time. 'When are we? What year?' he asked.

'1666,' answered Cosimo. 'September the second, to be exact.'

'A few years after the Restoration, then,' remarked Kit. 'Samuel Pepys and all that.'

'In Home World terms, it would be,' agreed Cosimo.

'Home World?'

'The Origin World,' he explained. 'Or, as you might say, the *real* world. It's the place where you and I were born.'

'But isn't this –?' began Kit, looking around. 'I thought –'

'No,' replied Cosimo, shaking his head. 'This isn't time travel, remember. We've gone to another place.'

'Which just happens to be in another time?'

'Precisely. This is not simply Restoration England revisited,' he explained. '*This* particular England has its own history and is developing along its own evolutionary route. Similar – given a common starting point – but different, and those differences multiply year on year.'

'An alternative history,' volunteered Kit, 'in an alternative world.'

'So to speak,' granted Cosimo. 'But in this particular England, we're not in the Restoration because there never was a cessation of the monarchy. Charles the First was never deposed. In fact, there was no Civil War at all.'

'Really?' wondered Kit. 'No Royalists, no Roundheads? No Oliver Cromwell smashing things up and bossing everybody around with pikes?'

'Oh, they're about. But in *this* England, Cromwell is an itinerant preacher. He's still a right pain in the arse, but relatively harmless.'

'You don't say.'

'In fact, the entire political climate is very different, as you will see.' Cosimo stopped and, fishing in an inner pocket of his coat, brought out a key ring. 'We're here,' he said. Stepping to the door of a modest timber building, he entered.

45

Kit followed, standing in the gloom of a long, unlit hallway as his great-grandfather fumbled the key into an unseen lock. There was a click and the creak of iron hinges. A voice drifted back to him. 'Stay there.'

The air was stale and heavy with the scent of mildew and rancid fat from cheap candles. Kit waited, listening to the tiny scratching of mice cavorting behind the wainscoting. In a few moments, he saw a faint, ruddy glow emanating from the room Cosimo had disappeared into, and then another and another as additional candles were lit. 'You can come in now,' Cosimo told him. 'Shut the door behind you.'

Kit entered and looked around the very spare room. A few items of wooden furniture – a table, a chair, a bed, a box of coal – seemed to be the sum total of the contents. There was another door at the far side, and Cosimo opened it and went in. He came back with an armload of clothes. 'We'll have to change,' he said.

'Is this your place?'

'Yes, I keep rooms here – saves all sorts of difficulties, as you can no doubt appreciate.' He tossed the clothes onto the bed and started unbuttoning his shirt.

'We can't do much for you just now, I'm afraid,' he said, glancing at Kit. 'But start with this.' He handed Kit a bundle of white linen.

Shaking out the cloth, Kit held up an enormous, very floppy, long-sleeved white shirt fully as wide as it was long. 'Say you don't mean it.'

'Sorry, old chum. We'll get you something better tomorrow. But right now we have to hurry. So, chop-chop!'

While Cosimo dressed, Kit removed his shirt and pulled on the voluminous, gown-sized garment that reached almost to his knees. He tried to tie the laces at the sleeves, but found it impossible and gave up.

'Now these,' said his grandfather, passing him a pair of baggy woollen breeches.

Kit removed his jeans and stuffed his legs into the breeches, pulled them up, and buttoned them at the waist; they were a size or so too big, but heavy and warm. Next came dark woollen stockings which tied at the knee.

'Not bad,' observed Cosimo, passing a critical eye over him. 'Shame we can't do something about those shoes,' he said, regarding Kit's ordinary brown lace-ups. 'Oh well, can't be helped. Now put this on.' He passed Kit a sleeveless, hip-length jacket – a doublet of fine broadcloth with a tight row of tiny silver buttons.

'So, are you going to tell me about those men?'

'Burley Men,' replied his great-grandfather. 'They are part –'

'Burly men?' said Kit. 'Is that what you said?'

'B-u-r-l-*E*-y M-e-n,' his grandsire repeated, spelling out the words. 'How best to describe them? Thieves, rogues, rascals, and highwaymen. They are in the employ of one A. P. Burley, the mastermind behind their nefarious activities.' Cosimo put his arms through a crimson satin waistcoat and began doing up the buttons.

'Organized crime, eh?' said Kit.

'Exactly,' confirmed Cosimo. 'The Burley Men are a law unto themselves and best avoided by any and all. They fear neither God nor man, and are each one as treacherous as their leader. Mayhem is their natural inclination, and murder second nature.' He drew on a short coat like the one he had given Kit. 'Cruel as the night is long, they are false-hearted fiends who wish no one well – even the best of them would not hesitate to sell their mothers to the devil for tuppence. They are as cunning and devious as they are relentless – all the more so if they think you have something they want.'

'Like this map of yours.'

'Quite.'

Kit considered this. It sounded reasonable enough. 'What was that animal? That cat with the blood-curdling roar?'

'*Panthera leo spelaea*,' declared Cosimo, tightening the lace on a garter holding up his long black hose at the knee of his black breeches. 'Better known as a cave lion – a creature from the Pleistocene epoch – oh, about six hundred thousand years ago, or thereabouts.'

'A cave lion,' echoed Kit in disbelief.

'A small one, yes,' affirmed his great-grandfather. He darted into the other room and returned with a wide lace collar which he proceeded to tie at his neck.

The thought of their narrow escape and what those scimitar claws might have done gave Kit an anxious feeling. He changed the subject. 'You look like a prince or something.'

'A merchant prince, actually,' replied Cosimo, passing Kit a wide-brimmed felt hat. 'Folk hereabouts think I'm something of a tycoon – sailing ships and whatnot – which is why I'm not around very much. It is a useful deception. We'll have to think of something to explain you. For tonight, however, I would advise you to speak only when spoken to, and then say as little as possible. That way, there will be less to untangle later.' Fetching another wide-brimmed hat, he put it on and smoothed the front of his red satin doublet. 'Ready?'

Kit put on his hat and adjusted it to what he imagined was a rakish angle. 'Ready as I'll ever be.'

Leaving the house, they were soon charging along the near-deserted streets once more, and Kit was trying to reckon where they were in relation to the London he knew when they stopped again. Extending his hand, Cosimo said, 'Shall we go in?'

Kit glanced up to see that they had come to stand before a large and imposing grey stone building with a wide flight of steps leading up to a set of brass-bound doors; two oily black torches fluttered either side of the entrance. They ascended the stone steps and entered a grand vestibule with a sweeping, carved oak staircase leading to a balustraded balcony. Doors opened off the vestibule in three directions; Cosimo chose the one in the centre and, laying a finger to his lips as a caution for Kit to keep silent, quietly opened the door and slipped in.

Kit followed and found himself at the back of a handsome and very old-fashioned lecture theatre filled row upon row with bewhiskered men formally attired in sober black gowns and plain white neck bands. The room was lit by the lambent glow of innumerable candles in sconces and massive brass chandeliers suspended from the ceiling. By Kit's rough estimate there must have been upwards of two hundred men in the audience, and their attention was wholly directed to the platform at the front where a very tall, lean man in a long, black gown and black silk skull cap was speaking. Below a trim, spade-shaped red beard erupted a veritable fountain of intricate lace. The great silver buckles on his high-topped black shoes glimmered in the light from the row of candles along the front of the stage; his gleaming white stockings were perfectly tight and straight, and he was holding forth in a dramatic, stentorian voice.

'What language is he speaking?' whispered Kit after listening for a few moments and failing to make head or tail of what the energetic fellow was saying. 'German?'

'English,' hissed Cosimo. 'Just let it wash over you.' He raised his finger to his lips once more and slipped into an empty chair, pulling Kit down beside him. The room was warm and hazy with the fug of candle smoke and body heat.

Kit listened to the flow of speech and, with a considerable amount of concentration, began to pick out, first, individual words, then separate phrases. A little more effort and he was able to piece together whole sentences. The fellow seemed to be banging on about some sort of new theory of energy, or something – but in the most convoluted and stilted manner possible.

'You will appreciate, my lords and gentlemen all, that there remain many unanswered queries in the diverse, but nevertheless intimately related, fields of natural mechanics and animal magnetism. The subtle energies of our earthly home are even now beginning to surrender secrets long held and jealously guarded. We in our present generation stand on the cusp of a new and glorious dawn when mastery of these energies lies fully within our grasp as secret yields to inquiry, which yields to experimentation, which leads to verification and duplication, which, in the final course, leads to knowledge.'

He paused to allow a polite spattering of applause to ripple through the auditorium.

'In conclusion, I beg the indulgence of this body in allowing me to reiterate the central premise of my lecture this evening, to whit: that an expedition numbering no fewer than five, nor more than eight, Royal Members in good standing shall be made to a location to be decided to undertake the experiment outlined in your hearing this evening. The experiment will commence as soon as the expeditionary force has been selected and proper arrangements can be made for travel, lodging, and matters attending. Therefore, it is with the greatest anticipation that I look forward to addressing this august assembly once again in the near future to divulge the results of the aforementioned experiment.'

There were shouts of, 'Hear! Hear!'

The lecturer took a few steps towards the other side of the stage, and resumed. 'My friends, esteemed colleagues, noble patrons, and honoured guests, I leave you with this: when next you turn your eyes to the vast reaches of heaven, gentlemen, you would be well advised to remember that not only is it far more vast than the human mind can fathom, it is far more subtle. All the universe is permeated, upheld, knit together, conjoined, encompassed, and contained by the Elemental Ether which we recognize as an all-pervading, responsive and intelligent field of energy, eternal and inexhaustible, which is nothing less than the ground of our very being and the wellspring of our existence – that which in ages past and present men have been pleased to call God.'

Enthusiastic applause concluded the speech, and the man on stage bowed low and received the accolades of his colleagues. Another man joined the first on stage and made a brief announcement of which Kit failed to understand a single word, and then the audience was on its feet, crowding the aisles, and moving towards the doors. 'This way!' said Cosimo, pushing into the aisle. He proceeded to fight his way upstream towards the front of the auditorium, dragging Kit behind him.

'Sir Henry!' called Cosimo, waving his arm. 'Sir Henry!'

'Mr Livingstone!' came the reply. The tall, lanky man surged towards them using his long black walking stick to ease his passage through the throng. 'Welcome, dear friend,' he cried, gripping Cosimo's hand. 'I trust this meeting finds you as well as you appear.'

'Never better. It is good to see you, Sir Henry. I must say, it has been far too long.'

'I was beginning to fear you had forgotten our rendezvous,' said the lecturer. 'I am delighted to discover my trepidations were completely unfounded.'

'Wild horses could not keep me away,' replied Cosimo. Turning to the young man beside him, he said, 'Sir Henry, I am delighted to present my great-grandson, Christopher.'

The nobleman turned his attention to Kit, who was in no way prepared to be the object of an almost blistering intensity of interest. One glance into those razor-keen eyes and Kit felt he had been peeled to the pith. 'A pleasure, sir!' cried the lecturer, seizing the young man's hand in a ferocious grip. 'An unalloyed pleasure.'

'Likewise,' mumbled Kit.

'Kit,' said Cosimo, 'I present to you my dear friend and colleague, Sir Henry Fayth, Lord Castlemain, a man of extraordinary accomplishments in many fields – astronomy, chemistry, geology, and engineering to name a few. In short, a polymath and scholar of the first order.'

Lord Castlemain gave a tap of his walking stick and bowed low. 'As always, dear friend, your flattery overreaches its humble mark.'

'Nonsense! It is the simple truth, nothing more,' replied Cosimo grandly. 'Now then, I believe I requested the pleasure of your company at dinner tonight. Will you honour me with your presence at my table, Sir Henry?'

'Nothing would delight me more, dear fellow. Indeed, I have held myself in the utmost anticipation all day. But – and I really must insist on this – it shall be my pleasure and mine alone to treat you to table.' Cosimo opened his mouth to object, but Sir Henry held up his hand. 'No, sir! I will not hear nay. Come, let us not fall out over trifles.'

'What can I say?' Cosimo bowed in deference to his friend's wishes. 'We accept your hospitality.'

'Splendid! I do hope you are hungry, good sirs.'

'Ravenous!' roared Cosimo – so loudly that Kit gave a start. But no one else seemed to pay the least attention. 'But might we first pass by Pudding Lane? I have that errand we discussed.'

'Certainly, sir. Let us not suffer a moment's delay,' said Sir Henry and, stick held high, charged off through the crowd. 'Please, this way, my friends, if you will. My chariot awaits.'

Kit fell into step behind the two men and, although labouring under the strong impression that he had wandered onto a movie set in mid-film, he had to admit that he was taken in by the very formal, and wholly archaic, manner of the man. And in all his wildest dreams, he had never once imagined he would ever hear anyone actually say the words 'my chariot awaits' and mean it literally.

The vehicle in question turned out to be a large and well-appointed coach with an enclosed passenger box and large windows. As the night was good, the windows were open and, taking the seat facing rearwards opposite the two older men, Kit settled into the sumptuous upholstered leather. The door closed, the driver flicked his whip, and they were soon bumping along the darkened streets of Olde London Towne to the fine clip-clop of a matched pair of enormous chestnut mares. This, thought Kit, feeling more and more like minor royalty, was the only civilized way to travel.

Hard on the heels of this thought came another: None of this is real.

This thought led inevitably to a third: You've fallen and struck your head on a rock and when you wake up in hospital, three weeks will have passed and you will be on a ventilator with tubes up your nose and wires attached to your broken cranium.

That was surely a safer explanation than the one where he was forced to admit that what was happening to him was in some way really happening.

Still, weren't those horses a lovely sight?

Chapter 6

In Which Kit Acquires an Apostle Spoon

The carriage clattered along the darkened streets of an alien London, the iron-rimmed wheels bouncing over uneven cobbles, until at last it rolled to a stop outside a tumbledown thatched house in a cramped street of low timber dwellings. 'Please remain seated, gentlemen,' said Cosimo. 'It is but the work of a moment.' He disembarked and hurried to the rough plank door which sported a crudely hand-lettered placard: Thos. Farryner, Baker.

Glancing up and down the narrow street, Cosimo banged on the door with the flat of his hand. When that failed to produce a result, he picked up a loose cobble and began beating on the planks, rattling the door on its hinges. In a moment, there came a cry from inside and the door flung open. 'Here! Here now! Wot'r ye about then?'

'Sorry to bother you at this late hour, my good man,' said Cosimo. 'I wonder if I might trouble you for a loaf of bread?'

'I be closed!' cried the somewhat woozy man. 'You've woke me up, you have!'

'I do most heartily apologize and beg your pardon,' replied Cosimo. 'But seeing as you are awake now, might I purchase the bread? Any old loaf will do.'

'Hold yer water, then,' grumbled Thomas the baker. He shuffled back inside, reappearing a few moments later with a round lump of bread. 'That's a ha'penny to you.'

'Here's tuppence for your trouble,' said Cosimo, passing over the coins. 'You can thank me later.'

'Tch!' replied the baker and slammed the door.

Cosimo returned to the coach with the bread under his arm. 'That should do it very nicely,' he chortled, climbing back into the coach. 'Drive on!'

As the coach jolted to a start once more, Kit puzzled over the meaning of the charade he had just witnessed. Finally, when he could no longer help himself, he asked, 'What was all that about? What do you want with stale bread?'

'Oh, this?' His great-grandfather glanced at the loaf beside him on the seat. 'But I don't want it at all.'

With that, he took the loaf, and calling, 'Free bread!' tossed it from the carriage to a clutch of poorly dressed women who had gathered around a lantern that cast a pale circle of light onto their bare heads and shoulders. One of them caught the loaf and at once began dividing it up among the others. 'Thank-ee!' she called with a gap-toothed smile.

'Don't you remember *anything* you learned in school?' asked Cosimo.

'Not much,' confessed Kit.

'Second of September... year 1666... Pudding Lane? No?'

'Sorry, not with you so far.' Neither the date nor the place rang any bells.

'Why, it's the Great Fire, dear boy. Never heard of it? What *do* they teach in school these days?'

'*That* I've heard of.' Kit thought for a moment. 'So, by waking the baker you've prevented the fire — is that it?'

'Well done! There might be hope for you yet.'

'But isn't that hazardous — messing with events?'

'Well, why not?'

'You're changing the course of history. I thought that sort of thing was strictly forbidden.'

'Forbidden by whom?' enquired Cosimo. 'Who's to say the reality in which we find ourselves is the best one possible?'

'Yes, but —' Kit objected.

'See here, if a simple act of kindness or generosity, such as buying a loaf of bread for some poor working women, can mean that wholesale death and destruction will be avoided – why, a man would be a monster who had it in his power to alleviate all that suffering yet stood by and did nothing.'

Sir Henry took no part in this conversation. Indeed, he seemed oblivious to the exchange; he smiled and nodded benignly from time to time at the two Livingstones, and it occurred to Kit that modern English was virtually a foreign language to him. Most likely, he simply could not follow very well.

This, and the thought of messing about with history, occupied him until the coach rolled up outside a large torch-lit house with a painted sign hanging above the door. The sign read *The Pope's Nose,* and had a picture of – it was difficult to tell in the flickering light of the torches – what appeared to be the plucked rear end of a somewhat startled goose.

'Ah, here we are, gentlemen!' cried Sir Henry, snatching up his walking stick and leaping to his feet the moment the coach creaked to a stop. 'This is my preferred chop house. The food is uncommonly good, but it is ferociously noisy, I fear, and likely to be crowded. I do hope you will not mind.'

'Not in the least,' replied Cosimo. 'As usual, Sir Henry, you have anticipated my desires precisely. Lead on!'

They stepped from the landau and marched up to the public eating house arm-in-arm, with Kit bringing up the rear. As they approached the entrance, Kit caught Cosimo's elbow and pulled him back for a word. 'Look, I'm hungry as anything – but what's going on here? Aren't we worried about Wilhelmina? I thought it was important to find her.'

'Rest assured, dear boy, it is my main concern and the focus of all our efforts. Trust me. We are definitely working on it. But it will do no one any good if we starve ourselves into a state of mental and physical exhaustion. We've got to keep up our strength and acuity, do we not?'

'I suppose so,' Kit allowed dubiously.

'And does not Sir Henry strike you as exactly the sort of ally who might aid our search?'

'I guess so.'

'Well then!' Cosimo waved him through the wide open door.

The ground floor of the house was given to two large public rooms with smaller, more private chambers upstairs. They were met inside the door by a red-faced man in a shabby leather jerkin with a greasy white apron around his more-than-ample middle and a sweat-stained blue scarf knotted around his neck. A limp cap of folded linen, balanced atop his round head, was listing to the side and causing him to hold his head at an angle. 'Welcome, gentlemen! Come in! Come in! I am honoured, good sirs. Honoured, I declare.' He clapped his hands and a boy came running to take charge of any hats, cloaks, swords, or pistols they might wish to shed for the evening.

They handed over their hats, and the landlord gave a flick of his hand and sent the boy away. 'I have prepared your customary room, Sir Henry. The fire is made up and fresh cloth is laid.'

'Thank you, William, but we will begin down here,' declared Sir Henry, indicating the large open room before them. 'I feel like eating in company tonight. If you please, we will make our way upstairs in due course.'

'Certainly, sir,' replied the landlord. 'Whatever your pleasure. Right this way.' He led them into the room, as into a den noisy with feasting lions. They passed among three long tables crowded with other diners of which there were perhaps twenty or so, all munching and chomping with true abandon. Lord Castlemain appeared to know many of these and he paused often to exchange a greeting or a word, shaking hands and bowing, before moving on.

The landlord conducted them to a small table near the hearth where a coal fire burned brightly in the grate. They settled into large, heavy carvers and Kit surveyed the table, which was spread with a spotted and stained blue tablecloth and white napkins folded into vaguely boat-like shapes. There were no utensils, so he reached for the napkin closest to him, took it, and shook it out just as a gangly young adolescent wearing a faded, much stained yellow turban approached the table and plonked down three wide-bottomed crockery jars overflowing with frothy ale. Sir Henry raised the jar before him and cried, 'To friends old and new! May they always remain true!'

'Was hael!' answered Cosimo, and drank.

The ale, though flat, was sweet and nutty with a warming flavour of cloves. Very nice, Kit decided, sipping liberally from the jar. Meanwhile, the turbaned lad had begun laying wooden bowls of soup before them. Sir Henry lowered his face to the bowl and sniffed. 'Ah! Periwinkle! My favourite.' Taking a large silver spoon from an inner pocket of his coat, he began to ladle soup into his mouth.

As no other spoons – or anything else – seemed to be forthcoming, Kit simply gazed at his watery reflection in the clear, twany liquid.

'Not to your liking, my friends?'

'Far from it!' remarked Cosimo. 'I'm terribly sorry, Sir Henry, but in our haste to meet you we seem to have come away from the house without our spoons.'

'Quite,' agreed Kit.

'We shall soon put that to rights,' said Sir Henry. He raised his hand and snapped his fingers. 'Two of your best spoons for my friends here, William, if you please.'

'Right away, Sir Henry!' cried William, shouting to make himself heard above the general din. He returned on the trot bearing two large and very handsome silver spoons. 'Peter or Paul?' asked the landlord, wiping the spoons on his soiled apron.

'Pardon?' replied Kit.

'Which saint, sir? Peter?' He held up a spoon. 'Or would you prefer Saint Paul?'

'Ah, um, yes,' said Kit, glancing at his great-grandfather for advice and received only an expectant nod. 'Paul, I suppose. No! Make it Peter – definitely. It's Peter for me all the way.'

'A very wise choice, sir,' replied the landlord, handing him one of the deep-bowled spoons which, on closer inspection, turned out to have a handle fashioned in the bearded likeness of said saint.

Kit dipped his utensil into the steaming broth and brought it to his tongue. To Kit's untutored palate, the soup had the musky savour of seashells stewed with old socks. Unable to match Sir Henry for the gusto with which the nobleman attacked this delicacy, he sampled a few spoonfuls politely. While his companions slurped down the soup, he looked around the room at his fellow diners: all men, and all wearing the same dark wool clothing with minor variations. All sported elaborate lace neck wear and a marvellous profusion of beards. This, Kit decided, was really where they splashed out. Indeed, his fellow diners seemed to be in some sort of tonsorial competition to see who could achieve the most outlandish whiskers. And, judging from the results on display, the contest was at a highly advanced stage.

There were men with sideburns so thick it looked as if they were peeping out from behind a scrubby bush; others with moustaches which had long since covered their mouths and threatened to engulf their chins; there were pointed beards, pencil-thin beards, ornately sculpted beards, goatees, and full-blown Father Time beards. Several had immaculately pin-curled their facial hair, and one especially hirsute fellow had grown his neck hair long and brushed it upwards to meet his face, rather than vice versa. Kit ran his fingers over his own scruffy growth and knew himself to be something of a pitiful specimen to the others.

The soup bowls were removed and exchanged for a platter heaped with steaming, half-open shells of mussels and clams; on the rim of the platter were shelled oysters interspersed with little round dollops of pale, squidgy meat Kit could not readily identify. Sir Henry and Cosimo fell to with a vengeance, and soon the discarded shells were clicking like castanets.

Kit, whose notion of acceptable shellfish extended only to prawn vindaloo, stared at the small mountain of glistening, gaping shells before him and felt his throat seize up. He picked at one or two of the shells closest to hand and tried to make it look as if he was enjoying himself. When that failed, he turned his attention to the rounded dollops decorating the perimeter of the platter. They looked harmless enough, so he tried one and decided it was not only edible, but positively delicious.

'Wise choice, sir!' exclaimed Sir Henry, glancing up to take a pull from his ale pot. 'Poached eel! A delight!'

Ordinarily, this knowledge would have somewhat dampened Kit's appetite for the morsels, but the heavenly taste outweighed any squeamishness he might naturally have felt and he proceeded to devour them one by one. He was genuinely sorry when the boy returned to take away the platter; when the debris was cleared away, he was given a clean crockery vessel the size of a generous mixing bowl. Two more lads followed bearing a wooden plank which, at first glance, appeared to contain the disjointed carcass of an entire pig. In fact, it was what Kit considered a mixed grill of the highest order containing not only chops of pork, but beef steaks, veal stuffed with brawn, lamb shanks, assorted ribs, a plump loin of venison and, around the whole, slices of pale pink flesh that Kit could not identify.

Knives had been stuck into some of the cuts, and Sir Henry wasted not a moment, but seized the handle of the nearest knife, speared a chop, and began eating it from the blade. Kit did likewise, impaling one succulent cut after another, sampling them all. The pork was excellent – all smoky, juicy and hot from the flames. The lamb and ribs were next, and equally toothsome, as was the stuffed veal. He skipped the beef – it was a little too rare for him – and went for one of the pale pink slabs of flesh he did not recognize. The meat was somewhat chewy, but with a fine, delicate flavour unlike any other meat he had ever tasted.

'Ah-ha!' exclaimed Sir Henry, watching him with amusement. 'You are a very trencherman, sir. I salute you!'

'It is wonderful,' enthused Kit around a large mouthful. 'This one is especially delicious. What is it?' He held up what remained of the slice for inspection.

'Oh, yes!' answered Sir Henry appreciatively. 'You have hit on it there, sir. For *that* is hart's tongue – a speciality of the house – aged and then brined, and slow roasted. I daresay you've never tasted the like.'

'I don't get out much,' remarked Kit. He finished the slice, and another, before moving on to taste a little more of the venison. Two additional bowls, largely overlooked, were also present on the board. One contained a mash of turnips and parsnips mixed with cream and drenched with melted butter, and the other held some sort of sautéed greens. He spooned up a hefty helping of the mash and politely tasted the greens, then resumed his steady work on the heap of ribs and shanks before him. By the time Kit pushed himself away, his bowl was a slaughterhouse tangle of bones and gristle, and his cheeks, chin, and hands were dripping with grease. He felt as if he might possibly explode from internal pressure and that, all things considered, this would probably be for the best.

'Well done, sirs!' cried Sir Henry. He commended them on their gustatory prowess and sat back in his chair, smoothing the fat from his trim beard with glistening fingers. As the serving boys appeared to clear away the carnage, he announced, 'I believe we shall take our port and sweetmeats in private, gentlemen.' Rising from his chair, he paused to wipe his mouth and hands on the tablecloth. 'This way, if you please.'

Kit rose to follow. Sir Henry paused, picked up the apostle spoon and turned to Kit. 'Any man who would hold his own at table with me must wield a ready spoon.' He handed the silver utensil to him. 'It would please me to offer you this as a commemorative token of our new friendship.'

Kit glanced at his great-grandfather for guidance. Cosimo smiled and gave him a slight nod of encouragement.

'Then I would be honoured to accept it in the spirit in which it is offered, Sir Henry,' he said, in imitation of the high-flown style of address. 'I shall treasure it.'

Sir Henry beamed and then led them back through the dining room and up a staircase to one of the smaller upper rooms where, as the landlord had said, a table had been made ready and a fire glowed in the grate. Sir Henry settled into one of the big, leather chairs and waved his guests to others. A small, bald man appeared with a decanter of ruby liquid which he proceeded to pour into shallow silver cups.

'Thank you, Barnabas. We will see to ourselves. You may go,' said Sir Henry Fayth when they each had a cup in hand. When the serving man had gone, he lifted his cup and said, 'Here now, let us discuss the issues of the day.'

'Nothing would please me more,' replied Cosimo. 'First, however, I would hear more about this experiment that you have proposed in the hall tonight.'

'Oh, that,' replied Sir Henry. 'The merest trifle, a bit of subterfuge – nothing more.'

'But do you think it wise?'

'I think it wise to nip the weed in the bud,' replied Sir Henry reasonably. 'Too many of our members are expressing interest in this so-called ley discovery. By leading and conducting an experiment which not only fails, but is seen to fail – and fail spectacularly, I might add – then no respectable member will dare raise the subject again for fear of being considered...' he paused, searching for the right word, '... ridiculous, yes – a laughing stock, let us say.'

'I see,' replied Cosimo doubtfully.

'You disagree, sir?'

'Not entirely.' Cosimo shook his head. 'No.'

Sir Henry took a sip from his silver cup and waved his hand as if swatting a fly. 'Tosh! You and I both know we cannot allow any outside interference. The rumour has spread and it is beginning to attract interest. We must eliminate any serious inquiry before someone stumbles upon the truth.'

'My chief concern is that they might see through your sham experiment,' said Cosimo, swirling the sweet liquid in his cup.

'One or two might,' conceded Sir Henry, 'given the chance. The rest would not recognize a genuine scientific principle if it jumped up and bit them on the bum. I shall, of course, choose my participant observers from among the latter.'

Kit listened to this exchange and it occurred to him that Sir Henry moved easily from his antique English into Cosimo's and Kit's modern version. From this, he surmised that the two had enjoyed a long acquaintance. However that might be, in one thing he was confirmed: Sir Henry, for all his lofty airs, was a level-headed, trustworthy, and honourable man. *How very civilized*, Kit decided. *It should be like this always*. Suddenly, he wanted nothing more than to stay here and be a part of whatever it was the two grand gentlemen were cooking up between them. He was thinking how this might be accomplished when he heard his name mentioned.

'... and Kit here can help,' said Cosimo. Both men turned to him and seemed to expect some sort of reply.

'I – uh,' ventured Kit, 'would be happy to assist in any way I can, of course.' He was not at all certain what he had agreed to just then, but felt it was the right thing to do.

'Splendid!' said Sir Henry. 'More Oporto?' he said, proffering the decanter.

'I don't mind if I do,' said Kit, smiling the muzzy smile of the mildly intoxicated.

While Kit nursed his drink, the other two talked about the impending experiment and how to sabotage it. Eventually, they agreed on a plan and Cosimo said, 'There is just one small thing that's come up, and I'd welcome your advice, Sir Henry.'

'Of course, dear fellow. Anything. How can I be of service?'

'We seem to have lost someone on our way here,' said Cosimo. 'A young lady friend of Kit's has gone missing. It appears she followed Kit and failed to complete the crossing.'

'That is most unfortunate, I daresay.' The lord scientist clucked his tongue with disapproval. 'What the devil was she playing at, if you don't mind my asking?'

'Sorry,' said Kit, speaking up. 'It was all my fault. I was showing her about the leys and, well…' he gave a shrug of helpless ignorance. 'I guess something went wrong.'

'So it would seem.' Sir Henry gave a questioning glance to Cosimo. 'One would have thought you might have taken the proper precautions.'

'He has received no training from me,' replied Cosimo. 'It seems he has picked up the knack on his own.'

This information caused Sir Henry's eyebrows to rise sharply. 'So!' he said. 'Our young chap is a prodigy? A natural?'

'So it would seem.'

'Runs in the family, I suppose.' Sir Henry turned an appraising gaze towards Kit. 'So much potential. I, for one, would not like to see it wasted.'

'He will be schooled, never fear,' said Cosimo with conviction.

'What about the young lady in question?'

'I know nothing about her whatsoever,' Cosimo said, turning to Kit.

'Please believe me when I say I didn't know I was doing anything wrong,' said Kit in his own defence. 'I only meant to show her what had happened to me and, well, it happened again. In any case, all I know is that we were together in the alley and then we weren't. She's my girlfriend –'

At Sir Henry's puzzled expression, Cosimo interjected, 'He means sweetheart.'

'Ah!' said Sir Henry. 'Pray continue.'

'Wilhelmina's gone and I feel responsible,' concluded Kit. 'I said I'd take care of her, but lost her instead. We have to rescue her.'

'Find her we shall, sir! Never fear,' replied Sir Henry. 'And once we have found her, the young lady will be returned to her place of origin – of that you may be sure.'

This made Kit feel better. 'Then shouldn't we start looking right away?'

'Indeed, sir. I stand ready to offer my fullest assistance.'

'As always,' said Cosimo, 'your generosity runs far ahead of our request. We are most grateful.'

The nobleman waved aside the compliment. 'Tosh, sir! Think nothing of it.' 'I was hoping you might have some idea about where we might start our search,' Cosimo continued.

'Of course. Tell me, exactly where did the young woman go missing?'

'On Stane Way,' answered Cosimo.

Sir Henry pursed his lips for a moment, then took a sip of port. After a moment's reflection, he sighed and said, 'Yes, well, it would have to be there, I suppose.'

'Is that bad?' asked Kit.

'Let us say that it will multiply the difficulty of our task inestimably.'

'Why is that?'

'Stane Way is a particularly old and active intersection –' began Cosimo.

'More circus than intersection!' offered Sir Henry. 'There are at least five major crossings along that line – if not more. Your friend has presumably parted company with you at one of them. But consider the Stane ley as a corridor with doors opening to other rooms, do you see? Each of those other rooms has doors and there is no telling where the doors from those other rooms might lead. In any case, I warn you,' he said sternly, his beard quivering at its point, 'it will be dangerous. There are forces that wish us ill –'

'Like those men?' wondered Kit.

'We met Burley Men outside Sefton,' explained Cosimo.

'Ah!' confirmed Sir Henry. 'So the enemy are nosing around again.'

'They know about my piece of the map.'

'Do they now!' exclaimed Sir Henry. 'This changes everything.'

The nobleman grew reflective. Kit and Cosimo exchanged an uneasy glance. Sir Henry nodded to himself, then said, 'I feel I must warn you both: Burley and his brutes are not the only danger we will face. There are others. Also,' he cautioned, 'you must accept that it may not be a swift search. Such an undertaking will require a great deal of patience.'

Kit considered this. 'Is there no way to speed up the search? Thing is, Wilhelmina's not a very strong person. She is barely able to cope with normal life – something like this could kill her. I feel terrible about getting her involved and if anything happens to her, it'll be my fault.' He shook his head. 'I don't know how she's going to survive on her own.'

'Be that as it may, we dare not rush headlong into a rescue,' replied Sir Henry. '*Alea iacta est.*'

'Sir?' wondered Kit.

'The die has been cast.'

'No kidding,' said Kit.

Part **2**

The Macau Tattau

CHAPTER 7

In Which Wilhelmina Lands on Her Feet

Stinging rain and a savage blast of wind left Wilhelmina standing in a muddy puddle gasping for breath. Wet to the skin, she smeared the water from her eyes with the back of her hand and looked around – instantly closing her eyes again: an instinctive reaction, the rational mind's desperate attempt to maintain coherence in the face of a displacement so severe as to shatter reality to smithereens.

London had vanished.

In place of the lively, thrusting metropolitan conurbation was an empty rural wilderness of damp brown fields under low autumnal skies. In that briefest of glimpses, she had seen enough to know that whatever had happened to her threatened not only her perception of herself in the world, but sanity itself. In the grip of such a devastating shock, she did what anyone would do: she opened her mouth and screamed.

She put her head back and wailed, opening her soul to the sky, broadcasting her dismay to the four winds. She screamed and kept on screaming until black spots danced before her eyes, and then she screamed again – loud, ragged, ugly bursts that rent the air and made her red in the face. When she could scream no more, she clenched her fists and stamped her feet, her boots splashing up mud from the track until, forces spent at last, she crumpled, subsiding into whimpers and moans, shedding tears for her fractured world.

Some part of her mind maintained a stubborn detachment, refusing to yield to the madness. Eventually, this practical awareness asserted itself, saying in effect: Get a grip, girl. You've had a nasty shock. Okay. So, what are you going to do about it? Sit all day in the mud and throw a tantrum like a two-year-old? It's cold out here; you'll freeze to death. Drag your wits together, and take charge!

Shaking water from her hands, she got to her knees and, placing a palm against her soggy bottom, looked around. Her quick survey confirmed that she was on a simple one-track lane in the midst of a bleak countryside of tended fields, and she was very much alone. 'Kit?' she called, but heard only the lonely call of a low-flying crow.

He's toast, she thought, rising unsteadily to her feet. *I'll murder him in tiny little pieces.* 'Kit!' she shouted – and then it hit her: a rising wave of nausea that left her heaving in the middle of the track. She vomited once, and then again, and felt better for it. Wiping her mouth on the sleeve of her jacket, she made her way towards a field marker she could see a few hundred yards along.

As she walked, she told herself that something very weird had happened and that whatever the explanation, it was all her loser boyfriend's fault. The thought did not comfort her as much as she might have hoped, nor did imagining what she would do to him when she caught up with him again. The enormous strangeness of her undreamed of situation at once dwarfed and engulfed all other concerns.

People did not go jumping from one place to another with nothing in between. It simply did not happen. She had been sure Kit was up to something, but she had never – not even for a nanosecond – imagined that he might be telling some loopy version of the truth. And yet, here she was in the middle of nowhere – plucked off the teeming streets of overpopulated Islington and dropped in a lonely country lane – more or less as Kit had said. So this must be Cornwall.

She reached the marker stone and paused. There was nothing more to be seen except gently undulating hills – some wooded, some in grazing land, and ploughed fields – stretching in every direction. She had no choice but to continue on until she reached a farmhouse or village where she could beg the use of a phone to call a taxi. Wrapping her arms around her, she plodded on, and in a little while saw a wooden signpost with fingers pointing in various directions. Her heart leapt at the sight. She picked up her pace and hurried on, soon to learn that the sign marked a significant road: paved with flat, hand-set flagstones.

She strode to the sign and paused to read it. The faded writing was in two languages, neither of which she recognized: Cornish, she decided, and something else. Gaelic, maybe? Or were those two the same thing? In any case, the nearest place indicated on the greyed and weathered signpost was twelve something. Miles, probably. Or kilometres. She hoped it was kilometres.

Determined to put the unsettling strangeness of her predicament behind her and find the nearest human habitation, she stepped onto the road and began walking with purpose. After perhaps two or three miles or whatever-they-were she heard a sound behind her – a slow, steady creak-clack-creak-clack. Turning around, she saw a horse-drawn wagon trundling along the road towards her. Obviously a farmer, Mina thought. She hurried to meet the wagon, intent on hitching a ride to wherever he was going.

As the vehicle drew nearer, she realized that it was not, as she had first imagined, a simple field conveyance, but a much more substantial vehicle: a large, high-sided affair with a cloth top drawn over curved hoops to form a round tent-like covering. The wagon was pulled by not one but two rangy, long-eared mules, and sitting on the driver's bench was a very plump man in a baggy cloth hat. She stopped and allowed the vehicle to meet her, whereupon it slowed and rolled to a halt.

'Hiya!' she called, putting on a chirpy voice in the fledgling hope that her damp and bedraggled appearance might be overlooked.

'*Guten Tag*,' came the reply, which sent Wilhelmina instantly back to her childhood and her German grandmother's kitchen.

The unexpected oddity of encountering a *Deutschsprachigen* on the road only served to deepen her already fathomless confusion. Bereft of speech, she could only stare at the man.

Thinking, perhaps, that she had not understood, the stranger smiled and repeated his greeting.

'*Guten Tag*,' Mina replied. Grasping for her long-disused German, she said, '*Ich freue mich, Sie kennen zu lernen.*' The words felt lumpy and wooden in her mouth, and her tongue resisted making them. '*Sprechen Sie Englisch?*'

'*Es tut mir Leid, Fräulein. Nein*,' answered the man. He eyed her curiously, taking in her odd clothes and short hair, then squirmed in his seat and searched both ways down the road. '*Sind Sie alleine hier?*'

It took her a moment, but the words came winging back to her as if from a very great distance. He's asking if I am alone out here, she thought. '*Ja*,' she answered. '*Alleine.*'

The fat man nodded then spouted a longish sentence which again sent Wilhelmina right back to the German she had learned as a child – the long outdated language of her grandmother who had learned it from *her* immigrant grandmother, and very different from the *Hochdeutsch* Mina had studied in school. Nevertheless, she worked it out that he was offering her a lift to the next town. She accepted on the spot. The traveller put down the reins and stood, leaned over, and indicated the iron step ring projecting from the base of the wagon bed behind the front wheel, then offered his hand. She placed a muddy boot on the step and accepted the offered hand, and was pulled effortlessly up and onto the wooden seat. As soon as she had settled on the bench, the man picked up the reins and gave them a snap. '*Hü!*' he called; the wagon gave a jolt, the wheels creaked, and the mules resumed their languid clip-clop pace.

They proceeded in silence, rocking over the uneven road. Now and then, she stole a glance at the driver of the wagon. Her companion was a well-upholstered man of indeterminate age, with a mild, pleasant demeanour. His clothes were clean and tidy, but so very basic as to be nondescript – consisting of a plain wool jacket of dark green over a rough but clean linen shirt and spacious breeches of heavy dark hopsacking. His shoes were sturdy ankle-high boots, well crafted, but scuffed and worn and badly in need of a shine. The plump fellow presented an altogether unremarkable appearance –

save for his face: smooth, pink as a baby's; round, even-featured, with pale blue eyes beneath pale eyebrows, and ample cheeks that glowed in the brisk autumn breeze beneath the fine haze of a thin, stubbly blond beard.

It was that sweet-natured face that made him, she decided, for the countenance with which he faced the world wore an expression of benign cheerfulness – as if all that met his gaze amused and delighted, as if the world and everything in it existed only for his pleasure. He seemed to exude good will. In short, he was a plump, pink cherub clothed in simple brown wool.

Finally, Wilhelmina cleared her throat and said, '*Ich spreche ein bisschen Deutsch, ja?*'

The man looked at her and smiled. '*Sehr gut, Fräulein.*'

'Thank you for stopping for me,' she said. '*Ich bin* Wilhelmina.' My name is Wilhelmina.

'A good name,' replied the man, his own accent broad but light. 'I, too, have a name,' he announced proudly. 'I am Engelbert Stiffelbeam.' Lifting a plump hand, he raised his shapeless hat and made a comical little bow from the waist.

The old-fashioned gesture touched her strangely, and made her smile. 'I am happy to meet you, Herr Stiffelbeam.'

'Please! Please, Herr Stiffelbeam is my father. I am simply Etzel.'

'Etzel it is.'

'You know,' he confided cheerfully, 'I almost did not stop for you.'

'Oh?'

'I thought you were a man.' He indicated her strange clothes and short hair. He smiled and shrugged. 'But then I said to myself – think, Etzel, maybe this is how they are dressing in Bohemia. You have never been out of München, so how do you know what they do in Bohemia?'

Mina heard the word Bohemia and wondered at it. She had to think a moment to phrase the next question in German, then said, 'If you don't mind my asking, how did you come to be in Cornwall?'

He gave her a strange look. 'Bless me, Fräulein, but I have never been to England. This Cornwall is in England, *oder*?'

'But we are in Cornwall now,' she informed him. '*This* is Cornwall.'

He put back his head and laughed; it was a full and happy sound. 'Young people must have their jokes, I suppose. No, we are not in England, Fräulein. We are in Bohemia as you surely must know,' he told her, then added by way of explanation: 'We are on the road that leads to Prague.'

'Prague?'

Engelbert regarded her with a look of pitying concern. '*Ja*, I think so.' He nodded slowly. 'At least, this is what the signs tell me.' He examined her again for a moment, then said, 'Could it be that you are lost, Fräulein?'

'*Jawohl*,' she sighed, slumping back in her seat. 'Most definitely lost.' The desperate strangeness of her plight came crashing in upon her with renewed vengeance. First London had disappeared, and now Cornwall. What next? Tears of fear and frustration welled up in her large dark eyes. She wondered what in God's name was happening to her.

'There, there, *Schnuckel*. Not to worry,' said her podgy companion as if reading her mind. 'Etzel will take good care of you. There is nothing to fear.' He reached behind the seat back and produced a heavy woollen blanket, which he passed to her. 'Here, your clothes are wet and it is getting cold. Wrap yourself in this. You will feel better, *ja*?'

Accepting the blanket, she brushed at the tears with the heels of her hands. Schnuckel – it was what her grandmother had always called her, the same grandmother, in fact, whose German she spoke and whose name she bore. '*Vielen Dank*,' she sniffed, gathering the travel blanket around her. As the warmth began to seep into her, she did feel a little better for his reassurance. Keep it together, girl, she told herself. You've got to keep a clear head. Think!

Her first thought was that without a doubt her current predicament was all her low rat of a boyfriend's fault. All that talk about laying lines, or whatever it was, and crossing thresholds into other worlds and all that malarkey. It was so… she searched for a word. Impossible. So utterly impossible. No rational and sane person would have, *could* have, believed him.

Yet, here she was.

But where was that?

'Excuse me, Herr Stiffelbeam –'

'Etzel,' he corrected her with a smile.

'Excuse me, Etzel,' she said, 'but where are we exactly?'

'Well, now,' he said, sucking his teeth as he considered, 'we are a little way from the village of Hodyně in the Province of Bohemia which is part of the great Empire of Austria.' He gave her a sideways glance. 'Where did you *think* we might be, if I may ask?'

'I hardly know,' she replied. At least she was growing more comfortable with the language as, like a rusty pump that only required priming, the words began to flow more easily. 'I was travelling with someone who has gone missing. There was a storm, you see, and I seem to have become a little confused.'

Engelbert greeted this explanation with placid acceptance. 'Travel can be very confusing, I find. And yes, the storm – it was very strong, *ja*?'

'*Jawohl!*' she agreed. You have no idea.

They continued along in silence. Mina gazed out at the drab countryside, all brown and grey beneath dark October skies – if it *was* still October; she assumed it was, but couldn't be sure. The fields were small, and neatly kept behind their stone fences. Wooded hills clothed in the gold and brown of autumn rose to either side of the cobbled road and, here and there, she saw small wooden houses, weathered grey, with shake shingles covered with moss; whitewashed houses with low thatched roofs. It all looked so very old-fashioned…

'What is the time?' she asked suddenly. 'I mean, what year?'

'It is the thirtieth year of Emperor Rudolf's reign,' answered Etzel promptly. He seemed to sense that the confusion surrounding his hitch-hiking companion encompassed not only place, but time as well. 'It is the year of Our Lord 1606.'

'I see.' Wilhelmina's brow lowered. It had been bad enough when she imagined she was in Cornwall. This was worse. But if anything was to be done about it, she failed to see what it might be.

Don't panic, she told herself. Something will come to you. Until then, you've got no choice but to roll with it.

'Are you hungry?' asked Etzel.

'A little,' Mina admitted.

'I myself am always hungry,' he proclaimed, as if it was a singular achievement. 'Behind the seat you will find a *Tasche*, *ja*?'

Mina swivelled around in the seat, parted the cloth which covered the wagon and formed an entrance to the wagon box, and saw barrels and casks, and large bags of what looked like flour, or maybe sugar. 'Do you see it?'

'Here it is!' She spied a lumpy sack, and snatched it up.

Placing it in her lap, she loosened the drawstring and folded down the sides to reveal half a loaf of heavy dark bread, a muslin-wrapped wedge of cheese, a scrag end of sausage, three small apples, and a crockery flask of something that appeared to be wine.

'Take whatever you wish,' Etzel invited. He reached over and broke off a chunk of bread. 'Like so, *ja*?'

Mina followed his example, broke off some bread, and popped it into her mouth. It was chewy and flavoured with caraway – just like her mother and grandmother used to make. 'All those barrels and bags in the back,' she said, speaking around a second mouthful. 'Are you a travelling salesman?'

'*Nein, Fräulein*,' he replied, helping himself to an apple. 'Try some cheese,' he urged. 'To tell the truth, I have never before travelled outside Bavaria.'

'You are Bavarian?'

'*Ja*, I am from Rosenheim. It is a small town not far from München. You will not have heard of it.' He raised the apple to his lips, nipping it neatly in half in a single bite. 'Do you like the bread?'

'Yes, very much – it is delicious,' she replied.

'I made it,' Etzel confessed, a touch of shyness shading his tone. 'I am a baker.'

'Really?' wondered Wilhelmina. 'What a coincidence – I am a baker, too.'

Etzel turned on his seat and regarded her, his blue eyes wide with surprise above his chubby pink cheeks. 'There is no such thing

73

as coincidence, Fräulein. I do not believe so. *This,*' he announced grandly, 'is a most fortuitous meeting.'

'Fortuitous?' She puzzled over the word. 'Fate, you mean?'

'Fate!' He said it as if the word itself was sour. His round cheerful face scrunched up in thought. 'It is…' he paused, then declared with a shout of triumph, *'Providence!* Ja, it is Providence that has brought us together. You see, I am a baker who is in need of a helper,' he placed a hand on his chest, 'and you are a baker in need of a friend, I think – and perhaps more, *ja*?'

It was, Mina had to admit, true.

He then revealed the reason for his trip to Prague. 'Times are hard in Bavaria just now – all over Germany, too, I think. Very difficult. In München I am a baker with my father and brother, but there is not enough business to support all of us any more. My brother Albrecht has a family, *ja*, and what little trade we have, he needs it more than I do. I am second-born,' he said sadly, 'and I have no wife, no children.' He paused, nodding to himself as if confirming that this was, in fact, the case. 'Last month we sat down together, the three of us, and after many beers we made a plan. So! They are sending me to Prague to see if I can start a new business there.'

'Well, I hope it works out for you.'

'*Werks aus*?' The meaning escaped him. '*Arbeitet aus, klappen*?'

'Ah, *gelang* – succeeds, I mean.'

He nodded. 'Do you know what they are saying?'

'No,' Mina admitted, liking his gentle manner. 'What are they saying?'

'They are saying that in Prague just now, the streets are paved with gold.' He laughed. 'I believe no such thing, of course. It is just a way of saying that things are better there.' He offered an amiable shrug. 'I don't say so myself. I only know things cannot be worse than they are in München.' He nodded. 'Things must be better there.'

'I hope you're right,' she said.

The wagon bumped along and as the dull day began to fade at last, they began to see a few more farms and houses scattered around the hillsides and beside the road and, finally, Hodyně: a dishevelled little farming town. 'We will see if there is an inn, *ja*?'

'All right,' agreed Wilhelmina doubtfully. 'But I should warn you, I don't have any money.'

'Not to worry,' replied Etzel. 'In a town like this it will not cost much. I have a little silver.' He smiled reassuringly. 'God willing, it is enough.'

CHAPTER 8

In Which Wilhelmina Proves Her Mettle

Prague in 1606 was a fairytale city of massive encircling walls with high towers at every corner, huge gates of timber and iron, crooked streets filled with tiny houses whose roofs of red clay tiles almost touched the ground, a fortified castle with turrets and a drawbridge. Green and yellow banners hung from the battlements, gilded angels kept watch over the city from the top of soaring church spires and, rising on a hill in the very centre of the city, gleamed the sparkling white-washed facade of a grand palace. To Wilhelmina it looked like something the Brothers Grimm might have concocted as a backdrop to a story about a spoiled prince and a selfless pauper. Mina had treasured such a book as a child – a gift from her namesake grandmother – and had always thrilled to the subtle horror of those ancient stories.

'It's like a dream,' she gasped upon seeing their imposing destination suddenly revealed in all its glory.

They had come upon the many-towered city quite without warning. The open, rolling countryside gave little hint of what was lurking just over the next hill. There was but a slight build-up along the road – a few more farms, a tiny settlement or two – and then, as they came over the rise, they were all at once confronted by the majestic city walls and a view of the imposing brown stone castle, banners aflutter in the breeze. A generous river skirted the south-eastern quarter of the town and a great many shack-like dwellings had been erected on the low ground. Engelbert did not approve of this, as he imagined the area would be prone to flooding. 'They should know better,' he huffed. However, he did approve of the hefty stone walls that encircled the city and the sturdy, ironclad city gates, and pronounced them very good work. 'Strong walls are important,' he declared.

The weather had turned cold. There was a shimmering skin of frost on the grass and trees. Travelling in the country, they had had the road mostly to themselves, but the traffic greatly increased the nearer they came to the gates. Engelbert left his seat and guided the mules as they joined the slow-moving parade which included ox-carts, horse-drawn carriages, and more than a few hand wagons: mobile businesses of several varieties, all pulled by their proprietors – tinkers, shoemakers, weavers, carpenters, and the like – as well as scores of people on foot, and even a goat cart or two. Most of those on foot carried bundles on their backs: sticks, straw, rope, and bales of hay for fodder.

They passed through wide-open gates and rolled on into the heart of the city. Wilhelmina took in the sights and sounds – geese honking, dogs barking, and from somewhere she couldn't see, the plaintive bleating of sheep – and the *smells*! The whole of Prague, as far as she could tell, stank of cheese and, unaccountably, apples. Why this should be so, she could not say, but under the pungent scent of rancid milk and rotting apples she detected, unmistakably, the sour, nostril-curling pong of the cess pit. The latter did not surprise her in the least since the gutters of the rough-paved streets ran with raw effluent, and there were mounds of rubbish heaped willy-nilly over footpath and pavement everywhere she happened to cast her eye.

Engelbert led his wagon directly into the spacious central square of the city, an area marked out and dominated by four immense buildings: a military barracks, a *Rathaus*, a guild hall, and the great hulking mass of a gothic cathedral. Numerous other structures crammed themselves between the larger buildings, wildly random in size and style – tall and thin brick next to short and squat half-timber, next to ornately plastered and painted and neatly curved facades – forming a sort of mad infill which gave the extravagant city square an outlandish, and slightly demented, character.

The sprawling open space played host to a generous number and variety of pedestrians, human and otherwise. A market appeared to be in full cry: merchants and customers haggling over the various wares on offer outside flimsily constructed booths; hawkers stalking, shouting for attention; dogs barking at ragged, quick-darting children; jugglers juggling, dancers prancing, and stilt-walkers swaggering through the milling throng.

All in all, Wilhelmina thought it breathtaking. And when Etzel announced, 'Here is where I shall have my bakery!' she felt a genuine tingle of excitement.

'Why not?' she replied.

'*Ja!*' He beamed at her with his happy cherub face. 'Why not?'

Etzel drove his wagon to a corner of the square where he found a stone trough and hitching post. He halted and climbed down, tied the mules to the post and allowed them to drink. 'We have arrived!' he called happily. 'Our new life begins.'

His inclusion of her was so easy and natural, she accepted it herself. In any case, it was not as if she had any better option.

The strangeness, the utter impossibility of her plight, was not lost on Wilhelmina. But benign acceptance of the peculiar situation was steadily, stealthily creeping up on her. She had to keep mentally pinching herself to force her wandering and easily distracted mind to remember that what she was experiencing was in no way normal. Yet, bizarre though it surely was, more and more she was discovering that her otherworldly sojourn was also curiously compelling. The weird cavalcade of events exerted its own beguiling influence. Old world Prague was winning her over.

Engelbert was gazing about him with equal amazement. Finally, he drew himself up and turned to her. 'I am wanting to ask you something, Fräulein,' he said, his voice taking on a note of unexpected gravity.

'Go on then,' she said warily.

'Would you watch Gertrude and Brunhild for me?'

Mina gazed back in bewilderment.

He indicated the mules.

'Oh! Of course.'

'I will not go far,' he told her, climbing down from the wagon box.

'Don't worry. I'll stay right here.'

But he was already gone, disappearing into the wheeling, swirling traffic of the square. Mina sat in the wagon and continued soaking in the sights and sounds around her, trying to gain some measure of the place. Prague, she thought, in the thirtieth year of Emperor Rudolf the second – is that what Etzel had said? What did she know about the seventeenth century? Not much. Nothing, really. Didn't Shakespeare live in the 1600s? Or was it Queen Elizabeth? She couldn't remember.

If she had ever once in her life given the realities of life in seventeenth-century Bohemia a fleeting thought – and she most certainly had not – she would have pictured a world of superstition and suffering where obscenely rich and powerful aristocrats oppressed the miserable mass of grimy peasants whose lives were nasty, brutish, and short. Yet the folk she observed bustling around her, while admittedly grimy and short, seemed a fairly happy lot – judging solely from the air of amiable bonhomie permeating the Old Town square. Everywhere she looked, people were smiling, laughing, greeting one another with formal handshakes and kisses. Uniformly dressed in dull browns and drab greens – long knee-length cloaks and breeches for men, and short bodices with long, full skirts for the women – they nevertheless seemed prosperous enough.

It was the ladies who caught her attention, and from what she could see from her seat in the wagon, long hair was definitely in fashion – piled high and extravagantly curled or braided. Nearly everyone wore some sort of head covering; a scant handful of women covered their elaborate locks with fine, lace-trimmed hats; simple linen caps were in abundance, as were scarves. While their skirts might have been plain, their shawls were not; whether fringed, tasselled, square-cut, rounded, fine-woven, or knitted – all were as colourful as the weaver's art could achieve: crimsons, yellows, blues, and greens, in any and all combinations. In fact, both men and women wore shawls. And children, of which there were many, were dressed exactly as their elders, adults in miniature.

The market crowd occupied her complete attention so that when the great clock in the city hall tower struck for the second time since her arrival in the square, she stirred and realized sitting so long in the wagon had made her cold. She rubbed her arms and blew into her cupped hands. Where had Etzel got to?

As if in answer to her thought, she heard a piping call and turned to see her companion, his arms laden with cloth-wrapped packages, bowling towards her through the throng, a small tribe of ragged foundlings around him. 'Wilhelmina!' he called as he came to the wagon. 'Our luck is good!'

He began handing up packages to her which she took and stowed behind the wagon seat. The children were clamouring in a language Mina did not understand. What did they speak in Prague? Czech? Slovak?

'There is only one bakery on the square,' he announced, 'and it is very small.' He passed her another package. 'This one is for you.'

'For me?' Wilhelmina savoured an unexpected delight. 'What is it?'

'Open it and see.'

She pulled one of the strings and unwrapped the parcel to reveal several small glazed cakes with chopped nuts and tiny seeds. 'Honey cakes!' she cooed. 'How sweet of you.'

He beamed. Taking another package, he handed it to the nearest and tallest of the ragamuffins around him. 'Share with your brothers and sisters,' he instructed firmly in German, which the children seemed to understand.

The young lad opened the bag and distributed little white biscuits to his noisy comrades who were now leaping up and down to receive their treats. The bag was soon empty and Etzel shooed his entourage away, telling them to be good, attend mass, obey their parents, and come back tomorrow.

'These are *lecker!*' exclaimed Mina, dusting off another of her grandmother's words. She held out one of the cakes to him.

'I am glad you like them,' he said, biting into the little pastry.

'This is a good place,' he observed, chewing thoughtfully. 'I like it here.'

'What should we do now?' Mina wondered.

'We will start looking for a place to have my bakery.'

'Now?'

'Why not? It is a good day.'

'Very well,' she agreed. 'Where do we start?'

'We begin here.'

After leaving the mules and wagon with a nearby livery service, Engelbert and Wilhelmina made a thorough circuit of the square. They went shop-by-shop around the large open plaza that formed Prague's busy commercial centre, and talked to many of the shopkeepers. Yes, the Old Square was the best in the city, the best in the entire region, even. And, yes, it was very expensive doing business in such a prime location. No, they did not know of any empty shops or premises on the square. 'The landlord charges any price he wants for rent,' complained the butcher, who worked out of a shop hardly bigger than a wagon bed. 'Yet, even at such high prices, these places do not stay empty long.'

The sentiment and explanation was echoed with only slight variation by everyone they approached. In the end, they were forced to conclude that even if there was a shop available, Engelbert would not be able to afford it with the limited funds he had brought from Rosenheim for the venture. 'Everything is very expensive. I am beginning to think I have made a mistake in coming here,' he confessed. The thought cast a pall over his cheerful demeanour.

'How can you say that?' Mina chided. 'It's a big city, and we've only looked in one place.'

'We've looked in the best place,' he sighed. 'Everyone says this.'

'Maybe,' she allowed. 'But there are bound to be others just as good. We just have to expand the search.'

Engelbert allowed himself to be prodded into action once more and they began scouring the interlocking network of side streets. These, they quickly discovered, were uniformly dark and narrow, and a far cry from the salubrious square. The shops and businesses were of a poorer, scrappier, even vaguely disreputable quality – as were the people frequenting these down-market establishments. The premises tended to be shoddy, the facades in need of cleaning and repair; there was rubbish everywhere; a few overly dressed ladies loitered about and, out of the corner of her eye now and then, Mina glimpsed rats.

The side streets were depressed, to be sure, and ultimately depressing to Engelbert, whose hopes dwindled with each dingy urban corridor they explored. His sighs became heavier and more frequent. Yet these grubby back streets did offer the one thing the more respectable and prosperous square lacked: cheap space, and plenty of it. Indeed, every third or fourth shop seemed to be either empty or going out of business; and those that weren't gave every impression of clinging precariously to their existence.

'I have seen enough,' said the now disheartened baker. 'Let us go back.'

Mina felt sorry for her dejected companion, and concern over her own prospects which were now enmeshed with his. She gave him a pat on the shoulder and they started for the open air and sunlight of the square. Working their way back through the tangle of interwoven byways, they turned onto a street they had not searched. Halfway along, they saw that the way was blocked by a horse and wagon drawn up outside one of the shops. There was a man in the wagon stacking furniture and boxes into a very tipsy pyramid. Now and again, a woman appeared in the doorway of the shop with another box which she handed up to the man to be added to the unstable mound.

'I think they're moving out,' surmised Mina.

'Who can blame them?' commiserated Engelbert.

Drawing near the wagon, they paused. 'Good day to you, sir. God bless you!' called Engelbert, who seemed incapable of passing anyone without offering a greeting.

The man looked up from his labours, and grunted a reply. The woman appeared in the doorway with a rolled-up rug. On a whim, Mina felt moved to address her. 'Good day,' she said. 'Are you moving out?'

'*Achso, Deutsch!*' The woman gave her a dark, disparaging look and answered in her own language. 'Are you blind, girl?'

The surly response knocked Wilhelmina back a step, but made her more determined. 'Please,' she said, 'it is just that we are looking for a place to open a shop.'

'You can have this one,' the woman told her, 'if you can hold your water until we've gone. And good luck to you.'

'Now, Ivanka, there's no cause to be rude,' said the man in the wagon, pausing to wipe his face with a dirty rag. 'It is not her fault.' The woman lifted her lip at him, turned without another word, and went back inside. To Wilhelmina, he said, 'Landlord is inside. You talk to him, good woman, and find out all you wish to know.'

Without consulting Engelbert, she stooped to enter the shop, which was almost empty save for two more rugs and a few wooden boxes. A long-faced, sallow man with a neatly trimmed goatee beard which only served to accentuate his already elongated face was standing at a wooden counter writing in a tiny book with a quill pen. Like so many of the men Wilhelmina had seen, he wore a long black coat and a white shirt with an odd little white-starched neck ruff; his head was enveloped in a large bag hat of green silk with the flourish of a white feather sweeping out to one side. 'Yes?' he said without looking up. 'What is it?'

Wilhelmina tried to think how best to phrase her request, and wondered if he, too, would understand her German.

'Well? Speak up, man! I am very busy.'

'Sir,' said Mina, 'are you the landlord?'

'Yes, of course.' He glanced around at her without moving his head more than necessary. 'Who else should I be?'

'I am certain I don't know,' answered Mina. 'Is this shop for rent?'

'Why? Do you want it?'

'Yes,' replied Mina rashly.

'Sixty *guldiners*.'

'Pardon?'

'Sixty guldiners – for six months.' He returned to his little book. 'Away with you. Come back with your father.'

'We will give you fifty,' she said, 'for a year.'

'Get out!' said the man. 'You don't know what you're talking about. Get out of my shop – and do not come back.'

'Wilhelmina,' called Engelbert from the door. 'What are you doing? Come away.'

Reluctantly, she rejoined Engelbert on the street outside. 'He wants sixty guldiners,' she told him, 'for six months.'

'That is too much,' said Engelbert. 'For a place like this,' he wrinkled his nose, 'it is too much.'

'I agree.' She frowned. 'What *is* a guldiner anyway?'

Etzel gave her a curious look. 'Do they not have such as this where you come from?'

'They have similar,' she allowed. 'But not guldiners. What is it?'

He lifted the hem of his coat and after a moment's fuss brought out a small leather pouch. He untied it and reached inside. 'This is a groschen,' he said, producing a small silver coin. 'It is worth six *kreuzer*.'

'I see,' replied Mina, repeating the formula to herself. 'One groschen equals six kreuzer.'

'There's more,' he said. 'Ten groschen make a guldengroschen – or guldiner, as we say.' He fished inside the pouch and brought out a larger silver coin. 'This is a guldiner – very good.'

Mina nodded. 'Ten groschen make up a guldiner. Got it. Are there any more?'

'There is a new one called a thaler – this is also very good, though you may not see so many of them. They are worth twenty-four groschen.'

'So, thalers are even better,' observed Mina. She plucked the silver guldiner from between Engelbert's thumb and forefinger.

The departing woman reappeared with another rolled-up rug under her arm. 'How much?' she asked as she passed. To Mina's puzzled look, she jerked her head towards the shop door and said, 'Him inside – how much did he demand?'

'Sixty guldiners,' replied Etzel.

'The greedy miser,' scoffed the woman, handing up the rug to her husband in the wagon. 'We only paid him thirty for the entire year.'

'How long were you –' she hesitated, amending her thought: 'How long did you rent from him?'

'We were here four years,' replied the woman, 'and never a good day in all that time. May the devil take him *and* his shop. I never want to see either of them again.'

'Do not take on so, Ivanka,' chided the man. 'It is hard to lose a business.'

'Where will you go now?' asked Etzel.

'We are going to Bratislava,' replied the man. 'My wife has a sister there and we will get a new shop.'

'What kind of shop did you have?' Mina wondered.

'It was a candle shop,' answered the man. 'I make candles.'

'The best in the city,' put in his wife proudly. 'No more. Let them live in the darkness.' She spat in the doorway for emphasis.

'She's very angry,' explained the man.

Wilhelmina thanked the couple for their help, and went back into the shop. 'Fifty guldiners is more than you will get from anyone else,' she announced. 'We want it for a year.'

The man in the green hat laid aside his book and stood. 'Am I not to be rid of you?'

'No,' said Mina, 'not until I get a reasonable answer.'

'Sixty Guldiners is reasonable,' replied the landlord.

'Not when the current occupants are paying only thirty a year.'

'Times change.'

'I agree,' replied Mina. 'That is why we are offering fifty.'

The man in the black coat snapped shut his tiny book. 'Very well. Fifty, then. It is done.'

Engelbert, standing in the doorway, opened his mouth to object.

'Not so fast,' said Wilhelmina. 'This room will need to be painted – and the outside as well.'

The landlord frowned. His eyes narrowed. 'A woman?' he wondered. 'And you talk to me like this?'

'Fifty Guldiners,' Wilhelmina reminded him.

'Very well, anything else?'

'Yes,' she said, 'there is one other thing. We will need an oven.'

'An oven…' He did not seem to appreciate the nature of the request.

'This is to be a bakery,' she told him. 'We need an oven.'

'A large one,' put in Engelbert hopefully, 'with four shelves.'

The black-coated landlord pulled on his beard in a way that suggested he thought he might be talking to crazy people, but could not be sure. 'No,' he said at last. 'It is too much.'

'Fine,' replied Mina. 'Come, Etzel, I saw a better shop closer to the square. It is empty and I am sure the landlord would be happy for our business.' Taking Engelbert by the arm, she started through the door.

'Wait,' called the landlord.

She turned back, smiling.

'If I do this, I will need a full year's payment in hand.' He tapped his open palm.

'We have the money,' Wilhelmina assured him before thinking to ask Engelbert if that was, in fact, true. 'Assuming the rooms upstairs are suitable for living, of course. We will need furniture – beds, tables, chairs. Simple things.'

'You will find all you need upstairs.' The landlord waved at the staircase at the back of the shop.

A quick look around the four rooms on the second floor assured Mina that this was indeed the case. There were beds in two rooms, and a table with four chairs in another, and a spare room with two chairs more and a large chest.

'It is acceptable,' said Mina upon returning to the ground floor. 'Two new rugs would make it more acceptable.'

'And the money?' asked the landlord.

Wilhelmina looked to Engelbert, who brought out his leather pouch. He turned his back and made counting noises, then faced them once more, extending his hand to the landlord, who reached out to receive his pay.

'Not so fast,' said Mina, intercepting the pouch in mid-air. 'We will pay you half now, and half when we have signed the papers.'

'Papers?' wondered the landlord. 'What are these papers? I know nothing of papers.'

'The legal papers,' she said. 'The *lease*, or whatever you call it. I want papers to say that we have paid for a year and that there will be an oven and new paint – all that we have agreed upon. I want it in writing.'

'My word is my bond,' sniffed the landlord. 'Ask anyone, they will tell you. Jakub Arnostovi is honest. I have never offered legal papers to anyone before.'

'Times change,' replied Wilhelmina sweetly.

CHAPTER 9

In Which Fragile Hopes are Cruelly Dashed

'You are a wonder, Wilhelmina,' breathed Etzel. Awed by her display of business acumen and tough-minded negotiating prowess, the big, gentle man could hardly speak. 'However did you do that?'

'Do what?' she asked, genuinely puzzled by his amazement.

'The way you bent Herr Arnostovi to your will. I have never seen the like. He is a landlord, after all.'

'Oh, that,' replied Mina. 'I live in London, remember? I've been dealing with landlords most of my life.'

'I would never have dared to speak to him like that. It was…' he sighed with admiration, '*wunderbar.*'

'That was nothing,' she said, smiling as she basked in his praise. 'You should see me rip into a Tottenham landlord – and they're the worst.'

'You have a good head for business, Mina,' he told her. 'We shall do very well together, I think.'

'I hope so, Etzel.'

'Now then!' He rubbed his chubby hands together. 'You stay here and wait for Herr Arnostovi's return. I will go and get the wagon, and then we can begin moving in.'

He hurried off down the street towards the livery stables, and Wilhelmina stood for a moment outside the shop, examining the exterior and trying to decide what colour to paint it. White, of course, was always good for a bakery; it made a place look clean and wholesome, like bread. And the deep-shadowed street could certainly do with brightening up.

But, no, dark blue was better – a royal blue, with gold trim. That would look posh and professional. She cast another glance up and down the street. No… white would stand out better and that was what they needed more than anything just now. A good solid white enamel, and a sign – judging from the street view, all good shops had signs – with a picture of a fresh baked loaf of bread.

Now, what to call the shop? Probably Etzel would have some ideas about that.

'It is Stiffelbeam and Sons Bakery,' he said when she asked him what his father's shop was called. 'It is a good name, I think.'

'Yes,' agreed Mina, doubtfully. 'But people here don't know you or your father. We need a new name – something that will be easy for people to remember.' She thought for a moment. 'Do you have a speciality?'

His broad, good-natured face bunched up in thought. 'I make very good Stollen,' he declared proudly. 'The best in München – that is what people tell me.'

'Great!' said Mina. 'And when Christmas comes we will make sure everyone hears about Stiffelbeam's Special Stollen. But I was thinking of something we might use for a name.'

'*Ahso.*' He thought some more. After a few moments' furious silence, he said, 'What if we called it Stiffelbeam's Bakery?'

'Yes…' Mina replied slowly. 'Well, we can think about it some more. Let's unload the wagon and get this place tidied up. I'm sure something will occur to us in the next day or two.'

They spent the rest of the day cleaning the premises top to bottom, and organizing their meagre store of supplies and Engelbert's few belongings. They planned where the equipment should go; how much space they'd need for a counter and shelves and workspaces; where to keep the fuel for the oven; and general household organization – such as who should take which bedroom and what items of furniture should go where.

In Wilhelmina's view, the place was primitive in the extreme: no electricity or running water; no radio, television, telephone, of course. Only fire for heat and light; only foot power – human or animal – for transport. Whatever else could be said, in the realm of creature comfort, Prague in the thirtieth year of Rudolf left a lot to be desired.

Everywhere she turned, some new – or rather, ancient – oddity presented itself, reminding her that the world as she knew it had mysteriously and radically changed. Thus, she remained in a state of continual low level shock. While giving every outward appearance of a person resigned to her lot, if not entirely content, the question of how she was to make her way back to what she considered the *real* world was never far from Mina's mind. Like a loose tooth the tongue cannot leave alone, she returned time and again to the question – all to no avail. She simply did not have enough of whatever she needed to advance the matter in any practical way.

In the meantime, Wilhelmina determined to make the best of her situation, peculiar as it might be. She occupied herself with the mundane chores of setting up the house and making the rooms inhabitable. She took inventory of her private quarters: a wooden frame bed with mattress and tented curtains; a pine table with one slightly wobbly leg; a good stout straight-backed chair made of oak; a large wooden chest for clothes; a small crate of imperfect candles of varying length, diameter, and straightness. The bed, like the chest, was heavy and well made; the mattress on the soft and lumpy side, stuffed as it was with straw and horsehair. The single coverlet smelled of stale sweat and she refused to sleep with it until it had been beaten within a thread of its life and aired out for a day in the sun.

In all the to-ing and fro-ing, Mina was pleased to see that Engelbert was a dutiful and diligent worker, unfailingly cheerful and optimistic; and, if not the fleetest fellow on foot, he seemed to be well nigh tireless. Over the next few days the shop began to shape up nicely. Masons and carpenters appeared, to construct the oven, and Mina talked them into building a simple counter and some shelves in exchange for a supply of free bread for a month.

Engelbert considered this needlessly extravagant, she could tell from the shocked expression on his face, but she explained that tradesmen worked in many households and for wealthy, or at least well-off, patrons. 'Word of mouth is the best advertising,' she told him. 'And it will cost us little enough. Once folk begin hearing about our wonderful bread, they'll be lining up in the street to get their hands on it.'

Every chance she got, Wilhelmina explored the city – starting with the great Týn Church in the square where, on Sunday, Engelbert dragged her from blissful slumber to attend the service. 'To thank the Lord for our good fortune, and the saving of our souls,' he said. Though Wilhelmina understood little of what went on, she enjoyed the service; she liked the pomp and pageantry, the smells and bells, the thundering music of the hymns, the splendour of the architecture and the robed majesty of the many priests. Most of all it made Engelbert happy, and she felt a better person for having gone.

Other times, she roamed the city wherever whim took her. She borrowed a little money from Engelbert and outfitted herself with a good, durable skirt, two long-sleeved white linen smocks, a set of small clothes, a handsome bodice, an apron, a red shawl, three pairs of heavy stockings, and sturdy leather shoes with brass buckles and stout soles. All the items, save for the undergarments, were second-hand but good quality. She donned the colourful headscarves to hide her too-short hair and help her blend in better, and so she would no longer be mistaken for a man. Thus disguised – as she thought of it – she allowed herself to wander here and there as her feet took her, always on the lookout for a bakery in order to do a little light industrial spying – sometimes following her nose to the source. What she learned was enlightening and practical.

She immediately discovered that the bread of Prague was heavy, dense, and dark. It was made almost entirely of rye flour, most often flavoured with caraway, and had a bitter, not altogether pleasant taste. Also, it dried out quickly; everyone was well accustomed to soaking it in milk or water if they were to have any chance of eating it after the first day or so. For reasons Wilhelmina could not readily perceive, the city's bakers insisted on fashioning this important staple of life into enormous loaves which were then cut into slabs of various sizes and sold like butchered meat: prime centre cuts fetched the highest price, scrag ends went for much less.

It was the same everywhere she went: the same black bread, the same lumpen slabs, the same prices and, she suspected, the same uninspired recipe in use across the city, if not the entire country. Everyone seemed sanguine about this arrangement – although why this should be so Mina could not say. In her opinion, the bread was vile. Clearly, the gentle folk of Prague were nothing if not long-suffering.

'We can do better,' she told Engelbert one day after her latest foray. 'We *will* do better. We will give our customers something new and different – something they've never seen or tasted before. We'll soon be the most successful bakers in the city – in the whole country even. Everyone in Prague will sing Etzel Stiffelbeam's praises.'

'Do you really think so?' he wondered, delighted by her assurance and enthusiasm.

'I would not be surprised if by this time next month, we were baking for the royal household.'

'For Emperor Rudolf himself?' gasped Engelbert. 'Oh, *ja*, that would be something.'

Indeed, a royal warrant would have been the guarantee of success. With that in hand, all loyal, right-thinking consumers would beat a path to the door of the bakery shop called, simply: *Etzel's*.

They opened for business on a bright, brisk morning three weeks after arriving in the city and waited for the custom that would make their fortune. The first week of trade came and went without causing so much as a ripple of interest, and the second followed in much the same way. A few curious or intrepid folk appeared and were artfully persuaded to try some of Engelbert's lighter, softer, tastier bread. Those who did so professed themselves pleasantly surprised, impressed, and satisfied.

'They'll come back,' Wilhelmina told Etzel. 'With every nibble, we catch a fish. We just need to cast the net wider, that's all.'

This left Etzel scratching his head. But Mina was in no doubt; as soon as word spread that a new baker had arrived with delicious new recipes, they would be inundated with orders and customers.

Still, as time passed and the days went by, Etzel's bread, delectable as it undoubtedly was, remained unsold. As the third week threatened to go the way of the previous two, Wilhelmina, feeling increasingly desperate, took several loaves down the street and out into the Old Town Square where she gave away free slices of their freshly baked product to passers-by. A few of these she was able to coax back to the shop to purchase a loaf of the same for themselves. Happily, the day ended with a profit for the first time.

Sadly, it was also to be the last time they would close up the shutters with coins in the cash box — the last, at least, for a very long time.

The trouble, Wilhelmina had begun to suspect, was twofold. First: they were foreigners. There was no getting around that. They were *Ausländer* and viewed as such by the self-considered sophisticates of Prague. Second: the location of the shop — down one of the old city's disagreeable streets — did not inspire either confidence *or* curiosity in the solid God-fearing citizens they hoped to lure through the door. There were possibly other reasons, too, of which Mina was unaware, but any way she looked at it the situation had every appearance of a disastrous error of judgment in the choice of location.

As the days drew on, and the glowing autumn began to ebb into the dull, chill, drab of winter, so did Wilhelmina's confidence wither and fade. She greeted each grey day with dread, and finished with a sense of grim relief that at least she would not have to face it again. Engelbert tried to remain cheerful, but his natural optimism was eroding with each renewed failure. And that was the hardest part for Wilhelmina — watching that great good joyful soul dwindle by degrees into ever bleaker despair as the bread so lovingly baked went untasted, unsold, and uneaten.

The bright hopes that had sped them so fair and free on favourable winds appeared set on a collision course with the treacherous coast of a harsh and bitter reality. When the two collided — it was only a matter of time now — their happy little shop would, like a storm-tossed ship broken on the rocks, sink without a trace.

CHAPTER 10

In Which Kit Entertains
Second First Impressions

Kit, yawning from a restless night on a lumpy horsehair mattress, could hear muffled voices through the panelling. Cosimo and Sir Henry were deep into a lengthy conversation which had begun as, 'Would you excuse us, Kit? Sir Henry and I have something to discuss in private. Don't wander away. Shouldn't take but a moment. We'll call you.' But they were still going at it hammer and tongs and, with no end in sight, Kit was bored with sitting in the vestibule and fed up with counting knots in the floorboards. He decided to stretch his legs.

Planning to be back before anyone realized he had gone, he tiptoed down the corridor and found a rear staircase that led to an outside door. The day was cloudy and trending towards rain; availing himself of one of Sir Henry's heavy wool cloaks hanging from a hook by the door, he slipped out, leaving the stately stone pile of Clarimond House with no other aim than to get some fresh air into his lungs and treat himself to another look at Olde London Towne. Flitting out through the back garden gate, he walked along the mews until reached the Musgrave Road and was instantly shocked anew by the unfathomable conundrum of a place at once so utterly strange and yet uncannily familiar. Perhaps it was like meeting in the flesh someone you knew very well but only through entries in a diary. Or maybe it was like meeting, as an infant, a friend you knew only as a grown-up adult. This, Kit thought, is what it is like to get a second first impression. So much was recognizable and unchanged, so much alien.

He proceeded down the road, passing half-timbered buildings that were not only unspoiled, pristine – not having suffered the ravages of time and remodelling – but also less desirable, since they were dwellings of common people and not the treasured darlings of the historic preservation set. No hanging baskets, blue commemorative plaques, or BMWs parked kerbside; no kerbs. Rather, they featured dirty little windows, dingy render, mildewed thatch, chimney tops black with soot. Long rows of such houses gave the scene a curious monochrome appearance, as if he had stepped into a black-and-white photograph. The streets were either roughly cobbled or, more frequently, rutted dirt tracks; and every city thoroughfare, as far as Kit could see, was sullied with horse and cattle manure. Cows, pigs, sheep, geese, chickens were herded along the city byways by farmers on their way to or from one of the city's livestock markets. Trees and plants were few; the little greenery visible was confined to the small out-of-the-way patches where feet did not tread, nor cattle graze.

A more subtle, yet no less profound, difference was one he noticed only as he walked along: the altered soundscape. His first thought was that something had gone wrong with his hearing. Not deafness – he could hear the occasional dog barking, the whinny of a horse, the rusty groan of the iron gate as he pushed it open, the voice of a street merchant calling attention to his wares a little further along – all that and more he could hear without difficulty. But the city seemed subdued, as if an occluding veil had been drawn across the world.

Kit's promenade very soon proved extremely taxing of his mind and senses. The continual noticing and cataloguing of innumerable diversities was exhausting and, unused to the rigours of such mental labour, Kit soon wearied of his ramble, and made his way back to Sir Henry's mansion.

Approaching the house from the road, and still a short distance away, Kit saw both Cosimo and Sir Henry emerge from the main gate and step out into the street, searching both ways. Cosimo saw him first and hurried to meet him.

'Where have you been?'

'Nowhere,' Kit replied. 'Just out for a walk.'

'Did you speak to anyone?' he challenged.

'No,' replied Kit, somewhat defensively. 'Not a word to anyone. I don't think anyone even noticed me.'

'Well, get inside.'

'Why? What did I do wrong?'

'I'll explain inside. Come along.'

Feeling like a naughty schoolboy, Kit followed the two men back into the house; his coat was taken from him by a servant, and he was hustled into Sir Henry's book-lined study. 'I don't suppose you have any idea of the havoc you might have caused?'

'No, but –' Kit began, then changed tack. 'Look, why am I even here? You two have your big powwow and don't include me. Fine. Whatever. I just want to find Mina and go home.'

'You're here because we need you. *I* need you.'

'Yeah? I don't see why. So far, everything you've done could have been done without me.' He shoved his hands in his pockets, adding, 'Nobody tells me anything.'

'I am sorry,' Cosimo said, softening his tone. 'Yes, of course, you're right.'

'We should not have kept you in the dark,' Sir Henry volunteered. 'See here, young Christopher. You have a gift – a rare and special ability. However, as with all such endowments comes great responsibility. There are dangers as well as benefits, and you must be made aware of them before the gift can best serve you. You must be educated.'

'Sounds good to me,' replied Kit. 'I'm all for it.'

'We begin here and now.' His great-grandfather turned back to the table heaped with piles of books, and scrolls of parchment. 'Have a look at this.'

Kit stepped to the table as his great-grandfather spread an elaborate diagram of what looked like a tree lying on its side – albeit a very stubby, short-trunked specimen with a mass of spindly, curling, tendril-like branches in unruly profusion. Some of the major limbs of this unusual tree were labelled in a neat cursive hand. A quill pen and ink pot lay nearby, and Sir Henry's fingers were stained.

'What am I looking at?' wondered Kit. 'Is this the map?'

'Oh, no,' said Cosimo. 'This is merely an attempt to chart the possible routes your Wilhelmina might have travelled. As you can see,' he waved a hand across the diagram, 'we have narrowed our search considerably.'

Kit regarded the tangled confusion of branching and intersecting lines. 'What did it look like before?'

'It has taken considerable effort to get this far. I doubt we can reduce it much further,' continued Cosimo. 'The point is, we'll have to search each of these pathways to find your friend.'

'All of them?' said Kit.

'Every last one of them – until we find her, that is.' Observing Kit's stricken face, he added. 'Cheer up, old son. You never know – we might find her on the first try. The thing to remember is that, complex though the whole might be, each single path leads only to one particular place.'

Kit looked doubtfully at the impressively complicated chart.

'Not to worry,' Sir Henry chimed in. 'This is just the opportunity we needed to spur us to the exploration of several pathways we have been meaning to trace – not to mention one or two basic theories that need testing and verifying.'

'Happy to help,' replied Kit. He stared at the diagram, trying to make sense of it. 'So where do we start?'

'Right…' Cosimo's forefinger hovered over the diagram, then stabbed sharply down. 'Here!' He ran his finger along a main limb off the central trunk; from this three smaller branches diverged, and each of these split again, and yet again.

'This one is called the Oxford Ley,' Sir Henry informed him.

'It runs right down the middle of the High Street,' confirmed Cosimo. 'It's a fairly static ley, as these things go, but responsive with the right manipulation.'

Kit turned this over in his head for a moment. 'Okay, but why not go back to Stane Way? That's where Mina and I parted company, as you have already pointed out. Why not start from there?'

'I investigated Stane Way, as you will recall, and failed to find her.'

'And, since the young woman did not arrive with you at your destination,' explained Sir Henry, 'we must assume that she has gone somewhere else. It is this *somewhere else* that we are doing our utmost to locate.'

'And Oxford,' Cosimo continued, 'is where I keep my copy of the map. We must collect it and take it with us on our search. As it happens, we can leave from there, too.' He paused, studied the diagram for a moment, then looked up. 'Have you ever been to Oxford?'

'Not lately.'

'Splendid place,' offered Sir Henry. 'You will like it immensely.'

Returning to the chart, Kit said, 'This is the same map the Burley Men want, right? What's so important about it? Buried treasure?'

'So to speak,' replied Cosimo. 'The map was made by a man named Arthur Flinders-Petrie. It is in the form of numerous tattooed symbols –'

'Whoa there,' interrupted Kit. 'By *tattooed* you mean…?'

'Exactly. Flinders-Petrie had the map indelibly inscribed onto his torso so it could never be lost nor separated from him. Upon his death, in order to preserve the map, his skin was made into parchment.'

'A skin map,' breathed Kit. 'Priceless.'

'Indeed, sir! We suspect it is far more valuable than that,' put in Sir Henry. 'Among the Questors, there are various theories, of course – some hold with one, and some another.'

'Hold on – not so fast,' objected Kit. 'These questers you both keep talking about – who are they?'

'Ah! Yes, the Questors. I suppose they are best described as a loose confederation of colleagues, all of whom belong to the Zetetic Society.'

'You guys have a society?'

'For obvious reasons, it is an extremely secretive organization,' Cosimo told him. 'Very small and informal.'

'How small?' Kit wanted to know.

'Seven or eight – perhaps.'

'You don't know?'

'Things happen,' replied Cosimo. 'People die.'

'Charming.'

'The important thing is that we are all of us united in the quest.'

'The quest to find the Skin Map.'

'That is the chief goal of our glorious enterprise, young sir,' confirmed Sir Henry, his tone taking on a note of pride. 'To find and re-unite the pieces of the Flinders-Petrie map so that we may learn what it was that he discovered. To this end we are pledged to aid one another and share all knowledge and resources in furthering the quest.'

'You will be inducted into the society in due course,' put in Cosimo, 'and we will introduce you to the other members then.'

'Okay, so about these theories,' said Kit, returning to the original question. 'What did old Flinders discover?'

'Your grandsire and I believe he may have discovered the secret of the universe – or something even more significant and momentous.'

What, thought Kit, could be more significant than the secret of the universe? Before he could voice this question, Cosimo said, 'We really won't know until we have found all the pieces of the map –'

'It's in pieces?' Kit shook his head. 'This just gets better and better.'

'Unfortunately,' said Sir Henry, 'we possess only one fragment.'

'And that's where you come in,' Cosimo continued. 'Finding the pieces is an arduous, not to mention *dangerous*, enterprise. It is a young man's game, and I am no longer a young man. Not to put too fine a point on it, I am getting old and may not live to see the end of this quest. What little knowledge and expertise I have been able to acquire over my many years in the chase, I would like to pass along to someone who can carry on the work.'

'You skipped a couple of generations, great-grandpapa,' Kit pointed out. 'Why didn't you hand over the reins to your own son?'

'I would truly have liked that,' Cosimo said gently, and to Kit's surprise the old man's eyes misted. 'Nothing would have pleased me more, believe me. But you have to understand that when I made my first leap it was pure chance and accident. It took me years to understand what had happened to me and find out how to get back home. By the time I was able to return, my son had grown up, lived a full life, and died an old man. In due course, I approached your father –'

'Dad? You can't be serious!'

'But John had inherited neither the knack nor the inclination. He refused to see me again after our first meeting. I suspect I am the reason your family moved from Manchester.'

Kit nodded, trying to comprehend all he was being told. 'So, tell me, what does this map look like?'

Before he could reply, there was a knock on the door and a liveried servant entered to say that the carriage was ready and waiting. 'Hold that thought,' replied Cosimo, rolling up the diagram. 'We can talk on the way.'

CHAPTER 11

In Which Efforts are Made and Actions Taken

The journey in Sir Henry's coach was, Kit considered, enjoyable if not exactly comfortable. Gentle autumn sunlight poured down like honey, suffusing the genteel English landscape with a fine amber glow. The fields and small towns rolled slowly by, unfolding one after another in stately progression at the regular steady clip-clop pace of the two chestnut mares. Sir Henry himself, in his smart black hat with the silver buckle, black leather gloves, and silver-topped ebony walking stick, was the very picture of gentlemanly style and grace. Occasionally, they met or passed other travellers: farmers with donkey carts, traders with pack mules, a hay wain pulled by heavy horses; more often, they encountered foot traffic: country folk carrying baskets of produce, or pulling fully laden handcarts; more rarely, they saw riders.

The only drawback in travelling this way was the road, which was more in the way of an endless series of potholes joined by ruts than a seamless ribbon of pavement. At intervals there were streams to be forded, or rocky steeps to be negotiated. The latter required the passengers to alight while Sir Henry's young driver expertly led the team and coach over the rough terrain. The jouncing, bouncing jolt and sway of the carriage took some getting used to, but once mastered became oddly soothing.

What his two companions were telling him, however, was anything but soothing. Kit tried to keep his mind on what they were saying, but it was proving a struggle. Most of what they were telling him he simply could not comprehend, and the small portion he *did* understand sounded too fantastic to credit – even by his own increasingly relaxed standards – and he could not help feeling that his companions had parted company with the solid ground of reality and were now floating high over fantasy land.

Then again, why quibble? Why strain at a gnat, his father used to say, when you've already swallowed a gnu – hooves, tail, horns, and moo?

'See here now, Kit,' his great-grandfather was saying, 'pay attention, this is important. When you travel to another world, the best policy is to interfere with the locals as little as possible and only when strictly necessary. Why, you ask? Because every interaction changes things in unexpected ways. Small, insignificant changes may be absorbed without undue strain, but large changes result in wholesale alterations in the universe, and we don't want that.'

'I don't know anyone who does,' replied Kit. 'But hold on a second – what about the other night? You know – when you woke up the baker and prevented the Great Fire of London? Isn't that just the sort of interference you're talking about?'

'Precisely!' exclaimed Sir Henry. 'It would be best to refrain from that sort of thing.'

'Excuse me?' protested Kit. 'If interference is forbidden, then how do you explain tampering with something as significant as the Great Fire of London?'

'Our actions,' his great-grandfather replied, adopting a superior tone, 'were taken only after a long and serious consultation. We discussed it for several years and arrived at the conclusion that it would serve no one's interest to allow all the suffering and upheaval of that disaster if it could be prevented.'

'Not even in the rebuilding of the city in stone?' wondered Kit. That was the one thing historians always pointed to when discussing the Great Fire: a new world-class city arising phoenix-like from the ashes.

Cosimo nodded. 'We considered that, too, of course. But how many human lives would you trade for a stone building or two?

Anyway, nothing emerged from the fire that would not have come about by other, less destructive, means. The fire merely lent speed and urgency to a process already begun. In short, there was no reason for all those thousands of innocent townsfolk to suffer and, as is most always the case with any disaster, it is those who can least afford to lose who lose the most.'

'Not to mention the enormous obstacle on the road to enlightened learning,' added Lord Castlemain.

'Sir?' wondered Kit.

'Saint Paul's Cathedral, of course,' replied Sir Henry, as if this should be self-evident.

'It is where London's booksellers stored their wares,' explained Cosimo. 'All the books on medicine, science, mathematics, history – everything lost. The fire would set learning back a hundred years, and at a time when reading was just beginning to catch on, so to speak.'

This sounded reasonable. 'So, until you can be sure you know the effects of what you're changing, the best course is not to interfere too much.'

'Some change is unavoidable,' Cosimo allowed. 'Merely by your presence, you alter the present reality of the world you are visiting. But just remember that every change, however small, has consequences. If the universe is altered enough, the effects can ripple through the entire omniverse.'

'The what? *Omniverse*?' Kit shook his head. 'Where *do* you get these words?'

'Omniverse,' repeated his great-grandfather. 'Put simply, it is everything that exists. It is this universe and who knows how many others – because there may well be more than one.'

'That has yet to be proven,' said Sir Henry. 'Though it does seem much the likeliest explanation.'

'Think of it as the grand total of all that is, was, or will ever be,' Cosimo told him. 'It is the Great Universe which may contain an unquantifiable number of smaller universes – like seeds packed in a pomegranate.'

'Why do we need so many?' wondered Kit.

'I don't know,' confessed Cosimo. 'But we seem to have them all the same – each in its own dimension, separated from the others by the thinnest of skins.'

Kit frowned and scratched his head. Multiple universes, cosmic pomegranates, dimensional skins… what next? 'I imagine you think this makes sense.'

'It helps to have the proper perspective to appreciate it,' suggested Sir Henry. 'That, I grant, is not easy to acquire, yet I have every confidence that you will gain it in good time.'

Kit thought for a moment, then said, 'I understand about travelling to other worlds and how they aren't in the same time zone, so to speak. But if you already know where the ley lines are and where they go, why do you need the map?'

'You're not thinking big enough,' Cosimo chided. 'How best to describe it?' He put his chin in his hands and looked out of the window for a moment, musing. 'I know!' he said suddenly. 'You're familiar with the London Underground train system, yes?'

'My home away from home,' remarked Kit.

'How many different lines make up the Underground system?'

'I don't know – a dozen, maybe.'

'And how many stops?' enquired Cosimo. 'In total, how many stations would you say there are?'

Kit shrugged. 'A couple hundred, I suppose – give or take.'

'Indeed,' affirmed Cosimo. 'Now the lines on the London Undergound are on different levels – some higher, some lower, and some very low – and they criss-cross through the earth in three dimensions, linking up at various points along the way.'

'The connecting stations,' added Kit. 'So you can change lines.'

'Yes, but not every line connects with every other – they merely connect wherever they will and there is no guessing where those connections might be. It is an ingenious system, but also very complicated. People can easily become confused when they use it – is that not so?'

'It has been known to happen,' granted Kit who, as a regular victim of Tube travel, knew the feeling only too well.

'The best way to avoid this confusion is to use a map – that rather clever schematic drawing with all its colours and crossing lines.' Cosimo's gaze grew keen. 'Now then, what if you attempted to travel from Whitechapel to Uxbridge without that little map? What if there was no helpful diagram posted above the door of the carriage, no signs on the platforms, nothing to show where you were or where you were going? You'd be quite lost, would you not? You could not tell where the line went or how many stations the train might pass along the way, or whether those stations linked up to other trains on other lines, or how many other lines there might be, where those lines crossed, or where they led. So, here you are, on the train without a clue where it's going – how, I ask you, do you navigate your way out of that?'

'Okay, okay, I get it,' conceded Kit. 'You need the map to find your way around a very complex system.'

'Exactly,' agreed Cosimo, warming to his argument. 'Now, imagine if you will that you discovered a Tube system that was several million times larger than the London Underground, and that there were an inconceivable number of individual lines linking billions of stations and a simply unimaginable number of trains…'

'That would be some big system,' observed Kit.

'And just to make it more interesting imagine that there was a time element involved so that you never knew when you arrived somewhere what year it might be, or even what century!'

'Awkward,' Kit allowed, beginning to grasp something of the awful complexity.

'That is very near the situation we are in, my son,' said Cosimo, leaning back on the bench. 'As it happens, Sir Henry and I have visited and committed to memory a few of the lines and several of the stations in our local neighbourhood, as it were. But the far, far greater part of this gigantic system remains a complete and utter mystery –'

'We don't even know how many other systems there might be,' suggested Sir Henry helpfully. 'More than there are stars in the sky, it would seem.'

'Furthermore,' added Cosimo, 'to even attempt to travel without the map beyond the few lines we know is incredibly dangerous.'

'Right, so what do you do if you get lost?'

'Dear boy, getting lost is the least of your worries,' his great-grandfather declared. 'Consider – jump blind and you might find yourself on the rim of a raging volcano, or smack in the middle of a battlefield during a savage war, or on a swiftly tilting ice floe in a tempest-tossed sea.' Cosimo spread his hands and shook his head. 'Anything could happen. That is why the map is monumentally, vitally, crucially, life-and-death important.'

'Hear! Hear!' said Sir Henry with a tap of his stick. 'We owe Arthur Flinders-Petrie the highest debt of gratitude.'

There was more he wanted to ask, but Kit felt his brain beginning to glaze over. Yet there was one worry that had been gnawing on his conscience. 'Getting back to Wilhelmina,' he said. 'What happens if, after all we do, we still can't find her? Tell me the truth. What's the worst that can happen?'

'Who knows?' said Cosimo. 'She could of course fall prey to any number of assaults, or she herself might cause unimaginable damage, unleashing catastrophe after catastrophe of unreckoned proportions –'

'Unwittingly, of course,' suggested Sir Henry.

'Or she could merely settle into a new life as a peculiar stranger in a foreign land, get married, raise a family, and do no harm whatsoever. Then again, depending on the local circumstance, she could be burned at the stake as a witch.' Cosimo lifted an equivocal palm. 'There is simply no way to predict the outcome.'

'The chief difficulty, you see, is that being out of joint with her temporal surroundings as she undoubtedly is, the young lady might introduce an idea or attitude alien to the natural course of development of the world in which she now finds herself.' Sir Henry, hands folded over his walking stick, turned his face to the coach window and took in the scenery. 'It is such a very complicated business.'

'I'll say. So if she changed something in *that* world,' ventured Kit, who was finally beginning to grasp something of the awful magnitude of the problem, 'the changes would spread throughout the universe.'

'Drop a stone into a mill pond and watch the ripples multiply until the whole pond is disturbed.'

Cosimo nodded. '*Thou canst not stir a flower without troubling of a star,*' he declaimed.

Sir Henry smiled at the quotation. 'I have never heard that. Who said it?'

'It's from a poem by a chap named Francis Thompson – a bit after your time, I'm afraid. Nice though, isn't it? Here's another: *The innocent moon, that nothing does but shine, Moves all the labouring surges of the world.*'

Turning once more to Kit, he said, 'The point is that through some innocent action your girlfriend might, like Pandora of old, wreak havoc great and small throughout this universe and beyond.'

'Then we'd better find her fast,' said Kit. 'Knowing Wilhelmina, she's probably stirred up a whole field of flowers by now.'

CHAPTER 12

In Which a Notable Skin is Honourably Inscribed

Macau sweltered beneath an unforgiving August sun, and the Mirror Sea was calm. The tall ships in Oyster Bay, the few wispy clouds in the sky, the lazily circling sea birds – all were faithfully replicated in precise detail in their liquid reflections. And none of it evaded the hooded gaze of Chen Hu as he sat on his low stool outside the entrance to his small shop on White Lotus Street, above the harbour.

A small, nimble man of venerable age, his squat form swathed in a light green silk robe, he leaned against the crimson doorpost and smoked a long clay pipe, watching the aromatic wisps drift lazily up to heaven. Every now and then he turned his eyes to the bay, to take in a familiar summer sight: a ship being rowed into harbour by its tender. During the dull summer season, when the gods slept and the weather was still, there was often not enough wind to drive the big trading ships into harbour, so they must be rowed by their crews – sometimes from many miles out at sea – into port.

The ship was Portuguese, of course: a large full-bellied sea hound with three sky-scraping masts and a great curved scimitar of a prow. Fully laden with trade goods, it required three tenders to haul its bulk into the bay, while lifeless canvas hung limp on the spars. Soon the docks would shake off their slumber and resume the business of transporting goods from hold to shore. For the next few days at least, there would be work and money for the dockyard lackeys. And eventually work, too, for Chen Hu.

Sailors were the principal source of income for Wu's Heavenly Tattau. Portuguese sailors were the chief contributors to his modest personal wealth.

From his lofty vantage point on White Lotus Street, he watched as the ship was slowly berthed and roped, and the gangplanks extended. There was a scurry of activity on deck as the cargo vessel was made secure. In a little while, the welcoming delegation arrived: a body made up of the harbour master and his assistants, several customs officials, heads of the various trading houses concerned, and the local labour broker. There would be the obligatory exchange of gifts, speeches read out, official documents presented and signed, and then – and only then – would the first voyagers be allowed to come ashore.

The dutiful servants of the emperor were highly skilled bureaucrats. Such ceremonies employed and honed the arts of official obfuscation and obscurantism that, from the highest sceptre-wielding magistrate to the lowest ink-dipper, served to protect someone's position in the imperial pecking order. The Qing Dynasty revelled in its bureaucracy.

Chen Hu knew all about bureaucracy. As one of the few private businessmen allowed to deal directly with foreign devils, he had attracted more than the usual amount of official interest in his affairs over the years. Everyone from tax officials to building inspectors knew, and respected, the House of Wu. He saw to it that the right palms were lubricated with the right measure of monetary grease to ensure that his business ran smoothly and with a minimum of interference.

He rubbed the back of his neck and put on his straw hat to shade his eyes, and continued to watch the ship. Soon – if not tonight, then surely tomorrow or the next day – the sailors would begin to find their way to his door. He thought of sending a boy or two down to the docks to advertise his services; better still, a girl. Sailors liked the young girls and followed them blithely.

But it was early yet. It was best to wait and see. If the expected trade did not appear, or proved a little too sluggish for his liking, he could send in the girls.

Chen Hu finished his pipe and gently knocked the bole against the leg of his stool to tap out the ashes, then rose and went into his shop. He removed his hat and knelt beside the hearth and took up the little iron kettle, filled it with water from the stoup, and set it on the brazier. He settled himself cross-legged with eyes closed, and waited. When he heard the burbling sound of water beginning to boil, he counted out nine green leaves from a pouch at his belt and dropped them into the steaming water. A few moments later, the aroma rose to his nostrils and he removed the kettle from the coals. He was just pouring the fresh brew into a tiny porcelain cup when the room darkened.

He turned to see the shape of a large man silhouetted in the doorway.

From the ungainly and graceless stance, he could tell his visitor was a *gaijin*. He sighed, poured his tea back into the kettle, stood, tucked his hands into the wide sleeves of his robe, and moved to the door, using the shuffling gait that indicated humility.

'Good luck to you,' he said in his best Portuguese. 'Please to come in.' He bowed low to his visitor.

'May good fortune follow you all your days,' said the stranger in a voice at once distinctive and familiar. He stepped back into the light and began unbuckling his shoes.

'Masta Attu! It is you!' cried the Chinese aritsan.

'I have returned, Chen Hu,' replied the dark-haired gentleman with a reverential bow. Switching smoothly to English, he said, 'Tell me, old friend, how fares the House of Wu?'

'All is well, Masta Attu,' replied Chen Hu with a wide, betel-stained grin. His facility with English was only slightly less assured than his Portuguese; both had been earned through long association with sailors. 'How could it be otherwise now that you are here?'

'It is good to see you, too, Chen Hu,' replied Arthur Flinders-Petrie, his own grin wide and handsome. 'You are the very picture of health. Your daughter Xian-Li – how is she? Well, I hope?'

'Never better, Masta Attu. It will bring her great joy to know that you have returned. I will send for her at once.'

'It would be lovely to see her, of course,' said the Englishman. 'Later, perhaps – *after* we have done some business.'

'Let it be as you wish.' The Chinese merchant bowed.

'Then let us get to it!' said Arthur in a voice much too loud for the little shop. 'I am itching to get this new design safely tucked away.'

'Please to come this way.' Chen Hu led his visitor to a low couch beside a large window covered with a bamboo screen. 'Be seated, sir, and allow me to bring you a cup of chá.'

'Thank you, my friend.' Arthur sat down on the silk-covered settee and began unlacing his shirt. 'It is a very oven out there. We've been a'stew in our own juices for a fortnight. Hardly a breath of wind to stir the sails. Dead in the water these last two days.'

'Ah, yes,' replied Chen Hu, pouring out the pale yellow infusion. 'It is the Season of the Dog. Very hot everywhere. Very bad for business. No one sells because no one buys. Very bad.' He presented the small porcelain cup with a bow, then turned to pour one for himself.

Arthur raised his cup. 'Health to you, Chen Hu!' He sampled the hot liquid gingerly. 'Ah! How I have missed the chá.' He smacked his lips in the accepted sign of satisfaction. 'Thank you, my friend.'

'The pleasure is mine,' replied the merchant, inclining his head slightly.

They drank for a while in silence; it was rude to intrude on another's enjoyment of chá. When the formalities had been concluded and the cups set aside, Arthur thanked his host and said, 'If you have no pressing business, I would like to begin at once.'

'Your servant awaits your command, sir.'

A fair-sized man with a compact frame, Arthur stood and removed his shirt, pulling the capacious garment off over his head to reveal a well-muscled trunk covered with hundreds of neatly etched designs – some no larger than a walnut, others as big as a fist; most the size of a clam shell – all meticulously rendered in deep indigo blue.

'The work of a true artist,' remarked Arthur happily. He ran a hand over the swathe of *tattaus*. 'Each and every one a miniature masterpiece.'

'I am honoured, sir.'

'Now then!' Arthur gave his belly a slap. 'I have a new one that will tax your skills, Chen Hu. I believe it is the most important of them all.'

'They are all important to me, sir.'

'Of course they are.' He gazed down the bare length of his long torso. 'I have just the right place for it here.' He touched a place in the lower centre of his chest just below his breastbone. 'In the centre, surrounded by all the others.'

Chen Hu bent near to scrutinize the proposed location. 'How big is the design to be, sir?'

'Oh! Yes, I have made a rendering of it.' He fished in the pocket of his breeches and brought out a small, much creased bit of parchment, soft with use. He sat down and smoothed the scrap over his knee. 'Here it is,' he said, his voice dropping low – whether through his customary fear of being overheard, or awe for the symbol was not certain. 'I found it at last, my friend – the ultimate prize, for I do believe it to be the greatest treasure ever known.'

The Chinese artisan fixed his gaze on the swirl of lines, half-circles, dots, triangles, and odd geometrical symbols. He scrutinized them carefully, pulling on his long moustache all the while. 'Treasure, sir? Does this one have a name?'

'The Well of Souls,' declared Arthur Flinders-Petrie reverently.

'Ah, so...' mused the Chinaman. 'Well of Souls.'

To Chen Hu, who did not understand the significance of any of the curious designs he had rendered for his friend over the years, it looked exactly the same as all the others: a tightly controlled spattering of abstract ciphers. They were, he considered, elegant in their own way as the Pinyin script was elegant, but utterly devoid of any comprehensible meaning.

But then, all foreign devils were mad. Everyone knew this. And in any case, it was not the place of the House of Wu to question the desires of its patrons.

'Very fine, sir,' Chen Hu assured him. He examined the bare patch of skin on Arthur's chest. 'May I?'

112

At a nod from his client, the artist took up the small rag of parchment and lifted it into place, observing how it would sit in the space indicated. If turned slightly, the design would fit perfectly well, he decided. As always, Arthur had laboured over his drawing and had planned it precisely – not like the roaring host of besotted sailors who came to him drunk in the small hours of the night demanding the names of lovers or ships or mothers entwined with anchors or angels.

Concluding his inspection, the Chinese merchant grunted with satisfaction.

'All is well?' asked Arthur.

Chen Hu inclined his head. 'I need only a moment to assemble my instruments.'

'Then do so. I wish to begin as soon as possible. You don't know how I have fretted over this *tattau* – I was afraid something would happen before I could reach you.'

'You are here now. There is nothing to fear.' The merchant rose slowly. 'Please, relax. I will rejoin you when all is ready. Would you like some more chá?'

'Yes, I think I would.'

Chen Hu poured another cup of chá from the steaming kettle and departed, leaving his client reclining on the couch. He padded silently into the tiny back room to prepare his engraving instruments: a phalanx of long bamboo rods tipped with very sharp steel points. He gathered up a handful of the rods and placed the pins in among the burning coals of the brazier, turning each one before withdrawing it and setting it aside to cool. When this was finished, he prepared some of his precious ink. The ink, always freshly made using a secret recipe developed over twenty years in the trade, was only ever mixed in small batches. A Chen Hu creation was a vivid blue: never muddy or, worse yet, washed out – like those of the cheaper waterfront vendors. This, as much as the skill of the practitioner, set Wu's Heavenly Tattau high above all the rest.

A Chen Hu masterpiece was made to endure. He had no doubt his work would last the lifetime of its owner, and beyond.

With slow, deliberate movements, he dribbled a few drops of the rich blue ink into a small stone vessel, took up the steel-tipped rods, and arranged them on a teak tray with a stack of clean, neatly folded rags. When all was ready, he carried the tray back into the shop, and placed it on a low table beside the couch. Next, he crossed to the hearth, knelt, and took up a bunch of joss sticks, lit them, and as the fragrant smoke ascended, he offered prayers to all the relevant gods to guide his hands auspiciously.

'Shall we begin?' he asked, seating himself on a stool before the settee.

'By all means,' replied Arthur with a magnanimous wave of his hand. 'I place myself in your capable hands, my friend. Do with me as you will.'

The small silk-robed man settled on his stool and, leaning near, placed the scrap of parchment on his reclining client's bare chest. He studied it for a moment, and then began to lightly sketch the design in blue ink. When he was satisfied that he had rendered the proposed drawing perfectly, he rose and retrieved a small brass disc and held it against the still-damp drawing.

'Splendid!' exclaimed Arthur happily. 'You may proceed.'

Replacing the brass disc, Chen Hu picked up one of the thin rods, dipped the steel point into the ink pot and then, stretching his client's pale skin between thumb and forefinger, he pricked it: deeply, cleanly, and repeatedly. The jabs were so quick, they seemed to merge into one. The process was swiftly and deftly repeated and a smooth rhythm established, punctuated by brief pauses to dab away the odd drop of excess ink or consult the parchment before the incessant pricking resumed.

When the first pass was finished, Chen Hu carefully wiped away the ink and the ooze of blood his needling had drawn, then gathered up four more of his sharp instruments. Holding them in a cluster, he dipped them in the ink pot. When the threads of each were well soaked, he began again, this time using a small wooden paddle to drive the tightly gathered points into the skin. Soon the hot summer air was fairly humming with the rapid clickity-clickity-click of the wooden paddle in the artist's hands.

Arthur Flinders-Petrie lay with his eyes closed, accepting the punishment like the willing victim that he was.

The second phase of the work was much the more painful and was longer in duration. Eventually, Chen Hu rose, bowed, and went to imbibe a cup of chá, leaving Arthur to restore himself. Many of the House of Wu's clients, if insufficiently drunk to be insensitive to the pain, required a moment to gather their fortitude for the final push. Arthur, however, required neither alcohol nor recuperation; a true veteran of over sixty tattau sessions, he had long ago grown accustomed to the pain. In any case, it was a small price to pay for the peace of mind the procedure brought in the end.

Still, he welcomed the respite from the needles and was relaxing with his eyes closed and was on the verge of sleep when he felt a shadow pass over his face. Thinking Chen Hu had returned, he opened his eyes and raised his head to see not the smooth, round countenance of his Chinese tattauist, but the long, angular features of a dark-haired Caucasian. 'Oh!' he sat up.

'Sorry!' said the man. 'Didn't mean to startle you. Pray, forgive the intrusion. I thought you were asleep.'

'I very nearly was,' replied Arthur. He cast a quick glance over the imposing fellow. The stranger was a large, rangy man with dark eyes, a long, somewhat narrow head and broad features which, when taken together, gave the strong suggestion of the equine. This horsy impression was only strengthened by the stranger's bushy sideburns and extravagant moustache. 'Look here,' said Arthur, finding himself as much an object of scrutiny as the interloper. 'Do I know you, sir?'

'I should think not,' said the man. 'But I *do* know you.'

'Sir?'

'Allow me to introduce myself,' replied the dark man genially. 'I am Lord Archelaeus Burleigh, Earl of Sutherland, at your service.' The fellow gave a slight bow and clicked his heels smartly. 'I welcome this meeting. It is most fortuitous. For several years now, I have been coming to Macau on business and I have recently begun hearing of your exploits.'

'Indeed?' wondered Arthur. 'I was not aware that any of my

trivial doings were public knowledge. In fact, to be blunt, sir, I have made rather strenuous efforts the other way.'

'Oh, I am certain of it,' agreed Burleigh. 'Otherwise, I have no doubt our paths would have crossed far sooner.'

'Is there something I can do for you?' asked Arthur politely, all the while thinking how he might rid himself of the stranger's unwelcome intrusion.

'Quite the contrary,' said the earl. 'I am here to offer my services in your very interesting endeavours.'

Arthur realized then that the man had been intently studying the symbols etched on his skin. He quickly pulled his shirt over his chest. 'Forgive me,' he said. 'I fear your offer, generous as it undoubtedly is, would be of little use to either of us. I require no assistance just now. You have my thanks all the same.'

'Let us not be too hasty,' replied the earl. 'Dine with me tonight, and allow me to convince you of my sincerity of purpose.' He paused, the light glinting in his keen glance. 'I promise to make it worth your while.'

Chen Hu entered the room just then, and Burleigh turned to the compact Chinaman, who froze in mid-step. A silent sign of recognition seemed to flit across the merchant's visage – there and gone again before anyone saw it. 'Please, be so kind as to wait outside,' said Chen Hu. He held out a hand to indicate the doorway. 'We are soon finished.'

'But of course, forgive me,' replied the earl. He moved towards the entrance. 'You will find me at the waterfront inn, sir,' he said to Arthur. He gave another little bow. 'Until this evening, then.'

Arthur watched from the open window as the stranger disappeared down the street. 'Extraordinary fellow,' he said. 'Have you ever seen him before, Chen Hu?'

'Maybe once,' replied the Chinaman, lifting a shoulder in a half-shrug. 'Maybe twice.'

'There is something about him that sits uneasily.' Arthur glanced at Chen Hu, who gazed back without expression or emotion. 'I wonder what he wants, eh?'

'This you will discover tonight, not so?'

CHAPTER 13

In Which Respectability Suffers a Serious Setback

The Portuguese trading house, Bertrand, maintained a rough and ready inn down in the docklands. It had been built to serve the few foreign worthies allowed to stay ashore during the trading season. Despite its name, *A Casa de Paz* was anything but a peaceful house. A notorious centre for gambling, drinking, whoring, and the inevitable fisticuffs that served as entertainment for the guests – none of which appealed to Arthur – he stayed well away from the place, preferring instead the safe and snug confines of his shipboard cabin whenever he came to Macau.

Curiosity, however, exerted a powerfully attractive force and, as a flaming orange sun began to lower over the Mirror Sea, Arthur's feet found their way to the door of the House of Peace Inn. One whiff of the muddy yard and he was of a mind to turn right around and head the other way. Indeed, he was about to do just that when he heard his name called from within the cavern-dark interior. 'Flinders, my good man! I've been waiting for you.'

Arthur turned and Lord Burleigh appeared in the low doorway. 'I am so glad to see you. I have ordered refreshments for us. Do you drink sherry?'

'Don't we all?' he replied stiffly.

'Then please come join me, my friend.' Burleigh extended his hand and ushered his reluctant guest inside. The interior of the inn was a murky fug of smoke and stale air mingled with the stink of rancid fat and sour beer, and other things too vulgar for a man of

117

gentle breeding to dwell upon. But a table had been placed under the only open window and it had been set with a range of dishes with bread, meat, goat's cheese, pewter goblets, and a heavy black bottle of the sweet Portuguese wine called sherry.

Two chairs were drawn to the table and Burleigh offered one to his guest. 'I hope you don't mind my saying that I have been looking forward to this meeting for some considerable time.' He smiled. 'You are a most difficult man to locate.'

'I was unaware that anyone should wish to, as you say, *locate* me. I simply go about my business.'

'Yes,' agreed his smiling companion; reaching for the bottle, he began pouring the cups. 'I am certain that you do.' Putting aside the flask, he lifted the cups and handed one to his guest. 'Let us drink to friendship and mutual profit.'

'As you say,' echoed Arthur. He put the cool pewter to his lips and sipped the sweet liquid, which warmed his mouth agreeably. They drank for a time in silence, and Arthur felt the pain of his new tattau begin to ease under the balm of the sweet wine. He finished his cup and put it down. 'Perhaps we might begin our discussion with an explanation,' he suggested.

'Why not?' said Burleigh, pouring more sherry. 'What would you like to know?'

'For a start, I'd like to know why you have been following me.'

'Nothing could be simpler,' replied the earl lightly. 'As it happens, we have a mutual friend – Fatheringay Thomas. I have lately been helping him establish the Oxford library. I believe he serves as a consultant for your various expeditions, yes?'

'I speak to him about them sometimes, it is true. We have been friends for many years. Friends talk, as I'm sure you will appreciate.' Arthur smiled stiffly. 'Although he has never mentioned you in any of our conversations.'

'Has he not? Oh, well. Nevertheless, he has told me of you, and your amazing exploits.'

'Hardly that, sir,' asserted Arthur, rebuffing the suggestion that his affairs were in any way adventurous. 'Hardly that.'

'Pray, don't be modest. I know a great deal more about this than you may suspect, and I know a true explorer when I meet one.'

Arthur offered a non-committal shrug and changed the subject. 'And what, may I ask, brings you to this part of the world? There is only one Englishman for every five Portuguese in Macau.'

'I am a partner in a mercantile establishment that wishes to make friends in this part of the world. I travel to advance my affairs and investments – although it takes little enough to get me out of London these days. I adore travelling. It makes a man quick on his feet and clear in his thoughts, I find. This is my third sojourn in the Orient – China, the Japans, India… and what have you.' He gave the list a diffident wave of his hand. 'The sun rises in the East, as they say. The future is here.'

'Do you have family in England?' Arthur sipped more sherry, his mood mellowing with every swallow.

'I have never married. Sadly. I should like to, of course, but I could not in good conscience inflict my wanderlust on anyone who looked to me for that kind of close companionship. Perhaps one day – when the urge to see new worlds under new skies has abated somewhat. Who knows?' He rolled his cup between his palms. 'And yourself?' He smiled again quickly. 'If you don't mind my asking?'

Arthur hesitated, then offered, 'I am a widower. It was several years ago now – she died in childbirth.'

'My sincere condolences.'

Arthur accepted the sympathy with a nod and a sip of sherry.

Burleigh indicated a tattau on Arthur's forearm. 'Was that her name?'

Arthur glanced down, then covered the tattau protectively. 'Yes – Petranella Livingstone.'

'Of the Staffordshire Livingstones?'

'The same. Do you know them?'

'Only by name. I've never had the privilege of their acquaintance. Her loss must have been devastating for you.'

'I try not to think about it. In any case, my work keeps me busy.' Arthur knew he was saying too much to this stranger, revealing too much of himself. But the sherry had begun to loosen his tongue and lower his defences.

Burleigh filled their cups again. 'We are men of the world, you and I,' announced the earl confidently. 'We are survivors. More, sir – we are conquerors. I have no doubt you could have the pick of any genteel young lady in England… if that was what you wanted.'

'Once, perhaps,' allowed Arthur. 'I fear I've grown too crusty and set in my ways to entertain any hopes in that direction now. Besides, I have my work.'

'And what important work it is, too, I must say.'

Even in his relaxed state, he sensed a warning in the words. 'Again, I fear you have me at a disadvantage, my lord earl –'

'Burleigh, if you please – just Burleigh.' He spread a bit of soft cheese on a chunk of bread and raised it to his mouth. 'You will find that I am not one to put on airs.'

'An admirable trait,' granted Arthur. 'Still, I greatly fear that our mutual friend has misled you. I am not an adventurer of any sort. I merely travel for my own amusement and the few business interests that keep me in coin.'

'I believe you are disingenuous, sir,' countered Lord Burleigh quickly. 'Fatheringay was most emphatic that we should meet.'

'I can hardly think why,' protested Arthur. 'Really, there is very little to say of interest to anyone –'

'Stop! I simply will not permit it.' Earl Burleigh raised a hand. 'If we are to get on together you must resist this false modesty. It does not become you in the least.' Burleigh's tone was light, but his meaning as sharp as a dagger in the ribs. Placing his hands flat on the table, he straightened in his chair. 'Let us speak frankly. You have a most rare and peculiar gift, Mr Flinders-Petrie. It is no use trying to deny it. I have seen it in operation for myself.'

'I must protest,' said Arthur, sobered somewhat by the man's abrupt change in manner. 'I have no idea what you are talking about.'

'These travels you speak of – they are not always by way of common transportation, are they?' His tone had become accusatory. 'In point of fact, they are not on the physical plane of this earth at all. They are, in fact, otherworldly.'

'Really!' said Arthur, shooting up unsteadily from his chair. 'How dare you presume –'

Lord Burleigh waved aside the objection. 'Please, do sit down. We are not finished yet.'

Against all his instinct and better judgment, Arthur sat.

Burleigh poured more sherry into the cups and pushed his companion's nearer to him. 'I have gone to some considerable trouble to arrange this meeting and it is my sincerest hope that you will hear me out.' The earl gave him a sly smile. 'We are two Englishmen far from home. We can at least listen to one another.'

'As you say,' Arthur allowed, but did not reach for the cup again.

'Now then,' the Earl of Sutherland continued, 'you have borne the burden of your gift alone until now. You have had to guard it jealously. I understand. Indeed, I respect you the more for it. There are not many men who, put in your place, could have resisted the impulses to power, wealth, and who knows what else – but you have, and I commend you.' The dark man leaned forward, narrowing the distance between them. 'But it seems to me that you could use a partner.'

Arthur stared at the stranger. 'What sort of partnership do you have in mind?'

'I propose to supply a ship and crew to sail at your express command wherever you wish to go for as long as you have need of it. Further, I am ready to outfit an expeditionary force of any practicable size, and this is also to be placed at your command. In short, any and all material assistance for the advancement of your work is to be extended to you – along with a generous stipend for your personal use, of course. All decisions concerning the disposition of support staff and use of resources would be yours and yours alone.' He seemed to be about to add something more, but paused and concluded simply. 'What do you say?'

Fatigued by the sherry, the conversation, and his ordeal with the tattau needles, Arthur felt himself to be very much at a disadvantage. 'Well, sir,' he replied after a moment, 'I hardly know what to say.'

'Then say me a simple "yes", and let us join forces at once and without delay.'

'You haven't told me what you hope to receive in return for such largess.'

'Only this,' replied the earl with a modesty that had not been much in evidence before this moment. 'That I may be allowed to follow in your footsteps, to walk, as it were, in your shadow, to nurture in my own small way your fabulous work.'

'I see,' said Arthur doubtfully.

'I am a very wealthy man,' Burleigh continued, parting company with his modesty. 'I make no bones about it. Why should I? I am as rich as few men can ever hope to be in this lifetime. But riches of themselves bring no lasting fulfilment, a curious fact which I am certain you can appreciate. In the time I have left on this earth, I hope to use my material means to further the reach of my fellows – fellows such as Thomas and his colleagues at Mr Bodley's library – in the acquisition of knowledge for the improvement of our race. Nothing less.'

Arthur gazed at his host silently, considering how best to respond. 'Well,' he began slowly, 'I am flattered you would consider me of sufficient worth to aid you in your noble quest. However, I cannot help but think you have made rather more of me and my peculiar interests than is warranted. You praise me too highly. My work may one day find a practical application, but try as I might – and I *have* tried, mind – I cannot think what it might be. Moreover, I have no need of ships or expeditionary forces. My own wealth, though certainly less than your own, is nevertheless sufficient to my needs. Add to that the fact that what I do is best done alone, and you will see that the partnership you suggest is of very little use to me.' He pushed his chair back slowly and stood. 'In short, I am sorry but I must decline your exceedingly generous offer of assistance.' Stepping away from the table, he bowed slightly. 'Thank you for the excellent sherry. I will wish you a good night, and a pleasant sojourn in Macau.'

'I understand,' sighed Lord Burleigh heavily. 'Yet I must ask – is there no chance you might be persuaded to change your mind?'

'I think not,' replied Arthur, looking for the door. 'Farewell, my lord earl.'

Burleigh rose then, as if to shake the hand of his departing companion, but instead he made a furtive gesture and clicked his fingers.

Out of the shadows appeared two heavy-shouldered, rough dockworkers. One carried a short, thick cudgel, and the other a long, thin knife.

'Take him!' commanded the earl, on his feet now and moving swiftly towards a shocked and alarmed Arthur Flinders-Petrie. 'If he gives you any trouble, you know what to do.'

Part 3

Black Mixen Tump

CHAPTER 14

In Which the Intrepid Travellers are Nobbled

The road into Oxford was busy, and busier still as it dropped down Headington Hill, through the East Gate and into the town. Draymen and their heavy horses clogged the narrow road, their great wagons heaped high with barrels, casks, and nets filled with coal, dung, and in one instance cabbages. Around and among them, like small fish swimming in the protection of larger creatures, darted pushcarts and barrows and men toting wicker baskets from the ends of wooden yokes across their shoulders.

Approaching the centre of town, they passed the newly finished facade of Queens College, now recast in Costwold limestone. The sun was low and soft, setting the honey-coloured stone alight with a warm, buttery glow. The clear autumnal air held the dry scent of falling leaves. Sir Henry directed his driver to the Golden Cross, a coaching inn off Cornmarket Street, and there booked in for the night. Kit was relieved to learn that he would be allowed the freedom of the city provided he remained in the company of either Sir Henry or his great-grandfather.

The room was large enough for two beds and a low couch, a table, two chairs, and a tallboy wardrobe; a single window opened onto the courtyard below, and there was a small hearth with a simple brick fireplace on one wall. Kit thought it a small space with the three of them sharing – but, as Cosimo informed him, they wouldn't be spending much time in the room. 'We're away as soon as we've washed off the road dust. Follow me, Kit, old son – I hear the call of the night jars!'

The main room of the inn was a dark, fetid den, but they found a table by a window onto the courtyard and ordered three jars of the best. When the ale came, the publican brought a bowl of roasted and salted cob nuts. Sir Henry raised a toast and they all quaffed down the sweet ale. 'As soon as we've finished here,' Cosimo announced, 'we're off to fetch the map.'

'And then?' wondered Kit.

'Then we shall determine the best course of action from the several that are open to us,' answered Cosimo. 'If my hunch is correct, we'll be heading off to one of the nearer leys – the Cotswolds is full of them, and there are several within striking distance.'

They drank in silence for a while, then Kit said, 'Tell me, is it always the past we visit? I mean, do you ever travel to the future?'

'The absolute future?' His great-grandfather shook his head of wavy white hair. 'No. Never. At least I've never heard that it was possible. Now, the *relative* future – well, that's something else altogether.'

'Come again?' said Kit, beginning to wish he had not asked the question.

'See here,' Cosimo said, 'the relative future is what Sir Henry would visit if he were to travel to London in, say, 1920.'

'The past for us, but the future for him. It's relative to where you started from. I get it.'

'Precisely,' agreed his great-grandfather. 'But no one – not Sir Henry, myself, you, or anyone else can go beyond the present time of the Home World. That's the absolute future and no one can travel there.'

'Why not?'

'Well, the simplest explanation is that the future hasn't happened yet.'

'Which is why they call it the future, I suppose.'

'You must think in Home World terms,' continued Cosimo, ignoring Kit's snide comment. 'Our world, the world you grew up in, is the origin world. It is the centre of all creation. For the

Home World, the future exists as a field of pure potential, where every possible outcome of any particular action occupies a separate divergent path. Until something – or someone – comes along to choose a particular path the various pathways remain in a state of indeterminate potential and therefore do not inhabit the realm of time.'

While Kit mulled over this explanation, Sir Henry added, 'If those events which might imprint a ley on the landscape cannot have taken place, there can be no ley, hence no travel to the place indicated by said ley.'

'I get it, I think,' said Kit. 'You can't travel somewhere if the road doesn't yet exist.'

'Exactly,' agreed Cosimo. 'And the simple human act of choosing a particular path forces the collapse of all possibilities – except the one chosen. One might say that human free will crystallizes raw, indeterminate potentiality into concrete reality.'

'Let me get this right,' said Kit, struggling to take it all in. 'Let's say I wake up one morning with a choice – I can go to the game or do the weekly shopping. Both those things exist as potential events, right?'

'Yes, and many more besides – all the things you might do with your day exist as a cloud of pure potentiality.'

'But I choose to go to the game – and that collapses all the other possibilities, right?'

'Yes. Because all the things you did not do cannot exist for you. Only the path that you chose exists as reality for you.'

'What happens to the other paths?' wondered Kit. 'All the other possibilities, what happens to them? They simply vanish, or what?'

'That is the best of current thinking on the subject, yes.'

'Whoa! The best current thinking? That sounds like weasel words to me.'

'I wasn't going to go into this, but since you insist… try to keep up,' replied Cosimo. 'There is another school of thought that argues for the continued existence of all possibilities for any given action or decision.'

'You mean –' began Kit.

Cosimo raised his hand and cut him off. 'Using your example – suppose you have a choice whether to go to the game or go shopping. Well, in this other school of thought *both* things happened. You chose to go and do the weekly shop – that was your conscious decision, and that became your reality. But, and this has yet to be confirmed by observation, there might exist a world where you went to the game instead. Both things happened, but in different worlds.'

'Wow!' breathed Kit, as the sheer magnitude of the implications went spinning beyond his feeble grasp.

'I don't say that theory is valid, but it is an interesting thought.' Cosimo drained his cup, wiped his mouth on his cuff, and rose. 'Ready, chaps? *Tempus fugit!*'

Leaving the Golden Cross, they walked out into the courtyard and entered Cornmarket Street. The sun was down and though the sky still held a glimmer of light, the evening gloom cast deep shadows along the already dark streets. A few scrawny dogs stood watching them pass as they came to the crossroads where, unaccountably, Kit felt the hair on his arms prickle and rise.

'Yes,' Cosimo observed, raising an eyebrow, 'we've just passed the intersection of Oxford Leys. I got a tingle just then, too.'

'Really? I never felt that before,' said Kit.

'Oh, you probably did,' his great-grandfather pointed out, 'but I imagine you didn't know what it was, so you ignored it.'

'This is a good sign, young Kit,' Sir Henry said with a tap of his walking stick, 'inasmuch as it shows you're growing more sensitive to your gift.'

They continued on to Christ Church a little further down the road, and presented themselves at the porter's lodge just inside the half-closed gate. Two torches blazed in their sconces outside the booth. 'Sir Henry Fayth and guests to see Bursar Cakebread, if you please,' said Cosimo by way of introduction.

The porter – a podgy man of middling age dressed in ample knee-length breeches and thick wool stockings, a long jerkin of faded red brocade, and a brimless black hat shaped like an upturned pot – took one look at the three before him, recognized the lord, and said, 'Bless me! But of course, sir! I will take you to him straightaway.'

The man lifted one of the torches and proceeded around the corner and into the quad with its unfinished, roofless cloister to a small room at the end of the paved walk. He knocked on the door and a voice within bade him enter. The porter stepped in, returning a few seconds later with the bursar, a short, pear-shaped man with a grey chin beard, but no moustache. His balding head was covered with a brimless round hat of soft red velvet, which he whisked off as he bowed to his visitors. 'Welcome, Sir Henry. It is, as always, an especial delight to see you once again. How can I be of service this fine evening?'

Sir Henry thanked the porter, took the torch and dismissed him. Handing the torch to Cosimo, he replied, 'Good evening to you, Simeon. It is good to be here again. We won't trouble you but for the key to the crypt.'

'No trouble at all, sir. No trouble at all.' The bursar darted back inside and returned with a ring of keys. 'This way, gentlemen, if you please.'

They were led to the college chapel and to a door set inside the entrance; Simeon Cakebread produced a large iron key from the ring, unlocked the door, and led them down a set of spiral stairs into the darkness below. A second door was unlocked and pushed open. As soon as Kit's eyes adjusted, he saw that he was in a vaulted room with a narrow grate high up in one wall. The six-sided room smelled of dust and age, but was dry. Ranks of iron-clad chests of assorted sizes – some no bigger than shoeboxes and others larger than tea chests – lined the perimeter wall, and in the centre of the room stood a low table with a large candle on a brass plate. 'Shall I light the wick for you, my lord?'

'Thank you, Simeon, but that will not be necessary. We will fend for ourselves, if you have no objection. We intend only the briefest of visits.'

'Then I will leave you to your business, Sir Henry.' He opened the ring and removed one of the smaller keys, passing it to his lordship, then departed by the staircase.

'My friend, you do the honours,' said Sir Henry, handing the key to Cosimo. 'It is your map, after all.'

Cosimo gave the torch to Kit and moved to one of the strongboxes; he bent down and fumbled with the lock for a moment. There was a chunky click, and a rusty squeal as the heavy lid raised on stiff hinges. Cosimo stooped and reached down into the chest, felt around a bit, then lifted out a roll of coarse cloth. Returning to the table, he drew off the cloth covering to reveal a scroll of parchment tied with a black satin ribbon. He loosed the ribbon and carefully unrolled the scroll.

Kit moved closer and held the torch over the table.

Gazing down in the flickering light he saw an oddly shaped piece of parchment roughly five or six inches long and ten inches or so wide. The surface was covered with weird little symbols – dozens of them: small, curious shapes that owed nothing to either nature or language. At least, no language or nature Kit knew.

'Is this…?' he started to ask.

'Yes,' said Cosimo. 'I brought it here for safekeeping some years ago. It was Sir Henry's idea. Cakebread is completely trustworthy and asks no questions. This crypt is virtually unknown outside of the few who use it, and is protected from the elements as well as casual observation. I keep it here because it would not do to have the map fall into the wrong hands.'

'Quite,' agreed Sir Henry as, with a fingertip, he lightly traced one of the symbols – a tiny spiral with dots along its outer rim and a jagged double line through its heart. 'It has been a long time since I saw this.'

Cosimo fished in his pockets for a pencil and paper – brought from another place and time – and bent over the parchment. 'Here, Kit, hold this down, will you? I need to copy this section.'

Kit put a hand on an unruly corner of the map and gazed at the meaningless scrawl and swirl and interlacing lines of the strange symbols. 'They tell you where we're going, is that it?'

'They do, and more,' answered Cosimo, busying himself with the pencil. 'I shall teach you how to read them, of course, but right now…' He paused, gazing at the parchment before him. 'Hello!'

He jerked upright, still staring at the map.

'What?' asked Kit.

Cosimo turned to him, eyes wide with shock.

'Seen a ghost?'

'Worse than that,' muttered Cosimo. 'Far worse.' Seizing the parchment in both hands he brought it to his face. 'More light,' he ordered.

Kit, grasping the torch, brought it as near as he dared.

'Just as I thought!' cried Cosimo, flinging the map at Sir Henry. 'A fake!'

'Upon my word, sir,' gasped Sir Henry, looking at it closely. 'Are you certain?'

'There is not the least shred of doubt. See here! The symbols are sloppy, poorly rendered imitations. Why, the thing is almost illegible. Obviously, whoever made this had not the slightest idea what he was copying.' He snapped the heavy parchment with an angry finger. 'This is *not* the map. Someone has purloined the original and left an inferior copy in its place. In short, chaps, we've been nobbled!'

'Outrageous!' cried Sir Henry. 'This trespass shall not be allowed to go unchallenged. Bursar Cakebread will know who has been down here and when. He will have a record of their names. We have only to –'

'Wait! Wait,' said Cosimo. He ran a hand through his hair, and turned around in a full circle. 'Forgive me, Sir Henry, but no – we will do nothing, say nothing.'

'Nothing? But surely this crime must be reported. We must –'

'We must *not* let on that we know anything is amiss, lest we risk warning the thief to be on his guard.' Cosimo flung the fake map onto the table. 'Don't you see? Whoever has done this must remain confident that his subterfuge goes undetected.'

'False confidence will make him careless,' declared Sir Henry, 'and thereby hasten his downfall. Very wise, sir. I yield to your superior intellect.'

'What about the map?' asked Kit. 'Can we still use it?'

'Sadly, no,' replied Cosimo. 'I fear it is worthless. We'll have to think of something else.' His brow creased with concentration, and then he brightened somewhat. 'I have it!' he announced. 'Black Mixen.'

'Ah, yes,' agreed Sir Henry with slow appreciation. 'I concur wholeheartedly. That will be our best course.'

'Black Mixing?' interrupted Kit. 'What is that when it's at home?'

'Black Mixen Tump,' replied Cosimo, 'is in the Cotswolds, not far from here.' At Kit's puzzled expression, he said, 'Never mind, you'll see soon enough.' Turning, he carefully rolled the parchment, retied the ribbon, and wrapped it in its cloth. He placed it back into the chest, which he locked. 'There – that's that. Now, not a word to Cakebread or anyone else about what we've discovered down here tonight. Agreed?'

'Absolutely,' said Sir Henry. 'Not a word.'

'Just one thing,' wondered Kit, as they started up the circular stairs. 'Whoever stole the map went to a lot of trouble to cover the theft. Why not just take the map and abscond?'

'Haven't the foggiest, I'm afraid,' replied Cosimo. 'We may not find out until we catch whoever perpetrated the hoax.'

Outside, the evening had grown chilly and there was a haze of wispy, horsetail clouds high above the rising moon. A gaggle of black-robed students scuffled noisily along the cloister. The three visitors paused at the bursar's office to return the key. 'I trust you found everything to your satisfaction, Sir Henry?' asked Simeon, coming out to collect his key. 'Everything in order, then?'

'We are content.' Sir Henry replied politely. 'And now, Bursar Cakebread, I will wish you a very good night, and farewell until we meet again.'

'And to you, Sir Henry,' answered the official with a bow. 'God keep you right well, gentlemen – right well. Good night.'

As they were leaving the gatehouse, the cathedral bells began to toll, and those of Pembroke College chapel across the now-deserted street. 'Time for all God-fearing men to be at their prayers,' observed Sir Henry. 'Would either of you care to join me?'

'Why not?' replied Cosimo. 'No doubt we'll have need of a prayer or two before the end of this adventure hoves into view.'

Kit was not reassured by this announcement, but dutifully

followed the other two across the road to the church whose bells were cleaving the crisp night air with their knife-sharp voices. They entered the churchyard and, as the last peals rang out across the town, the three men slipped quietly into the sanctuary.

CHAPTER 15

In Which Kit Makes a New Friend

The Golden Cross was awake at the peep of dawn and heaving with activity. All the establishment's patrons were keen to be about their business and, after a breakfast of stale bread and a hastily gulped jar of steaming ale, they wrestled one another out of the door and into departing coaches. Sir Henry, commanding his own coach, was able to leave in a less fraught and harried manner – though still way too early for Kit's taste. He lingered over his ale and bread, wishing with every half-asleep nerve and sinew that it was a cup of strong, black coffee and a flaky warm croissant. Coffee houses, however, were still few and far between in Oxford just then, and were the exclusive haunts of the idle wealthy, intellectuals, radicals, and other misfits of various stripes.

Having made do with mulled ale, he followed Cosimo and Sir Henry out into a grey morning, the night's dew heavy on the ground. The horses, fresh from their warm stable, steamed in the cold air; it made Kit shiver just to look at them. He found a lap robe and wrapped himself in it and, with the crack of the coach driver's whip like a gunshot in the chilly air, the carriage rattled from the inn yard and out into the street. They proceeded at pace and were soon passing through the city's dilapidated North Gate; once through, they passed a huddle of humble dwellings clustered close about the crumbling ruins of the old town walls, and then out into the open countryside.

Kit watched the land slowly come to life under blazing blue September skies. The day grew warmer as they went and Kit soon shed the lap robe and basked in the bright sun while he listened to the other two men talk. In a little while, they passed a tiny hamlet, crossed a ford of the Cherwell and continued on, reaching the village of Banbury where they paused to refresh themselves on some meat pasties from the local baker before resuming their journey, now bending westward and down into the Windrush Valley on small roads and farmers' tracks. Kit watched the Cotswolds roll by, becoming almost mesmerized by the endless expanse of round, close-crowded hills with their gentle slopes rising above stream-lined valleys which, more often than not, sheltered tiny farming communities.

The short autumn day eased by. As the shadows began to lengthen on the land, Kit spied an odd-looking hill in the near distance – remarkable even in a landscape of hills for its absolutely symmetrical sides and its flat-as-a-table top. A trio of tall trees graced that level summit like three plumes in a sultan's turban. Oddly, too, despite the abundant daylight, the hill seemed to abide in shadow, exuding a dark and melancholy air – an impression that strengthened the closer they came.

'Ah, there it is,' announced Cosimo, stirring from a nap. He yawned and stretched his limbs. 'That is the Black Mixen.' He gave an involuntary shiver. 'Unpleasant place. Wouldn't want to be caught dead up there at night.'

'You must be joking,' Kit said. 'It's just a hill, surely.'

'Yes, and I suppose the bubonic plague is just a disease.'

The place did appear somewhat dismal, Kit allowed. 'What's so bad about it, then?'

'There are stories,' Cosimo said. 'Lots of them, accumulating over time like an old soldier's memories – growing darker and gloomier with the passing years.'

Kit regarded the ominous hill for a moment. There was, he had to admit, a distinctly sinister air about the place – the way it sat squat and brooding on the landscape, its unreasonably steep sides wreathed in doleful shadow.

'There is one well-documented case back in the Home World,' continued Cosimo blithely, 'where a young chap, just back from the First World War, went to court his sweetheart up among the Trolls – that's what the three big oaks on top are called, by the way. Poor bloke was stood up, it seems, and fell asleep waiting for his girl to arrive. Spent the night up there alone, brave soul…' Cosimo's voice trailed off.

'And?' prodded Kit.

'Never seen again. Amidst evidence of a colossal struggle, they found only his coat and hat, and part of one shoe.'

'Really?'

'Nothing of the sort, you daft thing,' laughed Cosimo. 'The young chap came down the next morning, ate a hearty breakfast and threw over the faithless wench for the pretty little barmaid in yonder village. Why?' Cosimo laughed at Kit's alarmed expression. 'What did you think happened?'

'You dirty dog!' complained Kit. 'I believed you.'

'Do try to keep your wits about you, dear boy,' laughed his great-grandfather, massively enjoying his joke. 'No, no – forgive me, but there was nothing like that. In all truth, the effects of the Black Mixen are much more subtle, if no less disturbing for the locals.'

'Such as?' ventured Kit warily.

'Compass readings are skewed within a half-mile radius of the place, cattle and sheep will not set foot on the slopes, and birds refuse to nest in the trees. There are even recorded instances of time slippage.'

'Time slippage,' echoed Kit. 'Right.'

'Oh, this one is perfectly true, I assure you. An Oxford don carried out some tests in the early thirties with clocks, and reflected light beams, and magnetometers, and who knows what else. Clocks left to run on the Tump invariably slowed down, or ran faster, or simply stopped altogether; spectrum analysis of reflected light beams showed a dramatic shift towards the red; soundwaves travel more slowly, and all manner of curious anomalies.'

'So, what's the explanation?'

'No one knows. The professor went away completely flummoxed; and his research, while still on record, has yet to produce any sensible theories,' said Cosimo. 'Among the cognoscenti, however, the Black Mixen is considered a portal or hub – a place containing numerous otherworldly intersections, a junction so to speak. There are several known in Britain – Stonehenge being the largest and most active, and you'd be well advised to stay far away from that portal.' He paused and asked, 'Ever seen those old hippies wandering around the fields surrounding Stonehenge – eyes closed, faces to the sun, fingers waggling – trying to pick up the mystic vibes?'

'I suppose,' considered Kit.

'Playing with fire,' remarked Cosimo. 'If any of them had even the slightest idea of the forces they were conjuring they would faint dead away on the spot.' He laughed. 'They'd run a mile in all directions. Wouldn't you agree, Sir Henry?'

'Oh, indeed, sir. The Ring of Brodgar is another and altogether more useful hub,' Sir Henry informed him. 'Different from a ley, of course, but operating in much the same way for our purposes.'

'I see,' said Kit with an understanding nod – although he didn't comprehend much beyond the fact that they had travelled to this place in order to find a way to track down and rescue Wilhelmina, which was becoming an ever more complicated endeavour with each passing day. 'It is a strange-looking hill, I'll give you that.'

'Strange, yes, perhaps because it is actually man made,' explained Cosimo. 'New Stone Age, I believe, or very early Bronze Age. Hard to tell. The place is so very ancient, and it has been used by successive tribes and races over eons.'

Kit nodded with appreciation, much impressed by the brute labour that must have gone into building such an enormous structure – just lugging all that dirt around without heavy machinery must have taken millions of man-hours: a stupendous effort any way you looked at it. Impressive – but ultimately misguided nonetheless.

'Why misguided?' asked Cosimo when Kit voiced this insight.

'Well, look at it,' he said. 'It's a hill – in a landscape full of nothing *but* hills. What's the point of that, for heaven's sake?'

'That is the point precisely,' replied Cosimo. 'It is for the sake of heaven that it was built.'

Sir Henry, snoring peacefully on the seat beside him, stirred just then and woke with a little jump. 'Oh!' he said, sitting up quickly. 'Bless me, I must have been dozing.'

'Quite all right,' Cosimo assured him. 'I slept a little, too. You came awake with a start just then. Anything the matter?'

'I had the strangest dream,' said Sir Henry. 'Very disturbing. It's gone now – vanished utterly – and I can't think what it must have been, but it filled me with a powerful sense of foreboding…' He turned and looked in the direction of the Black Mixen, and his eyes narrowed. 'So! I might have guessed.'

'Yes, nearly there,' confirmed Cosimo. He fished a gold watch from his waistcoat pocket and flicked open the case. 'We appear to be somewhat early.'

'Marvellous invention,' remarked Sir Henry, regarding Cosimo's timepiece with an envious glance. 'I would so love to own one.'

'Now, now, Sir Henry,' cautioned Cosimo with a raised eyebrow. 'You know the rules.' He snapped the case closed and returned the watch to his pocket. 'It seems we'll have to wait a little while.'

'Why?' wondered Kit. 'We're here. Let's get on with whatever it is we've come to do.'

'As with most things in life, timing is everything,' replied Cosimo. 'Leys, of course, are time-sensitive, as you should know by now – portals like the Black Mixen even more so. It simply won't do to go charging up there and messing about before time.'

'And the proper time is when?' Kit asked, feeling as much as ever out of his depth.

'Sunrise or sunset – either one. It is when day and night are in stasis, so to speak, that the portals become most active and travel between dimensions is more easily accomplished. There are other ways and means, of course, but without the requisite training or special equipment…' he shrugged, 'it is best to simply wait.'

Kit settled back in his seat, but the other two men were eager to stretch their legs. They decided a walk around the tump would be just the thing to energize the inner man. 'Coming, Kit?'

Kit regarded the driver, nodding on his seat, and decided in favour of a nap instead. 'I'll stay here and keep the hired help company. You two run along and have fun.'

'We'll return for you in a little while,' said Cosimo. 'Don't wander off. When it's time to go, we'll all need to be ready.'

Pulling the lap robe up around his chin, Kit closed his eyes and was soon asleep... waking a little later to the clatter and chatter of rooks flocking to the high branches of the surrounding trees. He sat up and looked around. The coach driver was gone – along with the horses; no doubt he'd taken them to graze. The sun was a dim and fading spot far in the western sky; the shadows were deep and long, and the air was chill with the promise of a frosty night.

Kit let his eyes travel up the steep slope of the nearby tump, and glimpsed two figures climbing to the summit; upon gaining the top, they paused, then disappeared over the rim and out of sight.

'Typical', huffed Kit. 'Forgot and left me here.' He bounded from the carriage and started up the smooth incline of the man-made hill. The grass was long and slightly slippery underfoot, which made the going tedious and tiring. Roughly halfway up, he heard a sound which might be produced by a low and very resonant trumpet. Kit stopped and waited, but when nothing more happened, he continued his slog up the hill. He was puffing by the time he reached the top, and paused with hands on knees to catch his breath. It was then he heard voices – raised and angry. Glancing up, he saw four men – Sir Henry and Cosimo, and two hulking strangers in long black coats and tall riding boots – in an attitude of flat-footed confrontation.

'Burley Men,' muttered Kit. 'Fan-bloody-tastic.'

He edged closer for a better look. Cosimo held a small silver bell-like object in his hands, but he saw no weapons. More to the point, there was no sign of the Burley Men's meat-eating mascot, the dreaded cave lion. That, it seemed to him, tilted the balance somewhat. It would be three against two; with those odds they should be able to subdue the thugs, or drive them off.

Between himself and the others stood the Trolls, the great old oaks. Keeping the gnarled boles of the venerable trees between

140

himself and the others, Kit crept slowly around the perimeter of the flattened hilltop, trying to stay out of sight as much as possible. As he came closer, he caught snatches of the ongoing argument.

'… we know you have it…' said one, the voice of one of the strangers.

'… haven't the least intention…' answered his grandfather.

This was followed by, '… give it up, or suffer the consequences…' from the other stranger.

'And if we refuse?' countered Sir Henry.

They're after the map, thought Kit. *They think we have it.*

Uncertain what to do next, Kit imagined the best thing might be to create some kind of distraction, which would enable Cosimo and Sir Henry to seize the upper hand. Taking a deep, steadying breath, he drew himself up to full height and burst from his cover of the trees with what he hoped was a terrifying shout.

The surprise had the desired effect. The two dark strangers gave a start and turned as one. Cosimo leaped to one side, pulling Sir Henry with him.

'Kit!' cried Cosimo. 'He's got a gun!'

It was then that Kit saw what he should have seen before: one of the Burley Men held a flintlock pistol. Without the slightest hesitation, he raised it and levelled it directly at Kit, who threw himself to the ground. There was a dull clap as the flint chip hit the pan, followed by the sharp fizz of the powder igniting and the report of the explosion. Kit felt the whiz of a lead ball passing bare inches above his head. Without waiting to see what might happen next, he jumped up and threw himself headlong at the nearer of the two Burley Men. The thug lunged at him, but Kit launched a near-perfect rugby tackle; he caught the man in the stomach, and drove him to the ground and onto his back.

Having tackled the man, Kit's plan reached its natural conclusion. Before he could think what to do next, he felt a sharp elbow smash into his ribs. Kit rolled away, clutching his side as his attacker struggled to his feet.

Sir Henry darted forward. Wielding his walking stick like a cricket bat, he swung it up and into the Burley Man's face, driving him back. Cosimo took a wild haymaker swing at the second attacker; the punch failed to connect, but it threw the man off balance nonetheless. He staggered backwards and Cosimo stomped on his foot – which sent the rogue sprawling.

'Kit!' shouted Cosimo. 'Here! Hurry!'

Kit, squirming on the ground, looked up through tear-smeared eyes to see his great-grandfather standing on a square stone marker; his arms were raised high and he was surrounded by what appeared to be an inverted cone of radiant shimmering turquoise fog. Sir Henry stepped quickly into the unearthly haze, and took hold of one of Cosimo's upraised hands.

The nearest Burley Man lashed out with his boot, catching Kit in the stomach. Kit doubled over, gasping for breath.

'Kit! Now!' shouted Cosimo. 'There is no time!'

But the Burley Man was not finished with Kit yet. He stooped and snatched up a hunk of rock. He stepped closer, lifting the jagged stone high over his head, ready to smash it down on Kit's unprotected skull.

'Oi! You!' came a shout from behind them. 'Stop!'

Into his blurry field of vision, Kit glimpsed Sir Henry's coach driver charging towards them with the carriage whip in his hand. Kit pushed himself up on hands and knees, and tried to rise.

The coachman bulled forward, uncoiling the whip. The Burley Man standing over him took aim with the rock and heaved himself up on his toes to deliver the crushing blow.

The whip cracked.

A coil of braided leather snaked around the thug's arm and ripped it sideways. His grip torn, the stone toppled from his grasp, colliding with his own head on the way down. The Burley Man gave out a cry of rage and pain and, turning away, rushed towards the glimmering cone of light. His black-coated companion shouted something Kit did not catch and both men dived headlong into the shimmering light, joining Cosimo and Sir Henry.

Kit had a fleeting glimpse of the four men enveloped by the shimmering light. For the merest breath of a moment, all became very still, and then the men appeared to both stretch and diminish simultaneously. The turquoise cone shrank to a mere spark and disappeared with a little frazzled crack of static electricity. Kit, on his feet now, ran to the stone marker, but nothing remained of the brilliant shimmering cone, or the four men.

He jumped on the stone square where the men had been standing, but nothing happened. Lacking even the remotest clue what to do next, he gave another feeble jump and then sat down.

'Are you injured, sir?' asked the coachman rushing to him.

'Sore ribs,' replied Kit, pressing a hand to his side. 'Oh, I don't feel so good.'

'I came a'running soon as I heard the uproar,' explained the driver. 'Seems I was too late.' He coiled his whip and gazed around. 'Well, I reckon Sir Henry and the other gentleman are off on one of their journeys – in rough company, I reckon.'

Kit regarded the coachman closely for the first time and was mildly surprised to discover him to be a young fellow, more or less his own age, with a round head of short hair and a compact, stocky build. He had a wide, honest face, thick shoulders and a bull neck. His hands were strong and well calloused from his duties, and he wore a white kerchief knotted tightly around his throat.

'What's your name?'

'Standfast.' He made a curious gesture at his temple, which Kit realized was the symbolic doffing of an invisible cap. 'Giles Standfast.'

'What do your friends call you?'

The servant gave a puzzled look, then offered a half-hearted shrug. 'I do not have any friends, sir.'

'Well, you do now.' Kit stuck out his hand. 'You saved my life, and for that I thank you. Call me Kit.'

The driver regarded the offered hand with hesitant interest, then accepted it with a vigorous shake.

'Glad to meet you, Giles,' said Kit, wincing at the strength of the young man's grip.

'Likewise, sir.'

'So, you know about Sir Henry's journeys?' wondered Kit, removing his hand as from a bear trap.

'That I do, sir,' replied Giles the driver.

'Well, then,' replied Kit, accepting him at his word. 'Maybe you can tell me what we do now?'

'Well, sir, I am to go home and await Sir Henry's return,' he answered simply.

'Back to London?'

'Aye, sir. Back to London.'

Kit nodded. He took a last look around at the flat circular top of Black Mixen. The Trolls loomed overhead and the evening's shadows had claimed the top of the tump. All was quiet, peaceful in the coming of night.

'Very well,' said Kit, patting the dust from his clothes. 'Back to London it is. Lead the way, Giles, my friend.'

CHAPTER 16

In Which Wilhelmina Changes History Much for the Better

On the fortieth day of their steadily failing bakery enterprise, Wilhelmina rose early and padded downstairs to the kitchen to find Engelbert sitting in a chair with his head in his hands, the oven cold and unlit behind him.

'What's wrong, Etzel?' she asked, stepping lightly across the stone flagging in her bare feet. She knelt in front of him.

'What is the use?' he groaned without raising his eyes from the bleak contemplation of his empty hands. 'No one comes. No one buys. It is finished...' He sighed. 'We are finished.'

She bit her lip. She had never seen him so dejected and it tore at her heart. 'No,' she whispered, mostly to herself, 'I will not allow it.'

She stood and let her gaze sweep across the tidy shop. It was a fine place, a good place – too good to be driven down by the indifference of the locals. It only needed... something – some little refinement, a detail perhaps overlooked till now, or a new ingredient added. But what?

'Etzel,' she said slowly. 'Did they have coffee in München?'

'You mean *Kaffee*?'

'Yes, coffee, café, Kaffee – or whatever you call it – did you have it there? Were there shops that sold it?'

'This is a drink, *ja*?'

'That's right – a hot drink.' Wilhelmina began pacing before him, her brow scrunched in concentration. 'Did they have it there?'

'I do not think so,' he said slowly, raising his head at last. 'Though I cannot say for sure. I heard they had this Kaffee in Venice.' He shrugged. 'I have never tried it myself.'

'How far is Vienna?' she asked, mishearing him because her mind was already racing down the road to a certain destination. At his blank look she corrected herself. '*Wien*, I mean – how far is it from here?'

Etzel tapped his teeth with a pudgy finger and squinched up his eyes as he tried to work out the sums in his head. 'I think,' he said finally, 'it must be two hundred miles at least – a little more, perhaps. I have never been there, but my father went to Wien once as a young man. It is a very great city.'

'So it is. But, if I remember correctly, it is also the place where the selling of coffee in Europe began.'

Engelbert studied her carefully. 'What are you thinking, *liebchen*?'

'I am thinking that coffee will be the saving of us, Etzel.'

'But I know nothing of this Kaffee,' countered the baker mournfully.

'Don't worry about that,' Mina reassured him. 'I know all about it. All we have to do is get a supply of beans.'

'Beans?' he wondered.

'Coffee beans, Etzel – the grains used to make the drink.' She turned and stooped and, taking his hands in hers, raised him to his feet. 'Now then, you go and put on your coat and hat; then we'll go to the stable to get the mule cart ready.'

'Where are we going?'

'I'm staying here to make the shop ready,' Mina said. '*You're* going to Vienna – to Wien. Hurry along. We have wasted enough time as it is.'

A short time later, Wilhelmina stood watching as the mule cart clattered away down the empty streets of Old Prague. She sent her willing accomplice with a detailed description of the commodity – including a little drawing she had made – and instructions to purchase as many coffee beans from whatever source he could find. 'Get the black roasted ones if you can,' she had instructed him as he climbed up into the wagon box. 'If you can't get those, then get the green raw ones, and we'll roast them ourselves. It doesn't matter. Just get them.'

The plan was simply to go around the Viennese coffee emporiums and offer to buy beans in bulk. Thus when, after five days on the road, Engelbert arrived in the imposing city and began his search, he was heartily disappointed to find not a single *Kaffeehaus* anywhere. He walked the streets for a day and a half asking shopkeepers and businessmen and even idle passers-by where he might find a Kaffeehaus in Wien, but no one he met had ever heard of such a thing in the city. Weary from his travels, and woefully dispirited by the realization he had made a long trip for nothing, he began to wander aimlessly, not caring any more where he went. Eventually, he came to himself on the river banks of the wide, slow-moving Danube.

Looking around, he saw that he had inadvertently arrived at one of the many wharfs lining the busy river docklands. There were rows of warehouses and small shops serving the sailors, dockworkers, and day labourers. He strolled along the wharf and came upon a man pacing back and forth before a large heap of grain sacks. Two stevedores were loading the sacks onto a wagon. Dressed in expensive dark wool with a pristine white shirt and extravagant lace collar, the man was waving at passers-by and calling out something Etzel could not quite make out. He also held a small sign in his hands with which he seemed to be trying to attract attention.

Closer, Etzel heard the word *Bohnen*. That single utterance brought him up short. He stopped to observe the man as he waved his sign and shouted. 'Beans!'

Intrigued, Engelbert stepped nearer and summoned up the last ounce of friendliness from his vast reserve. 'Hello to you, sir,' he said. 'I give you good greeting, friend.'

'Would that I could offer the same in return,' answered the man, 'but I fear the hardship which I now endure would overcome you, too, even as it has overcome me.'

'I am sorry to hear it,' replied Etzel. 'I, too, am brought low by difficulties. May I ask what is the nature of your particular hardship?'

'I am a grain merchant, *ja?*' replied the man. 'I deal in barley, rice, and rye. From all over the world I buy, *ja?*'

'I pray your business thrives,' said Etzel.

'I make a good living,' conceded the merchant. 'Until today, that is.' He flung a hand at the heap of bags on the dock. 'What am I to do with all these beans?' He waved the sign at someone passing by just then. 'Beans! Buy some beans!'

The fellow hurried by, and the merchant returned to his subject. 'You see? No one wants them.'

'I do not understand, sir. What is wrong with them?'

'I have just this morning taken delivery of a long-awaited shipment – and now it is to be my ruin.' He turned to the nearest sack and opened it. 'Here! You see?' He dipped his hand in and brought out a fistful of shrivelled green berries.

'What are they?' wondered Engelbert.

'Ha! There it is, my friend. What are they? Who knows? I have no idea. Berries, seeds, grains – whatever they are, they are worthless to me. The merchants of Venice are pirates! I order rice and they send worthless seeds.'

'If you don't mind my asking, sir,' ventured Etzel, a tiny flicker of hope reviving in his breast, 'do these beans have a name?'

The merchant raised his head and called to one of the dockhands. 'What did the captain call these?'

'Kava,' the man replied, hefting another grain sack to his companion in the wagon.

'Kava,' repeated the merchant disdainfully. 'Have you ever heard of it? No! No one has! All I know is that I have been waiting for a shipment of rice and barley – three months I have been waiting! What do I get? A few bags of barley, two bags of wheat, and a whole load of worthless kava beans.'

Hardly daring to breathe, Engelbert licked his lips and asked, 'Might these kava seeds have another name, perhaps?' He gazed in earnest at the man, clasping his hands together as if in petition. 'Kaffee, perhaps?'

'I suppose so,' replied the grain merchant with weary resignation. 'Who knows? Who cares? Rice is what I need. What am I to do with these blasted seeds?'

Engelbert regarded the heap of sacks – at least twenty in all. 'Do you think it might be too much trouble to allow me to examine these seeds more closely?'

'Be my guest,' said the merchant.

Engelbert stooped to the open bag and peered inside at the mass of pale green, shrivelled bean-like pellets. He pulled out the picture Mina had made for him and compared it with the grains in the sack. They looked more or less alike. With trembling hands, he lifted a few into the sunlight. There was no doubt: they were the same.

'My dear sir,' Etzel said, clearing his throat, 'it may be that we can be of help to one another. I would be willing to purchase these beans from you.'

'You want to buy them?' wondered the merchant. 'Truly?'

'As it happens, I am a baker and I have a use for such as these. I cannot offer much, mind you, but I will pay what I can.'

The deal was not finalized then and there. The merchant, for all his complaining, knew well when he had a commodity someone else wanted and for which they were willing to pay good money. The negotiations took a little time and were not to be concluded until many sausages and much sauerkraut had been consumed at a nearby waterfront inn; but the deal was struck at last, and the sale solemnized over jars of sweet *Wiezenbier*. The afternoon was far gone when Engelbert loaded the last of twenty-three sacks onto his wagon, paid the grain merchant, and clambered up into the driver's seat. Without waiting for anything to mar his good fortune, he started at once for Prague.

In Engelbert's absence, Wilhelmina kept herself busy scouring the backstreet shops for tables and chairs. Occasionally, the strangeness of the world in which she found herself overwhelmed her anew and she had to pause to catch her breath. She resisted thinking about how she had come to be in this place and time. In truth, she could not think about her peculiar predicament save in bits and snatches; the bare notion was so very outrageous, she possessed neither the means nor the mechanism to process it in any meaningful way. Nevertheless, as the days passed a solitary thought drifted into her consciousness that seemed to offer a modicum of comfort: however it was that she had ended up in this singular position – and that did not bear thinking about – it did in some way feel right to her; that is, she felt more herself than she had for a very long time. Despite the incipient oddity of life in an alien time and place, the overall strangeness she perceived wherever she cast an unguarded eye, she felt good: physically strong, mentally alert, emotionally steady and, uncannily, content. In the deepest part of her heart, she felt a profound peacefulness she could not explain. That being the case, she determined not to dwell on the whys or wherefores, but rather to make the best of her situation in any way that presented itself to her.

Thus, she went about her business with extraordinary good cheer. She pestered the landlord Arnostovi into finding and securing a number of small ale cups of the kind used in public houses to serve mulled wine and hot ale in the winter, and an assortment of bowls and plates as well. Her persistence and no-nonsense demands impressed him, so he grudgingly obliged, delivering three crates of the requested items in person to find that the bakery had been transformed into something more in keeping with the main room of a public house – albeit a far brighter, cleaner, and cosier tavern than he had ever seen, with its great oven and wide counter and light-filled space.

'*Was ist los?*' he asked. 'Where is the bakery?'

'Never fear,' Mina told him, and launched into a breathless recital of her new ambition to be the first coffee house in Prague.

'Kaffeehaus?' he wondered. 'What is this Kaffeehaus?'

Rather than explain it to him, she chirped, 'Come back in a week's time and I will happily serve you one of the first samples of our new creation.'

Intrigued as well as impressed, he promised to do just that.

By the time Engelbert returned with the precious beans, Wilhelmina had transformed the little backstreet *Bäckerei* into an intimate den of tables and chairs, lamps and candles, warm with the smell of baking pastry. 'This is wonderful!' Etzel exclaimed. 'What is it?'

'It is a Kaffeehaus,' she told him.

He gazed around approvingly. 'Is this what a Kaffeehaus looks like?'

'Well, I suppose this is what they look like in Prague.' She examined her handiwork with a critical frown. 'Why? What do they look like in Vienna?'

'But Wilhelmina, there are no such places in Wien,' he replied, and told her how he had searched the entire city to no avail and was on the point of giving up when he met the grain merchant with the unwanted beans. 'Providence,' he pronounced solemnly, 'is on our side. I believe this.'

'So do I,' agreed Mina. 'We shall have the first coffee house in all Europe! The first in Prague, at least. We'll make history either way.' She walked to the two big bags Etzel had hauled to the doorstep. 'So, what have we here – black or green?'

'I have bought the green ones,' he replied, and went on to explain how blessed he felt to have obtained any beans at all. 'Green is good, *ja*?'

'Green is very good – better even than black, now that I think of it. They must be roasted, of course – we can use the oven for that. All we need now is to find some way to grind them. Can we get a good sturdy handmill, do you think? Maybe the kind you might use for hard grains?'

'*Ja*, I know the kind you mean,' he told her – which cheered her considerably since she wasn't at all certain what she meant. 'If we cannot find one, I will make it myself,' declared Etzel. 'This is not difficult.'

'Then I'll leave that to you.' She reached for the nearest of the two bags and put her hand to the neck of the sack. 'I will begin roasting them.' She made to lift the bag, and strained against the dead weight.

'No, no! I will do this,' said Etzel, moving quickly to her side. He smiled and it was good to see the light coming back into his eyes after so many days of gloom and despair. 'It is not work for a woman.'

She thanked him and fell into step behind him as, with ease, he hefted the sack onto his shoulder and hauled it into the kitchen, untied it, and carefully folded down the neck of the bag. Mina gazed at the multitude of pale green beans. 'Look at all the little darlings,' she murmured. 'Now to turn them into black gold.'

CHAPTER 17

In Which Wilhelmina Joins the Merchant Navy

The interior of Etzel's Kaffeehaus was filled with the almost intoxicating scent of coffee beans aroast in a wood-fired oven. This enticing aroma wafted out into the street, signalling the arrival of a new sensation in Old Prague. Very soon, the citizens of the city would be hearing about the latest fad which had suddenly arisen in their capital: the sociable drinking of a hot black, slightly bitter brew served up in small pewter cups in a quaint little shop down a side street off the square.

The day before the shop opened, the two bold entrepreneurs had tested their equipment and sampled the product. Using the beans Mina had lovingly roasted to perfection, Engelbert ground the shiny black specimens to a fine, gritty powder with the machine he had constructed from parts of an old hand-operated barley mill. Mina had then set a kettle to heat on the stove and warmed two cups. She had measured out the proper quantity of grounds and put them into a small sieve lined with muslin, then slowly poured hot water through the sieve and into a warmed crockery pitcher. 'We will have to find a better way to do this,' she remarked as she waited for the water to seep through the coffee grounds. 'Otherwise we'll be run off our feet trying to keep up with our customers' demand.'

Etzel smiled.

She saw him beaming and said, 'What?'

'I do not care about our feet,' he shrugged. 'I am only glad you think there will be some customers.'

'Oh, there will be great demand, never fear,' she assured him. 'Once the word is out and people have a chance to taste this, we won't be able to keep the customers away.'

When the coffee was ready, she poured it into the pewter cups and handed one to Etzel. 'To our glorious success!' she announced, offering her cup to be clinked.

'To our success!' cried Etzel gladly. 'May it please God.'

'May it please God,' echoed Mina softly, almost to herself. And something in her stirred at the thought.

Together they sampled the freshly brewed coffee, and though Engelbert wrinkled his nose and puckered his lips at his first taste of the steaming black, slightly oily liquid, Wilhelmina declared it a complete triumph. 'I would happily pay a guldiner or two for this!' she proclaimed.

'It is very bitter,' observed Etzel doubtfully.

'Bitter is better,' Mina assured him. 'Bitter wants sweet to complete it, and we will have sweet cakes and pastries to serve with the drink.'

'Ja,' agreed Etzel. 'Something *köstlich*.'

'Exactly.' Charmed by the old-fashioned word for anything scrumptious and delicious, she leaned close and planted a ripe kiss on the rotund baker's pink cheek. 'For luck,' she said, laughing at his round-eyed surprise.

Next morning, they were both busy from before sunrise, preparing the equipment and utensils. When all was ready, Mina sent Etzel out to secure the services of an *Ausrufer*, or town crier, to alert the unsuspecting inhabitants of the square that a new establishment had opened in their midst, bringing an exciting and exotic beverage to the city. She also applied her keen marketing mind to the problem of overcoming the natural reluctance of a very conservative population to try their singular product. This she did by preparing a tray of cups and a pitcher and sending Etzel out into the square to give away free samples. Each person willing to try their brew was given a small wooden token good for another cup in the shop itself.

This proved to be a shrewd success and steered a steady steam of custom into the Kaffeehaus. A few of their first patrons had heard of this new drink and were more than willing to try it and buy a second, and even a third cup at Mina's introductory rate of five groschen a cup. Seven trays of samples went out that day, and thirty-three customers found their way through the door. By close of business, Mina had sold forty-seven cups of coffee, and all of the honey buns she had made.

'We did it!' she cried as a very weary Etzel closed the shutters and bolted the door. 'We sold everything – all the coffee and all the pastries.'

'How much did we make?' he asked, sinking into an empty chair.

'By my best estimate,' she replied, 'we almost broke even.'

His face puckered in thought, but he could not make any sense of the term. 'What is this even breaking?'

'It means we almost reached the point where our profits equalled our expenses.'

'Oh, *ja*! Of course.' He was intimately familiar with the concept; he had just never heard it called by that term before. His face fell. 'Then we failed to make any money.'

'Well, strictly speaking, yes,' Wilhelmina replied. 'That's true. But we didn't set out to make a profit today.'

'No?' Worry wrinkled Etzel's smooth brow.

The mystified expression on his face so touched her that she put a hand to his head and smoothed back his soft blond hair. 'No, *mine Schatz*,' she said. 'Not today. And not tomorrow, either. I intend to give away as much or more than we sell – for the first three days only. That way we can be sure that the word will spread and bring enough customers to the shop.'

He nodded. 'This is a strange way to begin a business,' he said.

'Perhaps,' she allowed. 'But there has never been a business like this in Prague. Think of that!'

She then busied herself cleaning up the kitchen and washing the cups, getting the shop ready for the next day's trade. They ate a light supper and, before going to bed, Mina set another batch of dough to raise for the sweet buns. She went to sleep that night wondering if cinnamon was in any way obtainable in the city.

The next day's trading was the same as the one before – only a little busier, with more people crowding into the shop. The tables filled up from mid-morning to mid-afternoon and Mina exhausted herself running from the stove to the grinder to the tables to care for her patrons. After so many days of inactivity, it felt good to see the little shop full of people, and she distinctly enjoyed watching her customers take their first experimental sip of this new and unknown liquor. Etzel did his stolid duty ferrying free cups of coffee out to the square to give away to townspeople, and directing the more willing to the shop for more.

They ended the day tired, but delighted with the result – fifteen groschen to the good.

The third day of the free samples turned out to be a roaring success. Almost from the moment they opened the doors, the customers started arriving – most were folks who had been lured through the doors on the first two days and come back for more, some of them bringing friends along to share Prague's latest and quite possibly best innovation: fresh, hot Kaffee. Mina, despite anticipating a steady increase in trade, had seriously underestimated the demand. The sweet buns sold out by mid-morning and the last of the roasted beans were gone well before closing time. When Etzel finally put up the shutters and locked the door, Mina picked up the cash box and shook it to hear the heavy clink of numerous coins.

She opened the box and peered inside to see nine groschen, five guldiners, and one whole thaler. 'Etzel, we are going to make a million thalers,' she proclaimed, holding up the large silver coin. 'And here is the first one!'

Etzel laughed. He had rarely heard anyone even breathe such a number aloud. 'Then we will be the king and queen of Praha in our little Kaffeehuas.'

'Only one Kaffeehause?' wondered Wilhelmina. 'Why stop there? We are going to have at least six Kaffeehausen – and in München, too. Better still – a baker's dozen! Why not?'

'Why not?' echoed Engelbert, gazing at her with something very like awe.

The next few days passed in a pleasant, albeit hectic blur of steam and sweat and long hours in the kitchen. Wilhelmina was used to the routine of a busy shop, and Engelbert was no stranger to hard work. They knew one another's strengths and preferences, and adapted accordingly. By the end of the week, they had strengthened an already formidable partnership – as well as a small but increasingly loyal clientele, of which their landlord Arnostovi was an enthusiastic and influential member. As a longtime property owner in the city, he had connections stretching both ways, high and low, throughout Prague society. It was he who began conducting his business affairs from the Kaffeehaus, bringing clients and potential partners in his various schemes to the shop to talk and negotiate over cups of black coffee and plates of pastry, cakes, and fruitbreads which Etzel excelled at producing.

Word spread like a contagion through the city.

Rumours abounded, drawing more and more people to the shop. The new brew was said to be an extremely effective stimulant, a brain tonic, a blood regulator, and an aid to digestion and curative of various stomach ailments. The bitter black liquor was even whispered to possess potent aphrodisiacal properties. All this hearsay was discussed in low tones over the steaming cups.

Mina, in a light and pleasant manner, encouraged all this tittle-tattle as she went about serving the tables, chatting to her customers, learning their names and trades and personal tastes. She flitted about the room like an agreeable sprite, encouraging a hesitant first taste here, offering a free sample there, making sure everyone felt at ease and welcome in the cosy shop.

'We need more help,' Wilhelmina announced as Etzel locked the door one night.

'*Ja*,' he agreed, 'this is just what I am thinking.'

'Also, we need more beans. We are almost out.'

Etzel frowned. 'How much is left?'

'Two weeks – give or take a day or two.' She saw the frown deepen on his wide, good-natured face. 'Why, what's wrong?'

'This will not be so easy,' he said, reminding her how he had stumbled upon the beans by accident in the first place. 'I think we must go to Venice, and that is very far away.'

'How far?'

He gave his round shoulders a heave. 'A month – maybe two. I have never been there, so I cannot say.'

Mina's eyebrows puckered with thought. 'Obviously we should have begun searching the moment we opened the shop. This requires a permanent solution,' she said, thinking aloud. 'We need a steady supply. We must have a source.' She lay a finger to her lips and tapped lightly. 'What we need is…'

'Arnostovi,' said Engelbert. 'He knows everyone. Maybe he knows someone who can get the Kaffee beans for us.'

'You are right,' affirmed Mina. 'We shall ask him first thing tomorrow.'

The busy landlord was freshly installed at what had become his favourite table and the seat of his chair was not yet warm when Wilhelmina approached him with a gratis cup of coffee and a proposition. 'How is trade?' asked the man of business.

'Better and better, Herr Arnostovi,' replied Mina, drawing up a chair herself, which caused the bushy Arnostovi eyebrows to raise in mild surprise. 'In fact, business has been better than we anticipated. As you can imagine, this is not without its problems.'

'Good problems,' observed the landlord. 'I always prefer this kind of problem over the other kind.'

'Indeed,' agreed Mina lightly. 'Yet problems must be solved nonetheless. For example, the beans we use to make the Kaffee are beginning to run low. Naturally, we must have more if we are to continue bringing our fashionable and highly successful new product to Praha.'

'Naturally,' confirmed Arnostovi cautiously. A master of many meetings like this, he recognized a preamble to a proposal when he heard one. 'Pray, continue.'

'We would like to know if you know of any traders calling at Venice,' Mina told him. 'That is the best place to get our supplies.'

Herr Arnostovi took a sip of his hot Kaffee and thought before answering. 'Venice is very far away, *Fräulein* Wilhelmina. The only way is by sea, of course.'

'If you say so,' replied Mina.

'Alas, I know of no one who makes such journeys at the moment.'

'Oh.' Mina felt her hopes plummet. 'I see.'

'However,' added Arnostovi, 'I am not a man without some resource. It has been in my mind to acquire a participation in a merchant ship. If I were to do this, a journey to Venice for purposes of trade could be arranged.'

Mina bit her lip. She could feel the pinch coming. 'Yes?'

'Of course,' proceeded the man of business, 'I would require adequate compensation for this service.'

'I would have it no other way,' Wilhelmina assured him. 'Providing, of course, that the necessary supplies reached us in a timely manner. We must have supplies soon.'

'How soon, Fräulein?'

'Two weeks,' Mina told him, 'more or less.'

'That is not much time for such a venture.'

'No,' Mina allowed, 'but there it is.'

'Then let us come to terms,' said the landlord, as the plan crystallized in his mind. 'I will engage the ship at my own expense and obtain the supplies – not one time only, but in the future also as need requires. In return for this service, you will make me a partner in this Kaffee business of yours.'

'You want to be a partner?' Mina was already counting the cost of this proposal.

'Fifty–fifty.' Arnostovi watched her, stroking his pointed beard. 'Well? What do you say?'

'Seventy-five–twenty-five,' countered Mina.

'Sixty–forty.' Arnostovi took another sip of the hot, oily liquid.

'Sixty-five–thirty-five,' said Mina, 'but if I am to pay for the beans, then I also share in the profits from the ship.'

'No.' Arnostovi shook his head. 'Impossible.'

'Of course, I can always send Engelbert to Venice instead,' Mina reminded him. 'It would take longer, but…'

'Two per cent share,' conceded the landlord with a sigh.

'Five,' countered Wilhelmina.

'Three,' said Arnostovi, 'and that is all.'

'After deducting all expenses.'

'Naturally.'

'Also,' continued Mina smoothly, 'we will receive a reduction in rent on this shop, *and* first pick of your other properties as and when they become available.'

This caused the Arnostovi eyebrows to jump once more. '*Another* shop?'

Wilhelmina gave him a solemn nod.

'Very well,' conceded Arnostovi. 'You shall have this shop for half of what you pay now – which is little enough, I might add.'

'Nevertheless.'

'You are a shrewd woman of business, Miss Wilhelmina,' the landlord said approvingly. 'We have an agreement.' He put down his cup and extended his hand. 'We shake on this,' he said. 'From this day forward, we are in the shipping business together.'

CHAPTER 18

In Which Sir Arthur Meets an Avenging Angel

Arthur Flinders-Petrie was frogmarched from the House of Peace Inn and down a dark and narrow backstreet. The two dockland roughnecks either side of him maintained a powerful grip on his arms, which were bent painfully behind him as he was propelled along a noisome alleyway to a derelict yard. Earl Burleigh followed a short distance behind to discourage any curious onlookers from becoming involved in the proceedings.

The two toughs dragged their unresisting captive into the centre of the yard. Arthur gazed around, searching in vain for a means of escape. There was none. The deserted patch of waste ground was surrounded on three sides by the blind backs of the buildings fronting the dock – storehouses, boat sheds, fishing huts, dilapidated dwellings – and on the fourth by the alley entrance. 'What do you want from me?' Arthur demanded, looking from one to the other of his captors.

The answer came from Burleigh. 'I've already told you, Arthur. I want to share in your discoveries. I want to learn your secrets.'

'You don't know what you're asking,' he protested. 'You have no idea.'

'I think I do,' replied Burleigh. 'In any event, it doesn't matter. Since you refuse to share, I have no alternative but to take it all for myself.'

'Let me go,' pleaded Arthur. 'Hurting me will avail you nothing. I won't tell you anything. Believe me, I will not be forced.'

'Oh, I *do* believe you,' answered Burleigh. 'More's the pity.' He nodded to the thugs.

The one on Arthur's left reached behind him and produced a small cudgel – a lumpy iron ball attached to a crude wooden handle, and the whole bound in boiled leather. In the same moment, the thug on the right gave Arthur a violent shove, sending him sprawling to the ground. He rolled onto his knees and made to rise, but the cudgel came whistling through the air towards his head.

He jerked away.

The blow was haphazardly aimed and struck him a glancing blow on top of his shoulder. He gave a yelp and tried to pull free.

The cudgel whistled again and thudded into the back of his neck. A scarlet bloom erupted in his brain, and Arthur's knees gave way and he slumped to the ground, writhing.

Earl Burleigh moved to stand over him. 'I tried reasoning with you, Arthur,' he said quietly. 'We might have been friends.' He held out his hand and the bully with the knife placed the blade in Burleigh's palm.

'Please!' moaned Arthur through the roar of blood in his ears. He thrust out his hands to fend off the knife, but one of the brutes seized his wrists and yanked his arms over his head. 'What are you going to do?'

Burleigh grabbed his shirt and slipped the tip of the knife through the fine fabric and gave a sharp upward stroke, narrowly missing his captive's jaw. Two more rough slices and the shirt-front was cut away, baring Sir Arthur's torso and revealing the host of curious tattaus inscribed there. Burleigh's eyes narrowed with approval at the sight of his prize: dozens of small, finely etched glyphs of the most fantastic and cunning design, intricately picked out in indigo ink.

Arthur saw the look and instantly realized what it meant. 'No!' he yelled. 'No! You can't.'

'I assure you, sir, that I can,' countered Burleigh. 'I'm the man with the knife.'

'Release me!' shouted Arthur, squirming in the grasp of his tormentors who were now holding his limbs, stretching him out and pinning him to the ground. Burleigh sketched a line along Arthur's ribs with the tip of the knife. Blood began to trickle down his side. 'You're insane!'

'Not insane,' offered Burleigh calmly, drawing the knife up across the top of Sir Arthur's chest along the collar bone. 'Determined.'

'Agh!' screamed Arthur, trying to squirm free. 'Help!'

'You will have to be quiet,' Burleigh told him. 'And be still. I won't have the map damaged.'

He gave a nod to the rogue at Arthur's head and the cudgel came down once more, with a thick and sickening crack. Arthur felt his slender hold on consciousness begin to slip. 'It won't do you any good…' Arthur murmured, black clouds of oblivion gathering before his eyes. 'You don't know how to read it…'

'I know a great deal more than you think,' replied Burleigh with malice as cold as the grave. The blade bit deep. 'And I will simply learn the rest.'

Arthur screamed again, and felt the icy sting of the blade slicing into his flesh.

His vision grew hazy and ethereal.

As through a dream he glimpsed the iron-tipped cudgel hover in the air above his head as Burleigh's man took aim for the killing blow. It seemed to hang there for the longest moment…

And then… Arthur could not be certain, for his mental acuity was occupied wholly with clinging to the last shreds of consciousness. But it seemed to him as if, inexplicably, the crude weapon jerked in the cut-throat's hand and struck its wielder in the face with a force strong enough to shatter bone. The cudgel, which appeared to have taken on a life of its own, then whirled in the air, striking the second thug a wallop across the nose and continuing on its arc, narrowly missing Burleigh, who dodged aside just in time to avoid a blow that, had it connected with his temple, would have cracked his skull.

The knife blade flashed in the dingy light – a cruel and cutting arc. Then, curiously, it halted in mid-flight, hovered and spun spent to the ground as an agonized cry split the warm evening air.

Arthur sensed, rather than saw, a rush of movement. Something – a hand perhaps or, more strangely, a foot – swinging lazily through the air to catch a forward hurtling thug in the throat, crushing his windpipe; Burleigh's man dropped heavily to the ground, clawing at his neck and gasping for air.

There was an incoherent shout.

The sound seemed to Arthur to come from a very great distance above, or possibly from somewhere deep inside him. Someone seemed to be calling on someone to stand and fight. Dutifully, Arthur struggled to rise, his head throbbing, his eyes bulging with the effort. The sound of his own blood surged in his ears with the roar of wild ocean surf.

Dizziness overwhelmed him and he fell back – but not before he saw an angel.

The heavenly figure was swathed in glowing white silk and took the form of a young Chinese woman, tall and lithe, with long hair as black as jet, braided to her slender waist. Her face was a smooth oval of absolute beauty and composure, and Arthur knew he had never seen anything so lovely in all his life. The angelic creature's movements were performed with a calm, unhurried grace as, with an exquisite kick to the forehead of a charging attacker, she snapped the fellow's neck, sending him crashing to the dust in a quivering heap of twisted limbs. Pirouetting with a dancer's poise, she lightly turned to address the pale-faced Burleigh, who was now backing away, stumbling, cursing, and cradling a loose and strengthless arm which appeared to have adopted a wholly unnatural bend.

Arthur, overcome at last by pain and shock, allowed himself to lie back and close his eyes. When he opened them again, the white-clad angel was bending over him, cradling his head in her lap. 'Peace, my friend,' she breathed, and her voice was the soothing music of paradise.

'Thank you,' he murmured, and tried to lift his hand to her face. The effort brought pain in shimmering silver cascades that stole the breath from his lungs.

Laying a fingertip to his lips, she hushed him, and smoothed back the hair from his forehead. 'Rest now,' she said. 'Help is coming.'

In that moment, the pain of his wounds receded, ebbing away on the dulcet notes of her low, whispered voice. Bliss enfolded him and he lay gazing up into the most beautiful dark almond-shaped eyes he could conceive – and would happily have spent an eternity in such delightful repose. Then, wrapped in the warmth of the knowledge that he would live and not die, he felt himself lifted up and carried on light wings from the derelict yard that was to have been his pitiful grave.

He was roused again some while later to the sensation of being laid upon a bed of fragrant linen in a room aglow with candlelight. There were other figures floating around him now – more angels, perhaps? – and one of these was dabbing at his still seeping wounds with a warm, damp cloth that smelled of camphor and stung him however gently applied. The pain caused him to cry out, whereupon another angel applied a folded cloth to his nose. He breathed in heavy, sick-sweet vapours and the room with its heavenly beings grew dim and vanished into a realm of white and silence.

It was pain that brought him to his senses once more, to find himself in a dim room, covered by a thin sheet and shaking uncontrollably. The smell of burning spices and oil in a pan, mingled with the barking of a dog, made him heave violently, but his stomach was empty and nothing came up.

Arthur lay back, panting and sweating, his head and chest and side burning as if live coals had been placed beneath his skin. When he could open his eyes again, he looked around. The room was small and neat – bare wooden floors, grass matting on unadorned walls, a low three-legged stool and a bed – the bed a simple straw-stuffed pallet; a roll of woven bamboo strips covered a wide door half open to a tiny garden. Through the slits of bamboo, he could see a plum tree and, beneath it, a large copper basin of water. In the shade of the tree sat his old friend, the master tattauist Chen Hu, his expressionless gaze fixed in meditation upon the surface of the water in the basin where a plum leaf floated.

Arthur raised his hand to wave and made to call to his friend, but even that small exertion proved such a fierce and insistent agony that the effort lapsed as soon as it began. Instead, he drew a deep breath and held it until the pain subsided, then turned his attention to his wounds. He could see little, for they were covered with strips of cloth that had been soaked in some kind of aromatic liquid. Gingerly, and with the minimum of movement, he lifted the edge of one of the cloths and saw an ugly, ragged cut, its red, inflamed edges oozing blood and pus.

He had just replaced the cloth and was about to close his eyes against the throbbing in his head when there was a movement in the doorway. He turned on the pillow to see a young Chinese woman enter the room, carrying a steaming bowl. Dressed all in white with long, black braided hair, he recognized her at once.

'You,' Arthur sighed. 'You are the angel of my dream.'

Her perfect lips curved in a smile. 'You are alive still. That is good.'

'It was you who saved me,' he continued, his voice an ineffectual whisper. 'My angel.'

'Please,' she said, placing the bowl on the floor beside the bed. 'What is *ainjel*?'

'A creature sent by God,' replied Arthur, 'to be a protector and helpmate of man.'

'Ah, Anjo,' she said, then smiled and dipped her head. 'For you, I am pleased to be ain-jel.' She drew the low stool close, seating herself primly on it. With the most graceful and gentle fingers, she began peeling away the cloth strips covering his wounds, rolling them up and placing the rolls into the hot liquid in the bowl.

'You speak English,' observed Arthur.

'Father sent me to Jesuit school. They teach me very well.'

Arthur's eyes widened with surprise. 'Xian-Li?'

The young woman smiled and dipped her head. 'I am. And you are Master Arthur.'

'Xian-Li, the last time I saw you…' he fell silent looking at her, amazed at the transformation as if it had taken place before his very eyes. 'You have grown into a beautiful woman, Xian-Li.'

'And you have been hit on the head,' she replied, carefully removing another strip of cloth. The bandage stuck to the skin and pulled at the wound, making Arthur wince. 'So sorry.'

'No,' he said, 'you continue. I am sure it is doing me a world of good.'

'So sorry, too, because I came so late.'

'So late?'

'To save you injury,' she said. 'Father foresaw trouble. We went to inn and waited. When you did not come out, Father went in. But you had gone. It was a little time to find you.'

'Yet you found me,' replied Arthur. 'For that I will be forever in your debt.'

'*Det*?' she wondered.

'It is a service I must repay,' he told her. 'I owe you my life.'

'You owe me new shoes,' she corrected lightly. She indicated her feet and he saw that her blue silk slippers were soiled and stained with blood.

He smiled. 'As soon as I am better, we will go out together, you and I, and we will buy you the best shoes in all Macau. On that, you have my sacred vow.'

CHAPTER 19

In Which Kit is Mistaken for a Footpad

The journey back to London was a glum affair. Upon leaving Black Mixen Tump, the weather grew increasingly dank and drear. Low clouds closed in and mist rose up from the marshy places. Just outside Banbury, rain began leaking out of the heavy sky and Kit, wincing and clutching his sore ribs with every jolt of the vehicle, decided they had had enough fun for one day and told Giles to stop at the inn. They ate a supper of lamb shanks and dumplings at a table with some other travellers and, after seeing the single communal room they would have to share with other late-arriving guests, elected to sleep in the coach instead. They were on the Oxford road by sunrise the next morning, paused at the Golden Cross for breakfast and then resumed their journey.

Just outside Headington it began to rain again – a nasty spitting drizzle. Kit felt sorry for Giles, sitting hunched on his bench alone, driving in the rain through a cheerless wet countryside. Once, Kit climbed up to sit beside his new friend just to keep him company; but, clearly, having his passenger up front made Giles uncomfortable – as no doubt it violated the iron-clad social protocol that firmly kept the classes in their respective places. So Kit crawled back to his seat at the first opportunity, and order was restored.

They reached Chipping Wycombe late, and stopped at the Four Feathers coaching inn. Having spent most of their funds the previous night, they made do with a few meat pies and a small beer and spent the night in the coach again. Next morning, they joined the London Road and settled in for another damp, dull day. The going was a long slow slog along muddy tracks, so Kit had plenty of time to contemplate the latest wrinkle in his peculiar plight. What he thought, chiefly, was that whenever it seemed that he just might manage to climb up out of the mire of misfortune, Lady Fate – that haggard old slapper – turned around and smacked him back down again.

There was, Kit noted, little satisfaction to be had pursuing such musings, but eventually he found that it helped somewhat to imagine himself a shipwrecked castaway, lonely and lost, marooned on a remote island called Seventeenth-Century England – a topsy-turvy place where everything was oddly familiar, yet vastly foreign at the same time. Like a good castaway, he took stock of his resources and realized that he was not completely alone, or without some considerable material assets. He had Sir Henry's roof over his head – or soon would have – and there were a few friendly inhabitants around. What is more, they shared a roughly common language: with a steadily increasing fluency he could talk to the natives.

He had to keep his wits about him. Even well-known words were often pronounced differently and could have unfamiliar meanings; connotations were not fixed, they were fluid. Definitions drifted. He was constantly brought up short by the sudden realization that what he thought he had said was not at all what he meant – at least as it had been understood by his hearers. Still, he was coming to grips with the slippery speech and his confidence was growing.

As for the rest: Cosimo's and Sir Henry's disappearance with the Burley Men sharp on their heels… well, there was nothing he could do about that now, so he set it aside. Next on the list of his meditations was the outrageous, multi-storey universe theory his great-grandfather was promulgating. The implications of that were simply too many and too monumental for him to entertain at any meaningful level. Without any substantive scientific training in such things, Kit did not know what to think. Indeed, he did not rightly know *how* to think about any of it. If only he had read that book – the one he'd always been meaning to read but that still sat dusty and unopened on his shelf: *A Brief History of Time*. That might have given him some mental ballast for his current voyage of discovery. As it was, the very idea of a near infinite array of universes made his head swim. So Kit decided to set that aside for the time being, too.

Thus, he shortly arrived at the conclusion that owing to his woeful ignorance – or, as he put it to himself, his lack of useful information – the wisest course of action seemed to be to simply accept things as he found them and advance his cause as best he could wherever opportunity allowed.

The next day on the road passed much as the one before and Kit grew bored with his enforced solitude. He dozed on and off and woke at one point just in time to observe that they were trundling into London – a city he knew so well, and yet not at all. The rain increased as they passed the outlying villages and hamlets. The mud-thick thoroughfares – roads churned to goopy grey soup by foot and wheel – made the going exceedingly tedious as one after another vehicle – whether farm wagon, coach, or handcart – became bogged in the sticky morass and had to be hauled free. Kit, chilled to the bone, slouched in the relative comfort of the carriage and watched the bedraggled host of foot travellers slogging along: many burdened with bundles and boxes on their heads in a vain effort to keep off the rain which ran in rivulets from the down-turned brims of sodden hats and from the ragged ends of tightly gathered shawls. Some few lucky ones rode in sedan chairs borne by servants sunk to their shanks in the soupy mire.

The drab-dressed citizens of the drenched capital reminded him of a flock of very sorry blackbirds, feathers matted, soaked to the skin and miserable with it. The rough board shops and merchant stalls crowding the margins of the road – the tailors and tanners, brewers and barbers, dyers and drapers, fullers and fishmongers, and all the trading ilk – were splashed with mud to the gunnels, and forlorn faces of shopkeepers stared out from darkened interiors at the unhappy cavalcade passing by their bespattered premises.

Daylight was rapidly dwindling when Giles at last steered the coach onto the great London Bridge and the wide stone-paved street; Kit breathed a sigh of relief – but, alas, the pace did not quicken. If anything it slowed even more as the water-logged population funnelling onto the bridge conspired to bring traffic to a crawl. Kit abandoned any hope of reaching Clarimond House before nightfall and stared dully out upon the wet, wet world. By the time the coach rolled through the gate of Sir Henry's manor, torches were being lit in front of the larger houses on the street.

They clattered into the yard and a footman came running to help unhitch the horses and lead them into dry stables. Giles climbed down from the driver's seat to open the door of the carriage for Kit, saying, 'Get yerself inside and get yerself warm, sir.'

'You come, too, Giles.'

'I will follow along as soon as the coach is put up.'

'Can it not wait?'

'No, sir, it cannot,' came the reply.

Kit accepted this and made a dash for the house and was soon standing in the rear vestibule, shaking water from his coat. A tall servant in a red doublet appeared with a clean linen cloth and passed it to him without a word. Kit wiped his face and rubbed his damp hair, then passed the cloth back with his thanks. The servant then addressed him. 'You will be hungry, sir.'

'Yes, indeed – famished,' replied Kit. 'Kill the fatted calf. We've had almost nothing to eat for two days.'

The servant merely nodded, then announced, 'I will inform the cook.'

'Great. Fine,' agreed Kit.

'Am I to understand that Sir Henry and Mister Livingstone have departed on their travels?'

'Oh, yes. They are well away,' replied Kit, uncertain how much to say. 'Giles and I came back alone.'

'As I see.' The servant turned, then hesitated. 'Do you require anything before dinner, sir?'

'A change of clothes – if that is not too much trouble,' said Kit. 'These will need washing.'

'Of course, sir. I will have something brought to your room. Anything else?'

'Just one more thing,' Kit said. 'What is your name?'

'Sir?'

'What should I call you?'

'I am Sir Henry's steward, sir. You may call me Villiers.'

'Thank you, Villiers.'

The servant smiled thinly, dipped his head, and moved off.

Kit found his way up the stairs to his room; little light filtered through the tiny, thick-paned windows and a definite chill had settled in. He was casting about, trying to find a way to light the candles when there was a knock at the door and one of the younger servants announced, 'Your clothes, sir.'

Kit opened the door and retrieved the bundle. He thanked the servant and asked if he would mind lighting the candles. While the fellow busied himself with this task, Kit spread out his change of clothes on the bed. The breeches were knee-length and the shirt immense, with a long floppy-sleeved waistcoat of blue brocade, buttoned to the waist, and with pockets the size of saddlebags either side. It was the fashion of the day, he reminded himself as, shivering, he removed his damp clothes and put on the dry things, impressed all over again with the unreality of his situation. A fish out of water, that was him all over, he thought, drawing on his thick wool socks. He tied the stockings at the knee and stuffed his feet into the big, boat-like shoes. Then, remembering his apostle spoon, he slipped it into a pocket and clumped down the stairs in search of a warmer room. He settled in Sir Henry's study where a fire burned merrily in the hearth. A large brown leather wing-back chair was drawn up near the fire. On a small round table next to the chair rested a crystal decanter and a small pewter cup. An iron holder with eight tall candles stood nearby.

'This is more like it,' Kit sighed, sinking into the deeply upholstered chair. He stretched his legs and put his feet towards the fire, then turned to address the decanter. It was filled with a fragrant liquid which, Kit decided after a sniff, was probably brandy. He poured a little into the cup and took an ill-advised gulp. The virulent stuff burned his throat and scalded his gullet, and threw him forthwith into a coughing fit – which hurt his sore ribs and made his eyes water.

Pouring the contents of the cup back into the decanter, he rose and went to examine the bookshelves lining one side of the cosy room. The books were uniformly large and blocky tomes bound in heavy brown leather. Kit had seen the kind before – under lock and key at his university library. Yet here they were, free to roam about. Intrigued, he fetched the candle stand and brought it closer so he could read the words on the spine. They were all in Latin, and all with incomprehensible titles like: *Principium Agri Cultura…* and *Modus Mundus…* and *Commentarius et Sermo Sacerdos…* and the like.

Kit's Latin was scant, if not utterly absent, but he could work out a few of the titles. He ran his fingers over some of the spines, tracing the titles and pronouncing the words to himself. 'Ars Nova Arcana…' he said aloud, and became aware that he was no longer alone in the room.

Thinking Giles had joined him at last, he turned to find himself under the intense scrutiny of a young woman standing in the doorway. 'Are you a robber?' she demanded, stepping smartly into the room. 'A thief? A blackguard?'

'Uh, no – I, um –'

'What manner of rogue are you? A housebreaker?' She fixed him with the most defiant, daring, and challenging stare Kit had ever seen on the face of another living human being. 'Well? Speak up! Are you a footpad?'

'I don't think so.'

'What do you here in Sir Henry's study? Why are you skulking about? Who gave you leave to enter?'

'You ask a lot of questions,' Kit answered lightly. 'I hardly know which one to answer first.'

That was the wrong tack to take. She grew even more irate. 'Impudent rascal,' she charged. 'I will have you thrashed and thrown out.' Without taking her eyes off him, she called for the steward. 'Villiers!'

'Please,' said Kit, 'I am none of the things you said. In fact, I don't even know what a *footpad* is.'

'Then who are you? Tell me the truth and be quick about it.'

'I suppose you could say I am a guest of Sir Henry Fayth…'

She took another step, coming a little more into the light and Kit beheld what was probably the most beautiful woman he had ever seen up close in the flesh. Her softly rounded form was encased in a gown of sky blue satin with shimmering silver embroidery all down the tightly fitted bodice; a row of tiny black ribbons decorated each lustrous satin sleeve which billowed at the shoulder revealing faintly scented white satin beneath, accentuating the long line of her slender arms. The heavy boning of her bodice pushed her breasts high, the delicate mounds half-hidden beneath translucent lace. Her long, elegant neck was adorned with a string of tiny black pearls. But the most striking thing about her was the clarity of her keen brown eyes; her sensual, full-lipped mouth; the fine line of her jaw; her high, smooth brow; the way her long, dark russet curls made tiny waves at the temple...

In truth, there were so many exquisite features Kit took in all at once that he could not decide which was the best of an extraordinarily stunning lot. All he knew was that he was in the presence of a rare vision of loveliness, a goddess, a transcendently radiant creature whom he was wholly unworthy to address. Yet address her he did. She insisted.

'Well?' she snapped. 'Speak, sir! It is insulting and ill-mannered to keep a lady waiting.'

'They are working on –' Kit hesitated again, uncertain how much to say.

'Their secret scientific experiments?' she snipped.

'You know about those?'

'I know *all* about them,' she replied carelessly. Her accent was softer than most of the others he had heard, and her manner of speaking more inclined to his own. She was easier to understand, and he understood that she was completely and utterly irate. 'But I do *not* know *you*.'

'I'm, ah –' He caught himself this time. He forced a smile. 'My name is Christopher. You can call me Kit.'

Her frown deepened.

'And you are?' he ventured.

'You may call me Lady Fayth,' she replied crisply and with a slight lift of her chin.

'Lady Fayth? Forgive me, I did not know Sir Henry was married.'

'I beg your pardon, sir!' she replied haughtily. 'I am his *niece* – not that *that* is anything to you.'

'No, of course not, my lady,' replied Kit. On sudden inspiration, he bowed to her and, for all his lack of practice, managed some degree of elegance. 'Pray, forgive my thoughtless and entirely reckless presumption. I do apologize.'

His conciliatory manner had the desired effect. She appeared to relax slightly, though still regarded him warily. 'What are you doing in my uncle's private room? What have you done with Sir Henry?'

Before he could answer, a chime rang from somewhere in the house.

'Ah, saved by the bell,' remarked Kit under his breath. 'Perhaps you would allow me to explain myself over dinner. Would you allow me to escort you to the table, my lady?'

He presented his arm the way he had seen it done in old movies. To his amazement, she accepted – but with a distinctly diffident coolness. 'We will discuss this further.'

'Nothing would please me more,' he told her, and meant every syllable.

Part 4

The Green Book

CHAPTER 20

In Which Cairo's Nefarious Trade is Advanced

Earl Burleigh sat mopping his brow with a limp handkerchief and tried yet again to remember why he had imagined that arriving in Egypt at the height of summer was a good idea. 'If the heat doesn't kill you,' he mused, 'the flies surely will.' With that, he gave another informal gathering of the small, biting devils a swish of his horse-hair swatter. 'Cheeky blighters!'

He sipped from his tall glass of cool apple tea and loosened the starched collar of his second shirt of the day. From the palm-fringed comfort of the Om Seti Lounge of the Continental-Savoy, he sat in his big wicker chair and watched the hotel traffic traipsing through the lobby outside: European businessmen in dark suits and panama hats with decorative ladies on their arms, the women in crisp cream-coloured linen, high heels clicking on the polished marble floor; swarthy waiters in white kaftans bearing hookahs or tiny cups of tea on covered silver trays; sandal-shod bellboys in short satin trousers and red turbans; cigarette sellers with wooden trays; wealthy Arabs in spotless white gallabiyas.

All passed in languid procession. No one hurried. When merely ambling around in the heat of the day was considered foolhardy, rushing would be suicidal.

Overhead, a fan creaked as its woven rattan blades sifted the stifling air. Burleigh pulled his watch from the pocket of his waistcoat and clicked open the case. He would, he decided, give it another half an hour and then call off the chase. If his quarry did not turn up, he would go down to the docklands and visit his business contact to arrange shipping for the items held in storage since his last visit. With this thought in mind, he retrieved his wallet from the breast pocket of the jacket hanging on the back of the chair. He opened it and quickly counted his remaining funds and found that he still had a little more than eighty thousand Egyptian pounds.

The main problem with the trade in ancient artefacts was that everyone had a finger in the pie – the looters, the brokers, the warehousemen, the ship owners, museum curators, the police and, last but by no means least, the customs officials. All had to be paid off *before* any sale could take place. It was an expensive business.

By dint of hard work, vigilance, innate good taste, and the uncanny ability to sniff out a trend before it developed Burleigh had succeeded in building up an extremely lucrative trade in a business that was growing more difficult by the day. Competition for the best pieces had increased season by season with ignorant, heavy-handed free-booters moving in, driving up the prices unnecessarily, and attracting greater attention from the authorities. It was to the point now where a fellow could not afford to put a foot wrong lest he find himself floating face down in the Nile.

No honour among thieves, Burleigh concluded ruefully. The greedy morons would ruin it for everyone.

He finished his tea and cast a last quick glance around the hotel lobby. It was empty now. Anyone with any sense at all was resting from the heat.

Replacing his glass on the silver tray, he stood, drew on his jacket left the lounge and walked to the front desk across the lobby. 'I will be out for the afternoon,' he informed the concierge. 'I shall want a cold bath when I return.'

'Of course, sir,' replied the man behind the marble countertop. 'Will his lordship be dining in tonight?'

'I think so, yes. Have my table ready for eight o'clock.'

'Very good, sir.'

'And make sure you have a bottle of Bollinger chilled and

waiting. It was warm last time and I won't have that again.' Receiving the hotel's deepest apologies and assurance of better service, he strolled to the revolving doors and pushed through. The sun hit him like a sweaty slap in the face. He stiffened under its onslaught and signalled the white-coated porter in the plumed pith helmet to summon a taxi for him. In a moment, he heard the slow tap of hooves on pavement and a mule-drawn trap rolled up to the foot of the hotel steps. He climbed into the back of the small carriage, saying, 'Take me to the riverfront. I'll tell you the place when we get there.'

The driver nodded and, with a flick of the reins, they jolted off through the narrow and noisome streets of Cairo, a sprawling tangle of a city that was already ancient when Moses was a lad. They proceeded towards the river through progressively unsavoury neighbourhoods, dropping down the ladder of respectability rung by rung. Upon reaching the edge of the warehouse district, Lord Burleigh leaned forward and gave the taxi driver a street name. 'I will tell you when to stop,' he added. A few minutes later, they approached a large, dilapidated building. 'This is it,' Burleigh told the driver. The carriage stopped outside the door. 'Wait here, and there will be a triple fare for you.' He held up three fingers to enforce the point.

'It will be done, *effendi*,' replied the driver, touching the fingertips of his right hand to his forehead.

Burleigh strode to the wide entrance door and gave a short series of rapid knocks. He stood examining the peeling plaster while he waited and at last heard the clink of a chain being unlocked and an iron bolt withdrawn. The door slid open to admit him and he was met by a thin black Ethiope in a large red fez. 'Earl Burleigh, the rich blessings of Allah be upon you,' said the man. '*Marhaban.*'

'*As-salamu 'alaykum*,' replied Burleigh.

'It is good to see you again, sir.'

'As ever, Babu, the pleasure is mine.'

The servant bowed low and stepped aside to allow him to enter. 'My lord Hakim Rassoul is expecting you, sir. If you please to follow me.'

'After you, Babu.' Burleigh fell into step behind his guide. 'Business is good?'

'Allah is ever generous, sir.'

The interior of the warehouse was dark, the air stale and dusty and hot. The little servant led him through rows of shelves stacked high with dusty objects: stone urns and jars; caskets; statues of owls, and cats, and hawks in wood and stone; boxes, chests, crates, and hemp-wrapped bundles of all sizes. *Ali Baba the shipping clerk*, thought Burleigh.

Back behind the towering stacks, at the far end of the warehouse, they came to a door set in a blank brick wall. Babu gave one small rap and opened the door. He bowed again, ushering his visitor in.

Burleigh stepped into a room that appeared to be a cross between a Bedouin tent and an accountant's office. Behind a great slab of polished mahogany sat a slender, hatchet-faced Egyptian in a glistening silk waistcoat over a tight-fitting jalabah which was buttoned to his chin. The air was blue with the smoke of a recently extinguished cigar. 'Burleigh! Come in! Come in! Peace of Allah be upon you, my friend. It is good to see you.'

'*Wa 'alaykum as-salam*, Abdel Hakim. You are looking prosperous as ever.'

'Tolerable – only tolerable. But why tempt God with complaints? Babu, you good-for-nothing, bring us whiskey!'

'Thank you, Hakim, but none for me. Too early in the day.'

'Is it?' wondered Hakim. 'Well, then.' He shouted again, 'Babu, bring us wine – and figs... and some of those dates.' He stepped around from behind his desk, took Burleigh by the shoulders, and embraced him. 'It has been a long time, my friend.'

'Only six months,' replied Burleigh.

'That long? It seems much longer.' He smiled and waved his visitor to a carved boxwood throne covered in the fleece of a spotted goat. 'I trust your journey was pleasant.'

'Pleasant enough.'

'Sit! Tell me the news of the world.'

'You know it better than I, Hakim. I only arrived yesterday.'

'Ah, yes, we had your message.' The antiquities broker settled back in his chair, lacing his fingers over his spreading paunch. 'So! Here you are.'

'Here I am indeed,' Burleigh agreed blandly. 'But I must say all the travel grows tedious – and buyers are more difficult to find. I'm thinking of giving it up and finding another line of work.'

'Nonsense!' cried the broker, outraged. 'Never say it, my friend. We have the most successful export business this side of China. We are partners, you and I. If you quit, Hakim and Sons will die. Like grapes left on the vine, we will shrivel and die in the hot sun.'

'You have many other partners, Hakim. I expect you'll survive.'

'True,' admitted the broker. 'But none of my partners is as successful as you.'

'None who pay you as much, you mean.'

Babu entered just then with a teak tray bearing a bottle of wine, two crystal goblets, and dishes with figs in syrup and dried dates stuffed with almonds. He placed the tray on the desk, poured wine into the cups, and then backed from the room.

'Why so quarrelsome, my friend?' wondered Hakim. Seizing a cup in each fist he held them up to the light and then offered one to his guest. 'Come, let us drink – to good trade always!'

'To good trade,' echoed Burleigh, raising his goblet. They moved on to discuss arrangements for a number of items the earl had left in storage from his last visit; when that was concluded, Hakim stood up and declared himself ravenous. 'I could eat a camel,' he proclaimed. 'Come, Burleigh, my dear friend. Dine with me. I will take you to a place I know on the river where they prepare a meal of such exquisite flavours the angels look down in envy.'

'I'm certain it is very nice,' replied Burleigh, pulling his watch from his pocket. 'But I had hoped to see some new things before I go.'

'Of course! Of course! And such things –' He brought his fingers to his lips and kissed them. 'Mmwa! Wonderful things! The best yet. All for you.' Hakim reached behind his desk and brought out a small white satin turban and an ebony walking stick. 'But a man must eat, and the restaurant is not far. The walk will sharpen your appetite.' He bounded across the office in long-legged strides and threw open the door. 'Babu, you son-of-a-dog! We are going out. Admit no one while I am away.'

Locking the door, he turned and walked to a potted palm in a huge brass pot. On the wall behind the palm hung an ornate prayer rug; Hakim lifted the corner of the rug to reveal a hidden door, which he unlocked and beckoned his guest through. 'This way. It is much closer.'

Abdel Hakim Rassoul led his visitor through a dark passage that opened out into a dim walkway – merely a space between two warehouses – at the end of which lay a sunny lane wide enough for horse and ox-drawn wagons to come and go. The Egyptian antiquities broker turned and started off along the grassy verge. The smell of the river wafted along a breeze a touch cooler than the sun-drenched air of the city, letting them know that the Nile was close by. One turning and then another brought them to the riverbank and a large old house built on stilts to raise it above the perennial floods. At the top of the stairs they were greeted by a waiter in a coffee-coloured kaftan.

'*Asalaam'u*,' intoned the waiter. 'Blessings be upon you.'

'*Salaam*,' replied Hakim Rassoul. 'My table, if you please.'

The waiter led them through the restaurant and out onto a shaded terrace overlooking the river. Two or three other tables were already occupied. Woven grass mats propelled by an old man on a stool in a corner of the terrace fanned the air and made a light rustling sound. 'Ahh,' sighed Hakim, folding himself into his chair, 'it is a refuge for the weary, care-worn soul.'

'You ought to be a poet,' observed Burleigh. 'Your only care is how to spend your secret fortune.'

'Oh, my friend,' pouted Hakim, 'have you no heart? Look! Behold that wonderful river.' He waved a long-fingered hand at the grey-green slow-flowing water. A graceful felucca with tawny sails was passing just then, joining the busy river traffic of boats and barges on their way downstream. Feathery fronds of papyrus swayed in the breeze off the water, tossing their golden heads in chorus. 'Beautiful, is it not?'

'Indeed,' agreed Burleigh. 'Very.' He leaned back in his chair.

'Now then, what do you have for me? What will I see when we return to your den?'

The waiter poured water from a silver ewer into small glass beakers, and into a silver bowl. 'We will have whatever Hammet has prepared today,' declared Hakim. 'Bring it at once – and a dish of his exquisite olives while we wait.'

That done, he turned to his guest. 'What will you see? You know that things have been very slow lately. The market has become stubborn. However, I have a very nice sphinx – exquisite detail, fully intact, red granite with eyes of sapphire and gold headdress, big as a housecat. I could have sold it seven times over by now, but I saved it for you, my friend. I wanted you to have first choice.'

'It sounds expensive. What else?'

'Alas, as I say, it has been a slow season. Still, there has been some heavy excavation in one of the valleys north of Cairo this past winter. Some very good pieces are becoming available just now.'

'Who is excavating?'

'A man named Carter. He is funded by a wealthy backer – a lord somebody – I forget his name...' He drummed his fingers on the table. 'Cavanaugh, perhaps.'

'Carnarvon,' corrected Burleigh.

'You know him?'

'Not yet. But I hope to before the week is out.'

The waiter returned with a bowl of plump purple olives, pitted and stuffed with a white pasty substance. 'Taste these and know what a delight an olive can be,' said Hakim, offering the dish.

Burleigh took one and popped it into his mouth. 'Very good.' He chewed a moment. 'Are they finding anything? Anything worthwhile?'

'They are digging up the entire desert. It is all very hush-hush...' He smiled, reaching for a fistful of olives. 'But, naturally,' he continued, tossing stuffed olives into his mouth, 'I have my sources.'

'Naturally.'

Hakim swallowed, then leaned forward, dropping his voice, although there were no other diners within earshot. 'Rumour has it that they are on the very brink of a major discovery – a royal tomb, no less.'

'Is that so?' wondered Burleigh thoughtfully.

Hakim nodded. 'Any day now – so my sources inform me.'

'It seems I have come at the right time.'

'Most fortuitous,' agreed the broker. 'Trade will flow again soon, *Insha'allah!*'

Three kaftanned waiters trooped to the table bearing armloads of plates and platters. Without a word, they began laying down the food: honey-glazed quails stuffed with plums and pine nuts on a bed of delicate jasmine-scented rice, flavoured with coriander. This was accompanied by dishes of pickled slices of Nile perch and tiger fish with onions and whole peppercorns, pale green slices of melon, and figs in wine.

Hakim Rassoul smacked his lips and, tucking his white linen napkin into the neck of his robe, fell to with gusto, never once resorting to the use of knife and fork. His pleasure in the meal outstripped enjoyment and proceeded well on the way to rapture. Burleigh, whose appetite had been annihilated by the heat, watched in amazement, his own efforts feeble by comparison.

It was some time before Hakim could speak again. 'Heaven should have such food,' he announced, pushing his plate away at last. 'You have been in the presence of greatness, my friend.'

'I do not doubt it,' agreed Burleigh mildly.

Coffee was brought and they finished their meal in amiable conversation about the international trade in antiquities, then returned to the warehouse to resume their business. It was late afternoon when Burleigh took his leave; the taxi was still waiting – he had to wake the driver – and Burleigh settled into the back, deep in thought. Upon reaching the hotel, he roused himself, paid the driver a handsome tip, and went in. Three paces inside the lobby, he spotted his quarry: a tall, slender impeccably dressed man standing at the front desk, drumming his fingers on the marble counter.

Burleigh paused, straightened his jacket, then strode forward, coming up behind the man whose back was turned to him. He gave a little cough to announce himself, and said in a firm, resonant voice, 'Excuse me, but is it Lord Carnarvon?'

The man turned, took him in at a glance, and offered a polite smile. 'Yes? Whom do I address?'

'Allow me to introduce myself,' he said, offering his hand. 'I am Archelaeus Burleigh, Earl of Sutherland. I was informed you were staying here. We have mutual friends, I think. May I offer you a drink?'

CHAPTER 21

In Which Social Climbing is Indulged

'I'm sorry, Etzel,' Wilhelmina said, clasping the big man's hands in both her own. She gave them a squeeze for emphasis. 'I should have talked to you first. I know that. It happened so fast I didn't have time to think, and before I knew it, we had agreed.' She watched the wide, round face for any flicker of forgiveness; but the pale blue eyes remained downcast, the mouth pressed firmly together.

'We are partners,' he said, without raising his head.

'I know,' Mina assured him. 'I know – and that's why I feel so terrible about this. I just… please understand, I just saw the opportunity and took it. It was wrong of me to do that, and I am sorry. I really am.'

She felt herself caving in under her friend and partner's unhappiness. Her lower lip quivered and her voice became shaky. A tear rolled down her cheek. 'Please, say something, Etzel. Tell me you forgive me. I'll never do it again.'

Engelbert drew a deep breath and heaved his round shoulders. 'Ah, *mein Shätzchen*,' he sighed. 'How can I say no? We are partners, you and I.' He looked at her sadly. 'Of course I forgive you.' He raised a hand and rubbed away her tears with his thumb. 'Do not cry. I am not angry with you.'

'Then you do forgive me?' she sniffed.

'I have already said that I do,' he replied. 'How could I stay angry with you? If not for you, Mina, I would be back in München trying to please my father and brother. I would not have a Kaffeehause at all. Of course I forgive you.'

She took his hand and kissed it. 'Thank you, Etzel. It will all work out fine. I promise.'

He pursed his lips and nodded, thinking to himself. In a moment, he said, 'I have no doubt it is for the best. To be in business with Master Arnostovi — who could have imagined such a thing?'

'He is giving us a refund on the rent of this place, *and* we get first pick of his best properties as soon as any become available. Oh, Etzel, we'll have the finest coffee shop and bakery in all of Prague — in all Europe!'

At this, his good-natured face broke into a cherubic smile. 'We already have this, I think.'

'But the new shop will be better still. And it will have a proper bakery for you — with big ovens and a good kitchen. We'll even get some kitchen staff to help us. It will be wonderful, you'll see.'

He laughed then, and as low as Wilhelmina's heart had been at hurting her friend, her spirits revived and took wing on that happy sound. 'You are a good man, Etzel,' she told him, and planted a big wet kiss on his round cheek.

His smile swelled to bursting and his face turned red.

A few days later, Arnostovi made good on his promise. 'Fräulein Wilhelmina, come,' he said, striding into the Kaffeehaus with his little black book tucked under his arm. 'I have something to show you.'

'Would you like your Kaffee first, Herr Arnostovi?'

'Not now. We must hurry. Come along.'

He turned and stepped back out of the door and into the street, beckoning her to follow.

Mina turned and called to Engelbert who was just then taking a tray of pastries from the oven. 'Yes, go,' he replied. 'I will watch things here. Go. I trust you.'

'What is the rush?' Mina asked, catching up with him a few steps later. His heels clicked along at a fair pace, making the long white plume in his green hat ripple in the breeze of his passing.

'There are people coming to meet me at the property,' he told her. 'They will have it, unless you take it first.'

'Oh,' replied Mina, not quite understanding. 'I see.'

They proceeded at pace to the Old Town Square. 'There!' declared Arnostovi, pointing across the market area to the north side and a row of fine shops that shared a copper-faced awning that shielded the doorways to the shops from wind and rain. The shops were south-facing and fronted with large glass windows the likes of which were enjoyed by very few buildings on the square. 'That one,' he said, indicating the rank of shops with the point of his spade-shaped beard.

'Which one?'

'The one on the end nearest the clock tower.'

Wilhelmina's eyes widened at the sight. 'That one?'

'Yes.' He bent his head around to look at her, slowing his pace only slightly. 'What is the matter?'

'Nothing! It is … the best property on the square!'

'So some would say.' He started away again.

'And you are giving it to us?' she asked, scrambling to catch up with him again,

'I'm not giving you anything, Fräulein. I am offering it to you for rent, as we agreed.' Once across the square, he moved quickly to the door of the shop and withdrew a large iron key from the leather satchel at his side. 'Come. Hurry. We have not much time.'

As if to lend urgency to his words, the clock in the great stone tower began to chime the hour. Herr Arnostovi unlocked the door of the shop and opened it wide for Mina to enter. She stepped in.

The single large room was bare of furnishings, but what she could see spoke of luxury and quality – all brass and crystal, with white marble on the floors, and walnut wainscoting on the walls, and rows of expensive blue tiles around the windows and door. A three-tiered chandelier hung from a painted ceiling over the centre of the room, and the eastern wall featured an ornate *Kachelofen*, or ceramic stove, in glittering white and blue tiles.

'Well?' said Arnostovi. 'What do you think?'

'It is beautiful!'

'Good. Then it is settled, yes?'

'I'd love to have it, of course, but how much is it?'

He took out his book and began flicking through the pages.

'The men who are coming have offered twenty-five guldiners a month in rent. You will agree to thirty.'

'Oh, Herr Arnostovi,' said Mina, 'it is too much. We will never be able to afford that.'

'Maybe not today,' he allowed. 'But you will – and very soon.'

'But how…?'

'On the increase of business this place will bring. Also, you will raise your prices. You charge too little.'

Wilhelmina bit her lip. She looked around doubtfully. 'I cannot think what Engelbert would say.'

'He said he trusted you to make the decision,' replied the shrewd man of business. 'Now I ask you to trust *me*.' He fixed her with a fierce, demanding stare.

'What about storerooms and apartments?' she wondered. 'What about a kitchen?'

'On the floors above,' answered Arnostovi, 'you will find everything you need. I will build and furnish any kitchen you desire.'

Wilhelmina looked around, a frown of concentration creasing her forehead. Did she dare risk so much?

'My dear girl,' said the landlord gently, 'think what I am offering you. This place will be the talk of all Prague. The best people will come. Your clientele will pay any price to be seen here. It will be an unrivalled success, but please hear me when I say you must agree at once.'

Gazing around the empty space, Mina could see it filled with gleaming, polished tables where fine ladies and gentlemen sat, conversing and laughing, drinking coffee and eating Etzel's fine pastries. It was an attractive picture the landlord was painting, and she wanted it. 'I agree.'

Arnostovi closed his book with a snap. 'Good.'

A shadow darkened the doorway. 'They are here. Go in the back and see where you wish the kitchen to be. Say nothing. These men will be disappointed and angry. I will deal with them.'

Mina nodded, and moved to the rear of the premises where she did as the landlord had suggested and began planning how best to organize the space to accommodate the ovens and work surfaces she envisioned. At the far front of the shop she heard a rap at the door and Arnostovi answering it. There were voices, greetings exchanged, and then things grew quiet. She allowed herself a glance over her shoulder to see what was happening. Arnostovi and three men in loden cloaks and plumed hats were standing huddled just inside the entrance.

Then, even as she watched, one of the men gave the floor an angry thump with the end of his walking stick. Words were exchanged. Voices sharpened. Herr Arnostovi spread his hands and shrugged. Holding open the door, he ushered the men from the building, returning a few moments later, smiling and humming to himself.

'Well, what was *that* about?' Mina could not help asking.

'The truth is I do not own this building,' he confessed. 'As much as I would love to own such a place, my means do not yet extend to such a height.'

'Who does it belong to, then?'

'A building so grand...' He gazed around appreciatively. 'It belongs to Archduke Mattias.'

Wilhelmina took a moment to consider this. In her relatively short time in Prague, she had begun assembling a rough working knowledge of court affairs. 'The archduke – you mean the emperor's brother?'

'The same,' confirmed Arnostovi. 'The archduke owns many properties in the city in addition to his country estates, of course.'

'Of course,' agreed Mina, perplexed. 'But if that is so, then how...?'

'How did I rent it to you just now?' The man of business indulged in a crafty, conspiratorial smile. 'Naturally, Archduke Mattias does not manage these properties himself. Far from it. He employs ministers for that. Chief of these is one Herr Wolfgang von Rumpf, very high up in court. As it happens, Von Rumpf is a gambler and card player. He spends many an evening at the card tables of the more fashionable houses in the city. I also play cards.'

'You do surprise me, Herr Arnostovi,' tutted Mina. 'Go on.'

'Do not tell anyone – I am a terrible card player,' admitted Arnostovi cheerfully. 'Nevertheless, I am better than Von Rumpf.

I have been trying for months, years perhaps, to be invited to his table. Last night, it happened. We were both at dinner together with mutual acquaintances and we played.' His smile spread wide. 'I won.'

Wilhelmina's eyes grew wide. 'You mean…?'

'No,' replied the man of business with a shake of his head. 'He may be a bad card player, but he is not a fool.'

'Then what did you win exactly?'

'I obtained from him the promise to allow me to manage this property for him – and for the archduke, it must be said – for a small share in the profits.'

'I see.' Wilhelmina frowned.

'No, no! It is not like that. For me it is not the money. I want only to use this as a means of gaining access to court. It is all to the benefit of my business interests – yours, too, I might add.'

'Mine?'

'Venetian shipping. The archduke owns ships.'

'Oh, I think I am beginning to understand.'

'But Von Rumpf did not make it easy for me,' continued Arnostovi, pacing around the room. 'The terms of our agreement were such that I had to find a tenant – someone other than myself, understand – and before the others came to take possession this morning –'

'Those men just now.'

'The same. If I did this, Von Rumpf said, I would become manager of the property.'

'Otherwise, it would fall to them,' concluded Mina. She nodded with appreciation. 'You used me, Herr Arnostovi.'

'I did, yes – but you will not find yourself ill-used, Fräulein. This is just the beginning,' he told her, spreading his arms to take in the whole city. 'You have helped me, my friend, and you will not regret it. That I promise you. Our fortunes are on the rise.'

'Well and good,' replied Wilhelmina, casting a more critical eye around the premises. 'We will need a fair-sized fortune if we are to furnish this place in a suitable manner.'

'Do not worry,' chortled Arnostovi, delighted with himself and the world. 'Leave everything to me.'

Back in the Kaffeehaus, Engelbert was dubious. 'It is a very great sum of money,' he pointed out.

'Worth every little silver groschen. Wait till you see it, Etzel. We will be the talk of the town. It is truly *wunderbar!*'

He nodded, but remained unconvinced.

She paused, considering how best to reassure him. 'Think of it, Etzel – the archduke's property. It will be the perfect place to show off all the wonderful pastries you shall make. People will come from miles around to see and be seen in our beautiful new Kaffeehaus. And,' she concluded, 'they will all leave with a loaf of your heavenly bread.'

'A good location makes all the difference,' Engelbert conceded, warming to the idea.

'And this is the best location in the whole city – better even than the palace.'

'You have done well for us, *Liebchen.*'

The word made Mina's heart swell; it seemed a lifetime since she'd heard it. She smiled all day.

At the end of the week, they closed the little shop on the narrow side street, telling their small but increasingly loyal clientele that they would reopen very soon in a splendid new shop on the square. The next morning, a messenger from the shipping company came to say that the shipment of coffee beans was secured and the ship on its way home. Upon receiving this news, Engelbert and Wilhelmina sat down and, over steaming cups of coffee, began planning their new Kaffeehaus and *Bäckerei.*

There would be round tables of three sizes, and a generous *Eckbank* in one corner near the *Kachelofen*; the chairs would be well made and comfortable to allow patrons to linger and enjoy their daily cup – which would be served up in pewter pots with polished wooden handles and drunk from cups of the finest crockery they could find. In addition to coffee there would be a new line in pastries and cakes specially created by Wilhelmina for the new shop, and never before seen in Bohemia. 'Don't worry,' she told Etzel when he wondered where they would find the recipes for these new pastries. 'I have enough for three or four new shops right here,' she said, tapping her temple with a finger, then added in a slightly wistful tone, 'If we only had chocolate… but never mind. We'll make do with almond paste and kirsch.'

'What about the kitchen help?' he asked.

'We will have four extra staff to begin with,' she decided. 'Two to work the tables – serving and clearing the dishes and making the coffee – and two to help you in the kitchen with the baking. And they shall all wear matching uniforms – green jackets and aprons, and little white caps.'

Engelbert was delighted with the idea. 'Like servants in the fine houses.'

'Yes, just like servants in the great houses. We want our customers to feel like highborn lords and ladies – as if they have arrived at the emperor's court.'

'Maybe Archduke Mattias will come, *ja*?'

'I would not be at all surprised if Emperor Rudolf himself came to buy Engelbert's special Stollen.'

Etzel beamed at the thought. 'Do you think so?'

Wilhelmina nodded solemnly. 'Why not? We are climbing up in the world, Etzel. Things are going to change.'

CHAPTER 22

In Which Confidences are Frankly Exchanged

'Why did you not tell me at once?' demanded Lady Fayth. 'Do you not think that a most necessary and pertinent detail to have omitted?'

'I do assure you I am sorry, my lady – most heartily sorry,' answered Kit. 'But you must concede that I was not afforded ample opportunity to explain until just this moment. Even so, the fault, I own, is entirely mine.'

The revelation that Kit was the grandson of Cosimo Livingstone had thawed the frosty opinion of Lady Fayth somewhat, but she was still wary, and far from mollified. 'It would have saved me considerable distress, I do assure you.'

'Again, I can but throw myself on the mercy of the court,' he told her.

'The *mercy* of the court?' She smiled suddenly, brightening the room and Kit's heart with a glow of happiness. 'I do like that. Did you invent it?'

'Alas, no. It is a well-known saying where I come from.'

'Oh. I see.' She frowned and the glad radiance vanished. 'Now you are mocking me.'

'Not at all.' Eager to change the subject, Kit glanced down at his soup plate. 'This broth looks good.' He pulled his apostle spoon from the pocket of his waistcoat. 'Shall we dig in?'

'How oddly you speak,' she observed, picking up her spoon.

They ladled savoury beef broth into their mouths and Kit was glad for a moment's respite from the task of having to converse in the obtuse tongue of the seventeenth century – difficult enough at the best of times – and tilting with Lady Fayth was demanding and exhausting. He was happy for a chance to regroup. Silence, broken only by the occasional slurp, stretched between them. When the extended pause began to grow awkward, Kit entered the lists once more. 'Do you live in London?' he asked.

'Good heavens, no!' she exclaimed. Setting down her bowl, she took a bit of dried bread, crumbled it into what remained in the bottom of the bowl, and began spooning up the sops. 'What about yourself?'

'London born and bred,' he replied, then quickly amended his assertion. 'Well, in truth, I was born in Weston-super-Mare. My family has moved around somewhat, but I've lived in London a long time.'

'Weston-super-Mare?' wondered Lady Fayth.

'It's in Somerset, I believe.'

'Is it, indeed?' she sniffed. 'My home is in Somerset – Clarivaux, our family's estate. Do you know it?' Without waiting for a reply, she continued. 'My father is Edward, Henry's older brother. I had a brother, Richard, who sadly died when he was three. I never knew him.' She nibbled daintily from the edge of the spoon, raising her head slightly. The candlelight caressed the curve of her throat and made her fair skin glow. The sight of such transcendent beauty within stroking distance made Kit feel a little dizzy. 'Do you have family?' she asked.

'Well, there's Cosimo, I suppose.'

'What do you mean, you suppose? Either he is your grandfather, as you claim, or he is not. There can be no supposition about it.'

'We *are* related,' Kit assured her. 'There is no doubt about that. But he is not, strictly speaking, my grandfather.'

'No?' The spoon halted, hovering in mid-air. 'Then who, pray, is he?'

'He is my *great*-grandfather.' At her disbelieving glance he added, 'I know, I know – it seems unlikely. In fact, I had trouble believing it myself. But it is the honest truth. Cosimo is my great-grandfather.'

'Upon my word. You do surprise me.'

'It's all to do with their, um – secret experiments.'

'*Leaping.*'

'Pardon?'

'Ley leaping – that's what *I* call it. When one jumps from one place to another…' She favoured him with a superior smile. 'Leaping.'

'A good word for it,' granted Kit. 'Anyway, all this leaping about from one place to another seems to interfere with the natural process of aging in some way. Cosimo should be a whole lot older than he seems to be.'

'Is that so?' She spooned up another sop, then pushed the dish away. 'Am I to understand that you have been allowed to leap?'

'Oh, yes. Several times. And you?'

'No,' she replied. Servants appeared to clear away the dishes and prepare the table for the main course. 'It is thought to be too dangerous – though I cannot imagine why – and so, of course, being a woman, I am not allowed.'

'Well, I'm not very good at it,' Kit said, by way of mitigating her disappointment. 'And I don't pretend to understand much about it. But I do agree it could be very dangerous. I mean, what if you leapt and found yourself in the middle of the sea, or a tiger-infested jungle, or an exploding volcano…'

'That is why you need the map.'

'Pardon?'

'The Skin Map.'

'You know about that, too?' said Kit, wondering what else she knew.

A platter of sliced mutton in gravy, mashed turnips, and carrots was placed on the table, and silver plates efficiently filled. The servants topped up the wine glasses and retreated once more.

'My uncle trusts very few people with his secrets,' she confided, reaching for a clean spoon and knife. 'Happily, I am one of that select number. My father thinks it all wool and nonsense. He refuses to allow even the merest mention of leaping in his presence – or any of Henry's other theories, come to that. In consequence, they have not spoken in years. Thus,' her smile turned sweetly satisfied, '*I* have become the sole repository of my uncle's scientific investigations.'

'I see.' Kit took her at her word, but there was something in what she said that niggled even as it sought to explain.

'Indeed, that is why I have come up to London,' she continued, slicing her meat nicely. 'It goes without saying that much of his work is complicated and extremely esoteric. Uncle has promised to show me his journals and teach me some of his more abstruse theories. In time, I may be allowed to make a leap myself.'

'His journals,' repeated Kit glancing up from his plate. 'Wait! You mean he writes it down!'

'Certainly, he does. He keeps it all in a little book,' she explained. 'All his thoughts and theories, and also the results of his various experiments. It all goes into the book. Sir Henry is nothing if not scrupulous.'

'How very admirable,' declared Kit. 'About these journals – I suppose you know where they are?'

'Where? In his study I should think – where else should they be?'

Kit felt the sense of helplessness that had dogged him since leaving Black Mixen begin to recede. He had only to get his hands on that book and all would be well. At least, this was the track his mind ran along at that moment. In a few days he would discover just how wrong he truly was, but by then this train of thought would have reached a wholly unexpected destination.

Laying aside his spoon, he placed both hands flat on the table. 'Lady Fayth,' he said, adopting a solemn tone to better communicate the sense of gravity he felt, 'I don't mean to frighten you, but Sir Henry and Cosimo are in serious trouble. I think it imperative that we find that book at once.'

'Trouble, you say? What sort of trouble?' she asked, cocking one perfect eyebrow. At his hesitation, she pounced. 'Come, sir! If we are to get on we must of necessity agree to a full exchange of confidences. We must keep nothing back.' He saw the defiance leap up in her eyes. 'Lest you harbour any misguided sense of chivalric duty to protect a poor weak woman, I do assure you I am fully able and prepared to protect myself.'

The idea of protecting this fiery spirit had not remotely occurred to Kit. Once suggested, however, he was caught in a proposition of powerful allure, the mere suggestion of which filled him with a sudden pleasure.

'Speak, sir!' she demanded.

He shook himself from his cave-man reverie. 'Yes,' he allowed, 'a full and frank exchange of confidences. It is precisely what I was about to suggest myself.'

'Then, as we are in agreement...' She patted her mouth primly with the edge of her napkin, and tossed it aside. 'Let us begin the search.'

Kit looked longingly at the mutton slowly congealing on his plate. 'After supper, perhaps –'

'That will not do, sir!' She pushed back her chair and stood. 'If finding his journal is as important as you claim, then we have not a moment to lose.' She strode from the room and into the corridor.

Kit snatched a last bite of the mutton, then hurried after her. She led him to the room where he had first met her: Sir Henry's library. Kit caught up with her at the wall of books. 'Do you know what it looks like?'

'I do not, for I have never seen it.'

'Well, it should not take long to find it in any case. You start there,' he pointed to the top left side of the bookcase, 'and I'll start at the opposite end. We'll meet in the middle.'

Kit began at his end. The books were all big, heavy tomes bound in thick dark leather, darker still in the flickering candlelight; he had great difficulty reading the titles hand-lettered in black ink on the spines which, he had noted before, were mostly in Latin. Giving this up as a bad job, he began pulling books off the shelf, one by one, and leafing through them. Some were handwritten on parchment, others printed on paper; occasionally, he came across one that contained a block print or etching – usually of some sort of machine or curious scientific apparatus; mostly, however, the pages were covered with small words crowded on pages with tight margins.

After examining a number of these volumes, Kit began to suspect that Sir Henry's journal, if it did indeed exist, would not be among the large and dense folios he was examining. He turned his eye instead to the smaller, more portable books he saw. These were fewer and more easily handled, and he had soon worked his way through all within reach. He moved a couple of paces closer to Lady Fayth and became aware that she was humming; although he did not know the tune, the melody was charming.

He was soon entranced by the lovely, lilting quality of her voice and no longer paying attention to what he was doing. He stood transfixed, the book unopened in his hand.

'What have you got there?'

'Hmm?' He glanced down at the little volume in his hand. It had a green cover and was closed by a leather strap which wrapped around a little brass boss; beyond that there were no other markings of any kind. 'I don't know.'

'Open it,' she instructed.

His fingers fumbled with the leather strap and he cracked open the cover to reveal a page densely covered with a script of such eccentric nature he could not make out what language it might be written in much less what it said.

'What have you found?'

'I don't know,' he said, handing the book to her. 'I can't read it.'

'It is in Sir Henry's hand,' she announced, her excitement contagious. He watched her lips moving as her eyes scanned the pages, and wished he was a page in a book just so he could have those lips moving over him like that.

With an effort, he turned his eyes back to the book. 'What does it say?'

'Here he is writing about the *manifest universe*,' she replied, running a white fingertip along the line. 'And something called the *omniverse*, whatever that may be.'

'The omniverse!' cried Kit. 'That's it! That's the thing they were talking about.' He tapped the page with his finger. 'This must be Sir Henry's ley travel journal. It has to be.'

'Are you certain?' she asked, glancing up. 'Do you want me to read more?'

'No... yes... possibly.' Kit reached for the book. 'Here, bring it to the light so we can see it better.'

Without relinquishing the little tome, Lady Fayth moved to the candle stand and, opening the book, cradled it in both palms, allowing Kit to turn the pages. Though he still could not decipher the archaic penmanship, he did manage to work out the word 'ominverse.' He turned more pages and found tiny diagrams of lines that looked like broken triangles and rectangles, some with numbers attached to them which might have been latitudes, degrees, or distances – he could not tell.

'We're going to have to spend some time with this, I expect,' he decided, 'if we're going to find what we're looking for.'

'For what, pray, are we looking?' she enquired.

Kit bit his lip. 'I'm not at all sure what we should be looking for,' he confessed after a moment's thought.

Lady Fayth frowned prettily.

He turned some more pages. 'But I think I'll know it when I see it.' He reached to take the book. 'May I?'

She closed the book with a snap. 'Certainly not!'

'But –'

'I will not have you pawing through my uncle's private journal. If you wish to examine this or anything else you must provide me with an explanation of greater persuasion than you have offered thus far.'

'Your uncle is in trouble. This book could help –'

'So you have already said.'

'After all this, you still don't believe me?' He regarded the dangerous set of her jaw. 'Apparently not.' Kit pushed out his lower lip in thought, then brightened as the solution came to him. 'I know! We'll ask Giles – he was there. He saw it all.'

'Who is Giles?'

'The driver – I mean, Sir Henry's footman or coachman, or whatever. He was with us at Black Mixen Tump. He saw what happened. He can tell you.' Kit started for the door. 'Send for him and let him explain.'

'He will have gone to bed,' said Lady Fayth. 'It must wait until tomorrow.'

'All right,' agreed Kit. 'First thing tomorrow morning, we'll call him in.'

'Until then, the journal stays with me.'

'Absolutely. Just don't let it out of your sight. I have a feeling that little green book is priceless.'

CHAPTER 23

In Which Lady Fayth
Takes the Lead

The decision to return to Black Mixen Tump had been swiftly reached – so swiftly Kit still harboured misgivings. Lady Fayth was confident enough for both of them, however, buoyed as she was by the prospect of at last being allowed to make a leap – the very thing, she proclaimed with endearing enthusiasm, she had been yearning for all her life. In fact, she was almost giddy with it – which made Kit's more sober assessment appear churlish and curmudgeonly by comparison.

'Believe me, if leaping was not dangerous enough –'

'Oh, yes – ferocious volcanoes and man-eating tigers and such, as you have already explained so very colourfully.'

'Right. Well, aside from all that, there is something I haven't told you yet. There are people – bad men, *very* bad men – murderers, in fact – who wish us harm. They always seem to show up. So, we must assume they will be nearby, waiting to attack. They were at Black Mixen and there was a fight. Sir Henry and Cosimo got away, but their attackers made the jump with them.'

'All the more reason to be on our way, I daresay,' replied Lady Fayth blithely.

'I'm not sure I follow,' said Kit, missing the link in her logic.

'If our eminent forebears were not in direst danger,' she explained, as if instructing a backward child, 'they would not stand in need of rescuing, and it would not fall to us to save them.'

'Well, yes,' granted Kit, 'but that doesn't lessen the danger to ourselves. We still –'

'Take courage!' she told him. 'All will be well.'

'I'm glad we got that settled,' he sighed, shaking his head. 'I feel so much better now.'

Sarcasm must not have been in fashion in the seventeenth century, apparently, for his remarks were taken at face value and Lady Fayth favoured him with one of her incandescent smiles. 'I am happy for you. We shall leave at once. I shall inform Villiers of our plans and have the servants prepare the things we require. Kindly inform Giles to ready the coach.'

'But we haven't deciphered the book,' Kit pointed out.

'We can do that on the way. You said it will take three days to reach this leaping place, is that not true?' At his admission that this was the case, she placed the book in his hand and concluded, 'Then we must not waste another moment.'

Having made up her mind, Lady Fayth was across the room and almost out of the door. 'Wait,' called Kit, 'there is one other thing.' He hesitated, uncertain how to put it.

'Yes? What is it?'

'Your clothes, Lady Fayth. Forgive me for saying it, but I sincerely doubt that you can make a leap dressed like that,' he said, indicating her dress.

She glanced down at her elegant satin gown. 'Pray, what is wrong with my attire?' The defiant expression on her face gave him to know that he was skating on very thin ice.

'It is not, ah – functional,' he offered.

'I suppose you would have me wear nothing at all!'

The mere suggestion of her lithesome form arrayed in its natural splendour proved so distracting that Kit, with heroic effort, pushed it promptly from his mind and tried his best to explain in a way that would not be taken amiss. 'My lady, we cannot know what we're leaping into – it might be rough country, a jungle, a desert, anything,' he told her. 'Also, there is the matter of time. We might be years or centuries ahead of the current date and age, or behind. In short, we simply cannot know what the people we encounter will be wearing wherever it is we're going. We must try not to be too, um… different.'

'Such disconformity could draw unwanted attention to ourselves as travellers,' she concluded. 'I understand. By my faith, your counsel is wise. I will find something more fitting to the purpose.' She turned again to go. 'Further to that, we will require money, I expect, and weapons.'

'If you can get them…' Kit began, but she was already gone. He stood gazing at the empty doorway. *Faith, my counsel is wise*, he reflected happily, his misgivings flittering away like dry leaves before the balmy breeze of her good opinion, if only for the moment.

They would return in force, but by then the would-be leapers were already beyond the outlying hamlets of London in a carriage loaded with three days' worth of food and drink, several changes of clothing, a purse full of gold sovereigns, two slightly rusty cutlasses and a handsome flintlock pistol. At Kit's suggestion, Giles, who agreed willingly, was brought into the plan. They departed as soon as the equipment and provisions could be loaded onto the coach, and were soon clattering through the northern suburbs and out into the belt of farming hamlets ringing the city.

During the hours of good light, Kit applied himself to the study of the green book, poring over page after page of Sir Henry's crabbed text. The book itself was as fine a specimen of the binder's art as could be found anywhere: tight pages of fine paper, gold-edged, with a place-marker of black silk ribbon, all smartly bound in lustrous jade green kidskin, and so well made that it opened smoothly and closed with a satisfying snap. After properly admiring the craftsmanship of the tome, they had got down to studying the contents. Kit could not easily read Sir Henry's idiosyncratic hand, but Lady Fayth, whose eye was more accustomed to the mode of the day, seemed to have little difficulty. Under her instruction, Kit began to gain some mastery of the script.

Much of what he gleaned was so far over his head it might as well have been Japanese for all the impression it made – the language was arcane, when not archaic – and the concepts discussed assumed a knowledge, or at least a vocabulary, Kit lacked. However, by dint of perseverance, and with Lady Fayth's patient help, he was able to tease out a few useful nuggets of information from Sir Henry's theorizing about the nature of ley travel, its purpose, its mechanism, and its possible uses. There was much mention of the Skin Map, and a lengthy discourse on its curious markings with one or two examples, along with a few suggestions about the meaning of the symbols. There were also meticulous diagrams of ley lines and detailed directions to their locations, including maps.

From his study of Sir Henry's little green book, Kit learned that, temporally speaking, it made a very great difference where one crossed over on the ley. He shared this observation aloud to Lady Fayth, who confessed to being utterly confused.

'I think it means you have a choice not only where to leap, but *when*,' he explained. 'He seems to suggest that it's like a road – like the one we're travelling on now, with signs and mile markers along the way, see?' He pointed out of the coach window to a pale white milestone they were passing just then. 'Well, if this was a ley line then each of the mile markers would correspond to a different time in the otherworld location connected to that particular ley.'

'If you insist,' replied Lady Fayth hazily.

'Now, suppose that milestone we just passed corresponded to the 1500s in the otherworld, then the next one might be the 1600s and so on,' Kit told her, waving the book in one hand. 'Depending on *where* you make the leap, you end up in different times in the development of the world you're leaping into. Incredible!'

Lady Fayth was unimpressed. 'It sounds needlessly complicated to me.'

'Perhaps,' granted Kit. 'In any case, it means that we must be far more precise in our calculations to have any hope of ending up where we want to go.' He thumbed a few more pages in the book. 'Precision – that's the key. And that is why we need the Skin Map.'

Lady Fayth's perfect lips formed a perfectly puzzled frown.

'Look at this,' said Kit, leaning near her in his zeal. He indicated one of the strange signs Sir Henry had copied there – a curious semi-circular whorl with two almost parallel lines crossing it, one of which sprouted a barb like that of a fishhook at the end; a row of tiny dots lined the outer edge of the whorl.

'This is one of the symbols from the map.' He leaned closer still, holding the book to her. 'Sir Henry indicates that this little symbol tells not only where to find a particular ley, but also where that ley leads and the location of the milestones along the line to help navigate the time.' He beamed with this revelation and felt the visceral thrill of the nearness of her warm flesh. 'You've got to hand it to old Flinders-Petrie – he thought of everything.'

Lady Fayth accepted this appraisal coolly. 'Those obtuse jots and tittles communicate all of that?'

'Apparently,' allowed Kit. 'Of course, one has to know how to read the symbols. That's the chief difficulty – they're written in a sort of shorthand –'

'I do beg your pardon? With a short hand, did you say? However does the length of a person's hand enter into it?'

'Ah, yes.' Kit regrouped and started again. 'I mean – a code. They're written in code, or a secret symbol language. One must possess the key in order to unlock the secret of the symbols.'

Lady Fayth gave a nod towards the book. 'And is this key of which you speak to be found among Sir Henry's pages?'

'I don't know. We haven't read the whole book yet.' He glanced at the book in his hand. 'Maybe. I hope so. It would make things a whole lot easier if it did.'

Thus, together they turned to the section describing those otherworldly portals he called ley hubs – of which Black Mixen Tump was a prime example. What Kit eventually decided, after the lord scientist's circuitous language had been deduced and distilled, was that at certain times – corresponding, Sir Henry believed, to the phases of the moon or the alignment of the sun or perhaps both – the portal would stand open, allowing the ley traveller to cross the threshold into another world. Unlike a ley line, which required movement as well as timing and other manipulations, all that was necessary to use a ley hub, according to Sir Henry's understanding, was to position oneself in precisely the right place at precisely the right time and the crossing would be effected. In the case of Black Mixen the right place was indicated by a stone which someone had thoughtfully placed atop the tump; the right time was thought to be either dawn or dusk on days when the moon could be seen above the horizon before the sun had either risen or set.

Simple.

'There must be more to it than that,' Kit had muttered, mostly to himself. 'Is that all he has to say about it?'

'The entry is quite complete, but he has left a space to write further observations.' She turned the book so that he could see. 'The next entry is about something called "manipulation of matter *via* harmonic vibration" or something called soundwaves. There is nothing more about this Mixen Tump.'

No doubt there was more to it than Sir Henry knew, but all things considered, the information provided did roughly correspond to what Kit had witnessed not long ago in that very place. Besides, is was not as if he had any better choice than to trust his lordship's veracity and judgment. Blinkered as it might be, the green book was the only guide he possessed.

They reached the village of Chipping Wycombe and took rooms at the wayside hostelry for the night, resuming their journey early the next morning after a good night's sleep and a hearty breakfast. They travelled easily through the day, pausing only to water and rest the horses, reaching the Tetsworth Swan well before sundown. They were on the road all the earlier next morning, following the road down into the wide Thames Valley.

Upon rolling into Oxford, they paused as before at the Golden Cross coaching inn and – while the horses were fed, watered, and rested – they enjoyed a hearty meal of good greasy pork chops, turnip mash, and boiled greens. Giles took his meal with the other coachmen in the yard, gathering information on road conditions and where to spend the night in Banbury. Then, as the sun was high and bright they decided to stretch their legs, so walked around taking in sights of the university town, watching the students flapping from place to place in their long black robes and mortarboard hats. Kit exulted in being seen with the lovely lady by his side – a new experience for him, and rare enough in the streets of staid Oxford – it was all he could do to keep the swagger out of his stride.

Leaving Oxford, they struck out on the road to Banbury, where they planned to spend the night – to be within reach of their destination at the crack of dawn when, according to the green book, the portal atop Black Mixen would stand open. It was well after dark when they arrived in the little market town, and the solitary inn, the Fox and Geese, had only a single room to let. Lady Fayth took that, leaving Giles and Kit the choice of spending the night in the tavern hall in chairs by the fire, or sleeping in the stable. They chose to sleep in the coach with the horses in the stable, which was warm enough and comfortable, if redolent of straw and leather, horseflesh and manure. Giles woke them while it was still dark and they donned their travelling clothes: both Kit and Giles put on heavy lace-up shirts and breeches, stout shoes, and wide-brimmed felt hats; Lady Fayth wore a pair of breeches, a man's shirt over her own smock and stays, sturdy stockings and somewhat questionable high-topped shoes. They all wore loose jerkins of fine, thin leather.

She had protested that the clothes made her look like a man – a view which Kit vigorously rejected on the grounds that no trifling pair of breeches could ever make her appear in the least way mannish. The fact that he found her comely form all the more fetching in simple clothes, he kept to himself. Fortunately, since she did allow that her costly silks and satins were wholly unfit for the work at hand, his opinion was not required.

Thus outfitted, they continued on their way, jogging easily through a dark and deserted countryside, reaching their destination as the eastern sky blushed with the rumour of dawn.

'There it is,' said Kit, indicating the unnaturally symmetrical flat-topped hill. It loomed into view through the early morning mist like the black prow of a gigantic ship cleaving white waves, all ghostly and silent in the fast-fading night. The sight of its menacing bulk sent an involuntary shiver through Kit as he remembered what had happened the last time he had been there.

He was well down the road to rueing the decision to pursue this ominous undertaking when Lady Fayth exclaimed, '*That* is the dread Black Mixen?' Her tone left little doubt that she thought the sight highly overrated. 'From your description, I imagined it a grim and desolate mountain, plagued by rampant evil and grotesquery of every kind.'

'Don't let its looks fool you,' Kit muttered. 'That is one ornery tump.'

'That, sir, is the *merest* hill,' she scoffed. The coach rolled to a halt and Giles called out that they had come as far as they could go, as the coach wheels were sinking into the soft earth. Lady Fayth opened the carriage door and bounded towards the dark flank of the hill, her long hair flouncing in the brightening breeze – the very picture of an exotic bird at last released from its gilded cage and exulting in its long-awaited freedom.

'My lady! Wait!' Kit called after her. 'We must all stay together.' Stepping from the coach, he looked up to Giles on the driver's bench. 'Let's get the food and weapons up there. We don't have much time.'

'Right, sir.' Climbing up onto the seat, Giles reached onto the roof and untied the bundles fixed there, passing them down to Kit one after the other. 'After you, sir,' he said, shouldering the larger of the two parcels.

Kit started off, then halted, turned back and said, 'What about the coach and horses?' He was still that much oblivious to the conventions of the age in which he found himself that it was the first time he had spared a single thought for the animals.

'I have already made provision for them, sir,' Giles assured him.

'Really? When?'

'At the inn last night. The landlord will send a boy to collect them. The carriage will be taken to the inn and the horses stabled until we return to claim them.' At Kit's expression, he added, 'Never fear, sir, I did not let on what we were about. For all they know, we have gone hunting in the woods hereabouts.'

'Well done, Giles. It completely slipped my mind.'

'There is no reason why it should have concerned you, my lord. The coach and horses are my responsibility.'

They hurried to catch up with Lady Fayth, who had found the spiral path leading to the top and was already striding her way swiftly towards the summit. The two men toiled along in her wake and reached the top to find her tapping her foot with impatience.

Kit dropped his bundle the better to catch his breath. 'The

marker stone is beyond those trees,' he said. Glancing away towards the eastern horizon, he saw the sky pinking up in a line above the wooded hills in the distance. 'It will be light soon.'

'Then we must by all means hurry,' said Lady Fayth, starting off towards the trees.

'Wait, my lady,' said Kit, drawing a cutlass from his bundle. 'Let Giles and me go first – in case any of the Burley Men are about.' Before her ladyship could mount a protest against this line of reasoning, he started towards the Trolls, whose black silhouettes soared against the steadily lightening heavens.

Keeping a wary eye peeled for any movement which might betray the presence of intruders, he passed beneath the spreading branches of the great old oaks, and made for the place where he knew he would find the square marking stone.

There was no one about. They had the place entirely to themselves and, as the sun began to peep above the horizon, Kit found the square flat stone. 'Here it is,' he called, waving the others to him. 'Hurry! The time is upon us.'

Giles and Lady Fayth quickly joined him. 'Stand on the stone,' he instructed, pulling them closer. 'Now, everyone join arms. Whatever happens, do not let go.' He linked arms with Giles on one side and Lady Fayth on the other. 'I repeat,' he cried, 'whatever happens, *do not* let go!'

'Why are you shouting?' asked Lady Fayth.

'The wind!' hollered Kit – and then realized the anticipated storm had not, in fact, materialized. The air remained dead calm. 'Strange,' he said. 'There was always wind before.'

They stood for a long moment looking at each other. The sky grew lighter. Still nothing happened.

Kit thought back to the day Cosimo and Sir Henry had disappeared. An image floated into his consciousness: his great-grandfather standing on the stone with his arms raised over his head like a prize-fighter in a pose of triumph. 'Um,' he said, 'let me try something.'

He raised one arm and instantly felt the hair on his arms and the back of his neck stand up. The air seemed to be charged with static electricity. Raising the other arm, the eerie feeling increased. The air seemed to have become leaden, thick and difficult to breathe.

'Hold on to me!' he shouted again, and this time with good reason for a roar had erupted out of nowhere to fill the sky directly above them. A wild wind swirled, tearing at their clothes, and they were enveloped by an unearthly blue glow. The world around them – hilltop, the Trolls, the hills beyond – faded, becoming watery and indistinct as with a sort of luminous heat haze. The roar became a scream.

'Don't let go!' shouted Kit, trying to be heard above the whine. It was increasingly difficult to hold his arms aloft – as if the drag of a dozen gravities hung from each upraised arm. He had not accounted for the immense, almost crushing pressure. It felt as if the entire tump was balanced on his upraised fists. His muscles burned and he began to falter. Then, when he thought he could not hold up under the strain, he felt Lady Fayth tighten her grip and slip one arm around his waist. He glanced into her face and saw neither fear nor alarm, but pure, elemental exhilaration; a wild and exultant fire lit her eyes. She returned his gaze with something approaching admiration.

The look renewed his strength. He gave out a cry and rose up on his toes. 'Jump!' he shouted, and as he did so he felt his feet leave the ground.

It was only a small hop, but he came back down with a jarring bump that travelled up from his ankles through his knees and all the way to his hips.

And that was it.

Between one breath and the next, the sound and fury died. The weird blue shimmering haze simply ceased. The static-charged air gave a puny, apologetic pop and fizzled. Glancing down, Kit saw they were all still standing on the marker stone. His heart sank.

'I guess we'll have to try again this evening when –' he began, then broke off abruptly. 'Ow!'

Lady Fayth's fingernails were digging into the flesh of his side. Her eyes were wide with wonder and her face and auburn hair aglow with the light of a golden sunrise. He turned his gaze to see that what had so absorbed her attention was a long straight stone-paved avenue: an avenue lined with a double row of sphinxes.

CHAPTER 24

In Which an Understanding is Reached

The air was still, the heat of the day abating as the sun drifted westward. The Mirror Sea was living up to its name, its surface as smooth as molten glass, reflecting a pale, cloud-dappled heaven. Arthur Flinders-Petrie gazed absently at the handsome prospect of the harbour and the crescent sweep of the bay spreading out below him; his thoughts were troubled and his heart heavy. The last weeks of convalescence, spent largely in the company of Chen Hu's spirited daughter, Xian-Li, had revived him in many more ways than one.

But now it was time to go.

Had the choice been his alone, he might have tarried indefinitely. But the trading season was ending and by decree of the Chinese authorities all foreigners must leave the country – the same as every year; nothing had changed in that respect. All ships would be sailing within the next few days. Ordinarily, he would be glad to return to England as fast as the winds could carry him; but this year Arthur discovered he had a reason to stay.

'I will miss you, Xian-Li,' he said, a note of longing rising in his voice.

'And I will miss you, my friend,' she replied, touching his arm shyly. She smiled, 'But you will come back one day.'

'I will – and soon,' he told her. 'I promise.'

'And until then, I have these beautiful shoes to remind me of your visit.' She smiled and lifted her hem and pointed the toes of her delicate, unbound feet so that he could see the glistening blue silk of her pearl-beaded slippers. 'Thank you.'

'It is I who stand in *your* debt, Xian-Li,' said Arthur, regarding the slender, dark-haired young woman beside him: how her red gown shimmered, how her black hair shone. 'Alas, it is a debt I can never fully repay.'

'Do not talk of debt and repayment,' she chided lightly. 'What I did, I did for the honour of my family, and —' She halted, dropping her head demurely.

'And?' Arthur asked, feeling her hesitancy.

'And for the sake of your friendship to my father.'

'Only that?' A surge of emotion welled up inside him then. Time grew short; he could not leave without knowing. 'Is there nothing else?'

Xian-Li did not look up. Arthur gazed upon her bowed head, her long black hair falling in a curtain. He could not see her face to know what she might be thinking or feeling at that moment. 'Please, Arthur,' she said at last. 'There can be nothing more. Do not ask it of me.'

'But I do ask, Xian-Li,' he said. 'I ask because in the short time we have had together, I have grown to love you very much.'

'You will always be my dear friend, Arthur,' she replied, her gaze still lowered. 'Always.'

'Yet I would be more,' he said. Then, casting his customary diffidence to the four winds, he added, 'Marry me, Xian-Li. Become my wife.'

She glanced up quickly, her expression stricken. 'Arthur, no... please, no. It cannot be.'

'Why not?' he said, emboldened now that he had spoken his inmost heart. 'What is to prevent us?'

Her face clouded with unhappiness. 'Must you make me say it?'

'I love you, Xian-Li. Marry me. We can be together always.' He reached for her hand. 'I need you, my love. I cannot foresee a life without you.'

She shook her head gently. 'I am Chinese. You are English. It is 'forbidden,' she said, but she did not pull her hand away.

'There is no power on earth to keep us apart if we do not wish it,' he assured her.

He saw the love and hope kindle in her great dark, luminous eyes, and pressed for an answer. 'Come, Xian-Li. You know I speak the truth. We can be happy together, you and I.'

She seemed to tremble on the edge of assent, but could not make the leap. 'They will never allow it,' she said, dropping her head once more.

'Then we will go somewhere else – a place where no one will mind our differences.'

She shook her head, tears falling to the floor. 'You do not understand, Arthur. I cannot leave China. They will never allow it. I would be stopped at the harbour before I could ever set foot on your ship. They would punish both of us – me most severely.'

'Xian-Li,' he said softly. 'All obstacles can be overcome, if you will it. Come, give me your answer. Will you marry me?'

Without looking at him, she clasped his hand again. 'I cannot,' she said, her voice breaking into a sob. 'It is forbidden.'

She gave his hand a last squeeze and then turned and started away. He watched her go, certain now as never before that more than anything in the world, this – this union – was what he wanted. *It will happen*, he thought to himself. *I will it.*

He let her go, remaining on the promontory above the bay to think and watch the sun go down. One by one the evening stars appeared as tiny lights in the sky, but Arthur did not stir. Later, when his feet turned back towards White Lotus Street, it was with a resolute and determined step.

He entered the house and quickly ascertained that Chen Hu was napping in the rear garden, which was just how he wanted it. He found Xian-Li in the tiny kitchen at the rear of the house and joined her there. She gave him a forlorn smile as he entered the room. 'My love, I –'

'Shh!' She raised her hand and placed her fingers to his lips. 'We must not speak of it again.'

Taking her hand, he kissed her fingertips, then removed the

round iron wok from the fire and led her from the room. 'Come, I want to show you something.'

In the room where Chen Hu performed his artistry, he sat Xian-Li on the tattau couch and took his place before her. 'Look here,' he said. Unlacing his shirt, he drew it over his head, and tossed it aside. He put a hand to his chest and lightly brushed the intricate deep blue designs there. 'These tattaus which your father has made for me these past few years are not mere fancies – meaningless scribbles as many believe. They are symbols of my own devising and each one bears a fantastic secret, an incredible secret.'

Xian-Li, all attention, sat with her back straight, her hands folded in her lap.

'My love,' continued Arthur, his voice low but earnest, 'I am going to tell you something I have never told another living soul. I am going to share with you the secret of the symbols.'

'Arthur, no,' she protested. 'It is not necessary.'

'But it is,' he countered, 'very necessary – because, you see, I have a way to travel the world without ships or any other man-made conveyance. Each of these tattaus,' he touched one of the indigo symbols, 'each one represents a different place I have travelled.' He paused and waited to see how she would receive this next revelation. 'Xian-Li, I am not a businessman as you suppose. I am a traveller and an explorer.'

Xian-Li bit her lip, but said nothing.

'Listen carefully,' he said, dropping his voice still further. 'The places to which I go are not of this world.'

'Arthur, no...'

'It is true,' he insisted. 'Difficult as it may be to believe, it is true. The universe is not only greater than we imagine, it is far stranger. There are dimensions unknown and unguessed by the mass of mankind, and I have discovered a way to travel through them to worlds beyond our own. Each place I have visited is on a different plane of existence –' He touched another tattau. 'These marks represent my travels. They are the record of not only where to find the alien world, but how to get there. They are a map written on my skin so that it can never be lost, never taken from me. It is written there so that wherever I am, however far across the universe, I can always find my way home.'

Xian–Li stared at him.

'Come with me, my love. I will show you wonders you never dreamed possible. There are endless new worlds to explore. We will explore them together, you and I. Only say me "yes" and let us make a start.'

He reached for her and she stood, and took one tentative step nearer. She stretched her hand towards his bare torso, fingers shaking slightly, and delicately traced one of the blue marks, and then another.

'I ask again, and I will keep on asking,' he said, folding her hand into his own, 'will you marry me?'

'It was impossible before,' she began, hesitantly. 'It is even more impossible now. I know nothing of this life of which you speak.'

'You will learn. I will teach you.' He smiled. 'It will be the most glorious adventure ever known. I do not ask you to believe me, Xian–Li. All I ask right now is that you trust me. Can you do that, my love? Can you trust me?'

She looked at him a long time, then nodded.

'Good. Marry me and let us make a beginning.'

She wavered before the force of his insistence, then pulled away. 'I must think, Arthur,' she said. 'Please, I need a little time.'

'If it were mine to give, I would give you all the time you needed,' he told her gently. 'But we have only tomorrow, and then I must depart.'

'Tomorrow will be time enough,' she said.

'Until tomorrow, then,' he allowed. He retrieved his shirt and pulled it on, did up the laces and tucked it into his breeches while Xian–Li padded away to the kitchen to resume her preparation of the meal. Wanting to allow her time to herself, Arthur went out to the back garden to join Wu Chen Hu, who was now awake.

The elder man smiled when he saw his friend, and poured another cup of rice wine from the small jar in his hand. 'It is good to see you looking strong again,' he said, handing him the cup.

'Thanks to you, Chen Hu, and your daughter, I am hale and healthy once more.' He raised the cup and saluted his host, taking a sip and passing back the cup. He sat down and leaned against the smooth trunk of the plum tree.

'And soon you must leave us.'

'Yes, tomorrow – otherwise the Gongbú will throw me into prison.'

'Those fellows can be very unforgiving,' sympathized Chen Hu. 'Perhaps next season you will return for another tattau.'

'For a certainty, I will,' vowed Arthur. 'I feel in many ways that my travels have only begun. I have many more places to visit,' he smiled and patted himself on the chest, 'and many empty spaces to fill with tattaus. Yes, I will come back.'

'That is good to hear.' The older man sipped some wine and returned the cup to his guest. 'I have another daughter, you know.'

'I did not know that.'

'Yes.' Chen Hu nodded slowly. 'She lives in Zhaoqin – two days from here. She lives with her husband and two little boys. But a few days ago I received word from a friend who was in Zhaoqin that her husband is being sent to Macau – he is an official on the Líbú and he goes where they tell him to go. He has been given a promotion and increased pay.'

'Good for him,' mused Arthur, 'and good for your daughter.'

'And good for Chen Hu, too. I will have someone nearby to help look after me, so Xian-Li's burden will be eased greatly.'

'I had not thought of that,' replied Arthur, wondering why his old friend had introduced this line of conversation. Were his feelings for the old man's daughter so obvious, so transparent?

Chen Hu, a little tipsy with the strong, sour wine, leaned forward unsteadily. 'To speak truth,' he confided, 'Hana-Li is a better cook than Xian-Li.' He grinned raffishly. 'I am sorry, my friend, but it is true. You should know this, I think.'

'And you should know, Chen Hu,' he said, 'that I worship your daughter. She is light and life to me. I do not care what kind of cook she might be.'

'You will!' chuckled the old man. 'You will!'

And the thing was done. An understanding had been reached between the two men and nothing more was said, or needed to be said. The agreement was made then and there. All that remained was Xian-Li's assent.

He still faced the difficulty of smuggling the young woman out of the country, but that, he considered, could be overcome one way or another. Where there was a will, there was a way: no one believed that more fiercely, more ardently than did Arthur Flinders-Petrie, who had greater validation for this belief than anyone might reasonably expect.

Later, after the three of them had shared the evening meal and walked a little in the night market, viewing the stalls of the merchants and artisans – looking for a few trinkets Arthur might take home to his young nephew and niece back in England – they said goodnight and went to their respective rooms. Arthur was sitting on the edge of his pallet, removing his shoes, when the door opened silently and Xian-Li entered. She took but two steps into the room.

One glance at the expression on her face and he put his shoes aside and stood, waiting for her to speak.

'My father told me about my sister returning to Macau,' she said. 'He has set me free to follow my own heart.'

'Where does your heart lead you?'

'It would bring me happiness to marry you, Arthur,' she said.

He crossed the room in three strides and gathered her into his arms. 'My darling,' he sighed. 'There is so much I would show you, share with you. We will make a fine life together.' He bent his head and kissed her; she returned his kiss fully and freely. He held her close, and felt her strong hands on his back and neck as she strained against him. 'We will be happy, my love,' he whispered, kissing her again. 'We *will* be happy.'

CHAPTER 25

In Which the Alchemy of Coffee is Discovered

The Grand Kaffeehaus opened on the Old Town Square to such heightened anticipation that a queue of patrons stretched from the door out into the busy marketplace. This, of course, drew even more attention, which caused the crowd to swell further. Engelbert and Wilhelmina, and their four uniformed assistants were very soon overwhelmed by the crowds. All were run off their feet before the day was half through, and the shelves were stripped of pastries, pies, and cakes by midday; after that, they served coffee only until they locked the door at sunset on the first day. Herr Arnostovi appeared just after they had closed the shutters bearing a bottle of Riesling, which he opened in celebration of their triumph.

'You should be proud of yourselves, my friends,' he said, filling the cups and passing them out to Mina, Etzel, and the serving scullions. 'A successful opening in this city is rare enough to be remarkable. Word will reach the highest levels of society. Even now, the news is spreading through the great houses. You will be famous in Prague.'

'Thank you, Herr Arnostovi,' said Etzel simply. 'We know it could not have been achieved without your help.'

'I only looked after my own interests,' replied the man of business. 'Nothing more.'

'You did far more than that,' Mina chided lightly. 'Etzel is right. We could not have come this far this fast without your guidance, Herr Arnostovi. Your help in these past days made all the difference.'

Delighted by this fulsome praise, the tall, thin man made a low, solemn bow, his arm swept wide. 'It has been entirely my pleasure,' he replied. Then, raising his cup, he cried, 'May God grant you every success!'

Engelbert, whose own joy could not easily be confined, joined the salute. 'It is right to remember God at this time,' he said when they had drunk the first toast. 'For without God, nothing is possible.' Lofting his cup, he said, 'To our Wise Provider, Benefactor, and Friend. May all our efforts bring praise and glory to his name!'

Herr Arnostovi smiled. 'Although I am a Jew, with this we can all agree, and I say to you "Amen, and amen"!'

They finished the bottle of sweet white wine and the helpers were dismissed to mix the dough and prepare the oven for the next day's baking. Wilhelmina and Engelbert were treated to a fine dinner by their landlord, who took his partners to an eating house where he often dined with his intimates. There they enjoyed a splendid night's celebration and the following morning opened their doors to another great crowd of curious and enthusiastic customers. For Wilhelmina, the clamour, though hectic, was most gratifying. Finally, for once in her life, her skills were being rewarded – lauded even – by a business under her complete control, putting into practice her own ideals, and being run to her exact specifications. Such, she reasoned, would never have happened back in London.

Thinking of London and of her former life there put her in a melancholy mood – not because she missed it very much… but because she did *not*. At first she had wondered how she would ever survive such a wrenching displacement – being stranded in an ancient time and strange, alien place – but the truth as it gradually dawned on her was that she had not only survived, but had thrived beyond all reasonable expectation – thanks largely to Engelbert, it had to be said, but prospering all the same. Her life before the leap had taken on the quality of a dream and, like a dream, had faded with the passing days, growing increasingly remote; her waking reality was here and now, and she liked it very much indeed. In all honesty, she was forced to conclude that she did not miss twenty-first-century London at all – not her friends, her apartment, her family, or anything else. Not even Kit. She had not spared her miserable boyfriend more than a fleeting thought since arriving in Prague. He, like everything else in her swiftly receding past, had simply relinquished any hold on her heart. Curiously, the thought made her a little sad, though she could not say why.

Perhaps the lack of sentiment revealed the poverty of her former existence, and it was that which cast her into a melancholy mood. In any event, this fit of introspection did not last long. Ever the practical person, Mina viewed such musings as wholly unproductive and when they threatened to interfere with forward progress, she shoved them firmly behind her. Instead, she got on with business – and what a business to be getting on with! She and Etzel, and their new helpers, found themselves in the centre of a whirlwind of sensation and acclaim. The worthy citizens of Prague simply could not get enough coffee. Every day, Engelbert was forced to close the shutters with customers still waiting to get in. Far from discouraging their patrons, this random exclusivity only made them more determined.

The first week passed into the second, and so on, the first month into the next, and still the flood of custom did not subside. It did, however, become slightly more regulated as people began working out when was the best time to arrive for whatever social gathering one hoped to meet. Wilhelmina saw patterns emerging and was fascinated by their relations: businessmen, many of whom were fellow merchants on the square, arrived as soon as the doors opened, but did not linger – they ate and drank, conversed quickly and then hurried off to their affairs. By mid-morning society's aristocrats, would-be aristocrats, and climbers were firmly installed; they dawdled over their steaming cups so that each and all could admire clothes, company, rank and bearing. The more ordinary worthies and the curious came next, mostly just to exchange gossip and partake of the city's latest sensation. The next group to colonize the Kaffeehaus Mina could only describe as the intellectuals and intelligentsia – professors and lecturers from the university along with some of the more exalted doctoral candidates and students – finishing their day and mingling with the creative class made up of poets, artists, musicians, and other bright young things whose day was just beginning. Lastly came what Mina considered the radicals – dark and furtive men who gathered to give vent to the dangerous ideas percolating in their fanatic and militant souls.

Around the margins of these more distinct groups were others who came and went, floating easily among the various tiers and strata, but not wholly part of any one faction or another: certain professional men – physicians and lawyers, for example – who mixed with any of several groups. There were also a variety of minor court officials, among whom Wilhelmina noticed an odd coterie she could not readily identify. They came dressed in vaguely academic garb complete with silly hats – bizarre shapes and unusual fabrics – long stoles, and fur-trimmed hooded gowns. Closer inspection revealed that their robes were invariably threadbare, the furs moth-eaten, the hats soiled, the stoles exhibiting a variety of stains. They kept mainly to themselves, their company exuding an air of benign secrecy. They came late and huddled head to head over their cups, speaking in low, earnest voices, often consulting books and scraps of parchment which they brought with them; and though they dressed as impecunious scholars, they paid in good new silver.

Intrigued by their mysterious presence, Mina determined to find out who they might be. One evening, after the main group had come and gone, she approached one of the younger men who remained behind, nursing his coffee at the table recently abandoned by his fellows. 'Would you like another cup?' asked Mina, brandishing her pewter pot. She liked walking through the room, meeting her customers and refilling their cups for free. 'No charge,' she said, smiling.

'Please,' said the fellow. He looked a little lost in his big dark robe and squirrel fur collar. His hat was two sizes too big and sat on his head like a limp rhubarb leaf. 'My thanks, good woman.'

'Your friends had to leave,' she observed, raising the pot. She poured and discovered that the pot was all but empty. The last splosh came out in a gush along with some of the grounds – she had yet to devise a completely satisfactory filtering system. 'Oh, I am sorry,' she said. 'You've got the dregs. Don't drink that – it will be too bitter. I'll bring you some more.'

'It is not necessary,' said the young man, but she was already gone.

When she returned with a new pot, she found him gazing into the murky liquid at the bottom of his cup. 'Here, I brought you a new cup, too,' she said, and made to take the old one from his hand.

'Please,' he said, still clutching the vessel with a tenacity that surprised Mina. 'This sediment – this bitter earth...' He indicated the mud awash in the bottom of his cup. 'What do you call it?'

'Um...' Wilhelmina thought of the proper German word. 'Grounds,' she said with a shrug. 'We call them Kaffee grounds.'

'If I may be so bold,' he said, 'what do you do with them?'

'*Do* with them?' She gave him a puzzled look, and sat down at the table. 'Why do you ask?'

'Believe me when I tell you that I mean neither disrespect nor malice in any conceivable form,' he replied. 'Indeed, I not only understand, but commend your instinctive reluctance. You wish to protect this unique and marvellous – some might even say *exotic* – creation. This I can well understand, as anyone might...'

The young scholar's articulate yet circuitous mode of expression made Mina smile.

'It is not too much to say that I possess the utmost esteem, reverence even, for your industry and acumen in bringing such an invention to its obvious fruition –'

'It isn't that,' Mina interrupted. 'I merely wondered why you might want my Kaffee grounds.'

'Ah! If you will, allow me to enlighten you, good lady,' replied the young man. 'Nothing less than the advancement of the scientific arts compels me to ask.'

'I see,' answered Mina, suppressing a laugh.

Nevertheless, the young man noticed the mirth dancing in her eyes. 'I discern full well that you are not wholly convinced of my veracity,' he sniffed a little haughtily. 'Even so, if you will indulge me yet a moment longer, I believe I have within my grasp the power to allay your disbelief and assuage any doubts that may still linger in your mind.'

'Do,' said Mina, growing more fascinated by the moment, 'by all means, continue.'

'Good lady,' he said, drawing himself up, 'you are addressing a member of His Highness Emperor Rudolf's court. My name is Gustavus Rosenkruez, and I am Chief Assistant to the Lord High Alchemist.' He dipped his head in a courtly bow. 'I am at your service, good lady.'

'The men who were with you this evening,' ventured Mina. 'Are they alchemists, too?'

'They are members of what the common rabble of this city, in their vulgar way, have named the Magick Circle, yes,' he answered stiffly. 'But not all are alchemists. We have astrologers, physicians, prognosticators, kabbalists, diviners, and other scientists among the members of our eminent fraternity.'

Wilhelmina nodded. 'I wouldn't worry too much about the common rabble,' she said. 'You are all more than welcome here.'

'On behalf of the Learned Fellowship, I thank you.' He swirled the dregs in his cup. 'And I hasten to assure you, by whatever means you will accept, that my interest in this substance is purely scientific. One of my duties is to determine the properties of various materials and explore their potential usefulness for alchemical purposes. It is work of great consequence to our aims.'

'Oh, yes? That would explain it, I suppose.'

'It has occurred to me that this elixir, this Kaffee, is a most potent and particular concoction. No doubt we are only on the cusp of discovering its manifold uses. Further, the potency of this elixir must derive from the primary body with which you formulate the liquid.'

'That is true,' Mina granted. 'You are very perceptive, *mein Herr*.'

'Seeing that you agree with my basic premise,' Gustavus continued, watching her closely, 'it follows that a closer examination of the prime essence would be in order – would you agree?' Mina nodded. 'Therefore, I would like to obtain a quantity of this bitter earth with which to perform experiments.' Noticing what he imagined to be a hesitation, he quickly added, 'You will be well remunerated, of course.'

'You want to *buy* my Kaffee grounds?'

'Realizing the value of such a rare commodity, it is only appropriate.' The young alchemist, anxious to secure her agreement, said, 'Your co-operation would be a most valuable contribution to the advancement of science and knowledge.'

'Since you put it that way, I don't see how I can refuse,' she told him. 'Would a pound or two be enough to begin?'

The young man, unable to conceal his glee, leapt from his chair, swept off his curious hat, and bowed low. 'Good lady, I salute you. When would it be convenient to collect the material?'

'Wait here but a moment, and I will have a package prepared for you at once. You can take it away with you now.'

The alchemist rubbed his hands with eager delight and returned to his seat to finish his coffee while Wilhelmina proceeded to the kitchen to fetch some spent grounds. She returned bearing a fair-sized bundle. 'Accept these as a gift of the Grand Kaffeehaus,' she said. 'Use them, with my blessing, for the advancement of science.'

The young man stared at the package. 'Your generosity overwhelms me,' he said, glancing from the bundle to Wilhelmina. He licked his lips.

'Think nothing of it,' she said, adding in a low voice, 'I think little enough of it myself.'

'The gift will be reckoned, you may rest assured,' he declared. 'All at court will hear of your unbounded munificence.'

'Tell them also about Etzel's fine cakes and pastries,' replied Wilhelmina.

'Indeed, I will,' said Gustavus. He dipped his head again and took up the bundle in both hands. 'And now I will wish you a good evening.' He all but bolted for the door.

'Goodnight,' Mina called after him.

A short while later, when the shutters closed on another day, she told Etzel about the exchange with the young alchemist. 'It was good of you to give him the spent grounds,' he said. 'It cost nothing to make him happy. We should all practise this more, I think.'

'Happy? He was ecstatic. You should have seen his face when I gave him the bundle,' she said. 'I could not bring myself to tell him that ordinarily we just throw them away.'

'One good deed breeds others,' Engelbert declared. 'Good will come of it.'

And he was right. The next day just before closing time, a message came to Wilhelmina from her young alchemist. It was delivered by a liveried servant of the court, who said, 'I am to await your reply.'

Wilhelmina accepted the parcel – a small square of parchment tied with red ribbon and sealed with wax.

'I wonder what it can be,' she said, turning the square in her hands and studying the seal carefully.

'Open it and find out!' urged Engelbert, eyes glinting merrily.

She broke the seal and unfolded the thick parchment, scanning the flowing script there. 'I can't read it,' she said, handing the message to Etzel. 'You read it.'

The big man grasped the parchment and, holding it close to his face, began to read it out loud, pausing to exclaim, 'It is from the Master of Royal Audiences!' He gazed at the parchment, his eyes growing large. 'Did you hear? We are summoned to the palace tomorrow to receive the thanks of the emperor's Lord High Alchemist. We are to be granted an honour.'

Mina expressed her amazement at the summons, and asked, 'What kind of honour?'

Etzel scanned the page again, very carefully. 'It does not say.' He glanced at the waiting messenger, then at Mina. 'What should we tell them?'

'Tell them that of course we would be delighted to attend,' she said.

Etzel relayed this reply to the messenger, who made a small bow and informed them that a carriage would call for them at this time tomorrow, and that they should array themselves appropriately for they could expect to dine with the emperor's retinue.

'This is because of your gift,' Etzel said when the messenger had gone. 'You have made friends at court – friends in high places.'

'Do you think so?' she wondered, flattered and impressed.

'In truth,' replied Etzel solemnly. 'What else can it mean?'

CHAPTER 26

In Which a Sealed Tomb
Gives Up its Secrets

Sunrise was still some while off, but Burleigh could feel the coolness of night wilting and the day's heat beginning to build – as if an oven had been lit and was being stoked somewhere beyond the horizon. It would be another scorching day, no surprise there, but he had prepared himself as best he could and was determined to enjoy the day. He had purchased a suit of loose, camel-coloured linen, complete with pith helmet, and a white kaffiyeh to keep the sun off his neck. Now, as he sat in the back of Lord Carnarvon's specially outfitted touring car, jouncing along an unmarked path, watching the pale arid hills undulate past his open window, he wondered what the day would bring. Certainly, his host was in exceptionally high spirits.

The location of the tomb was being kept a close secret. Although rumours were rife, and many knew that excavation was taking place, only four people in the world knew where to find the site. Despite this, it had proved no great difficulty to a man of Burleigh's skill and power of persuasion to wangle an invitation to attend the opening. His own knowledge and appreciation of Egyptian history and artefacts no doubt played a major part in convincing Carnarvon that he was genuinely interested in supporting the nascent science of archaeology; nor did his charm and good looks hurt his case where Lady Evelyn, his daughter, was concerned. After drinks and dinner on the terrace at the hotel, it seemed the most natural thing in the world to invite him, a fellow countryman of one's own class, to accompany them and witness what was surely going to be a monumental occasion.

'Have you visited excavations before, Lord Burleigh?' asked Evelyn. Dressed in a loose linen shirt and trousers, her hair hidden beneath a scarf, she sat in the jumpseat of the jouncing sedan facing her father and his guest.

'Once or twice,' Burleigh replied, forgoing mention of the fact that his visits tended to be after midnight when the site guards had been bribed to look the other way. 'I find it all endlessly fascinating, of course, but I never seem to be in the right place at the right time, if you see what I mean.'

'Today will be the exception,' Canarvon informed him grandly. 'I anticipate great things. Great things! I don't mind telling you I scarcely slept a wink last night. I rarely do on such occasions.'

'Father is like a fretful child at Christmas,' Evelyn confided lightly. 'He always feels someone else will get there before him and steal all his presents from under the tree. I myself slept like a baby.'

'This tomb,' said Carnarvon, 'is thought to be a royal tomb. Very rare. Although we cannot be completely sure until we open it, Carter is convinced – at least, as convinced as one can be at this stage of the dig – that we have found something very special.' He tapped his knee lightly with his fingertips. 'Very special indeed.'

'And I must thank you again for allowing me to be a witness to this historic occasion,' Burleigh volunteered. 'Incredibly generous of you.'

'Nonsense!' bluffed Lord Carnarvon. 'I won't hear of it. Your presence falls in with my purposes admirably well. We want credible corroboration for our finds, you know – even as we desire secrecy right up until the moment the grave is opened.'

'Publicity, in other words,' Lady Evelyn added in a lightly mocking tone. 'Father is never averse to a little publicity for his activities. It's the latent thrill-seeker in him. He used to race cars, you know, for the same reason.'

'Now, now,' chided her father, 'we'll not bore our guest with that old chestnut.' Glancing at the earl, he asked, 'Have you ever raced?'

'Horses, yes,' he replied, the lie slipping easily off his tongue. 'As a lad – until I grew too big. Cars? Never – though I've often wondered if I might like to try. I suspect I'm a bit too long in the tooth now.'

'Pish-tosh,' scoffed Lady Evelyn. 'You're never too old to race automobiles. Father only gave it up because he injured himself in a crash. Otherwise, I harbour not the slightest doubt you'd find him in a grease pit at Brooklands right this very moment.' She nudged her father's shin with the toe of her shoe. 'Admit it, Daddy,' she said, 'if not for the crash, we wouldn't be in Egypt now.'

'My daughter exaggerates terribly,' allowed the Earl of Carnarvon. 'But I did enjoy racing – *almost* as much as I enjoy a good dig. In retrospect, it was for the best – the crash, that is. Egypt has engaged me in ways that racing never could. I'll admit that after the accident it filled the gap. I've put all my energies into my excavations since then.'

'Will Mr Carter mind me tagging along, do you think?' wondered Burleigh.

'Can't think why,' said Carnarvon. 'I pay the bills. I can invite whomever I jolly well please. In any case, he's a most amenable chap, Howard Carter. Extremely knowledgeable. You'll like him once you get to know him.'

'I look forward to meeting him,' said Burleigh.

'You won't have long to wait. We're almost there,' Carnarvon announced. Leaning forward he pointed past the driver through the windscreen to the hilltop rising before them. 'It's just over the next rise. We'll be there in two minutes.'

At the top of the hill, the car braked and then started slowly down a steep, rocky incline along which a rudimentary serpentine road had been scratched for the few vehicles tending the site. They proceeded down to the valley floor and turned into a narrow, steep-sided ravine, or wadi. They followed the undulating gorge deeper into the hills, the vehicle headlights sweeping the sides of the wadi until at last it opened out at a junction where two other ravines joined the first.

Even in the pre-dawn gloom, Burleigh could make out a ramshackle camp made up of canvas and timber awnings stretched over shallow holes in the ground, and a few rough wooden shacks; three canvas tents as large as houses stood in a line to one side; several smaller black Bedouin tents with tiny campfires lay scattered around the periphery.

The sedan rolled to a crunchy stop outside the row of canvas tents and the passengers disembarked. The tents were empty, the occupants already at work. 'Carter will be at the dig,' called Carnarvon. 'This way. Follow me, but watch your step!' He strode off into the near darkness.

'After you, my lady,' said Burleigh, offering his hand.

'I hope we can get this over with before noon,' Evelyn confided. 'It gets so beastly hot out here. I positively liquefy.'

'Until today,' Burleigh confessed, 'I was seriously doubting my sanity for even setting foot in Cairo in the summer.' He paused. 'Mind you, winter isn't much better. Fewer flies, I suppose.'

'I daresay you'd never make much of an archaeologist, my dear earl. You've got to have a hide as thick as a rhino's and a love of dirt in all its glorious forms. Mr Carter, on the other hand, is desert born – with sand in his veins and the constitution of a camel. I myself think Egypt's past is best explored from eight to midnight on the terrace of the Continental-Savoy Hotel.'

'Spoken like a true daughter of the desert,' quipped Burleigh.

Lady Evelyn laughed, her voice deep and full. 'Archaeology is daddy's passion, not mine. Although I do enjoy the unveiling – like today. There is something terribly exciting about uncovering something that has been hidden from the world for untold centuries – that visceral thrill that one gets when one beholds the glory of a distant age so long submerged in darkness brought back to the light.' Suddenly self-conscious, she glanced at the tall man beside her. 'Wouldn't you agree?'

'Wholeheartedly,' Burleigh replied. 'Otherwise, I sincerely doubt I would brave the heat, flies, and scorpions to be here.'

They continued the rest of the way in silence, picking their way over a rough terrain of broken rock and piles of rubble, stepping over the stakes and guy lines of various awnings covering the works they passed. Up ahead, Lord Carnarvon had reached his destination:

yet another low awning of dirty canvas stretched over a gaping hole in the rocky desert landscape.

'Here!' he called, waving to them. 'Over here!'

He was standing at the rim of the excavation and calling down into it as they joined him. 'Are you down there, Carter?' he shouted. 'Carter?'

A faint and muffled voice came wafting up from the hole. 'Here!' It grew louder as it continued. '… a moment… let me get you a light. All is ready.'

A thin light wafted up from the dark heart of the hole before them, casting a pale illumination over the top step of a narrow staircase; a rope had been attached to one side of the hole to act as a handrail. Lord Carnarvon gripped the rope and quickly disappeared into the hole. 'After you, my lady,' said Burleigh, offering his hand to help steady the young woman as she prepared to descend.

Burleigh followed, descending the steep-stepped passage into a fair-sized underground chamber lit by kerosene lamps in the hands of half a dozen workmen directing their lights towards a stone doorway whose posts and lintel were carved with hieroglyphics. The door itself was stone bricks that had been plastered over with white-washed mud, and from which all the plaster had been chipped off.

'We've just completed the removal,' Howard Carter was saying to Carnarvon. 'In anticipation of your arrival –' He broke off abruptly. 'Oh, hello – who's this?'

'Ah, yes, forgive me,' Lord Carnarvon said, turning to his guest. 'Allow me to introduce my friend, Lord Burleigh, Earl of Sutherland.' He quickly made the introductions, proclaiming his new acquaintance an enthusiastic amateur archaeologist.

Lord Burleigh extended his hand to the renowned Egyptologist – a man of middling height and ordinary appearance who gave the impression of a chap who might be more at home behind a desk in the head office of an actuarial firm than raking up the desert in search of buried treasure.

'Delighted to meet you at long last, Mr Carter. I've heard so much about you. Your contribution to the increase in our understanding of ancient culture is incalculable.'

'I am glad you think so,' replied Carter in a thin, nasal voice. 'However, the popular press does tend to sensationalize things overmuch, I find.'

'Nonsense,' chimed Lady Evelyn. 'You are a most erudite and canny explorer, Mr Carter. You are far too modest for your own good.'

Carter smiled diffidently. 'I have been lucky,' he said.

'Never luckier than at this very moment!' declared Carnarvon. 'Shall we get on with it? We've waited years for this – the first glimpse of a royal tomb. Lay on, man! Let's see what we've found!'

Turning to the sealed doorway, Carter signalled to two workmen standing by, armed with mallet and chisel. The fellows began chipping away at the mortar between the blocks and soon the dead, still air of the chamber was filled with a fine gritty dust. As the mortar fell, the sense of anticipation in the chamber rose; the workmen murmured in Arabic; Carnarvon and his daughter whispered back and forth; Carter remained rigid, staring at the brick wall before him as if tearing it down by sheer will power alone.

Soon one of the central blocks had been freed. Carter raised his hand. '*Kata!*' He said. The workmen ceased their hammering, and he stepped forward. Carter ran his hands along seams of the block, working his fingers into the gap. He pulled, but the brick did not give. '*Takkadam*,' he said, stepping away again as the workers resumed hammering at the block. 'We'll have to break it to get it out,' he explained; his bookish face, betraying a sheen of eager perspiration, glistened in the lamplight.

'Won't take long,' Lord Carnarvon assured them. He rubbed his hands. 'Any moment now.'

With each blow of the hammers, the atmosphere grew more charged, the sense of anticipation more intense. The chink of steel on steel, and steel on stone, filled the chamber with a dull clamour; the dust grew thicker. The block fractured under the assault, and the crack was rapidly exploited.

'*Kata!*' cried Carter again.

The hammering ceased.

Moving to the sealed door, Howard Carter worked his fingers into the newly created crevice and pulled on the broken brick, slowly drawing the first half away. He tossed it behind him and the second half soon followed.

He peered in through the hole.

'What do you see?' asked Carnarvon.

'I see…' began Carter.

Earl Burleigh felt Evelyn lean close in her excitement. She pressed the knuckles of her right hand to her lips. 'Oh, please!' she gasped softly.

'Nothing.' Carter stepped away from the hole in the door. 'I can't see anything until we can get a light in.' He gestured to the workmen. '*Takkadam,*' he said, and the hammering began again.

The second stone fell more quickly than the first, and the third followed and the fourth and fifth in rapid succession. The dust in the anteroom chamber rose in clouds, filling the still air. All looking on covered noses and mouths with their scarves.

'*Kata!*' shouted Carter. Taking a lamp from one of the men, he stepped to the void in the door and shoved the lantern through. Trembling visibly, he leaned forward, pressing his eager face to the stonework.

'Well?' demanded Carnarvon, almost hopping with excitement. 'What? Tell us! What do you see?'

'Gold!' announced Carter. 'I see gold.'

The word sent a visceral quiver through Burleigh; he felt it in his belly.

Carter, still at the door, motioned for Lord Carnarvon to join him at the breach. The aristocrat muscled in beside him and pressed his face into the gap. 'Glorious!' he proclaimed. 'Open it! Open it at once!'

'Oh, Daddy!' cried Lady Evelyn. 'Let me see!'

'A moment more, my dear,' said her father, 'and we shall all be able to see.' To the workmen he commanded, 'Pull it down.'

'Selfish beast,' muttered Evelyn.

Burleigh patted her arm in mild commiseration, although he himself felt no such disappointment. He was supremely happy to, for once, be in at the sharp end of the discovery, to be present when the grave was opened and the objects that made his livelihood were brought back to the world of men and commerce. In fact, his cunning mind was already awash with schemes for insinuating himself into the profitable disposal of the artefacts soon to be revealed.

Brick followed brick as whole sections of the sealed doorway tumbled. Within moments, the breach was large enough to allow entrance. 'Here,' said Carter, handing around lanterns. When each member of the party had a light, he said, 'May I remind each one of us not to touch anything, please, until we've had a chance to photograph everything in situ?' After receiving assurances all round, he smiled. 'This way, please. Watch your step.'

Turning sideways, he shrugged through the gap and disappeared into the dark interior of the tomb. Lord Carnarvon went next, with his daughter close on his heels. Burleigh fell in behind her, stepping carefully over the pile of broken brick and rubble, passing through a narrow vestibule and into a chamber which had been hollowed from the living stone.

No one spoke. All remained silent in the grip of the mystery.

The air inside the tomb was dry and held the metallic scent of rock dust and, oddly, spice − as if a once-pungent mingling of pine resin and frankincense had faded away over untold time to a mere ghostly wisp of its former aromatic self. It tantalized, rather than tickled, the nostrils. Burleigh rubbed his nose and moved further into the tomb.

Slightly larger than the interior of a train carriage, the room was stacked with dusty articles of furniture − a black lacquered chair, a bedstead, the painted wheels of a chariot… and boxes, caskets, and chests of various sizes. The black chair's armrests were carved with the heads of lions that had been encased in gold leaf. This, Burleigh decided, was what Howard Carter had seen glinting back at him when he first looked in, for there was no other gold to be seen anywhere.

At opposite ends of the chamber, doors gave way to other rooms. Carter instinctively moved to the door on the right and Carnarvon to the left. Carnarvon was first to break the silence. 'Canopic jars,' announced the lord, his voice falling strangely dead in the close air of the tomb. 'What have you got?'

'The sarcophagus,' declared Carter. 'It's here – and intact. We're in luck. There has been no robbery here.'

While the others busied themselves with a cursory examination of the dead royal's elaborate stone sarcophagus, Burleigh made a quick mental inventory of the items he could sell, estimating what each might bring on the market. Over in one corner, he saw two very fine statues of cats carved of red granite; next to them was a small ebony owl; in among the wooden boxes was a large wooden hunting hound with a jewelled collar…

'Who is it? Can you see?' said Carnarvon.

Burleigh joined the others crouched beside the sarcophagus – an oversized buff-coloured stone coffin, the top of which was covered with hieroglyphics. 'It's here,' Carter was saying. 'Yes, here it is. Here is a name…'

'Well?' demanded Carnarvon, impatience making his voice shrill. 'What does it say? Who is it?'

Anticipation, Burleigh noticed, was quickly giving way to low-level frustration. And he thought he could guess the reason why.

'It is a male,' Carter intoned, his fingers tracing the glyphs like a blind man reading Braille. 'His name is Anen.' Glancing up from his examination, he said, 'He is – *was* a priest with the title of Second Prophet of Amun. Very high in the temple organization.'

'Not royal then,' observed Lord Carnarvon, unable to keep the disappointment out of his voice. 'Not a king, at least.' He paused. 'Pity.'

'No, not a king,' confirmed the archaeologist. 'But still an important find nevertheless.'

'Of course,' agreed Carnarvon, turning away. 'Extremely important.'

'Oh, Daddy,' chided Evelyn, 'don't pout – just because there is not a mountain of gold and jewels to be plundered. Look at all the marvellous paintings.'

She held her lantern to the wall and Burleigh saw what had, until that moment, failed to catch his notice: the walls of the tomb had been plastered white and covered with images. Every square inch of every surface was intensely, vibrantly, vivaciously decorated.

One enormous panel showed the tomb's occupant in a chariot beside the crowned figure of a pharaoh, spear uplifted, dogs racing ahead on the heels of a high-leaping antelope; another showed the priest in his colourful robes leading a ceremony where a number of animals were being sacrificed and which was being overseen by a huge figure of the bronze-skinned god, Amun, with his tall plumed crown. A third panel showed the tomb's occupant on his papyrus punt polling among the tall reeds surrounded by cranes and ducks and egrets, the sky above filled with birds of all kinds, the water below the boat filled with fish and even a crocodile... and more, floor to ceiling – and the ceiling, too, in glowing blue and covered with tiny white stars to simulate the heavens: wonderful, intricate, detailed paintings, with colours as fresh and bright as the day the artists lay down their brushes and retreated to the daylight.

'*There's* his wealth,' Burleigh observed, moving to Lady Evelyn's side and holding his lantern to hers. 'The chap spent all his money on art.'

CHAPTER 27

In Which the Emperor Awaits a Mysterious Visitor

Rudolf, King of Bohemia and Hungary, Archduke of Austria and King of the Romans, tapped his long fingers impatiently on the arms of his favourite throne. He hated waiting. And yet it seemed that the principal chore of the most powerful ruler of the Holy Roman Empire was not ruling, but waiting. Each day, every day, all day long the life of an emperor amounted to little more than a series of brief conversations, punctuated by lengthy intervals of waiting. He waited for audiences, waited for his edicts to be ratified and executed, waited for ministers to act on his decisions, waited for replies to his manifold messages, waited while the vast wheels of government slowly revolved to bring about a result, any result... and so on and – so far as he could see – forever.

The best that could be hoped for was to organize all this waiting into more productive heaps, overlapping as many delays as possible. Rudolf liked to think it made these more or less idle periods more productive than if strung out individually. Just now, for example, he was waiting for paint to dry, and for his first audience of the day, and for word from Vienna regarding the birth of an infant by his mistress. He was having his portrait painted and the artist insisted that he wait until the paint had dried sufficiently to allow a second layer to be applied before he could move from his pose; he was expecting his chief alchemist to attend him with the results of the latest experiments; heavily pregnant Katharina had been sent to

Vienna to bear his child, whose imminent arrival was expected at any moment. Later on, he could look forward to waiting for his ministers to present the state of his treasury, waiting for his friend Prince Leopold of Swabia to arrive for his annual visit and hunt, waiting for the coach to take him to the opera for his evening's entertainment. A full and productive day of waiting stretched before him.

'How much longer?' he asked, meaning the paint – it had become such a familiar phrase on his lips, his courtiers did not feel obliged to respond with any degree of precision.

'Not long, Highness,' replied the artist Archimboldo, wafting a cloth gently over the surface of the canvas. 'Soon. Very soon.'

The Holy Roman Emperor sighed and resumed drumming his fingers. The artist busied himself with mixing colours on his palette. An eternity elapsed, and the emperor was on the point of asking yet again how much longer he must wait before he could get up when a sharp rap came on the door of the chamber and his master of audiences appeared. 'Forgive the intrusion, Your Highness,' he announced, 'but Herr Docktor Bazalgette craves the pleasure of your attention.'

'And we his,' replied Rudolf. 'By all means, bid him enter at once.'

The courtier bowed and stepped backwards, ushering into the room Balthazar Bazalgette, the emperor's chief alchemist: a portly man of middle years, who possessed not only the jowls of a prize swine, but lavish eyebrows the artist might have envied for portrait work. He was also a man of immense erudition, and no small pomposity. If one was prepared to overlook the latter, however, one found beneath the expansive velvet robe a man of great industry and a sincerity of purpose that many princes of the church might have done well to emulate.

'Bazalgette!' cried Rudolf, happy at having this latest round of waiting interrupted at last. 'Come here to us!'

The Lord High Alchemist swept into the room in a rush of robes, his tall, fur-trimmed hat slightly askew in his hurry. 'Good news, Highness! I bring very encouraging word. We have succeeded in producing the Elixir of the Wise. Our experiments can now continue without delay.'

'That *is* good news,' Rudolf agreed. He liked anything that promised to minimize the dread *delay* in any of its insidious forms. 'Sit you down.' He indicated the painter's stool nearby. 'Tell us all about it.'

'Gladly, Sire,' said the alchemist, drawing the stool close to the throne. 'As you will recall from our last conversation, the prime difficulty of producing red sulphur lies in the inherent instability of the constituent ingredients.'

'Yes,' affirmed Rudolf, 'we do recall the particular conversation right well.'

'To be sure, another part of the difficulty lies in securing sufficient quantities of feculent earth needed to produce the righteous oil.'

'Of course.' Rudolf nodded. Alchemy was a complicated business. He marvelled that anyone could maintain his wits in the face of such monumental and implacable intricacy.

'By a most fortuitous coincidence,' continued Bazalgette with mounting excitement, 'my assistant – remember young Rosenkreuz? – was at this new Kaffeehaus in the square, and adroitly obtained a goodly quantity of a new and hitherto unknown substance – a bitter earth called ground of Kaffee.'

'Did he indeed?' The imperial eyebrows lifted in mild surprise. 'How very enterprising of him.'

'He is a most capable assistant, Sire,' commended the chief alchemist benignly. 'We have already begun experimenting with the substance, Highness, and though a complete assay will take some time, I am pleased to say that preliminary results appear extremely promising.'

'We have heard of this Kaffee,' the emperor mused. Turning his face towards the door. 'Ruprecht!' he shouted.

The door opened momentarily and the master of audiences appeared. 'Highness? You called?'

'We have heard of this Kaffee, have we not?'

'I believe so, Highness.'

'But we have not imbibed it?'

'No, Sire. Not as yet.'

'Have some brought to us,' Rudolf commanded, then hastily added, '– today! Without delay.'

'It will be done, Your Highness,' intoned the master of audiences.

'If I may interrupt, Sire,' ventured the alchemist, 'I have already taken the liberty of inviting the owners of this Kaffeehaus to visit me at court to discuss supplying us with the bitter earth for our experiments. Inasmuch as their co-operation is of inestimable value to our experiments, I thought we might bestow an honour upon them – the better to secure their future goodwill for the aid and advance of the Great Work.'

Rudolf smiled. 'Good thinking, Bazalgette.' To the lingering Ruprecht, the emperor commanded, 'Send a coach for them at the arranged time, and make sure they bring some of this Kaffee with them. We would like to taste it.'

'It will be done, Highness.'

Turning once more to the alchemist, Rudolf said, 'It is a momentous age we inhabit, is it not?'

'Indeed, Sire,' agreed the alchemist. 'All the more when I tell you that just this morning I received word from an acquaintance of mine who is soon in Prague and wishes to engage certain members of our enlightened brotherhood in the construction of a device to further his astral explorations.'

Rudolf blinked at the alchemist. 'His *what* explorations?'

'Astral, Sire,' answered Bazalgette. 'The etheric realms, you might say. It appears that he is even now perfecting the means to travel the astral planes by means known to him and wishes our help in furthering his endeavours.'

'Spirit travel?' wondered Rudolf. That, in itself, seemed of little promise, and less interest.

'Oh no, Sire,' countered the alchemist quickly. '*Physical* travel – moving bodily between various planes or dimensions of existence. I believe he can demonstrate this ability.'

'*That* we should like to see,' said Rudolf, his interest piqued.

'No doubt it can be arranged,' offered Bazalgette.

'Summon him to us,' commanded the emperor. 'We will grant

him a place here in the palace should he so desire. We wish to see what he can do, this astral explorer. It may be that this mode of travel could prove a boon to humanity if it could be perfected for good.'

'I could not have said it better myself, Sire,' agreed the alchemist. 'I will engage him directly he arrives in the city.'

'Good. Speak with Ruprecht. We would like to meet him.'

'Of course, Highness.'

'Excuse me, Your Majesty,' said the court painter Archimboldo. 'I would never dare to interrupt, but you asked me to tell you when the portrait was ready for viewing. I have finished for the day, so if you would like to see it, I humbly offer it for your inspection.'

'Come, Balthazar, let us see how this portrait is developing.' The emperor rose and crossed to the artist's easel. 'Tell us what you think,' he said, casting a critical eye over the expansive canvas. 'The truth, now. We will not hear flummery.'

'Exquisite, Highness,' remarked the chief alchemist in a reverential tone. 'Undoubtedly a work of genius. Just look at that melon – and those peaches! – wondrous to behold. The grapes are a revelation, if I may say it. And the asparagus is astonishing.'

Giuseppe Archimboldo had made a name for himself by painting fruit and vegetables in a most remarkably lifelike way. Lately, he had hit on the idea of portraiture as still life – rendering his patrons as if they were agglomerations of items from a greengrocer's stall. Although the enterprise was still in its infancy, it was hoped that the style would catch on.

'This pear,' said Rudolf, indicating a large fruit in the centre of the canvas. 'What kind is it?'

'It is a Fiorentina pear, Majesty – an Italian variety.'

'Do you think an Italian pear was an appropriate choice for my nose?' wondered Rudolf. 'Does not its shape make my nose look bulbous?'

'By no means, Sire. With peaches for cheeks, a pear for a nose makes perfect sense.'

'Ah, but would not a fig be better?'

'Perhaps a Turkish fig –'

'Do not speak to me of Turks!' snapped the emperor. 'I am sick to death of all things Turkish.'

'I am sorry, Your Highness,' said Bazalgette quickly. 'Pray, forgive me.'

'And then there is the issue of colour,' suggested the artist delicately. 'Ripe figs being purple, you see.'

'Let it stand as it is,' commanded Rudolf.

'A wise decision, Sire. The painting is approaching perfection. I feel as if I could reach out and take hold of that artichoke, or smell those roses,' offered the alchemist, happy for a chance to distance himself from any mention of the hated Turks. 'And the aubergine… oh, the aubergine is a magnificent specimen of its kind.'

'Yes,' agreed the ruler of all that remained of the Holy Roman Empire. 'It is truly masterful.' Half-turning to the painter, he said, 'Well done, Archimboldo. You surpass your craft.'

'Thank you, Your Exalted Highness,' replied the artist, who stood looking on. 'Your praise is food and drink to me.'

'We will see you tomorrow,' Rudolf told him. He crossed the wide floor of polished walnut to the chamber door, which was opened by one of the two pages standing to attention there; he entered the mirrored corridor. Turning to his chief alchemist following two steps behind him, he said, 'We will expect you to inform us when this traveller fellow arrives. We wish most ardently to converse with him.'

'Never fear, Highness,' said Bazalgette with a respectful bow. 'It will be a most interesting meeting of the minds, and I welcome it with greatest anticipation.'

The emperor gave a slight flick of his hand to dismiss his courtier and proceeded down the corridor, led by the regal figure of his master of audiences and the two young pages. 'Ah! Bazalgette,' he called behind him. 'Do not forget the Kaffee. We want very much to try it at the earliest opportunity.'

'Worry for nothing, Highness,' answered the Lord High Alchemist. 'It will be done.'

Part 5

The Man Who is Map

CHAPTER 28

In Which Promises are Made to be Broken

The crossing had been rough for Xian-Li, and Arthur felt bad about that. He put a comforting hand on her back and murmured encouragements as she bent over retching. It was only her third otherworld leap and she had yet to develop the physical mastery which would greatly reduce the more unpleasant effects and make travel between dimensions bearable if not entirely comfortable. He remembered his first few times – leaping blind into the unknown and arriving in a strange world disoriented and incapacitated. To be so helpless in an unknown place and time was alive with dangers of every kind, some of them lethal. He shuddered now to think what might have happened to him in those early days of ignorant experiment: he might have plunged headlong into an arctic, blizzard-lashed ocean, or arrived on an alien battlefield in the midst of a desperate clash, or landed in a steaming tropical jungle surrounded by ferocious carnivorous beasts – *anything* might have happened. That he had survived those early exploits, he put down to Providence looking out for him when he did not know how to look out for himself. For that he was grateful, and remembered always that what he did, he did with the merciful sufferance if not the subtle guidance of his Benevolent Protector.

'There, there, my love,' he cooed. 'Breathe deeply. The worst is over. The sickness will soon pass.'

She retched again.

'You'll feel better now,' advised Arthur.

'I'm sorry,' she gasped, wiping her mouth with her husband's offered handkerchief.

'Not a thing in the world to be sorry about, my dear.' Taking her elbow he raised her up. 'There. Better?' She nodded without conviction. 'The important thing to remember is that it won't always be like this. Your timing and skill will improve, as you will see. And your body will soon grow adept at weathering the changes.'

'I hope so for your sake.' Xian-Li offered a weak smile. 'But I want you to know that even if it never gets better I still want to come with you. I can happily endure a little travel sickness if that is the cost of joining you on your journeys.'

Her determination made Arthur proud. His young wife was a fighter, no doubt about it. As she had so ably demonstrated that day in the back alley when driving away the odious Burleigh and his thugs with nothing but her own two bare hands, she was a capable and cool-headed combatant. For that, if for no other reason, he was glad to have her by his side.

'Are we here?' she said, looking around for the first time. They seemed to be standing in a great expanse of desert with nothing but shattered, buff-coloured, rock-strewn hills in every direction. 'I do not see the temple.'

'The old temple is in the city, and the new one has not yet been built,' he told her. 'But it will be, and very soon. This is the Eighteenth Dynasty, as we would call it – probably somewhere around the twentieth year of Amenhotep III. I won't know for certain until we talk to my friend here.' He shouldered the small pack he had brought. 'Ready? The city is just beyond those hills.'

'The priest, yes,' replied Xian-Li, falling into step beside her husband. 'I remember.'

'You will like him. He's a wise and gentle man – very high up in the royal family, too, as it happens. His mother was married to Yuya – who was Grand Vizier of Egypt, second only to Pharaoh, and his sister is Great Royal Wife to the current pharaoh.'

'Brother-in-law to the pharaoh,' considered Xian-Li. 'He sounds very powerful.'

'It is useful to have friends in high places,' replied Arthur lightly. 'There is none higher than Anen. I wouldn't be at all surprised if he became high priest one day.'

They walked easily in the dawn light. The land was as dry as sun-burnt bone and there was not a blade of green to be seen anywhere, apart from a single, blasted, dust-covered acacia bush. The early morning air was alive with coveys of sparrows and gangs of starlings and, high, high overhead, larks sent down their liquid song. 'Insects,' said Arthur in answer to his wife's wondering glance. 'They will vanish again before noon and not be seen again until this evening at sundown – the birds, too.'

'Where do the insects come from?' asked Xian-Li.

'You wouldn't guess by looking,' Arthur said, indicating the bleak landscape surrounding them, 'but just beyond that line of hills ahead, there is one of the greatest rivers of the world watering one of the most fertile valleys in the world.'

'The Nile,' declared Xian-Li proudly.

'The very same,' confirmed Arthur. 'You have been studying, my dear.'

When they reached the foot of the nearest hills they found a narrow and very crooked sheep trail winding up the hillside. 'Our ladder to the stars,' he said. 'After you, my dear.'

They followed the path and, upon reaching the top, paused to survey the landscape. To the north, at the wide mouth of a valley leading back into the desert, lay a jumbled assortment of low stone buildings, some obviously under construction. To the south, asprawl in the brilliance of the early sunlight, spread the city the Egyptians called *Niwet-Amun*, the City of Amun. Nestled on the edge of the desert between the arid desert hills and the fresh verdant fields of the Nile valley, it gleamed with the marbeline lustre of a moonstone. They gazed down upon the tangled clusters of white-washed houses scattered arbitrarily along the lowland which stretched off towards the majestic river just visible as a clear blue line dancing on the far horizon. The air was bright and clean, the breeze soft. The sound of barking dogs could be heard drifting up from the nearer houses below.

'It seems our arrival has been noticed,' said Arthur. 'Dogs are always the first to know, it seems.'

'They are alert to every change in their world,' Xian-Li observed. 'In China the old ones say a dog can hear and smell change before it happens.'

They descended to the valley, keeping an eye on the houses below. Though the dogs kept barking, no people appeared until they reached the road scratched on the hard-packed earth. Once on the track leading to the city, they noticed faces appearing briefly at the small dark windows and doorways of the white-washed mud houses they passed. 'We're being watched now,' murmured Arthur. 'Don't be afraid; just smile and keep walking.'

Glancing behind them, she saw two brown men standing outside their houses, arms crossed, dogs by their sides and children hiding behind their bare legs. Xian-Li was glad of her linen robe – not all that different from what she had worn in China, but more in keeping with the local dress. Arthur had the harder part; even dressed in his loose-fitting full-length shirt, he would never blend in with the locals: he was too tall and, it had to be said, too white.

The further into the city they went, the closer and more crowded the houses became, the streets and pathways between them more tangled and twisted. They passed through districts of wealth and ease, hard by areas of mean description. In the more affluent quarters the dwellings were made of cut stone, shaded by fig trees or date palms, and surrounded by well-tended gardens; in the humbler neighbourhoods, homes were made of mud brick and plaster, chickens and pigs wandered among rows of cabbages and beans, and the yards were used for small industry: pottery making, carpentry, weaving, and the like.

Xian-Li found fascination in everything she saw. Even the smallest glimpse brought a frisson of excitement as some new surprise revealed itself: young girls dressed in sky blue shifts carrying reed baskets of laundry wet from the river; little boys herding flocks of geese with willow switches, stirring up more chaos than order; women spinning raw flax into thread and weaving at outdoor looms; all-but-naked youths working in dye pits, their limbs stained bright blue and green and yellow; stone-cutters roughing out grindstones for hand mills; a butcher cutting up the carcass of a cow with an axe and hanging the bloody pieces on hooks all over the front of his house; a potter and his wife toting their wares to the oven on boards balanced on their heads... all of the life of a busy city was on display.

'It is wonderful!' she breathed. 'The people are so... so beautiful.'

Slender, lithe, with black hair and eyes, their skin colour darker than her own – as dark as some of the folk from the islands in the south China sea – Xian-Li swiftly formed the opinion that they were some of the most attractive people she had ever seen.

'They are a handsome race,' Arthur agreed. 'Very peaceable, in the main. Inquisitive as the day is long, too. Very little passes their regard, and they're terrible gossips.'

'Just like in China.'

'Worse,' laughed Arthur. 'They will all have noticed that we are here, but they don't want to be *seen* to notice. I can tell you they're all itching with curiosity right now, but they prefer to pretend otherwise. That's why they're making such a show of ignoring us.'

The roads and paths grew more crowded as they approached the centre of the city. Here also, the Egyptians maintained a polite distance and an aloof air of indifference towards the obvious strangers in their midst. At the heart of Niwet-Amun lay the sprawling Temple of Amun, a square stone building on a low platform of three tiered steps; an odd conical pillar stone stood before the entrance. Three young priests dressed in loincloths were busy anointing the surface of the pale stone; their hands and arms glistened with oil, their cinnamon-coloured skins gleamed with sweat.

Arthur stopped. 'Here's our man,' he whispered, watching the priests slather oil over the stone, rubbing it slowly over the smooth surface.

'Which one?' wondered Xian-Li.

'The one with the flowers.'

A little apart stood a fourth priest; tall and elegant in a pale blue pleated robe of crisp linen and a breastplate and belt of gold discs, his head newly shaved but for his thick braided plait that hung down his back; he held a garland of yellow flowers looped around outstretched arms that were decorated with many golden bracelets and armbands. He called a word to his fellow priests, who straightened from their work, then bowed and, extending their hands, palms horizontal to the ground, backed away. The gold-belted priest stepped forward and placed the garland over the newly oiled stone. He raised his hands to shoulder height and chanted in a loud voice. Then, stepping away, he bowed, then turned and with his fellow priests started back to the temple.

'Anen!' called Arthur.

The priest halted and turned around, scanning the people milling around the temple square for the one who had called his name. His large dark eyes swept the crowd, falling eventually on Arthur and Xian-Li. 'Artus!' he cried.

A moment later, the priest was before them. 'Artus,' he said, seizing the forearms of his friend. The two men brushed cheeks on each side, and then the tall man turned to Xian-Li. Smiling, his eyes merry with delight, he took her hand. '*Iaw*' he said. '*Ijetj! Ijetj! Nefer hemet.*'

Although she could not understand his speech, the man's voice was nicely modulated and gentle, and the goodwill shining from his gleaming countenance was unmistakable. She felt instantly at ease and comfortable in his presence.

'He says you are welcome here, beautiful lady,' Arthur explained. 'He wishes you peace.'

'You speak Egyptian?' Xian-Li asked, her eyes growing round.

'I spent many months here a few years ago. I was assigned a young priest to teach me their language. I learned as much as I could in the short time I had.'

The two men spoke briefly to one another, whereupon Anen called out to his fellow priests who had been participating in the ritual with him; they were dressed in simple yellow robes now, and they hurried to meet their master. The priest gave them a series of rapid commands, then turned to his visitors and explained.

'He has ordered the guest house to be prepared for us,' Arthur translated. 'We are to stay with him in the temple precinct while

247

we are here. He hopes we plan to stay a long time. He has much to show us.'

Turning to Anen, he relayed their acceptance and thanks, whereupon the priest pressed his hands together and then turned, indicating that the two travellers should follow him. He led them past the temple entrance to a gate set in a low wall, through the open gate and into a compound containing an assortment of low buildings. The compound was paved with white stone, but with numerous islands of greenery containing flowering bushes and small trees; larger trees planted along the periphery wall shaded the open places, keeping the compound cooler and a world away from the crowded, dusty streets outside. Iridescent blue peacocks strutted in the sun and roosted in the lower branches. Four skinny youths with shaven heads, bare to the waist in short knee-length yellow kilts, swept the already spotless pavements for errant leaves and peacock droppings. From somewhere close by, the trickle of water into the bowl of a fountain lent the compound a calm and soothing air.

'This reminds me of the prince's gardens at the Jade Palace in Maccau,' Xian-Li said. 'So beautiful.'

While the two men talked, Xian-Li strolled around the grounds, feeling the sunlight on her hair and skin. After the cold and rainy winter in England, the sun felt like a long absent and much missed companion, and she luxuriated in the warmth. Even as she was enjoying the garden, she was reminded once again how utterly unimaginable her life had become. When Arthur had shared the secret of his tattaus with her, she believed him – in the same way that a child, not understanding anything of the world, will believe its parents when they tell it that money is valuable; but like that child, Xian-Li did not, could not, begin to imagine the fathomless implications of what he had told her.

To take even the first shaky steps towards understanding, she had to experience ley travel for herself; although it had to be admitted that the experience raised many more questions than it answered. This was her third time – the first two were but short hops within England and were mere rehearsals for this trip. Those first two modest leaps had shocked her enough to take it all very seriously. And now as she looked around, what she saw simply beggared belief. Nothing in her previous life could have prepared her for the things she was learning and seeing, living under Arthur's tutelage. She had no words to describe it – at least, any description she attempted always fell far short of the staggering astonishment she felt. Enthralled, enchanted, reeling with wonder, she loved it – almost as much as she loved the man who had opened this fantastic universe to her.

In a little while, she heard Arthur call her back. 'The guest house has been made ready,' he said. 'We can rest a little if you like. There will be food later. They tend to eat their largest meal at midday, but Anen has ordered some light refreshment for us.'

'I am not tired,' Xian-Li replied. 'And I could not eat a thing right now. I want to see the city. I want to see everything.'

Arthur laughed. 'Then let us take a walk. I can show you around a little. Anen wants to take us to the royal palace to meet the royal family. Tomorrow, maybe. Pharaoh is travelling upriver, but his return is expected any day. Wait a moment, while I tell Anen that we're going for a short walk in the city.'

The priest would not hear otherwise but that his visitors should be given clothing more suitable for their station, and for the weather. When they had changed into their lightweight robes, he seconded one of the temple acolytes to attend them as guide and interpreter, and the three ventured out from the temple compound and proceeded around the square. Arthur's intent was to let his young wife get her feet under her a bit, and learn something of the land and its people. Once she had the measure of things, he would take her to see the Nile and travel upriver to the temple complex at Kahira, the place that would, given time, become known in this world, as in the other, as Cairo.

After making a circuit of the square, they started up the single main street. 'These are the dwellings of the wealthier merchants,' Arthur explained, pausing before a line of large stone houses either side of the wide, palm-lined street.

'And the small huts?' wondered Xian-Li. Squatting in the shade of the expensive houses with their well-appointed gardens were simple hovels of mud brick thatched with palm leaves.

'For the slaves,' replied Arthur. 'All higher caste Egyptians keep slaves – Nubians, Ethiopes, and others. All in all, it is not so bad for them. Life in Egypt is very good.'

'Aha!' cried their guide suddenly as Arthur made to continue up the street.

Arthur halted in mid-step, putting out his hand to stop Xian-Li. 'Wait,' he said. They turned as the first of a long line of fully laden donkeys passed, their drivers walking beside them with corded whips. The bundles heaped high on the beasts' strong backs contained cut cane, raw flax, produce – melons, leeks, nets of radishes and beans and chard – and lengths of aromatic wood.

'They're heading for the marketplace,' Arthur told her as they watched the passing train. 'Tomorrow is market day, I should think. Would you like to see it?'

'Oh, yes! I want to see everything.'

'Then in the morning we'll go,' promised Arthur.

They continued their walk into the city, but did not get much further because Xian-Li, dazzled by the diversity of this strange and exotic culture and overwhelmed by all she saw, grew fatigued. 'I am sorry, husband,' she confessed. 'I think I must rest a little.'

'Of course, my dear. It can be daunting – so much all at once. We'll go back now, rest and have a little something to eat. You'll begin to get used to it. Tomorrow will be better, you'll see.'

But the promises of tomorrow, however sincere, are fragile paper boats launched on a vast and uncertain sea: easily swamped by the least rippling wave or errant breeze.

CHAPTER 29

In Which Dragons are Not Confined to Statues

The coach rumbled over the bridge and Wilhelmina received her first good look at the emperor's palace. A massive, looming presence – more bunker than castle – it put her in mind of the stolid, grey eminence of Buckingham Palace back home in London. Uniformly lacking in charm and elegance, Emperor Rudolf's palace was a colossal stone crate devoid of towers, keeps, battlements or outward decoration of any kind, presenting a brooding blank aspect to the world. Directly across from the dull bulk of the palace, however, soared the serried spires of the cathedral dedicated to Saint Vitus. Glowing ruddy gold in the early morning light the great church appeared an almost magical construction by comparison with its hulking neighbour. Clinging to the highest point in the city – for all its chapels, steeples, and the colossal copper-domed bell tower – the heroic structure seemed poised to take flight into the heavens.

Once across the bridge, the palace passed from view as the carriage began the steep climb up the palace mound. Mina turned to her companion. 'You're smiling, Etzel,' she observed. 'What are you thinking?'

'I am thinking that, whatever happens, today I will stand before the emperor and give him some of my baking.' His smile grew into a wide and easy grin. 'That is something even my brother and father cannot take from me.'

In the time they'd worked together, Wilhelmina had formed a picture of Engelbert's life before she met him. 'It was hard for you – living under the thumb of your father and brother.'

He gave a little shrug. 'I suppose it was hard for them, too, maybe.'

'Well, I wish they were here to see you. Wouldn't that be something?'

He laughed. 'Their eyes would fall from their heads to see their Engelbert serving pastry to the emperor.'

She glanced at the box of equipment and supplies on the floor of the coach next to her – she would not allow it to be placed outside on the baggage carrier out of her sight – and wondered if she had remembered everything. Was anything missing?

Etzel followed her gaze. 'It is all there, Schnuckel,' he said. 'We made a list and we put everything in the chest. We have forgotten nothing.'

They had checked and double-checked the items that went into the box – everything they would need to make coffee for the emperor and a few select members of his court. 'Today,' she said, gazing back at Etzel, 'is one of the most important days of my life. I just want to do well. Our future depends on it.'

'No,' replied the gentle man, 'our future is in God's hands. Nothing can change that. So let us just enjoy today and be happy.'

'I *am* happy, Etzel,' she said, reaching across the space between their seats to squeeze his hand. 'I want you to know that. I am very happy to be here with you today. I wouldn't want to be anywhere else.'

He made as if to speak, but could not find the words, so instead rubbed his hand through his blond hair and nodded his round head in agreement.

The royal coach crossed another bridge – this one separating the upper town from the lower – and continued up increasingly precarious streets on its climb to the palace precinct on top of the city's highest hill. A short while later, the carriage approached the palace walls and the grand gatehouse guarding the entrance. The gate was open and guards waved the vehicle through. Mina felt butterflies in her stomach as the horses clattered into the yard and rolled to a stop. Soldiers with long pikes and crested silver helmets and breastplates stood either side of the red lacquered doors between stout pillars which supported a pediment with a statue of Saint George who, with a hideous and extremely realistic dragon curled about his feet, stood with one foot on the angry beast's neck, his gallant sword upraised to deliver the killing stroke. The dragon – all teeth and scales and slashing claws – writhed in its dying rage, while the sainted George gazed down with implacable sternness of purpose.

The statue, poised as it was directly over the palace entrance, made Mina shiver as a pang of foreboding shot through her. She looked away. The feeling passed in an instant as footmen sprang to attend them and, opening the carriage compartment, placed steps beneath the door so that the occupants could climb down easily. Meanwhile, from out of the palace emerged a man in gleaming royal livery, his plump, red-stockinged legs bearing him forward with all speed.

'Welcome, subjects,' he intoned in a perfunctory voice. 'The emperor bids his honoured guests to attend him. He awaits you in the Grand Ludovic Hall.' He made the briefest gesture of a bow. 'I am to lead you to him. If you will follow me?'

Without waiting for a reply, he turned and started back to the palace.

'Sir! We have baggage to carry,' Engelbert called after him.

Without pausing, the official tossed a command to the footmen. Engelbert indicated the box in the coach and the first lackey took it up; the other footman reached for the smaller box in Engelbert's hands, but the big man shook his head. 'This one I carry myself.'

The party resumed its progress through the door and into a spacious vestibule painted red and white, and filled with marble busts of illustrious men, most of them royal and all of them dead. Two more soldiers stood guard either side of the door, and the royal usher whisked them through and into the main hall: a gargantuan room with vaulted ceilings from which hung no fewer than eight four-tiered chandeliers. Enormous glass windows pierced the walls on either side allowing a tide of sunlight to wash through the room; and from them the entire city of Prague spread out below, the rooftops of the houses making a chequered patchwork in various shades of red, green, and brown. Here they were met by another official, the master of audiences, a dour and imposing man in a long robe of deep green velvet. Without a word, he marched them through the hall, heels clicking on the polished inlaid floor; a few clumps of people stood huddled around the large gilt doors at the far end of the hall awaiting their turn to be called. Engelbert and Wilhelmina were led directly to the golden doors, past the envious stares of the loiterers and into a seemingly endless corridor lined with mirrors. Tiny oval windows allowed light to spill along the length of the passageway, and they passed door after door until arriving at one that was larger than the others and whose frame was carved with laurel leaves and ivy. Here the master of audiences paused and, taking a short knob-topped rod from a hidden holder at his side, he gave three short, sharp raps, then opened the door.

They heard a muffled voice from inside and then the senior court official summoned them through and into the presence of the Holy Roman Emperor Rudolf, sitting on a grand throne of ebony lined with red satin, his chin in his hand, shoulders hunched, looking bored. A man in a long blue robe with an odd conical hat stood nearby with a roll of parchment in his hands. A few paces to one side stood a large easel and canvas, behind which an artist darted a glance before disappearing behind his work again.

At the appearance of the two Kaffeehaus proprietors, the emperor smiled, straightened, and clapped his hands. 'Splendid!' he said, then waved the other man aside. 'Come! Come! We are delighted to meet you at last.'

'My Lord and King,' intoned the master of audiences, 'I present to you Engelbert of München, and Wilhelmina of England.'

This last caused the man in the blue robe to turn and stare at the young woman who was just then making a low and elaborate curtsy to the emperor. He pulled on his grey beard and watched her with interest.

Rudolf extended his hand to his subjects, allowing them to kiss the imperial ring, and said, 'We do hope you have brought this liquor with you, this Kaffee. We are eager to taste it.'

Engelbert glanced at the master of audiences, who whispered, 'You may address him when spoken to.'

The big baker swallowed and cleared his throat. 'Indeed, Your Imperial Majesty,' he said, somewhat shakily. 'We have brought everything we need to make it for you especially.'

'To *make* it?' wondered the emperor.

'Yes, Majesty. We will make it for you.'

Wilhelmina saw the misunderstanding and offered, 'It is a hot drink, Your Majesty. It must be prepared fresh and drunk from special cups while it is still warm.'

'Mind your place!' the audience master hissed. 'You will speak only when spoken to!'

'We permit it,' sighed Rudolf, forgiving the breach in protocol. 'You may go, Ruprecht.' He waved the courtier away. The man in the blue robe and curious hat started backing away, too. 'No – stay, Bazalgette, stay. We will all partake of this beverage together.'

'Thank you, Sire,' replied the man.

'This is Herr Docktor Bazalgette,' the emperor said, introducing his companion. 'He is Lord High Alchemist to the royal court.'

'At your service, my friends,' replied the man of science, doffing his cap.

'Can you produce enough liquor for two?' asked Rudolf.

'We have enough for *ten*, Your Majesty,' answered Etzel, delighted with the prospect of serving such esteemed courtiers.

'What do you require to facilitate your production?' asked the court alchemist. 'Perhaps I can aid your preparation.'

'Only a small fire,' answered Wilhelmina. 'We have brought everything else. It is in a chest outside.'

'Shall I have it brought in, Your Majesty?' offered Bazalgette.

'Yes, and tell Ruprecht that we will require a fire to be lit in the hearth. Have him inform the chamberlain that we want it at once.' To his visitors, he said, 'Is this agreeable to you?'

'Of course, Your Majesty,' ventured Wilhelmina. 'But perhaps it would be easier and quicker for me to simply go to the kitchen and prepare the Kaffee there. I will bring it to you when it is ready.'

'Excellent!' cried Rudolf. His excitement was dashed the very next instant when he considered what this meant. 'However, we were hoping to watch you prepare it.' He frowned.

'Then, if you would allow me to suggest,' said Wilhelmina, 'perhaps Your Majesty might accompany us to the royal kitchen and Your Highness will be able to observe everything we do.'

The King of Christendom started and stared, jolted by this revolutionary idea. 'We do not believe we have ever been to the royal kitchens,' he considered, his brow creasing deeply at the thought.

Lord High Alchemist Bazalgette rescued the imperial dignity by an apt recommendation. 'Might we repair to my laboratory instead, Majesty?' he proposed delicately. 'There is a fire in the hearth, and it is in this very wing of the palace.'

'Yes,' allowed Rudolf with some relief, 'perhaps that would be best. That way we will taste this Kaffee liquor that much sooner.'

It was thus agreed. The emperor rose from his chair and, escorted by his chief alchemist and followed by his guests, moved to the door.

'Exalted Majesty…?' called a voice from the far end of the room.

'Ah, yes, Signore Archimboldo,' said Rudolf, remembering himself. 'We are finished for the day. But do come along and join us if you like. We are going to partake of a new potion. You may find it inspiring to your work.'

'Your servant would be honoured, Majesty.' The artist put aside his palette and brushes, quickly doffed his smock, and joined the party, following them into the long corridor to a stairway leading up to the next floor and down another mirror-lined corridor to a suite of rooms at the far end of the passageway.

'Here we are, Highness, friends,' said Bazalgette, pushing open the heavily carved door. 'Please, come in and feel free to amuse yourselves. If you will excuse me, Majesty, I will see to the necessaries.'

The apartment was as big as a ballroom, but every square inch of available space was packed with all manner of gear and equipment: tables crowded with jars, pots, and jugs, each labelled with its contents; counters lined with a formidable array of bulbous decanters filled with murky liquids; mortars and pestles in a range of sizes and made of porcelain, glass, marble, and granite; crucibles, beakers and bowls of lead and copper and zinc and bronze; pottery and glassware articles in bizarre organic shapes; bundles of raw materials from dried herbs to animal fur; iron tools of many kinds. And if there were mortars and pestles in sizes a giant might find useful, there were hammers and tongs a fairy sprite would covet. Marking the perimeter of the room on three sides, floor to ceiling, stood great hulking bookcases filled with leather-bound volumes and parchment rolls.

Wilhelmina felt as if she had entered an Aladdin's Cave where instead of gold and jewel-crusted treasure, the thieves specialized in chem-lab equipment and biological specimens. Everywhere one looked the eye was arrested by some oddity or other – desiccated cats, stuffed birds, unborn pigs in brine, fully articulated lizard skeletons, and prehistoric insects in lambent lumps of Baltic amber.

At the far end of the room, the original hearth and fireplace had been extensively modified to accommodate a large stove with several apertures on top, two ovens below and, to one side, an open-flame bed something like a forge. Beside the stove, using its light to examine a diagram on parchment, stood two men whose presence Wilhelmina had not marked when entering. She did so now. One of the men was a tall, well-muscled fellow with striking good looks and a regal bearing; the other was the chief under-alchemist whom she had met at the Kaffeehaus.

'Ah! Here you are!' cried Bazalgette, hurrying towards the men. 'We have the honour of receiving the emperor.'

The two turned from their study of the diagram and the younger man bowed; the stranger merely stood and waited for the imperial party to approach, whereupon Bazalgette made the introductions: 'Your Highness, allow me to present my esteemed visitor, Lord Archelaeus Burleigh, Earl of Sutherland, newly arrived from England.'

Lord Burleigh put his heels together and made a crisp, elegant bow. 'Your devoted servant, Majesty,' he said in a full, resonant voice.

'We welcome you, my lord earl,' said Rudolf. 'Is this your first visit to Prague?'

'It is, Majesty,' replied Burleigh, his German flawless. 'But I assure you, it will not be my last.'

Other introductions were made then, which Mina ignored, finding herself wholly unable to take her eyes from the darkly handsome earl. *What luck!* she thought. *A fellow countryman.*

The formalities observed, the chief alchemist turned to his assistant. 'Rosenkreuz, clear away a space for the use of our friends here,' he commanded. 'They are here to produce an elixir of Kaffee for the emperor. Have chairs brought in.'

'At once, Herr Docktor,' replied the young alchemist, handing the parchment diagram back to the earl. With a nod and smile of acknowledgement to Etzel and Mina, the young man began moving beakers and pots, making room for Engelbert and Mina's simple equipment. The boxes were brought in and unpacked. Working quickly together, fresh water was soon on the fire, the beans ground, and the pot and cups prepared. At each stage of the operation, Engelbert with enormous gravity explained what they were doing.

While the company waited for the water to come to the boil, the chief alchemist offered a small tour of his laboratory and Wilhelmina sidled up beside Lord Burleigh. She caught his attention. '*Guten Tag, mien herr,*' she said, speaking low. '*Ich bin* Wilhelmina. But perhaps we can speak English?'

'Delighted to meet you, my dear,' he replied smoothly, his manner at odds with his old-fashioned demeanour.

'When Herr Bazalgette introduced you just now, I was a little surprised. I've not met many Englishmen in Prague.'

'Nor will you, I imagine,' he replied, offering her an ingratiating smile. 'But please, if you don't mind my asking, how did you come to be here?'

'Here in the palace? Or here in Prague?'

'Either,' he said, laughing politely. 'Both.'

Before she could answer, Bazalgette called to them, 'May I direct your attention to *this* – our latest discovery!' He lofted a large jug of green glass half-full of a cloudy whitish liquid. 'Come close, everyone.'

'Another time, perhaps,' said the earl, directing his steps to rejoin the others who were now gathered around a table heaped high with books and racks of glass vials and porcelain jars.

'Come to my coffee house tomorrow,' invited Wilhelmina, falling into step beside him. 'I'll give you a cup of coffee and we can talk then without interruption.'

'I'd be delighted,' replied the nobleman with a bow of his head. 'But tell me – which Kaffeehaus is it?'

'There *is* only one.'

CHAPTER 30

In Which a Mystery is Confronted

The screech of the wind seared through his skull and the world spun around him, but Cosimo, fighting with a skill born of long experience, ignored the discomfort, gritted his teeth and clung doggedly to the fast-fraying strands of his concentration. Keeping his eyes on the seething black void before him, he gathered his strength and the instant he felt solid ground beneath his feet once more, gave out a tremendous push with both hands. Solid muscle and bone met his fists. The Burley Man, momentarily disoriented by the crossing, was sent sprawling to the ground.

'Run!' cried Cosimo.

Spinning around, he glimpsed Sir Henry down on all fours, struggling to rise – an attempt made the more difficult by the Burley Man clinging to his back.

Three quick strides carried Cosimo to his side, and two swift kicks to the groin and instep freed his friend. 'Run!' he shouted, pulling Sir Henry to his feet. 'This way!'

Without waiting for a reply, he raced off down the long avenue of sphinxes towards the ruined temple.

He did not get far.

Cosimo, in full flight, felt his foot caught from behind and yanked out from under him. The broken pavement came up fast and smacked him on the chin. He rolled onto his back, lashing out with his legs as the Burley Man descended on him. One of his wild kicks connected, knocking his black-coated assailant back a pace or two.

Scrambling to his feet, Cosimo leapt to the fight, fists swinging. He managed to land a punch or two before being seized from behind and pulled off. Thrashing this way and that, Cosimo tried to shake off the steely grip. He sensed rather than saw a movement to his side, and heard a thin whistling sound. He ducked just as the silver knob of Sir Henry Fayth's walking stick flashed by his ear, striking the Burley Man squarely in the centre of the forehead. The man gave out a yelp, released his grasp, and sank cursing to his knees, arms flung over his head.

'Enough!' The shout was like the clap of a rifle shot in the still air. 'It's over.'

Cosimo glanced back over his shoulder to see three more Burley Men standing in the centre of the avenue; one of the men held tight to a chain on the end of which strained the great brindled brown shape of the cave lion. Muscles bunched, head low, it watched them with evil interest as it ran its red velvet tongue around its dagger-like teeth. Rattling along the rough-paved avenue behind them came a wagon drawn by a team of mules driven by a fourth Burley Man with a rifle across his lap.

'Mal, Dex – stand down. Con, get the gear from the wagon,' commanded the man who was clearly the leader of the cut-throat gang. Dressed in a loose white shirt, tall boots, and wide-brimmed straw hat with a red handkerchief knotted around his throat, he looked more like a farm hand than the mercenary soldier that he was. The face beneath the hat was as impassive as the stone statues around them. He strode forward to address his captives. 'I'm Tav,' he said. 'Which one of you is Cosimo?'

Cosimo and Sir Henry exchanged a glance, but neither spoke.

'Baby is hungry,' said Tav. 'I have half a mind to let her feed. If you'd rather not be on the menu, you'll answer me when I speak to you – and keep a civil tongue in your head. I ask you again, which one of you is Cosimo?'

'I do not deal with thugs, sir,' replied Cosimo.

The Burley Man's hand snapped out so quickly, Cosimo did not see it coming. The blow snapped his head back and a moment later he tasted blood on his tongue. 'Mind your manners, friend,' Tav warned. 'We're going to take a little walk, and you're coming along whether you like it or not. Now, you can make things easy on yourself, or difficult – it's up to you. I don't give a tinker's either way.'

The wagon came rattling up, and the one called Con hurried over, returning with two coils of rawhide rope.

'What do you want with us?' demanded Cosimo, rubbing his lip.

'You'll find out soon enough,' replied Tav. He signalled to his thuggish crew, who began shedding their coats, throwing them into the back of the wagon, and withdrawing bundles of lighter-weight clothing. 'You two want to change into something more comfortable?' he asked. 'It's going to get hot.'

'We're fine as we are,' replied Cosimo with sullen resolve.

Tav nodded, and called to his men. 'Ready, lads?' Turning away from the temple, he started back down the long avenue lined with sphinxes either side. Some had lost heads or feet; others had crumbled, their features eroded by wind and sand over time; but a good many were whole and in place, still guarding the pathway to the temple. When Cosimo and Sir Henry failed to fall into step behind him, he said, 'This way, gents.'

'I protest this treatment most strenuously, sir. I am not going anywhere with you,' Sir Henry declared.

'I think you'll find that you are,' replied the Burley Man. He gave a nod to Con, who advanced with the ropes. The one called Dex fetched two burlap bags from the wagon. Before either Cosimo or Sir Henry could protest further, the coils of rope were around their waists, their wrists were tied, and the burlap bags whipped over their heads. Thus bound and blinded, they were led away. The Burley Men with their wagon and cave lion fell in behind them and the party moved off down the rough-paved road.

Cosimo and Sir Henry shuffled along. A little light came through the uneven weave of the burlap, and they could see their feet and the patch of ground on which they walked, but no more than that. They could hear the heavy footfall of the men, the creak of the wagon wheels, and the low, breathy rumble of the lion padding dangerously close behind them. At the end of the avenue, Sir Henry and Cosimo stepped off the ancient pavement and into the desert where they were led in a more or less southerly direction towards a range of low dun-coloured hills. It was a thirsty region, a wasteland of shattered rock, dust, and sand in pretty much equal measures, ruled by the sun, and inhabited only by scorpions and lizards. The ground was rough and uneven, treacherous underfoot – like traversing an endless field of potsherds and broken brick. After trudging a good while in silence, Sir Henry moved fractionally nearer to Cosimo and whispered, 'Where are they taking us?'

'Not a clue,' Cosimo replied, his voice barely audible. 'I was here briefly a few yeas ago, but as far as I know there's nothing for miles around in any direction.'

'We should formulate a plan of action.'

'Agreed,' whispered Cosimo. 'But until we know what they intend –'

'Quiet, you two!' said the gang leader. 'Save your breath – you'll need it before we're through.'

'Stay alert, and look for an opening,' Cosimo concluded.

'I said, that's enough chatter!' Tav snarled, giving the rope binding their hands a painful jerk.

An hour or so passed; the sun rose higher in the clear blue sky and the heat increased. Every now and then the cave lion gave out a wounded-sounding growl, just to let them know it was still there. Aside from that – and the weary creak and crunch of the wagon wheels – no sound could be heard. The captives in their heavy dark clothes began to sweat. Through the burlap, they could feel the sun's burn and began to wish that they had changed clothes when given the chance. Sweat ran from their heads and ran down their necks. Their shirts and cloaks were soon drenched.

Still they trudged on. An hour passed, and then another. As a third hour commenced, Sir Henry gave out a sigh and stopped.

'Get moving, you!' came the command from behind.

'No,' he replied, bending to rest his hands on his knees. Sweat dripped from beneath the burlap bag to fall on the bone dry ground. 'I need water. I am near to fainting in this heat. I shall not take another step until I get a drink.'

'We're all thirsty, mate,' said Tav, not unreasonably. 'But there's nothing to drink out here until we reach the site.'

'No water?' sneered Cosimo. 'What manner of fools are you?'

'Shut your face,' snarled Dev. 'Get moving.'

'No,' said Sir Henry, planting himself firmly in place. 'I will not.'

'You can stay out here all day and die for all I care,' said the gang leader. 'But we're nearly there – a few more minutes is all. The sooner we get there, the sooner we all get a drink. Savvy?'

'Come along, Sir Henry,' urged Cosimo. 'It's too hot out here to argue.' To Tav he said, 'Lead on.'

The party resumed its march and a short while later reached the foot of a low bank of hills. Here they paused and the burlap bags were removed, much to the relief of the captives, who gasped and gulped down the air as if they had been suffocating. A few more minutes' walk carried them to the base of the nearest hill where an unseen seam opened in the much-eroded landscape: a wadi barely wide enough to admit the mule cart and team. Into this parched ravine the party turned and proceeded down the long, undulating corridor cut into the sandstone by water from the melt run-off during the last ice age.

The air inside the wadi, though dead, was at least a little cooler owing to the shadow cast by the steep walls; the sun did not penetrate to the valley floor save for only a few minutes each day. The shade was welcome, and Cosimo felt himself slightly revived. As they proceeded deeper into the gorge, he began to notice small niches carved in the soft sandstone. Some were square nooks, others rectangular; a few of the more elaborate niches had inscribed hieroglyphs alongside them, and many of these had pedestals fashioned into the floor of the nook as if to hold an object for display. Whatever the niches had held, all were empty now.

They came to a place where the wadi divided; Tav guided them into the wider of the two branches and proceeded as before. The wall niches became more numerous, larger, and more elaborate. Cosimo noticed that some few of these had been defaced – the hieroglyphics scratched or chiselled away, the pedestals smashed and broken.

The canyon snaked this way and that as it cut through the rock hills; the travellers followed the long, looping bend and came all at once to a dead end: a smooth wall of ruddy sandstone towering two hundred feet in the air, at the bottom of which was carved a doorway – a black square guarded either side by enormous effigies. On the right side, holding a rod of authority, stood Horus, the sun god, who possessed the body of a long-limbed, muscular man combined with the regal head of a hawk. On the left, his hand raised in warning, stood Thoth, ibis-headed god of all civilized sciences and magic, and judge of the dead.

Here they stopped.

'Sit 'em down, lads,' ordered Tav. He walked to the door and disappeared inside. The wagon and mules continued on, passed around a bend in the wadi and out of sight.

Cosimo and Sir Henry settled themselves on a rock in the shade, wiped sweat from their faces, and sat panting from their exertion. The cave lion, too, lay down, panting, its red tongue lolling from its mouth. 'I know just how it feels,' muttered Cosimo, unlacing his boots to cool his hot feet. He had rubbed one foot and ankle and was rubbing the second when the gang chief reappeared carrying a skin of water; in his wake came another man, tall and dark, with a face not unlike that of hawk-beaked Horus carved in the rock. Although clearly a European, he was dressed like an Egyptian in a long, loose-fitting black garment with a black turban on his head.

The newcomer gave a nod of acknowledgement to the others and said, 'Put Baby away. See she's fed and watered.' As the men gingerly prodded the overheated beast to its feet and led it away, the man in the turban filled a cup from the waterskin and offered it to Sir Henry, saying, 'Welcome, Lord Fayth. I have long been an admirer of yours.'

The nobleman accepted the cup without a word and offered it in turn to Cosimo, who refused it. Sir Henry then drained the cup in several deep gulps before handing it back. The black-turbaned one refilled it and passed it to Cosimo. 'Mr Livingstone, I presume,' he said with a smile.

'Very droll,' muttered Cosimo, his voice cracking. 'You come crawling out from under your rock at last, Burley.'

'Lord Burleigh, if you please.'

'Whatever you say.' He tipped up the cup and drank deeply, feeling the life-giving liquid sooth his sticky dry throat. 'Now that we're here, what do you intend to do with us?'

'That depends entirely on you and your friend here,' he said, passing the cup to his chief, Tav, who filled it and drank before passing the waterskin on to the others. 'You see,' Burleigh continued, 'I believe in choices. So, I will always give you a choice. We can do this either of two ways – easy or difficult,' he explained, his tone mild, good-humoured even. 'The first is gentle and profitable for all concerned. The second is slow, messy, and painful. If you're open to a little advice, I'd recommend taking the first option. Believe me, it really is simpler all round and, anyway, it is too bloody hot for making fires to heat up the instruments of persuasion.'

He retrieved the skin from Dex and poured out another cup. 'More water, gentlemen?'

Sir Henry nodded. 'If you please.' He gulped it down.

'Finished?' said Burleigh when Cosimo had drunk his second cup. 'There will be more later. I wouldn't drink too much all at once – it's bad for the stomach.' He tossed the cup to Tav. 'Now then, if you're refreshed, come along. I have something to show you.'

'On your feet, you two,' said Con. They needed no prodding, but rose and followed the earl's lead around the bend in the gorge to a hole at the base of the rock wall over which someone long ago had erected a wooden shelter. Here Burleigh paused and, withdrawing a key from a hidden fold of his kaftan, disappeared down a flight of wooden steps into the hole. There was a clink and the grating sound of rusty hinges, and his voice came floating up from the ground, 'One at a time, gentlemen, and do watch your step.'

Cosimo and Sir Henry descended the wooden stairs into the dry darkness, squeezed through a heavy iron gate at the bottom, and found themselves in a very small and cramped vestibule hollowed from the living rock. Tav followed, but no sooner had he joined the others than Burleigh sent him away again, saying, 'The generator, Tav.'

'Aye, sir.' He disappeared again and a few moments later the distant sound of a combustion engine coughed, then started to hum.

'You'll want to see this in all its glory, believe me,' said Burleigh. Cosimo glanced at Sir Henry as their captor bent down and fumbled with a black box on the floor. There was a click of a switch and a warm yellow glow emanated from the chamber beyond. 'This way, gentlemen.'

He led them into the next chamber, larger than the first – a simple rectangular box devoid of either furniture or feature, except for a blue-painted ceiling covered with white spots of stars. 'Through here,' said Burleigh, moving through a doorway into a further room.

Cosimo, his trepidation having given way totally to unfeigned interest, followed willingly. The room was empty save for a large granite sarcophagus in the centre of the floor and three naked light bulbs affixed to makeshift stands. The sarcophagus was missing its lid, and the lights wavered gently with the irregular pulse of the generator.

'Here we are, gentlemen,' Burleigh said, moving quickly to the far side of the room which was covered every inch, floor to ceiling, with incredibly lifelike and colourful paintings of life in ancient Egypt in all its glory.

Sir Henry, experiencing his first exposure to the science of electricity, could not take his eyes from the softly glowing bulbs.

'If you will allow me to direct your attention to this particular wall painting,' Burleigh said, 'you will, I think, find something of inestimable interest.'

Cosimo nudged his companion. 'Not now, Sir Henry. I'll explain later. Let's see what this drama is all about.'

Burleigh stood next to a nearly life-sized painting of a bald Egyptian dressed in the traditional knee-length linen kilt and heavy gold-and-lapis necklace. Although the figure was heavily stylized in the iconic manner of all tomb art, it was clear the painters had tried to give him a modicum of personality: his round face positively beamed with beatific serenity and humour; even in a two-dimensional rendering he seemed a pleasant, good-natured fellow.

'Allow me to introduce you to Anen, the High Priest of Amun, in whose tomb you are now standing.'

'High Priest Anen, you say?' wondered Sir Henry. 'I don't believe I have ever heard of him – have you, Cosimo?'

'Oh, he's a very interesting chap, as it happens,' continued Burleigh. 'Brother-in-law of Pharaoh Amenhotep III and who, at the time of his death, had scaled the heights to become Second Prophet of Amun. He enjoyed an extremely powerful and influential position in Pharaoh's court, as I think you can appreciate.'

'Very impressive, to be sure,' said Cosimo, 'but what does any of that have to do with us?'

'Patience,' replied Burleigh with a smile. 'We are getting to it.'

'Go on then.'

'Take a good look at him, if you will,' said Burleigh, indicating the somewhat stocky figure in the painting. 'You'll see him again just here –' He moved on to the next floor-to-ceiling panel, which depicted the priest Anen standing next to a pale-skinned man dressed in a long striped robe of many colours. The man's robe was open at the chest to reveal a cluster of tiny blue symbols on his chest. Behind the two figures a vast building project was proceeding – the raising of a palace or temple of some sort – the site swarming with hundreds of half-naked workers. 'Mark the man in the coloured robe?' said Burleigh.

'Incredible…' breathed Cosimo.

Burleigh moved to a third panel. 'Now then,' he said, 'things grow more interesting. Here is our man, Anen – older now, as you can see, and what is that in his hand?'

'Good Lord,' said Cosimo stepping closer to the wall and squinting his eyes against the shadows. 'Is that…? It can't be!'

The picture showed the priest standing alone in the desert under a brilliant blue twilight sky. One hand was raised skyward, forefinger extended; in the other hand he grasped what looked like a ragged banner shaped roughly like a truncated human torso. This curious banner was decorated with the same symbols that had appeared on the man in the striped robe of the previous painting.

'Gentlemen, I give you the Skin Map!' announced Earl Burleigh in triumph.

'Good Lord, indeed,' breathed Sir Henry. 'Of all places… here!'

'As if there could be any doubt,' said Burleigh, obviously relishing the effect of his revelations, 'I direct your attention to this particular cartouche.' He indicated a small lozenge-shaped panel decorating the border of the painting.

Cosimo bent near and, in the glow of the gently wavering electric light, examined the hieroglyphics contained in the cartouche, working out the meaning. 'The man… who is… map.'

'Precisely,' confirmed Burleigh. 'The Man Who is Map – none other than Arthur Flinders-Petrie.'

'He was here,' breathed Cosimo in astonishment. 'Graphic evidence that Arthur was here.'

'Moreover, the map was here,' said Burleigh.

'How do you know that?' asked Cosimo.

Burleigh gave him a sly smile. 'Because I was here with Carter and Carnarvon when this tomb was opened. I held it in my hands.' He gave his turbaned head a rueful shake.

'You knew Carter?' said Cosimo.

'Oh, yes,' replied Burleigh. 'In a former life, you might say.'

Stepping to the stone sarcophagus, he reached in and pulled out an ancient wooden chest and presented it to Cosimo. The pale yellow lacquer was dry and cracked, but the rounded top, on closer inspection, was seen to be covered with the same blue symbols as those represented on the wall painting. 'The map was in one piece, and it was in here,' said Burleigh, tapping the lid with a finger. 'Unfortunately, at the time I did not know what it was that I held.'

Cosimo carefully opened the chest. '*Was* here,' he said, examining the dusty interior. 'Once upon a time.'

'Yes,' replied Burleigh, 'but that is beside the point.'

'Then, pray, what *is* the point?' demanded Sir Henry, accepting the empty chest from Cosimo. 'Come to it, man!'

'Patience,' chided Burleigh lightly. 'We must tread lightly, for here we confront the elemental mystery.'

Moving again to the last painting, he said, 'Consider what our friend Anen the high priest is doing in this picture.'

'Certainly, he's holding the map,' volunteered Cosimo.

'Yes, as we've already established. But what is he doing with his other hand?'

Cosimo followed the raised right arm of the priest to the extended forefinger. 'Why, he's pointing into the sky…'

'He seems to be pointing at a star,' added Sir Henry.

'Indeed, he is!' replied Burleigh. 'But not just any star.'

'No?' wondered Cosimo.

'Think where we are, gentlemen,' coaxed the earl. 'Egypt – the southern sky, yes? And what is the brightest star in the southern sky?'

'Sirius,' answered Sir Henry. 'The Dog Star.'

'Bravo!' applauded Burleigh, his hand claps ringing loud in the empty chamber. 'High Priest Anen is holding the Skin Map and pointing to the Dog Star.' He turned a keen and questioning gaze upon his two captives. 'Now, why is that, do you think?'

CHAPTER 31

In Which the Quality of Mercy is Strained

A razor-thin line of daylight stole into the forechamber of the high priest's tomb, broadening as it sliced through the darkness. The tomb, empty now, scoured clean, its costly objects duly catalogued and carted off to Cairo's new antiquities museum, remained steeped in a centuries-old silence altered only by the early morning song of a desert bird perched high on the wall of the wadi, its piping note echoing through the canyon.

Inside the tomb, two bodies lay on a floor hewn from the living stone of the wadi: two men, both asleep, one breathing heavily.

At the sound of the bird, one of the bodies stirred and Sir Henry Fayth opened his eyes in the semi-darkness of the inner chamber. He lay for a moment, listening – to the birdsong, to the man a few paces away whose breathing had become laboured during the night – then rose and went to his friend.

'Cosimo,' he said, giving his shoulder a nudge. 'Cosimo, will you wake?' When that failed to rouse the sleeping man, he desisted, and crawled to sit with his back against the massive stone sarcophagus which dominated the centre of the room.

Now that he was awake, thirst came upon him with renewed ferocity – and with it his reawakened hatred of Burleigh. Enemy or no, it was inhuman of Burleigh to lock them away without food or water. Sir Henry would not have treated a mad dog so cruelly, much less another human being. Such behaviour was brutish and ignoble, far beneath the decency of civilized men.

He would, he vowed, protest in the strongest, most strenuous terms when the next opportunity presented itself, which would be... when? One full day and half of another had passed since they had last seen Burleigh or one of his toadies – thirty-six hours without food or water in the dark, airless tomb of Anen, the High Priest of Amun.

That the quest should end here, like this, seemed a needlessly malicious fate for a God-fearing man such as himself. In the early days of their friendship, when he and Cosimo had first begun exploring the inter-dimensional highways and byways of the universe, there had been little danger, save from the local environment wherein they might happen to find themselves. Before the rot set in, before the race to find the map – that is to say, before Burleigh and his men – things had been very different.

Perhaps, he thought, they should surrender to Burleigh's demands, give him what he wanted in exchange for their freedom. Or, better still, join forces, pool their knowledge. Obviously the rogue possessed information that they lacked, and that would be useful to know.

For example, it would be helpful to learn how it was that the villains always seemed to know where and when to find them. Such had not always been the case. There was a time, when the Burley Men first appeared, that they had been ridiculously easy to elude. After that first time, they would not encounter them again for a very long time – sometimes years might pass between episodes. Not any more. Now, each and every leap was likely to attract their interest and consequent involvement. How did they know? By what means or method were they drawn to the precise location at the exact time?

Burleigh also had knowledge of the map that they did not. Obviously he knew Flinders-Petrie had once sojourned in Egypt, and that the map had once resided in this very tomb. What else did he know? Would it not be useful to find out?

As Sir Henry sat thinking, the light grew faintly brighter. Outside, he heard the mechanical engine sputter to life. That meant the Burley Men were up and about their nefarious duties for the day. He considered calling out to them, asking for water – just the merest sip to take away the metallic taste on his thickening tongue. Indeed, he was on the point of doing just that when he heard footsteps on the stone-cut staircase leading down into the tomb. Climbing heavily to his feet, he straightened his clothes and went to stand by the iron grate that formed the door of their prison.

'Ah, Sir Henry, you are awake,' said Burleigh, his voice loud in the quiet of the tomb. He strode to the bars, holding a waterskin and tin cup. 'Good. It saves me the trouble of trying to rouse you.'

'We need water,' replied Sir Henry, his eyes going to the waterskin. 'And medical attention – Cosimo has fallen ill.'

'I am sorry to hear it,' said Burleigh with mock sincerity. 'Still, I feared this would happen. There is something down here, you see. I cannot say what it is – a plague miasma, a curse, who knows? Personally, I suspect that it is some compound or other the ancient Egyptians used to protect their tombs.'

'He requires immediate care,' insisted Sir Henry.

'I do not doubt it. Without treatment it is fatal.' He raised the waterskin, holding it just beyond reach of the bars. 'Are you ready to see reason?'

'Please,' said Sir Henry, 'help us.'

'Say the word, and you will have all the help you need,' Burleigh told him.

A low moan escaped Cosimo's lips. Sir Henry glanced back at his friend. 'Very well, what do you want me to do?'

'Tell me where your piece of the map is hidden,' answered Burleigh. 'Let's start with that, shall we?'

'Then you will let us go?'

'Not so fast,' chided Burleigh. 'First things first. If your information proves useful, then yes, I will let you go.' He smiled. 'Where is your map?'

'We don't have it any more. It was stolen.'

'Oh, dear. Oh, dear,' said Burleigh. 'That will not do at all. You're going to have to do better than that.' His voice became hard. 'Where is the map?'

'But that is the very truth,' maintained Sir Henry. 'Cosimo kept the map locked away in the crypt at Christ Church in Oxford. We went there to consult it and discovered that it had been taken, and a poor substitute put in its place. Truth be told, we suspected you had done it.'

'That part, at least, I do believe,' allowed Burleigh.

'Please,' said Sir Henry, holding out his hand for the waterskin. 'You have to believe me.'

'Let's try again,' suggested Burleigh brightly. 'What do you know about the Well of Souls?'

'The Well of Souls,' repeated Lord Fayth, puzzled.

'You have heard of it, surely?'

The sound of their voices had succeeded in waking Cosimo. 'Let us go, Burleigh,' he called, pushing himself up onto an elbow. 'Keeping us here will get you nothing.'

'Cosimo!' said Sir Henry, stepping quickly to his friend's side. 'Here, allow me to help you.' He shouldered Cosimo's weight and led him nearer the grated door.

'What have you told him?' demanded Cosimo.

'You are more than welcome to join the conversation,' invited Burleigh, forcing a smile. 'I was enquiring about the Well of Souls. In exchange for information, I am willing to offer medical assistance – and more.' He waggled the waterskin in his hand. 'I want to learn what you know about the Well of Souls.'

'It's a myth,' said Cosimo, pressing a hand to his head. 'A traveller's tale, nothing more.'

'And yet,' countered Burleigh smoothly, 'myths generally form around a kernel of hard truth, do they not? I intend getting to the truth at the core of this particular myth.'

Cosimo glanced at Sir Henry, worked his cracked lips, and said, 'All right, I'll tell you what I know – but first you have to give us the water.'

'No,' stated Burleigh firmly. 'Talk first, then the water.' He passed the tin cup through the grate.

'My throat is parched and I'm burning up with fever.' Cosimo reached through the grate for the waterskin. 'Give me a drink first.'

'When you've told me what you know.'

Cosimo, swaying on his feet, yielded. 'The Well of Souls is a legend with various strains,' he began. 'Jewish, Arab, Egyptian – they all have a version of it, but none of them agree on the precise nature of this supposed well, or even where it is located.'

'See? That wasn't so hard,' said Burleigh encouragingly. 'Continue.'

Cosimo swallowed. 'A drink.'

'You are wasting time. Talk.'

'Some tales have it that the well is an earthly place, an underground region where the souls of the dead congregate to await the coming judgment. Others hold it to be a heavenly place where the souls of those not yet born await their call to life in this world.' Breathing heavily at this mild exertion, Cosimo leaned over, resting his hands on his knees. 'That's all I know,' he concluded. 'As I say, it is a myth, nothing more.'

'Oh, I *am* disappointed,' said Burleigh. 'I had such high hopes for you. I really did.'

'What did you expect?' demanded Cosimo. 'There is no such place. It's just a story nomadic sheepherders told around the campfire.'

'You know very well it is much more than that!' charged Burleigh, suddenly angry. 'What did I expect? Seeing that your life is on the line, I expected you to tell me the truth.'

'I told you everything,' snarled Cosimo. The outburst caused a coughing fit which seemed to diminish him. 'I don't know any more than that,' he concluded weakly.

Burleigh stared at him. 'Why do I fail to believe you?'

'If you know more, then you have better information than I.' Cosimo, breathing hard, gulped down air like a drowning man. 'I can add nothing more.'

'Can you not see the man is ill?' Sir Henry intervened, pushing close to the iron grating. 'He needs immediate help. In God's name, I implore you to let us out.'

'Is this information so precious to you that you are willing to die for it?' asked Burleigh.

'We have told you what we know. What more do you want from us?'

'I want the location of the Well of Souls,' he said; then amended, 'Actually, I want a good deal more than that, but I will settle for that just now.'

'It isn't a real place,' insisted Cosimo. 'It is only a legend.'

'Only that? Are you certain?'

'I swear it.'

Burleigh regarded the two men for a moment, shaking his head slowly from side to side. 'Look at you – adventurers, gentlemen explorers… dilettantes, dabblers! You still don't know what this is all about, do you?'

Neither captive offered a reply.

'You poor deluded fools,' he said quietly, as if talking to himself. 'You have no idea what is at stake.'

'You want the map,' said Sir Henry, his voice rising in desperation. 'We would give it to you, but it is gone, stolen – as I have already made clear. If you did not steal it, then I have no idea who the thief might be, or where it now resides.'

'Pity,' sniffed Burleigh. 'Then you and your friend are of no further use to me.' He turned on his heel and started away.

'For the love of God, Burleigh,' shouted Cosimo. 'Let us go!'

He stopped in mid-step and turned around. 'There is no God,' he said, his voice flat and hard. 'There is only chaos, chance, and the immutable laws of nature. As men of science, I had thought you would know that. In this world – as in all others – there is only the survival of the fittest. I am a survivor.' He turned again and began walking away. 'You, apparently, are not.'

'You are wrong,' Cosimo called after him. 'Utterly, fatally, and eternally wrong.'

'If so,' replied Burleigh, moving to the doorway, 'then God will save you.'

'Have mercy!' pleaded Sir Henry. 'Leave us the water.'

The man who called himself Burleigh shrugged. 'It will only delay the inevitable, but –' He retraced his steps to the cell and placed the skin of water on the floor just within reach of the grate. 'I leave it for you to decide.'

CHAPTER 32

In Which Turnabout is Fair Play

The Kaffee-tasting at the palace was a triumph, the royal palate piqued and pleased by the exotic elixir and Etzel's excellent pastries. Following a most successful audience, they had been approached by the master of warrants, who offered them a wooden plaque carved and painted with the royal arms; the plaque was to be placed over the door of their Kaffeehaus, indicating King Rudolf's imprimatur of satisfaction and pleasure. Engelbert and Wilhelmina returned home floating on the heady vapours of victory. That night they celebrated in the Grand Kaffeehaus with a special dinner and a bottle of fine wine supplied by Herr Arnostovi, whose palace spies had confirmed the emperor's delight in the new drink and its accompanying sweet cakes and his intention to imbibe frequently in the future.

'Your success is assured,' Arnostovi told them, rising from the table to hoist his wine cup high. 'With the royal warrant, you will want for nothing in this city, my friends. Let us raise our cups to the Grand *Imperial* Kaffeehaus!' He tipped his cup to his mouth and, losing his balance, sat back down with a thump.

'The Grand Imperial now, is it?' Wilhelmina laughed. 'You are drunk, Arno.'

'Perhaps,' he admitted. 'And why not? It is not every day you conquer a city like Prague.'

'Hardly that,' scoffed Mina lightly. She smiled at the thought all the same.

'We have tickled the emperor's taste buds, I think,' suggested Etzel. 'He drank his Kaffee and ate three of my cakes. This is all we hoped for.'

'And yet,' said the landlord, 'your modest hopes have been rewarded in riches beyond your dreams. I salute you, my friends!' He waved his cup again, sloshing wine over the rim and onto his hand. 'What will you do with your fame and fortune, I wonder?' he asked, licking wine from the back of his hand.

'We don't have a fortune yet,' Mina pointed out. 'What with the rent of this shop, shipping expenses, the payment of staff – I think our fortune is far from secured.'

'Only a matter of time,' crowed Arnostovi. 'You should think about investing with me.'

'Right now, I only want to think about enjoying this delicious dinner,' Mina said. 'Thank you, Arno.' She reached across the table to pat his hand. Etzel saw the gesture and his mouth twitched. Mina, mindful of her partner's more tender feelings, reached for his hand also. 'Here I am with my two favourite people in all the world,' she gushed, the wine making her free with her feelings. Still, she realized even as she spoke the words that it was probably true. 'I thank you both.'

'Why are you thanking me?' wondered Engelbert.

'For being my friend,' she told him, giving his hand another pat. 'For helping me, trusting me and, above all, believing in me.'

'Mina,' said the big baker, his voice growing soft, 'it is *I* who should be thanking you for all those things… and more.'

'To friendship!' cried Herr Arnostovi, draining his cup. 'Let us eat and drink and rejoice in your victory today. But first –' He rose abruptly from the table and took two unsteady steps backwards.

'What is it?' asked Mina, half-starting from her chair.

'First, my friends,' said the man of business, 'we need more wine!'

The next morning the cluttered table stood as a silent reproach to the previous night's festivities. 'It looks as if *someone* made merry,' observed one of the kitchen helpers when they arrived to begin work. With much tut-tutting and shaking of heads, the minions set about clearing away the detritus of what had been a sumptuous, if slightly raucous, celebration.

By the time the shop opened for business, all was ready and in order. Wilhelmina, still exalting in the triumph of the previous day, floated about her chores, her heart light, a song playing on her lips. Etzel, too, hummed his way through his duties, taking great pleasure in the way their Kaffeehaus filled up with customers. Thus, the day passed in happy industry – right up until the late afternoon when the chief under-alchemist Gustavus Rosenkreuz appeared with the court visitor known as Lord Burleigh. The two took a table in the corner and ordered Kaffee and Etzel's cream cakes. They had been served and were deep in conversation, their sweets untouched on the table, when Mina saw them.

Curious, and eager to continue their brief conversation of the previous day, she paid a visit to the table.

'. . . the device must be small enough to carry on one's person,' Burleigh was saying. 'A traveller cannot afford to be burdened in any way.'

'I understand, *mein Herr*,' replied the young alchemist, studying a scrap of parchment spread out among many on the table. 'I think it is well within our skill to manufacture such an item to your requirements. Its size should not present undue difficulties.'

'Splendid!' Burleigh glanced up quickly. 'Ah! Fräulein! We meet again.' He stood, and the alchemist rose, too, as Burleigh took Wilhelmina's hand and gallantly kissed it. 'Your shop is wonderful. I congratulate you.'

Mina thanked him. 'And how was your Kaffee?'

'As good as any I've ever drunk.'

'You've had Kaffee before?' wondered Rosenkreuz.

'Oh, once or twice,' said the earl dismissively. 'I forget where. I congratulate you, too, on receiving the royal patronage. You must be very proud.'

'We are very grateful.' Glancing at their empty cups, she said, 'May I bring you more Kaffee, gentlemen?' Both accepted the offer and Mina went to fetch it; when she returned with a fresh pot Earl Burleigh was at the table alone.

'My young friend has remembered some urgent business,' he explained in his formal English. 'But this will give us a chance to become better acquainted.' He indicated the chair next to his own. 'Please, sit with me.'

Mina settled into the offered seat. 'Forgive me, lord earl,' she began, choosing her words with some care, 'but it seems to me that you are very far from home.'

'As are you, my dear,' replied Burleigh.

The reply was ambiguous, so Mina probed a little deeper. 'Yes, of course,' she said. 'I left more than London behind when I came here. I suspect you did also.'

The dark stranger's expression grew keen; his eyes narrowed. But he said nothing.

She took his silence for affirmation. 'So, where did you come from? Or should I say *when*?'

'Whatever do you mean, dear lady?' replied Burleigh, still watching her intently.

'I mean,' said Wilhelmina, lowering her voice and leaning forward, 'like myself, you have travelled in time. You're not of this century, and neither am I.'

'What makes you say such a thing?'

'I *know*, all right?' she said, glancing around quickly. 'Your little slip-up just now – about having coffee once or twice. You forgot this is still a new thing here. And yesterday, you betrayed yourself when you asked which Kaffeehaus was mine.'

'Ah,' replied the earl thoughtfully. 'Touché.'

'Then there are your clothes,' continued Wilhelmina, warming to her argument. 'Plain, good quality, serviceable they may be – but the cloth is machine woven. I had the same problem when I arrived. The things you're wearing might have been made in England – but a few hundred years from now, I expect.' She fixed him a sly, knowing smile. 'They may fool the locals, but they don't fool me.'

'What sharp little eyes you have, my dear,' replied Burleigh through his teeth.

'Thank you,' she smiled. 'I don't miss much.'

He took her hand as it rested on the table. 'Then I am certain,' he said, giving her hand a gentle squeeze, 'that you will understand,' he squeezed again, a little harder for emphasis, 'when I tell you...' he squeezed again, uncomfortably harder, and maintained the pressure.

'Ow!' yipped Mina, trying to pull her hand away.

Burleigh held her fast in his grip. '... when I tell you that you have suddenly become an unwanted intrusion in my affairs.' His grip tightened.

'You're hurting me!'

'I'll do more than that, sweet thing,' he muttered.

'Let me go!'

He brought his face close to hers the way a lover might. 'If you want to stay alive,' he said, his breath hot in her ear, 'stay far away from me.'

He released her hand and rose from the table. 'Thank you for the coffee,' he said, all smiles and good manners once more. 'I will say goodbye. I don't expect to see you again.'

He moved quickly to the door and was gone before Wilhelmina could think to call for Etzel.

She was still sitting there, rubbing her hand and staring at the door through which the treacherous earl had disappeared, when Rosenkreuz returned. 'Wilhelmina?' he asked, taking his seat at the table. 'Is all well?'

She started, coming to herself once more. 'No – I mean, yes.' She forced a smile. 'Never better.'

'What happened to Lord Burleigh?' asked the young alchemist. 'Where has he gone?'

'It seems he had to leave. No doubt he will meet you again later.'

Rosenkreuz accepted this without comment.

'But here,' said Mina, jumping up, 'your Kaffee has gone cold. Don't drink it. I'll bring you some more.'

'Thank you, but I should be about my own business.'

'It won't take but a moment,' said Wilhelmina, hurrying away. 'There is something I wish to discuss with you.'

'Is anything the matter?' asked Etzel, catching a glimpse of her preoccupied expression as she entered the kitchen. He placed on the baking table a tray of buns fresh from the oven.

'What?' she said. 'Oh, no – no. Everything is splendid. I was just thinking. Ummm, those cakes smell heavenly,' she told him. As soon as the pot was filled, she returned to the table in the corner bearing a tray with milk, a second cup, and a plate of Etzel's special pastries, which she placed before the chief under–alchemist. 'On the house,' she said, taking her seat.

The expression puzzled the young fellow, but he reached for a pastry as his cup was filled. 'I am in your debt, Fräulein,' he said, the crumbs falling from his lips.

'My pleasure,' she replied. 'But I need your help with something.'

'Anything.'

'Merely a little information.'

'But, of course. What would you like to know?'

'What is Lord Burleigh doing here in Prague? I'd like to know.'

'But it is no secret,' answered Rosenkreuz readily, then after a moment's hesitation added, 'at least I cannot think that it is a secret…'

'Well, then?'

'He has come to ask our aid in the manufacture of a device to aid his travels.'

'The device, yes,' said Mina, remembering the diagram she had seen in the earl's hands upon entering the alchemy laboratory. 'You were talking about it when I joined the two of you just now. Tell me about it.'

Rosenkreuz explained that the Earl of Sutherland was engaged in the exploration of the astral planes – the otherworldly dimensions which made up the unseen universe – and required a device to aid him. 'He is a very intelligent man,' the alchemist confided, 'and very brave.'

'Undoubtedly,' agreed Mina. 'Another pastry? Please, go on.'

'The astral realms are thought to be –'

'The device, I mean. Tell me about that.'

'I do believe it to be the most cunning invention I have ever seen.' His hands described an oval roughly the size of a grapefruit. 'This device is to be used to identify the invisible pathways by which the earl makes his travels. These pathways are all around us, apparently – if we only knew how to recognize them.'

'I see,' nodded Wilhelmina, making up her mind. 'Herr Rosenkreuz, how would you like to secure a ready supply of bitter earth for your experiments – free, at no charge whatsoever?'

'Of course. It goes without saying,' the alchemist agreed at once, 'but that is in no way necessary. We can easily pay.'

'I know,' she replied, 'and you are more than generous. But I want to exchange it for your help.'

'Very well,' agreed Rosenkreuz. 'What is it that you wish?'

'When you have manufactured this device for Lord Burleigh,' said Mina, her tone taking on an edge Rosenkreuz had never heard in a woman's voice before, 'I want you to make one for me.'

CHAPTER 33

In Which Nature Takes its Course

It began as a simple tickle in the throat. Xian-Li coughed once or twice, drank a little water and carried on making herself ready for the day. She and Arthur breakfasted with some of the priests on slices of sweet melon, dates, figs in honey, and goat's milk flavoured with almonds. While Arthur and the servants of Amun chatted over their food, Xian-Li sat quietly and enjoyed the warmth of the sun on her back, letting her mind wander where it would.

'You're not eating,' Arthur observed at one point during the meal. 'Aren't you hungry, darling?'

'Mm?' she shook off her reverie and looked down at her untouched plate. 'Oh, I was –' Her voice drifted off.

'You must eat something,' he chided. 'You simply can't meet Pharaoh on an empty stomach, you know.'

She nodded, picking up a fig. She put it down again after only a bite, and her mind flitted away once more. The next thing she knew the meal was over; the white-kilted priests were getting up and Arthur was on his feet, ready to go.

'Xian-Li?'

'Yes?' she said, glancing up.

'I was talking to you just now. Didn't you hear me?'

'Very sorry, husband,' she replied, offering a wan smile. 'I was cloud drifting.'

He laughed. 'In England we call it wool gathering.' His glance became serious. 'Are you sure you're well, my dear? You look a little pale.'

'A little tired, perhaps,' she allowed. She stood up and the world seemed to spin; the ground shifted under her feet. Her vision dimmed and, suddenly dizzy and light-headed, she sat back down with a thump. 'Oh!'

'Darling? Are you all right?'

She waved away his concern. 'I stood up too fast,' she told him.

'Here, let me help you.' He put his hand beneath her arm.

She stood again, more slowly this time. 'It is nothing.'

They walked across the sunny temple yard to the guest house to finish preparing for the short journey to meet the pharaoh's barge at Oma on the Nile. Anen was to be their guide and had gone to fetch a mule cart for them; the priest, as a member of the extended royal family, would travel in a horse-drawn chariot. They were to leave as soon as he returned.

'This is a very great honour,' Arthur was saying as they entered the small, spare house. His voice seemed to come to her from a very great distance. 'I suppose it would be akin to meeting your Emperor Qing –' He broke off abruptly, for his wife was leaning against the door post with her hand to her head.

'Darling! You are unwell.'

'I feel a little warm,' she confessed. 'Maybe I was in the sun too long.' She patted his arm and went to wash her face in the basin on the tripod beside the bed place. She bent over the basin and in her reflection in the still water she saw a drawn, hollow mask of a face looking back at her. Lowering her hands into the basin, she laved cool water onto her face and neck, and felt instantly refreshed. 'That is much better.'

She dried herself and wound her long, black hair into a coil and pinned it up for travel. She found the linen scarf she had been given to help keep the sun off her head and, thus prepared, sat down on the pallet that was her bed to await Anen's arrival with the cart. Meanwhile, Arthur heard a clatter of hooves in the courtyard and went out to greet the priest, and on his return found his wife stretched out on the bed, her arm over her face.

'Xian-Li,' he said, 'it is time to go.' He crossed the room and knelt beside the pallet. When she failed to respond, he gave her arm a gentle shake. 'Xian-Li? Wake up, my dear.'

She came awake with a start. 'Oh, forgive me, I must have dozed off. I –' She struggled upright, only to sink back down once more.

He put the back of his hand to her forehead. 'Darling, you're burning up! You've got yourself a raging fever.'

'I was in the sun too long,' she insisted, pushing herself up. 'I am well enough to travel.'

Arthur frowned doubtfully. 'I think you should stay here and rest.'

She scoffed at the idea. 'And miss meeting Pharaoh? It is nothing. It will soon pass. I can rest in the cart.'

Arthur helped her to her feet. He steadied her as she swayed. 'Still light-headed?'

'A little,' she admitted. 'But there – it is gone. I am better now. Let us go, and think no more about it.'

His wife strode briskly out into the sun-filled courtyard, drawing the scarf over her head. The priest Anen, holding the bridle of the lead chariot horse, called a greeting; a small two-person donkey cart stood waiting nearby, as well as a pack mule bearing simple provisions, and four other priests to accompany them. Xian-Li approached Anen and gave him a polite bow, then walked to the cart.

'My wife is determined to go,' Arthur explained, stepping close to his priestly friend.

The two men watched as the dark-haired young woman raised her foot to the step at the back of the cart; she gripped the hand rails and made to swing herself up into the open end of the vehicle. But it seemed that either her hand or foot slipped, for the next thing they saw was Xian-Li falling backwards, onto the stone-paved yard. A quick-thinking brother priest saw what was happening and leapt forward to catch her, breaking her fall, easing her to the ground.

Arthur and Anen rushed to her side.

'Xian-Li!' cried Arthur, kneeling by his stricken bride.

Her eyelids fluttered momentarily, and then she seemed to come to herself once more. 'Arthur… oh! What has happened?'

'You fell,' said Arthur. 'You must have fainted.'

'No,' she said, 'I –' She broke off as a spasm passed through her body. 'Oh…' she gasped, and tried to sit up.

'Rest a moment,' Arthur told her. 'We'll get you back inside.' He signalled to the priests to help him, and they lifted her up and carried her back into the guest house, and laid her on the pallet bed.

'I have sent Tihenk for the physician,' Anen said as he joined them. 'He will come at once.'

Arthur thanked him, and Anen ordered his brother priests to wait outside. 'You must go soon or you will not be on time to meet Pharaoh. You dare not keep him waiting.'

'Another will go in my place,' countered Anen. 'Pharaoh will understand.'

'Please, I will not have you stay here on our account,' Arthur protested. 'The physician will look after her, and we will join you in a day or two when Xian-Li is feeling better.'

'Then when she is well, we will travel together,' Anen replied. 'Until then, I am staying here with you.'

Seeing that no amount of persuasion would change the priest's mind, Arthur thanked him and fetched his wife a drink of water; he dipped the end of her scarf in the basin and used the damp cloth to bathe her forehead. A few minutes later, the physician arrived – a stocky senior priest with a smooth bald head and soft hands. Schooled in the healing arts since childhood, he possessed the easy manner of a competent, unflappable soul. He carried a simple woven grass bag on his shoulder and a small, three-legged stool. 'I am Khepri,' he said. 'I am here to help you.' Anen completed the introductions and, after a brief explanation, the fellow placed the stool next to his patient, sat down, and removed his bag.

Khepri sat for a moment, quietly, studying his patient, then clapped his hands and, raising his face, closed his eyes and uttered a prayer for Isis to attend him and aid in curing the ailment of the woman before him. Then, leaning forward, he placed his hand on Xian-Li's forehead, nodding to himself. He turned to Arthur to enquire what she had eaten in the last day.

'Very little,' Arthur told him, then went on to list the few items he knew she had consumed. 'Do you think it might be something she ate?'

'That is the most likely cause,' replied the physician. 'Many people of foreign origin suffer so when sojourning in our land for the first time. There is nothing to worry about. It will pass.'

'Good,' said Arthur. 'I am glad to hear it.' He glanced down at his wife, who lay with one hand over her eyes. 'What can we do to make her more comfortable while we wait?'

'I will give her some water mixed with honey and the juice of plums,' Khepri told him. 'Also, we will keep a damp cloth on her head and feet to draw the heat from the fire in her blood.'

The treatment sounded good to Arthur, so he gave his assent. Anen spoke a word to the doctor, who went to fetch the necessary items, and then said, 'I will leave you in his care for a while. I must go and see Shoshenk on his way to meet Pharaoh.'

'I thank you for your care, my friend,' said Arthur. 'But you do not have to do this.'

'It is done,' replied the priest.

He departed and Khepri returned with the honey water and gave some to his patient. Xian-Li drank as much as she could, then said she would like to sleep. Arthur translated her words for the physician, who nodded, saying, 'That is for the best.' He rose, taking up his stool. 'I must go and attend to a man with a broken arm. I will return when I have finished.'

'Please, go,' Arthur told him. 'I will stay with her until you come back.'

Arthur settled down to sit with his sick wife, holding her hand and, every now and then, dipping the cloth in the basin to wet it again before replacing it on her forehead. Xian-Li, for her part, drifted in and out of sleep. When she woke, Arthur offered her some more honey water, which she accepted, but rarely took more than a sip or two before laying her head back down.

'Do you hurt anywhere?' he asked her once after she had drunk a little.

'My neck is sore,' she said, her voice a dry rasp. 'On the inside.'

'Your throat, you mean,' corrected Arthur.

'Yes.'

'When Khepri comes back I will ask him for something to help.'

She offered him a weak smile. 'I am sorry, husband. I have disappointed you.'

'Never!' protested Arthur. 'I love you, Xian-Li. You could never disappoint me.'

She slept through the rest of the morning. Khepri the physician returned at midday and made up a mixture of honey and spices, thinned with a little almond milk, to ease the pain in her throat and make swallowing more comfortable. He noted that the fever had not eased, nor had it abated by late afternoon when he came back with his father – also a physician – to seek his wisdom and advice.

Arthur stood by as they held close conference with one another; he watched the two men nodding as they whispered back and forth on their stools. The elder man lifted Xian-Li's unresisting hand and held it for a moment before replacing it on her breast. They talked some more, and then Khepri rose and came outside to where Arthur and Anen were hovering at the door.

'It is our opinion that tainted food is not the cause of this illness,' he said.

'No?' said Anen. 'What then – can you tell?'

'My father has seen this before,' replied the physician. 'It is a fever which commonly afflicts children.'

'I see,' said Arthur. 'What can be done about it?'

'It gives me no pleasure to tell you, my masters, but there is no cure. I am sorry.'

'We just let nature take its course?' asked Arthur. 'Is there nothing else we can do?'

'We will make her comfortable and pray that recovery is in the will of the gods for this soul.' The physician, his dark eyes full of sympathy, put a hand on Arthur's shoulder. 'I am sorry.'

At a sign from Anen, the doctor returned to his patient. 'Come with me, my friend,' said the priest, 'and let us eat something.'

'I could not eat a thing,' sighed Arthur. 'I think I should stay here.'

'We have a long night ahead of us. I will have food brought here.'

A short while later, Anen returned with a company of priests bearing bowls of food, which they arranged on a low table with seating mats spread on either side. 'I have ordered a sacrifice to be made in the temple for the return of health,' Anen told him. 'They will perform the ceremony at the rising of the moon.'

'Thank you,' said Arthur.

They ate a silent meal together, Arthur picking at his food and watching the darkened door expectantly. Evening deepened around them, the stars kindling in the wide black expanse above. When it grew too dark to see, two young temple acolytes came with torches in iron stands; they placed one at the table and on either side of the door of the guest house, and then withdrew.

Night drew on. Occasionally, one physician or the other came to the table for refreshment; Arthur went now and again to sit at his wife's side. She slept the restless, troubled sleep of the sick, and though Arthur dutifully bathed her face and neck and feet with the cool water, it no longer seemed to bring her burning body any comfort.

As midnight approached, Xian-Li began to lapse in and out of consciousness. She moaned and murmured in increasingly fretful sleep, sometimes calling out, the words garbled and indistinct. Then, suddenly, she would wake and struggle to rise, fearful, no longer knowing where she was. Arthur did his best to calm her and soothe her restless spirit, all the time fighting his own growing fears.

The physicians, meanwhile, tried to get her to drink and continually refreshed the damp cloths. The last time she was able to drink, she vomited it all back up, and from then on could not be induced to take any more water. As the terrible night wore on, she began to sweat and shake with chills – so violently that once Khepri held her jaws together with his hands lest she shatter her teeth.

Gradually, the shaking grew less strenuous, which Arthur took as a good sign. But Khepri said, 'Her strength is failing. The fire inside is consuming her.'

Arthur could but look on in helpless anguish as his young wife's breathing grew ever more shallow and erratic. The sweating stopped. Her chest rose once and fell. Between one breath and the next, Xian-Li, her life devoured by the fever, expired. She was gone.

It took a moment for Arthur to realize what had happened, and even then he could not grasp the awful finality of it. The end had come so quickly and, right up until the moment she died, he had been certain she would pass the crisis. He had not had time to prepare for the possibility that she might not survive. Uncomprehending, he simply sat and stared at her body as the lines of tension in her face and limbs eased and she relaxed into death.

A few moments passed, and then the two physicians bent over the body and began to unfold a linen cloth to cover the corpse.

'No,' murmured Arthur. 'Leave her be.'

Khepri nodded to his father, who extended his palm in a gesture of respect and backed from the room. 'I am sorry,' Khepri said. 'It was the will of the gods. There was nothing to be done.'

'What?' Arthur roused himself. 'What did you say?'

'We were powerless before the mighty will of the gods.' He glanced with sadness at the still body. 'If you wish, I will begin making the arrangements for her embalming. It is best done quickly.'

'No,' Arthur said, shaking his head. 'Thank you, Khepri, but no. I will make my own arrangements.'

'As you will, master.'

Anen came in then and, seeing what he had already been told had taken place, he embraced his friend and expressed his sorrow. Then, spreading his hands over the body, he intoned a chant for the dead. Arthur listened, unable to make anything of it. When the priest finished, he turned and asked, 'If you wish, I will have the body prepared for its journey into the afterlife.'

'How long until the sun rises?' asked Arthur.

'Not long. The night is far gone.'

Arthur turned and rushed into the courtyard. Cupping his hands to his eyes to shut out the light of the torches, he quickly scanned the heavens. From among the billions of bright pinpricks of light he located the one he hoped to see: a star of piercing intensity, easily the brightest light in the heavens.

'Then we must hurry. There is not much time,' he said, rushing back into the guest house. Bending over the pallet, he gathered the still-warm body into his arms.

'What will you do?' asked the priest.

'I'm taking her to reclaim her life.'

Anen opened his mouth to protest. 'But –'

'Please,' said Arthur, cutting him off, 'I must be at the ley before sunrise.'

Anen saw from the set of his jaw that it was no use arguing. 'What do you require?'

'Your chariot – is it still here?'

'I will order another.'

While the priest went to fetch the vehicle, Arthur wrapped the body of his wife in the linen cloth Khepri had left for him. Then, when he heard the sound of the horses in the courtyard, he gathered up Xian-Li's body and walked out. Together, they laid the corpse on the floor of the chariot and Arthur started to climb up.

'Have you ever commanded such as this?'

Arthur admitted that he had not.

'Then allow me,' said Anen, taking the reins from his friend's hands. 'Stand behind me and hold tight.'

Arthur took his place in the chariot and they rolled out into the darkened street and were soon on the road leading out of the city. By the time they reached their destination, the sky was already pearling in the east. Wasting not a moment, they lifted Xian-Li's body and arranged it so that Arthur could carry it more easily.

As the first golden rays of the newborn sun struck the unnaturally straight path, Arthur started walking.

'Where will you go?' Anen called after him.

'There is a place beyond that star,' Arthur replied, indicating the solitary star still ablaze in the fast-fading sky. 'If Xian-Li can be healed anywhere, it will be there – at the Well of Souls.'

CHAPTER 34

In Which a Tour Guide is Engaged

'It has happened!' cried Lady Fayth. 'We have made –'

The leap-induced nausea overtook her before she could finish. Turning away quickly, she bent over and vomited politely. Though he felt sorry for her, Kit did admire her form. Giles was also affected; the sturdy coachman swayed on his feet and then crumpled onto hands and knees, emptying the contents of his stomach into the dust at the side of the road.

'Don't try to fight it,' said Kit, sounding like a veteran of the wars. 'Just breathe deeply through your nose and let it wash over you.'

This well-meant advice met with a cool reception from Lady Fayth. 'You knave!' she muttered as soon as she could speak again. She dabbed her mouth with the back of her hand. 'You knew full well it would make us sick.'

'Well, yes, unfortunately it does rather –'

'You might have warned us.'

'I thought I did,' replied Kit lamely. 'Did I not?'

'You most certainly did not,' she fumed. 'I would have remembered such a salient fact.'

'Then I do most heartily apologize, my lady,' replied Kit stiffly. 'It is in the nature of the leap, I'm afraid. It does monkey with your internal navigation system.'

She glared at him. 'What are you babbling about?'

'It makes you feel seasick,' he explained. 'But the feeling passes quickly, and you do seem to get used to it eventually. I feel quite normal, you see?'

'How pleasant for you,' she sniffed. Turning her eyes away from Kit, whom she held to be the source of her discomfort, she took in the sight of the sphinxes. 'Heavens!' she gasped. 'Where are we?'

'Egypt somewhere, I reckon,' answered Kit. He looked to Giles, who was still kneeling in the dust. 'How are you feeling?'

The servant nodded and rose unsteadily to his feet, his skin a pale, waxy hue. 'Better,' he said without conviction.

Kit quickly scanned their surroundings. A more desolate landscape he could not have imagined: not a blade or twig of anything green to be seen; nothing but empty sky above and dusty barren rock-crusted hills all around. There was no one about, and nothing that looked like human habitation of any kind – except, at the end of the sphinx-lined avenue, the immense black rectangle of a doorway carved into the side of the dun-coloured hill at the end of the long corridor of statues.

'It looks like a temple or necropolis or something,' observed Kit. 'If Cosimo and Sir Henry came here, they might have taken shelter there. I say we go and investigate – see if we can find out anything.'

Shouldering the bundles containing their provisions and weapons, the three started towards the temple, walking between the paws of the couched sphinxes whose stone faces gazed on with remote and imperturbable dignity. Some of the statues had hieroglyphs on their pedestals, and some had clearly suffered wear and tear from sandstorms and the simple ravages of time – cracks and fissures in the stone, damaged feet or faces – but most were in fairly good condition.

They proceeded along the broken road, alert to any sound or movement around them. The early morning breeze, though still cool, held the threat of heat to come. From somewhere high above, the lonely cry of a scavenging buzzard drifted down. Closer, they saw that the temple entrance rose on tiered platforms which formed low steps leading up to a massive door guarded by two enormous statues – one of a man in a tall plumed headdress holding an ankh in his hand, the other of a man in the striped headdress and heavily ornamented kilt of a pharaoh. Daunted by the yawning emptiness of the entrance and its giant guardians, they paused at the foot of the steps. 'Shall we?' said Kit.

'I think it only right that you go in first,' suggested Lady Fayth.

'Sure.' He mounted the steps to the doorway and tried to peer into the dark interior of the temple. 'Hello?' he called. 'Anyone there?'

No reply.

'Hello?' he called again. 'Anyone?'

His voice reverberated through the empty interior and died away in the dark recesses of the rock-hewn edifice.

'It's safe,' he said, motioning for the others to join him. 'There's no one here. We have the place to ourselves.'

Kit entered the temple. The air was dry and cool, the light dim. The roof had been pierced in places, allowing shafts of sunlight to penetrate the interior darkness and illuminate a veritable forest of stone pillars. In one of these rectangular pools of light a crude table had been set up using bricks from the temple and a piece of old planking. Dusty rugs lay in a heap beside the table. The base of the nearest pillar was black with soot where fires had been lit. 'Somebody has been here.'

'More than one somebody, I would say,' Giles added, pointing to an array of footprints in the dust on the floor. 'And perhaps not all that long ago.'

'There are all sizes here.' Kit bent down for a closer look. Most prints bore the marks of a simple shoe without heels – a sandal, most likely – and some were barefoot. Many were scuffed and overtrod, suggesting people milling about. He straightened again and looked around. 'Sir Henry and Cosimo might have been here as well, but there's no way to tell for sure.'

'Whether they *were* here or not is irrelevant,' Lady Fayth pointed out. 'They are not here now.' She turned in a slow circle, letting her eyes sweep the dim, cavernous interior. 'And there is nothing else of interest.'

'Then we continue the search.' Kit turned and walked back to the doorway and out onto the steps. 'Maybe we should leave the bags here while we have a look around.' He glanced at Giles, who was shaking his head. 'No?'

Kit followed the coachman's gaze and saw, coming towards them along the avenue of sphinxes, a travelling company made up of at least eight camels surrounded by a small army of people on donkeys and on foot. 'Oh,' said Kit. 'It looks like we've got company.'

'A genuine Egyptian caravan!' gushed Lady Fayth. 'How truly exciting!'

They waited and watched as the parade drew closer and it became clear that the group was coming to the temple and that it was, to Lady Fayth's disappointment, not an exotic desert caravan at all, but a pack of tourists; the Egyptians among them were guides and beggars. The lead camel stopped a few dozen yards from the entrance and the camel drivers made their beasts kneel so that the visitors could dismount. The newcomers were outfitted for a day's adventure: dressed in elaborate khaki desert gear with multi-pocket jackets and loose trousers stuffed into tall boots. The men wore pith helmets and carried riding crops, and the ladies wore wide-brimmed hats held in place by gauzy scarves, and carried fly swatters. The Egyptians wore simple white robes and double-strapped sandals; a few sported chequered turbans.

'By Jove!' shouted one of the men, throwing his leg over the crown of the saddle and sliding to the ground. 'It is magnificent! Someone get a photo of me at the doorway, what!'

'Tourists all right,' said Kit. At Lady Fayth's uncomprehending glance, he added, 'Travellers – they have come to see the temple.'

'Whoever they are,' she observed, 'they speak something very like English.'

'True,' replied Kit. 'Wait here, both of you. I'm going to talk to them.' He started towards the man who seemed to be the leader of the group. 'Hello!' he called, giving the fellow a wave. 'Hello! May I ask where you have come from?'

The man turned and saw the three travellers for the first time. 'Upon my word!' he exclaimed. 'You're here awfully early. I say! They told us we'd have the place to ourselves.'

'Yes, well, we wanted to get here early – before it got too hot, you see.'

'Yes, quite,' replied the man, squinting up at the sun. 'We've come from the Queen Hatshepsut.' Seeing Kit's puzzled frown, he added, 'It's a boat. On the Nile? Just over those hills back there.' The man gestured vaguely behind him. 'And you? I didn't see any other boats at the mooring last night.'

'No, we're on foot.' Kit regarded the tatterlings beginning to swarm around them.

'Ah! Roughing it, what?'

'Something like that,' Kit admitted. 'We were hoping –'

Before Kit could finish, he was mobbed by a gang of urchins – barefoot, half-naked beggar children, all of them clamouring to be heard above the others, grabbing at his shirtsleeves and shouting, 'Mister! Mister! You English, mister? You English? You have shillings, mister? Shillings!'

'Sorry, no,' said Kit. 'No – no shillings. Sorry.'

'Shillings, mister! You have shillings! Give, mister. Give.'

'I don't have any shillings,' Kit said, more forcefully this time. 'No shillings.' A dozen small hands snatched at his sleeves and trousers; small fingers wormed into his pockets. He raised his arms out of their reach and stepped back. 'Look, I don't have any money, see? No money. No shillings!'

'Give, please. Mister, give!'

'Looks like you've had it, mate!' called the tour leader. Chuckling, he walked back to join his group, who had dismounted and were moving towards the temple. 'You'll have to give them something to get rid of them.'

'Thanks for your help,' called Kit, still trying to extricate himself from the clutches of the insistent young vagabonds. His efforts aroused the attention of some older boys with donkeys; they rode their diminutive animals into the besieging horde, clicking their tongues and swatting their rivals with switches made from palm branches. 'Mister! You ride donkey! We take you! Ride, mister!'

'No! I don't want a donkey ride,' said Kit, backing away.

'What are you doing?' asked Lady Fayth, stepping up beside him.

'I've got a little tangled up here,' he said. 'But I'm working on it.'

'Pray, do not farce about. Ask them if they have seen Cosimo and Uncle Henry,' she suggested.

'I was just about to do that,' replied Kit. 'There probably isn't much that happens around here that they don't know about.'

'Well?' she demanded, swatting away the hands that were trying to find their way into her pockets.

'Excuse me!' shouted Kit. 'Excuse me! We are looking for two Englishmen. Two English – big men. Has anyone seen English men?'

Though his repeated inquiries appeared to have no effect on the bawling horde, one of the donkey boys left the pack and returned a moment later with one of the camel drivers. 'You English?' called the driver. 'You look for men?'

'Yes,' Kit answered, hurrying to meet him. His noisy entourage moved with him. 'Two Englishmen. They came here a few days ago. Did you see them?'

The camel driver waded into the throng and, with a few words and a flick of his camel whip here and there, instantly scattered the begging children. They ran to catch up with the tour group just now entering the temple. 'Old men,' said the Egyptian.

'Yes,' confirmed Kit. 'Old men – two of them. One was a big man, tall, with wavy white hair.' He rippled his fingers over his head to demonstrate. 'The other had reddish hair and a pointed beard.' His fingers made the sign of a beard at his chin. 'They were wearing dark clothes – black coats.' He patted his own shirt and breeches. 'Did you see them?'

'Yes. Them I see.'

'Do you know where they went? Can you show us where they went?'

'Why you want knowing this?'

'They are our friends. We were meant to meet them here.'

'They are bad men,' said the camel driver, and spat.

'No,' countered Kit quickly. 'No, please – they are good men. But they may be in trouble. Bad men were following them. We have come to help.'

298

The Egyptian considered this, his crinkled eyes examining Kit and his companions. 'I take you.'

Turning to Lady Fayth and Giles, Kit shouted, 'He has seen them. He says he'll take us to them.'

'Fifty dirhams,' added the driver.

'Ah, yes,' said Kit. 'Wait here.' Returning to his companions, he said, 'I need some coins – a few crowns should do it.'

'Sir Henry and Cosimo – the fellow knows where they are?' said Giles as he stooped to remove a satchel from the bundle he carried. 'He has seen them?'

'And he'll take us to them?' questioned Lady Fayth.

'That's what he says,' replied Kit. Taking the purse from Giles's hand, he opened it and poured out a handful of coins, took up two of the larger silver ones and passed back the rest. 'This should do it.'

He crossed to the camel driver, and held up the two coins. 'This one to take us to find our friends,' said Kit, handing the coin to the driver. 'And this one when we have found them.' He returned the second coin to his pocket. 'Agreed?'

The Egyptian whipped the coin out of sight into a fold in his kaftan, and made a little bow. 'I am Yusuf,' he said. 'We go now.' He turned and started towards the line of kneeling camels.

Kit called to the others, 'Come on! He's taking us now.'

They shouldered their bundles and hurried to join their guide and were soon clambering up onto the awkwardly sloping backs of three camels. Yusuf commandeered a donkey from one of the lads and without so much as a backward glance, they were soon jolting off along the avenue of sphinxes and into the desert. Of the three travellers, Giles most quickly mastered the odd swinging, lurching gait of their long-legged mounts, and Lady Fayth soon caught the knack; Kit, however, could not quite adjust to the jerky, undulating sway and resigned himself to an uncomfortable – and very smelly – ride. The camels, all but silent on their flat, padded feet, passed along a low rise of dust-coloured hills; away to the west, tawny dunes of sand undulated like the waves of a stationary sea.

The sun rose higher, growing steadily hotter beneath a cloudless sky. The line of hills stretched into the distance, disappearing into the silver shimmer of the burgeoning heat haze. It was not long before Kit began wishing he'd thought to bring a hat – and a canteen filled with something cool and refreshing. It was an unfortunate thought, because once it had entered his head, it quickly passed from idle fancy into fixation. The more he thought about it, the more it grew to occupy his mind, filling it and driving out all other thoughts. He began to feel as if his mouth was stuffed with cotton and his throat was made of tree bark; his vision became rimmed and distorted as if he were peering through cheap binoculars.

'Sir?' Kit became aware of someone calling him. 'Kit, sir?'

He turned his head to see that Giles had reined up beside him. 'Hmm?'

'Are you well, sir?'

'I'm fine.' Kit swallowed. 'A little thirsty is all.'

'I fear, sir, that we forgot to bring any water.'

'I know. We'll just have to wait.' Urging his mount forward, he came abreast of their guide. 'Is it much further?' he asked.

The swarthy Egyptian pointed to the rock-rimmed hills. 'There,' he said. 'Not far.'

Turning around on his saddle, Kit called back to Giles and Lady Fayth, 'He says we're almost there.'

Lady Fayth, shielding her face with her hand, nodded grimly.

They rode on a little longer, and then, quite unexpectedly, turned towards the same shattered hills the guide had indicated. As they approached the base of the nearest hill, they saw what appeared to be little more than a crease open out onto the desert. Yusuf turned into the crevice and, riding single file, they proceeded into a channel between two sheer rock walls – a wadi cut into the soft stone by the abundant rains of a much younger world. The air was dead still inside the wadi, but at least the high walls afforded some shade; it was cooler at the bottom of the gulch and Kit felt himself revive. They came to a place where the gap between the walls widened and here their guide halted. 'We leave the animals,' he said. 'We walk from here.'

Kit wasted not an instant scrambling down from his disagreeable perch, and hurried to their guide. 'We need some water,' he said.

'There is a well,' replied Yusuf. 'I take you.'

After securing the beasts, they gathered their gear and started down the wadi, soon arriving at a place where the walls flattened slightly and there, in a fissure at the base of one wall, a deep pit had been hollowed in the solid rock; the pit was covered by a stone which, after it had been removed, revealed the end of a rope of braided hemp. Yusuf pulled on the rope and up came a leather bucket dripping with water. The liquid was tepid, but fresh enough, and they all slaked their thirst. Kit was last to drink. 'Everyone okay?' he asked, passing the bucket back to their guide. He thanked him and asked, 'How much further?'

'We walk a little,' replied Yusuf. Taking a water skin from one of the camels, he filled and passed it to Kit. 'This way.'

They followed the gently meandering course of the ancient gully as it cut deeper into the arid hills. The sheer walls of banded rock soared on either side; sometimes their tops were so high they could not be seen from the bottom. They passed beneath low overhangs and around long curving bends – so many that Kit lost count – until Yusuf finally stopped and said in a low voice, 'We must climb.' The three looked around; they were standing at a crossroads of sorts where a smaller branch joined the larger. The walls here were lower, and much eroded. In looking at the broken walls, they saw that a set of narrow steps had been carved into the rock face on one side. Yusuf started up, gesturing for the others to follow.

They reached the top and proceeded overland along a crumbling goat track which ran along the edge of the wadi. Yusuf led them to a spindly acacia tree and stopped. 'They are down there,' he said, indicating the wadi floor. 'I stop here.' He held out his hand for his second coin.

'We thank you, Yusuf. If we have need of your camels again, I will look for you.'

'*Sala'am aleikem*,' said Yusuf, turning to go. The Egyptian paused, then glancing back over his shoulder added, 'Be careful, my friends. They are bad men.'

'Do you know how many are down there?'

Yusuf thought for a moment, then held up four fingers. 'May Allah the Merciful be with you,' he said as he hurried away.

Giles glanced around the barren cliff top, then turned to Kit. 'What would you do now, sir?' he asked, unslinging his bundle.

'Let's have a look down there and see what we can see,' suggested Kit. 'Stay out of sight and keep quiet.'

'If you please,' remarked Lady Fayth, 'we are *not* children. Kindly refrain from treating us so.'

'Sorry.' Kit turned towards the gaping crevasse of the wadi. 'Let's take a look.'

They moved to the edge of the cliff, crawling the last few feet on hands and knees, and then squirming on their stomachs to peer down onto the wadi floor fifty or sixty feet below, where to their wondering eyes appeared the chiselled statues of Thoth and Horus standing either side of a doorway cut into the solid rock of the canyon wall facing them. Another branch of the wadi angled off to the left and right and the junction of these branches formed a broad triangle; in times past, the ancients had filled the walls with niches, hundreds of little nooks carved into the sandstone. 'There's a temple or something down there,' observed Kit softly. Even as he spoke, a man in a long white kaftan wandered into view. He paused in the open area in front of the temple and looked around, casting his gaze up the three separate canyon branches in turn – almost as if he knew someone was watching him. Discovering nothing out of the ordinary, however, he called out to an unseen companion and then moved on.

The three rescuers continued to watch, but nothing more happened so, with the sun scalding their unprotected heads, they edged back from the overlook and returned to their bundled provisions and weapons. 'Well, I suppose if it is to be four against two' – Kit said, then hastily corrected himself – 'four against three, I mean, then I suggest we make our move tonight.'

'When everyone is asleep,' said Lady Fayth approvingly. 'Very shrewd.'

'I've watched a lot of movies,' muttered Kit.

'Sir?' wondered Giles. He and Lady Fayth exchanged a puzzled look.

'I'll explain later,' Kit said, looking around. The brave little acacia provided the only shade to be seen atop the overlook; it would be close quarters, but better than nothing. 'It's getting pretty hot out here. I suggest we get out of the sun and try to keep cool.'

'And then?' asked Lady Fayth.

'We wait.'

CHAPTER 35

In Which an Alliance of Consequence is Formed

The long hot day passed. As the blistering sun sailed high overhead, Giles passed around the water skin, then opened the bundle of provisions and made a meal of apples and barley bread. As they ate, Kit dug out Sir Henry's green book. He unwrapped it and, after orienting himself anew to the tight-crabbed script, began to read. 'This is interesting!' he announced, laying aside his apple.

When nothing more seemed forthcoming, Lady Fayth said, 'Pray, do you intend sharing what has so obviously piqued your interest?'

Kit thumbed back a page in the little book. 'Listen to this,' he said, and began to read aloud. 'Sir Henry writes, "I hold two precepts absolute: That the universe was created to allow Providence its expression, and therefore nothing happens beyond its purview."' He glanced up to see his audience wholly puzzled by this nugget. 'Wait, there's more. "Secondly, all was made for the benefit of each: man, woman, child, and beast, down to the curve of every wave, and the flight of the lowliest insect. For, if there be such a thing as Providence, then everything is providential, and every act of Providence is a special providence."' He looked up again. 'Do you see?'

'A curious musing, perhaps,' conceded Lady Fayth. 'Yet I fail to see that it has anything to do with the particular undertaking before us. Does it?'

'Well,' allowed Kit, 'not at the moment maybe. But see here –'

He turned the book towards her. 'What is it that he's scribbled in the margin?'

Lady Fayth bent her head to the text and squinted at the smudgy words Kit's finger marked. 'If I am not mistaken, it says, "No Coincidence Under Heaven."'

Kit pointed to another annotation. 'And this one?'

'Providence not coincidence,' replied Lady Fayth, glancing up again.

'No coincidence,' echoed Kit. 'I think he's trying to say that nothing happens that Providence does not permit.' Kit frowned, and amended the thought immediately. 'No, I mean — nothing happens that Providence cannot use to express itself.'

'Or,' volunteered Giles, 'nothing happens that Providence cannot use for the benefit of all things.'

'It is a fascinating notion, to be sure,' agreed Lady Fayth doubtfully. 'Do you believe it?'

Kit thought for a moment. 'I don't know. But Sir Henry seems to.'

Just then, a loud popping sound came echoing up from the canyon basin; it was followed by the rumbling growl of a combustion engine. 'Whatever is that?' said Lady Fayth, looking towards the canyon.

'It is a motor,' Kit explained, wrapping the book and tucking it back into his pocket. 'A machine that powers things. My guess is it's either a vehicle engine or a generator.'

They moved to the cliff top and gazed down. The engine rumbled on, growing louder, filling the wadi with its rough growl. A moment later, an ancient flatbed truck swung into view and the vehicle proceeded slowly down the wadi, trailing thick white plumes of smoke. 'We're in luck,' observed Kit. 'They're leaving.'

'What is it?' asked Giles, pointing to the truck rattling out of sight along the gully floor.

'I guess you'd call it a horseless carriage,' Kit told him. 'The motor powers it.'

'And a very disagreeable machine it is,' remarked Lady Fayth, holding her nose as the diesel fumes reached them. 'Most unnatural.'

'You have no idea,' said Kit.

They watched a while longer, but all remained quiet. 'Do you think they have gone?' asked Giles.

'Maybe,' allowed Kit. 'There is only one way to find out.' He stood. 'Let's go down.'

'Have you ever used a pistol?' asked Lady Fayth, brushing dust from her clothes and hands.

'No,' admitted Kit, with a shake of his head.

'Then *I* shall take the pistol,' she decided. 'You and Giles will do better with the cutlasses – if it should come to that.'

'Fine,' agreed Kit. 'Cutlasses it is.'

Giles opened the bundle and handed out the weapons. Kit gripped the hilt of the sword; fully as long as his arm, the slightly curved, tapering blade was somewhat heavier than he expected, but well balanced and reasonably sharp. After a few practice swipes, he felt suitably armed and dangerous. 'Ready?' The others nodded. 'Right. Stay alert and keep quiet. Here we go.'

They started down the broken staircase, picking their way among the rocks one step at a time, as silently as possible. Upon reaching the wadi floor, they stopped and crouched, waiting to see if they had been heard or observed. All was calm and silent. 'So far, so good,' Kit whispered. 'This way.'

They moved quickly to the temple, darting into the entrance so as not to be seen in the open. The interior, illuminated only by the light coming in from the doorway, revealed a simple square hollowed from the living rock. A stone ledge three feet off the floor ran around the perimeter of the room which, save for the sand that had drifted into the corners, was empty. Turning back towards the doorway, they looked both ways down the two connecting branches of the wadi. To the right a lean-to hut of rough timber had been constructed against the canyon wall and, beside it, a large tent; to the left, there was nothing but a series of door-sized niches carved into the rock – three of them, each a few yards from the next.

'Which way?' asked Kit. 'Right or left?'

'The fellow we saw earlier went that way,' suggested Giles, indicating the tent on the right. 'We might try the other way first.'

'Sounds good to me,' agreed Kit. 'Stay close.'

Leaving the temple entrance, the three flitted along the wall towards the first niche. 'Wait here,' said Kit. 'And keep a sharp look out.' He crept to the doorway and paused, listened, then ducked inside. An overpowering smell of diesel fumes in the close confines of the small chamber made him gasp. He could just about make out the black boxy shape of a generator, but nothing else.

'Not in there,' Kit reported when he stepped out again. 'Let's try the next one.'

As before he positioned his watchers either side of the doorway and then ducked into the rock-cut chamber; this one was slightly larger than the first and, from what Kit could make out, seemed to be filled with crates and casks and boxes. 'It's a storage room,' he reported, then motioned the others to follow him to the third doorway. A swift inspection revealed that the last chamber was filled with oil drums. 'Another storage room,' Kit said. 'That's it for this side.' He turned with some reluctance towards the tent. 'I guess we look there next.'

'There may be something down there.' Lady Fayth pointed further along the wadi.

Kit looked where she indicated and saw another opening thirty or so yards away and all but hidden in a fold in the smooth canyon wall. Smaller than the others, and narrower, Kit had mistaken it for a shadow. Lady Fayth was already starting for the place. Kit overtook her and hurried to the low doorway. 'Fourth time lucky,' he said and, stepping in, almost broke his neck when he lost his footing and plunged down a steep flight of stairs. The cutlass spun from his grasp and clattered down the stone steps with him.

The sound of his fall echoed up from the hollow chamber below. 'What happened?' asked Lady Fayth in a strained whisper.

'Careful!' replied Kit, his voice echoing in the empty chamber. 'There are some steps.'

'Are you injured, sir?' asked Giles. 'Shall I come down?'

'No, I'm all right. Just stay put,' answered Kit. 'There's another room down here.'

Light from the doorway above flowed down into the chamber, illuminating a small vestibule and revealing a doorway to a narrow connecting tunnel. Kit started forward; his foot struck the cutlass and sent it rattling across the floor. A voice rasped out of the darkness from the unseen room beyond. 'This is horrific! You must release me at once.'

Kit recognized the voice immediately. 'Sir Henry – it's me.'

'Kit?'

'We've come to rescue you.' He retrieved the cutlass and moved to the doorway. He had just put his foot on the low step when there came a shout from outside, followed by the sharp report of a pistol.

'Oh, great!' Kit muttered, already racing for the steps. 'Hold on,' he called behind him. 'I'll be back.'

Kit leapt up the stairs and scrambled out into the wadi where Giles was grappling with two attackers: Burley Men. Kit managed to be surprised by what was merely inevitable – that the Burley Men would always appear at the worst possible moment. Although dressed in light-coloured Arab garb – kaftans and kaffiyehs instead of their customary black coats, tall boots, and wide-brimmed hats – there was no mistake; Kit had seen them before. Giles seemed to be holding his own, so Kit turned his attention to the third attacker who was struggling to hold on to a very angry and animated Lady Fayth. Drawing a deep breath, Kit launched himself at the fellow's back. Gripping the cutlass with both hands, he raised it and brought the knob of the hilt down on the man's head. The rogue gave out a yelp and released Lady Fayth. Shaking herself from his grasp, she spun around, raking at his face with her fingernails while Kit, with a well-aimed kick, lashed out at his knees. The Burley Man's legs folded under him and he went down in a hail of blows from Lady Fayth's fists.

Kit rushed to Giles's aid. He closed on the nearest of the two clinging to the coachman's arms. 'Stop!' he shouted. 'Let him go!'

The brute half-turned to meet this new threat and Kit thrust the point of the cutlass at his unprotected chest – stopping just short of piercing the skin. The attacker growled and made an ill-judged swipe at the blade. Kit held firm. 'I said stop!' he shouted, driving the man back onto his heels with the point of the rusty blade.

'Tav!' cried the Burley Man. 'Over here!'

Kit gave another jab with the point of the blade and the man fell over backwards. In the same instant, Giles swung his free hand into the face of the thug still clinging to his arm, connecting with a satisfying crunch of bone on gristle. 'Agh!' shrieked the man, staggering back, both hands clutching his nose as blood gushed down the front of his kaftan.

Lady Fayth screamed and Kit turned to see her attacker on the ground, clutching her ankle as she swiped at him with the butt of the pistol. He raced back to her side, reaching her just as the Burley Man succeeded in toppling her. Kit caught her as she fell, taking her weight. Momentarily unbalanced, Kit felt his own foot clasped and yanked from under him. He sat down hard, loosening his grip on the cutlass as he crashed onto his rump. Lady Fayth fell on top of him and, as they lay in a tangled heap, Kit felt his weapon wrenched from his grasp. He made a wild grab, snagged the hilt, and hung on. 'Giles!' he cried. 'Help!'

With his free hand, Kit punched at his attacker and succeeded in landing a solid blow in the man's gut. He felt the blade loosen and, with a mighty heave, pulled the cutlass from the Burley Man's grasp. The rogue roared and smashed him in the eye with an elbow.

Kit, his eyes watering, clutched the cutlass hilt and rolled away. He pushed himself up and tried to rise – only to be met with a boot in the ribs. Unable to breathe now, he tried to squirm away. He heard Lady Fayth scream again, and swung blindly at his attacker with the cutlass, making a wide sweep of his arm, driving his assailant back. But before he could swing the blade again, the resounding crack of a rifle shot exploded in the canyon, and a chunk of rock above his head shattered, sending splinters and dust over him. Instinctively, Kit ducked; and even as he turned in the direction of the shot, a second, gut clenching sound rumbled through the wadi: the feral growl of a very large and angry cat.

Two more Burley Men in Arab dress were standing before the temple. One was tall and lank with a white kaffiyeh, the other thickset and bareheaded; the tall one held a rifle, and his muscular companion grasped the iron chain linked to the cave lion's heavy collar. The beast itself strained forward, the hair across its shoulders raised in bristling spikes, its mouth open, tongue lolling as it watched the newcomers with its pale yellow eyes. Giles and Lady Fayth, startled by the sight of the beast as much as by the rifle shot, ceased struggling. All grew deathly still.

'That's right,' said the man with the rifle, striding towards them. 'Everybody calm down now before someone gets hurt. Baby hasn't eaten today and she's getting a little restless. You there,' he waved the rifle barrel at Kit, 'put down that blade – nice and slow. We don't want you to cut yourself. There's not a doctor within a hundred miles of this place.'

'Who are you?' Kit demanded.

'I'm the man with the rifle. Now, do as you are told, and put down the sword.' Kit obeyed. 'Good. Kick it aside.'

'You won't get away with this.' Kit gave the blade a shove with his foot.

'No?' The man moved towards him. 'I think you'll find I already have.'

'Rogue!' spat Lady Fayth. 'You, sir, are a low criminal.'

'Oh, I am much more than that, my darling.' He gestured to his henchmen to seize and bring the others. 'Con, Dex – take 'em.'

Giles and Lady Fayth were seized by Burley Men. 'What do you ruffians intend doing to us?' Lady Fayth demanded.

'That ain't for us to say,' replied the one called Con. 'Lord Burleigh'll decide when he gets back.'

'Put 'em below,' said Tav. He gestured with the rifle barrel for Kit to join his companions. The would-be rescuers were taken to the low doorway of the underground chamber and shoved down the narrow stone steps.

'We've brought you some company, yer lordship,' announced Tav, his voice ringing loud in the stone chamber. 'I would offer to introduce you, but I think you all know one another.' He gave Kit a nudge with the muzzle of the rifle. 'Get on with you. Straight through there.'

Kit stepped through the short tunnel-like entrance into another, slightly larger chamber, the end of which was covered by a heavy iron grate door. Sir Henry shuffled into view behind the bars of his prison.

'Phew! It stinks something terrible down here!' said Tav.

'You devil,' spat the nobleman. 'Let them go. They have nothing to do with any of this. They know nothing of value to you.'

'With respect,' countered Tav, 'I do most heartily disagree.' To the one called Con, he said, 'Lock 'em up.'

A key was produced and the grate unlocked. Giles, Kit, and Lady Fayth were shoved roughly through the door and into the rock-hewn chamber to be instantly assailed by the sickly sweet stench of ripe death – a stink so strong it made them cough and gag. The room was bare, save for the bottom half of a large stone sarcophagus and walls covered with bright-coloured panels of almost life-sized paintings – most featuring a shaven-headed Egyptian in a kilt and ornate breastplate. Every inch of the room was painted – even the ceiling: a sea of blazing blue full of white stars.

Sir Henry opened his arms to embrace his niece. 'Haven, are you well? Have they mistreated you?' This minor exertion appeared to exhaust him; he staggered backwards and collapsed in a fit of coughing.

'Uncle!' she cried, rushing to his side. 'Here, let me help you. Do not speak.' To Giles she said, 'Is there water? Hurry! He's choking.'

Sir Henry raised a shaking hand to stroke his niece's cheek. 'You should not have come,' he said and coughed again, and Kit heard the deep rattle in his lungs.

Giles found a jar and bowl in one corner; he filled the bowl and brought it to his master.

'Drink a little,' said Lady Fayth, taking the bowl and raising it to Sir Henry's lips. He took a sip then slumped back against the chamber wall. 'What has happened here?' she asked.

'Where is Cosimo?' asked Kit, already knowing, and fearing, the answer.

Sir Henry, his skin pale and waxy, stretched out his hand and pointed to the sarcophagus in the centre of the room. Kit rose and stepped to the open stone coffin, dread making his heart thud; he looked inside to see the body of his great-grandfather, flesh pale and bloodless, eyes closed, hands folded across his still breast. Kit tried to speak, but his voice faltered. Giles stepped beside him and peered into the sarcophagus with him. Both men drew back as the noxious perfume of death rose from the corpse; their eyes watered and their stomachs squirmed.

'I am sorry,' rasped Sir Henry. 'He died in the night.' The words set off another fit of coughing, worse than the first. 'The rogues put him in there...' He gulped air, and continued, '... terrible thing. I must soon follow him.'

'We are here now, Uncle,' said Lady Fayth. 'We will help you.'

'No, no.' Sick sweat beaded on Sir Henry's forehead. 'Listen to me,' he said, his voice little more than a whisper. 'I have much to tell you.'

Kit, sick at heart and woozy with the smell, staggered back from the sarcophagus and marshalled his scattered faculties to listen to what Sir Henry was trying to say. 'Do not stay here,' he whispered. 'Use any means to get away... something in the air...' He coughed, and Lady Fayth helped him take another sip of water. When the coughing subsided, he continued, 'There – on the wall...' He pointed to a particular painting. 'Just before nightfall, the sun will shine through the doorway. You must...' he gasped, swallowed, and forced himself to go on, '... must be ready.' He began coughing again and this time refused the drink. Giles and Lady Fayth eased him the rest of the way to the floor and made him more comfortable lying down.

'Be ready for what, Sir Henry?' asked Kit, kneeling beside him.

'Copy... the map.'

'The map?'

'The Skin Map.' The nobleman gestured vaguely at the painting. Kit moved to it for a closer look. The panel depicted a bald Egyptian in ceremonial kilt and ornate jewelled breastplate, holding a curiously shaped flat object in one hand and pointing towards the heavens with the other. The object in the Egyptian's hands looked a little like a scrap of papyrus that had been decorated with a random scattering of hieroglyphics. Kit held his face closer and recognized the tiny whorls and line-pierced spiral designs. 'Copy them,' urged Sir Henry. 'Use them to further the search.'

'We will copy them, Uncle,' said Lady Fayth. 'But you must rest now. Do not speak. Save your strength.' She offered the bowl again.

'Ah,' he sighed. 'Thank you, my child.' He seemed to be sinking further beneath the illness that was killing him.

'The symbols on the map, Sir Henry,' said Kit. 'We don't know how to read them. Can you tell us?'

'He died peacefully,' said Sir Henry, almost dreamily, 'knowing he had passed the torch to you. He put all his hope in you, Kit. He was content.'

'The symbols, Sir Henry,' persisted Kit. 'Can you tell us what they mean? We don't know how to use them.'

But the nobleman had closed his eyes. 'Sir Henry?' There was no reply.

'He is sleeping now.' Lady Fayth pressed his hand, and then rose. 'We will let him rest.'

Kit turned to Giles. 'We have to find some way to copy the symbols,' Kit told him. 'We can put them in the green book, but we have to find something to write with.'

A quick search of the chamber failed to turn up a single useful item and, with great reluctance, both men turned towards the sarcophagus. 'Do you think he might have had something we can use, sir?' asked Giles.

'Maybe,' allowed Kit doubtfully. 'I suppose we should look.'

'With your permission, sir,' said Giles, moving to the coffin. Kit nodded and the coachman began going through Cosimo's pockets. He quickly finished and reported that he had found nothing.

'Then I guess that's it,' sighed Kit. He ran his hands over his face as a tremendous fatigue drew over him. 'What a mess I've made of this – this whole thing.'

'You were not to know, sir,' Giles told him.

Evening came on and, as Sir Henry had said, a shaft of sunlight through the vestibule brightened the interior of the tomb. Kit, feeling helpless, stood before the painting and tried to memorize the dozen or so symbols on the painted map so that he might reproduce them later. Giles and Lady Fayth joined him, each taking a section of the painting; but there were too many and the opportunity was all too brief. They were able to commit only a paltry few to memory before the sunlight faded, gradually dimming away until darkness claimed the tomb of Anen.

Sir Henry continued to sleep, his breath heavy and laboured. Kit, fatigued by the shocks and alarms of the day, began to hurt. His ribs ached, his head throbbed, the muscles in his neck and arms burned, and he seemed to have been peppered all over with bruises. He settled into a convenient corner and found himself next to Lady Fayth. 'So,' he said, sliding down beside her, 'your name is Haven. I didn't know that.'

'A lady does not give her name to just anyone,' she replied primly.

'But we've known each other for days and days.' He could not decide whether to be offended or by how much, but in any case was too tired to protest further.

'You were wonderful,' she told him, and he heard her sigh. 'So very gallant.'

'You weren't so bad yourself,' replied Kit, a sudden warmth spreading through his aching limbs. 'Where did you learn to fight like that?'

'I have two elder brothers.'

'That would explain it.'

'I am so sorry about your grandfather,' she said. Kit felt her fingers on his arm. 'So very sorry.'

'Thanks,' he said. Overcome by an oppressive exhaustion, he yawned and the movement brought instant pain to his jaw. When the pain subsided, he whispered, 'Goodnight… Haven.'

'Goodnight, Kit,' she whispered back. He closed his eyes and it seemed that he had just drifted off when he was being nudged awake again. 'Hmm?'

'Shh!' hissed Lady Fayth. 'Someone is coming.'

Kit made to sit up and the effort renewed all his aches and pains. 'Ohh…'

The chamber was still dark, but less dark than it had been before. A thin light trickled into the cell from the vestibule beyond. The light grew brighter and then there was a lantern being held up to the grate. 'Well, well, well – what have we here?' The booming voice resounded in the bare chamber. Kit came fully awake. He turned to look at Lady Fayth, who was on her knees beside him. 'Looks like everyone is present and accounted for now.'

The face at the grate, as revealed by the lantern, was vaguely handsome in a horsy sort of way, with a luxurious moustache and large dark eyes; but there was a ruthlessness about the mouth that gave the lie to the overall genial impression.

'Let us go, Burleigh,' said Kit, climbing to his feet. Giles rose and came to stand beside him.

'So, you know who I am. And I know you. Isn't this splendid?'

'Keeping us captive won't get you anywhere.'

'It may surprise you,' replied Lord Burleigh, 'but I am rather inclined to agree with you. Oh, I must say, the atmosphere down here is most foul! However do you put up with it?'

'That's all your fault. Cosimo is dead, and Sir Henry here is –'

'Yes, yes,' interrupted Burleigh quickly, 'it is all very grim. So, let us not waste time wallowing in blame and recrimination. I propose we work this out between us. The simplest thing would be for us to join forces to work together for the common good – one hand washing the other. Help me find the Skin Map. Pledge yourselves to my service, and I will set you free.'

'You can't be serious.'

'You will rot in here just as your great-grandfather did, and as Sir Henry soon will. It's the miasma of the tomb, or the mummy's curse, or some such thing, you see? Carries one off just like that!'

'We'd be crazy to join you,' spat Kit. 'Murderer!'

'So be it,' replied Burleigh with a shrug. Withdrawing the lantern, he prepared to leave. Then, turning back, he addressed Lady Fayth, who was kneeling at her uncle's side. 'What about you, Haven? Does this rash young man speak for you as well?'

Silence, deep as the tomb in which they stood, descended upon them. No one moved, hardly daring to even look at one another. Then, slowly, Lady Fayth rose to her feet.

'Haven?' Kit said, breaking the silence.

She crossed to him and held out her hand. 'Uncle's journal,' she said. 'I want it.'

'You can't –'

'Give me the book!' she demanded. When he made no move to obey, she snaked a slender hand into his pocket and extricated the cloth-wrapped book. Kit grabbed her wrist.

'He's your uncle – your own flesh and blood! How can you betray him?'

'Unhand me,' she said, pulling free of his grasp. She moved towards the door.

'Think what you're doing!' shouted Kit.

'I know full well what I am doing,' she replied coolly. A key clanked in the lock and Burleigh pulled open the door. She glanced at Giles. 'You can come with me if you like.'

The servant regarded Sir Henry stretched on the floor and then shook his head. 'No, my lady. My place is here.'

'I thought as much.' She walked through the open door.

'Nicely done, my dear,' Burleigh told her, relieving her of the green book. 'Nicely done, indeed.'

'Haven, no!' Kit darted after her. 'What about Sir Henry – you can't just leave him to die.'

'My uncle's life is over,' she replied as the door began to close once more. 'See for yourself. My life, on the other hand, has only just begun.'

'No!' shouted Kit. 'You can't do this.' He rushed to the door and threw himself against it. But the Burley Men on the other side forced the grate shut and locked it again. 'Listen, Burleigh – wait!' cried Kit. 'Don't leave us here. You have what you want; let us go.'

'You had your chance,' replied the departing voice. 'Goodbye, Mr Livingstone. I do not expect we will meet again.'

In Which it is Darkest Before the Dawn

The footsteps in the passage faded and silence reclaimed the tomb. Kit stood in the darkness, blind, mute, and unmoving. The enormity of the betrayal and the swiftness with which it had taken place took his breath away. He felt dead inside, hollow, as if his entrails had been carved out with a dull spoon. Whatever Giles was feeling, he kept it to himself. It was a long time before either of them could speak, and then it was Giles who said, 'That was ill done.'

Fairly shaking with anger and humiliation, Kit finally mustered enough composure to ask, 'Why didn't you join her, Giles? You could have walked free.'

'My loyalty is to Sir Henry.' After a moment, he added, 'And to those who are loyal to him.'

'Thank you,' Kit said. 'But it may well cost you your life. You know that, don't you?'

'Yes, sir,' came a soft reply. 'I do.'

'Well, then,' said Kit. He fumbled in the darkness for the nearest wall and sat down with his back against it. Kit heard Giles moving, feeling his way along the wall. He stopped at the place Sir Henry lay.

'Sir Henry is dead,' Giles confirmed, his voice ringing hollow in the chamber. 'He must have expired in the night.' He paused. 'Should we do something for him?'

'We will,' said Kit after a moment. 'As soon as it gets light.'

He closed his eyes, but sleep was the last thing on his mind. How, he wondered – how in the name of all that is holy could he have been so stupid? How could he have got tangled up in such a reckless and ill-conceived scheme? How could he have come here so staggeringly unprepared to rescue anybody? Rescue! The word mocked him. The whole affair was an absolute, unmitigated catastrophe: Cosimo and Sir Henry dead, he and Giles captured, and Lady Fayth allied with the enemy. *Well done, Kit. Pin a medal on your chest, you bloody genius.*

He was a stranger in a strange land: lost in the cosmos, a man with neither compass nor guide, sitting in a tomb in Egypt surrounded by the dead, with Giles – a man his own age, but separated by class and sensibility and four hundred years of enculturation – looking to him for answers. He had none: only questions, the chief of which was how could he have been so utterly asinine?

The internal accusations and recriminations scalded his psyche and seared his soul. The disgrace – the disgrace of so monumental a failure dragged at his heart with almost unbearable weight. Despite his best efforts to stifle them, hot tears of shame leaked from his eyes and rolled down his cheeks as Kit descended into abject misery. This failure was his alone, and now he would have to pay the price. Tragically, he had dragged others into his half-baked scheme and now they would pay, too: Giles with his life, and Lady Fayth with her honour, whatever might be left of it. And that was another thing! He had trusted her and, trusting her, had allowed himself to be manipulated by her. The realization that he had been completely taken in by that pretty face made the disgrace complete.

These unhappy thoughts, and a clamouring host just like them, occupied Kit through the remainder of the night. Eventually, the darkness of the tomb began receding with the dawn of a new day. As soon as he could make out the outline of the stone sarcophagus, Kit crept close and knelt down beside it. 'I am sorry, Cosimo,' he whispered, steeling himself for a glance at the cold, stiff corpse of his great-grandfather. 'I have failed you… failed everyone. I am so very sorry.' He forced himself to look into the pale, lifeless face, etching it in his memory. There was a peacefulness about it that surprised him, but it was clear that what he saw in the sarcophagus was the mere shell of the man that had been. Cosimo was no longer there. 'If I ever get a chance to make things right, I will. I promise you, I will.'

He put all his hope in you... were the last words Sir Henry had said to him. His own father and grandfather had, for some reason, proven unsuitable. Now it was Kit's turn. Was he any more capable than they?

Faint stirrings of determination quickened his heart. First they had to get out. Kit began pacing the length of the chamber – arms outstretched, fingers splayed, sifting the air for that tell-tale tingle of a ley field. He felt nothing, but still did not give up. He tried jumping – once and again – in various locations in the tomb, to no avail. Not that he had expected anything to happen. After all, if there had been a ley portal or hub in the tomb, Cosimo would have found it.

Admitting defeat, he went to where Giles sat by Sir Henry. He knelt beside the body stretched out on the floor of the tomb and observed him for a moment. No breath stirred his chest, no pulse flickered at his throat. Just to be certain, Kit lightly pressed his fingertips to Sir Henry's wrist, then applied them to the side of his neck. 'I'm sorry, Giles,' he said.

'We cannot leave him like this,' said the coachman. 'We should do something.'

'Come on, we can put him in the sarcophagus.'

Together they lifted the body and carried it to the huge granite coffin in the centre of the room; they gently lowered it in, carefully placing it beside Cosimo.

They then straightened the nobleman's limbs and folded his hands across his chest. 'Friends in life,' said Kit, 'they can keep one another company in death.'

Even as he spoke the sound of light footsteps on the stairs leading down into the tomb echoed from the vestibule beyond. Whoever it was moved quickly and quietly.

Kit rushed to the iron grate. 'Burleigh! Let us out. Killing us makes no sense. This is madness! Let us out.' He paused to listen.

The footsteps faltered as the intruder entered the vestibule and paused. Then there was the quick patter of feet as the newcomer hurried across the empty chamber. 'Burleigh! Do you hear me?'

'Kit? Are you in there?'

The voice was soft and feminine, and despite all that had transpired since he had left the only world he had ever known that day in an alleyway in Islington, Kit recognized it instantly. 'Wilhelmina!'

And there she was: Wilhelmina, tanned and radiant, gazing back at him through the grate. Dressed in a zippered military jumpsuit with a desert camouflage pattern, her long hair was upswept and tucked beneath a sky-blue scarf which she wore in the manner of the Egyptian women. Tall and slim as ever, the dark circles were gone from beneath her eyes, and her skin glowed with robust good health. She held a small oval-shaped brass object in one hand, and a large iron key in the other. The object was emitting a soft turquoise glow. 'Had enough of Burleigh's hospitality?' she asked with a smile.

'I can't believe it,' said Kit. 'What are you doing here?'

'I've come to break you out – you and your friends.' She put the key in the lock and jiggled it around.

'Mina! Mina, I was trying to find you. I never abandoned you – you have to believe me. I didn't know where you were, or how to reach you. Cosimo went back for you, but you weren't there, so we asked Sir Henry to help. That's what all this is about – trying to find you.'

'And here I am, finding you,' she said, smiling sweetly. 'We'd better hurry. We don't have much time.'

'But how – ?'

Giles put his head around the corner. 'Sir?'

'Oh, Giles, step up here. This is Wilhelmina Klug,' he said. 'Mina, meet Giles Standfast.'

'Glad to meet you, Giles,' said Wilhelmina.

'An unexpected pleasure, my lady,' replied Giles.

Wilhelmina jostled the key again, gave it a twist, and the lock clicked. She pulled and the heavy iron grate swung open, releasing the two captives. Kit stepped into the vestibule and into Wilhelmina's arms – their embrace the slightly hesitant and awkward clasp of familiar strangers. Kit understood in that moment that she was no longer the woman he knew; the change was fundamental and profound. 'Thank you, Mina,' he whispered, holding her close, trying to recapture something of their old intimacy.

'My pleasure,' she said, releasing him. 'We'd best be off.'

'I'm sorry,' he said. 'About losing you, getting everyone mixed up in this… I'm sorry about everything.'

'Don't be,' she said brightly. 'It was the best thing that ever happened to me.' She turned and started for the stone staircase. Kit hesitated. 'What's wrong?'

'It's Cosimo and Sir Henry – they're dead,' Kit told her, gesturing to the tomb behind him. 'We can't just abandon them – walk away as if nothing happened.'

'Oh.' She stood in the dim light of the chamber for a moment, gazing through the open grate and into the tomb; she made no move to enter. 'I'm sorry, Kit, I really am,' she said at last. 'But if we don't leave now we will join them. There's nothing more we can do. We have to go.' She softened then, adding, 'Look at it this way – what better resting place than a royal tomb?'

Giles came alongside him. 'She is right, sir. The gentlemen are beyond our help, and it avails us nothing to remain here. "Let the dead bury the dead" – so it is written, is it not?'

'I suppose,' allowed Kit, still unpersuaded. 'It just doesn't seem right.'

'If we go now, there is a chance we can come back and make it right,' suggested Wilhelmina. 'But we do have to go.'

Kit accepted this assurance and put aside his qualms. 'Lead the way, Mina.'

Crossing the chamber in quick strides, she paused at the foot of the steps to listen. Hearing nothing from the wadi above, she started up the stairs. 'Stay close,' she said, her smile beguiling. 'You really don't want to get lost.'

Epilogue

The stranger paused before the porter's lodge and rang the small bell attached to the doorpost. To the square-hatted head that poked out from the tiny window, he said, 'Bursar Cakebread, if you please.'

'And who might you be?' demanded the porter.

'Flinders-Petrie.'

'Oh!' exclaimed the stubby little man. 'Very sorry, sir. I did not recognize you.' He bowled from the lodge. 'This way, sir, if you please to follow me.'

The visitor was led through the gate and along the inner quad to the office of the bursar of Christ Church. The porter knocked on the door, and a voice from inside said, 'Enter!'

The visitor thanked the porter, removed his hat, and opened the door. 'Bursar Cakebread, is it?'

'I am, sir. I am. Whom do I have the pleasure of addressing, if I may be so bold?'

'I am Douglas Flinders-Petrie,' declared the visitor. 'I think you will have had my recent correspondence.'

'Ah! Mister Flinders-Petrie! To be sure, sir. I received your letter only yesterday. Please, do come in and sit down.' He escorted his visitor into his snuggery of an office. 'May I offer you some sherry?'

'Thank you, no. My visit to Oxford is regrettably all too brief. I must leave again within the hour, but I wanted to see you before I go.'

The bursar sat down behind his table, heaped high with account books and papers. 'How may I be of service to you, sir?'

'As I communicated in my letter, I have come into a considerable inheritance and wish to endow a chair at an Oxford college, to be named after my late grandfather, the philosopher and explorer Benedict Flinders-Petrie. Perhaps you have heard of him?'

'And who has not, sir? I ask myself – who has not heard of the illustrious Flinders-Petrie? His benefactions to this very institution are well known, sir – well known.'

Douglas smiled. 'As you can imagine, I will require the aid of someone strategically placed in college to help guide the process. To steer the application through the proper channels and keep it from running aground, as it were.' He reached into a large leather wallet and pulled out a bag of coins, untied it and began counting gold sovereigns into his palm. 'Naturally, I am prepared to reward the person who undertakes this charge on my behalf.'

The bursar gazed in wonder at the gleaming coins. 'It goes without saying, I hope, that I stand ready to aid your enterprise with all dispatch.'

'Splendid,' replied Douglas. 'I am so glad to hear it.' He placed a neat stack of coins on the table. 'We will consider this but the first blush of appreciation,' he said, pushing the money towards the bursar. 'Naturally, once the chair is established, I will require someone to aid in its maintenance – and for this I am prepared to be most appreciative.'

'Say no more, sir. Say no more!'

'Good.' Douglas Flinders-Petrie rose to go; he leaned over the desk, his lanky form towering over the squat bursar. 'I knew I could count on you, Mr Cakebread – even as I know I can count on your complete discretion.'

'It goes without saying, sir – goes without saying.' He rose and followed his guest to the door. 'Was there anything else, sir? Anything at all?'

'No, I do not believe –' began Douglas, who paused and, as if on sudden inspiration, added, 'Now that you mention it, I believe I will have need of somewhere secure to keep various items – important documents, charters, and the like – which will be used to support my application for the endowment chair.'

'Certainly, sir,' said the very agreeable bursar. 'I have just the place.'

'Could I see it now, do you think?'

'To be sure, sir.' Bursar Cakebread jumped to his feet. 'I can show it to you straightaway – it is in the chapel crypt.'

Douglas was led to the college chapel and down into the crypt where, in the flickering light of a hastily kindled torch, he saw a small, dry room with a table surrounded by wooden chests and iron-clad strongboxes. 'Yes,' he said, appreciatively. 'This will do nicely. Is there a chest I might use?'

'This one here is empty, sir,' replied the bursar. He fumbled with a large iron ring for the key.

'That won't be necessary,' said Douglas, relieving him of the ring. 'If you wouldn't mind waiting for me upstairs, I'll find it myself.' He smiled, backing the bursar towards the door. 'I won't be but a moment. I'll rejoin you in your office.'

'As you wish, sir – as you wish,' replied the bursar. 'I'll wait for you upstairs, then. Please, take your time.'

Closing the door behind the bursar, he listened until he heard the man's footsteps on the stairs, and then went directly to a chest in the corner. After a few tries, he found the key that worked, unlocked the chest and opened it. There, among some bundled parchments and scrolls, he spied a cloth-wrapped bundle tied with black ribbon. 'At last,' he whispered. 'I've moved heaven and earth to find you.'

He lifted the roll and placed it on the nearby table. There, fingers shaking with suppressed excitement, he untied the ribbon and drew away the cloth to reveal a long, irregular roll of parchment so papery and fine as to be almost translucent. Carefully, carefully, he unrolled a portion of the scroll to reveal a number of bright blue symbols etched on the surface of the scroll.

'How do you do, Grandfather?' he said. 'Am I pleased to meet you! You have no idea.'

Then, as if fearing to be overheard, he pulled a roll of parchment from an inside coat pocket and quickly wrapped it, retying the ribbon. Replacing the substituted scroll, he locked the chest, tucked the purloined parchment into the inner pocket and left the room.

Bursar Cakebread was waiting for him when he emerged from the crypt. 'I hope you found everything to your satisfaction, sir.'

'It was nothing less than I expected,' Douglas replied, passing the key back to the bursar. 'I will return one day soon. I trust you will keep my visits to yourself – until such time as the announcement of the chair is made public.'

'My lips are sealed, sir.'

'Then I will wish you a good day, Bursar Cakebread.'

'And to you, sir – and to you.'

Upon leaving the college, Flinders-Petrie walked up the road towards Cornmarket Street. As he neared the crossroads, he saw a crowd of people had gathered in the street around a small one-horse chaise. He slowed as he drew near and saw that there had been an accident: a small boy had been hit and knocked down in the street. The little fellow was bleeding from a cut to the side of his face and he was crying, but he was sitting up and some of the townsfolk were ministering to him. A little to one side stood another small boy and it was this lad's remarkable appearance that arrested Douglas's interest.

The boy, barefoot and dirty-faced, dressed in filthy rags, had a head two sizes too big for his small sturdy body. That, along with pale flaxen hair and tiny eyes the colour of slate, gave him an almost supernatural appearance. He stood glowering at the injured lad, clearly hating him with every fibre of his little being, though he was but six or seven years old.

His interest piqued, Douglas stopped. 'What's happened here?'

One of the nearest bystanders replied, 'That one there pushed t'other in front o'carriage, the little devil. Like to have killed the child. Lucky thing t'driver saw him an' pulled up.'

'Is he hurt?'

'Don't think so. Got a nasty jolt, I reckon.'

Then, even as they were discussing the situation, the odd-looking ruffian stepped forward and kicked his young adversary in the head. The injured boy collapsed and his attacker kicked him again – and would have gone on kicking him in full view of the bystanders if he had not been roughly pulled away. 'Here, you!' shouted the man restraining him. 'Stop that! Someone call the bailiff!'

'That won't be necessary,' said Douglas Flinders-Petrie, pushing through the crowd. 'I'll take responsibility.'

He moved quickly to the smouldering child, interposing himself between the boy and the crowd. 'Listen, you little guttersnipe,' he hissed, bending over him. 'Come with me now if you want to stay out of gaol.' Then, taking the boy by the hand, he began leading him away.

'Oi! You there!' called one of the citizens. 'You know that boy?'

'Yes,' called Douglas over his shoulder. He kept walking. 'It's all right.'

'Are you his father?' called another onlooker.

'Yes,' he answered, then added under his breath, 'I am now.'

CHAPTER 1

In Which
Some Things are
Best Forgotten

From a snug in the corner of the Museum Tavern, Douglas Flinders-Petrie dipped a sop of bread into the gravy of his steak and kidney pudding and watched the entrance to the British Museum across the street. The great edifice was dark, the building closed to the public for over three hours. The employees had gone home, the charwomen had finished their cleaning, and the high iron gates were locked behind them. The courtyard was empty and, outside the gates, there were fewer people on the street now than an hour ago. He felt no sense of urgency: only keen anticipation, which he savoured as he took another draught of London Pride. He had spent most of the afternoon in the museum, once more marking the doors and exits, the blind spots, the rooms where a person might hide and remain unseen by the night watchmen, of which there were but three to cover the entire acreage of the sprawling institution.

Douglas knew from his researches that at eleven each night the head watchman retired to his office on the ground floor to make tea. He would be duly joined by his two underling guards, and the three would enter their observations in the logbook and then spend an enjoyable thirty minutes drinking their tea, eating pies, and exchanging gossip.

While they were thus occupied, he would strike.

The pub was quiet tonight, even for a damp Thursday in late November. There were only five other patrons in the place: three at the rail and two at tables. He would have preferred more people – if only so his own presence would not be as noticeable – but he doubted it would make much difference. In any event, there was nothing he could do about it.

'Everything all right, sir?'

Douglas turned from the window and looked up. The landlord, having little to do this evening, was making the rounds and chatting with his customers.

'Never better,' replied Douglas in a tone he hoped would dismiss further intrusion. But the man remained hovering over the table.

'Mr Flinders-Petrie, is it not, sir?'

'Indeed so.' He offered a bland smile to cover his annoyance at being recognized on this night of all nights. 'I fear you have me at a disadvantage. I was not aware that my name would be common knowledge.'

The landlord chuckled. 'No, I suppose not. But do you not recognize me, sir?'

Douglas looked more closely at him. There was a vague familiarity about the fellow, but… no, he could not place him.

'Cumberbatch, sir,' the landlord volunteered. 'I worked for your father, I did. Oh, quite a few years ago.' At Douglas's dubious expression, he said, 'I was his footman – Silas.'

'Silas! Certainly, I remember you,' Douglas lied. 'Do forgive me. Yes, of course, now that you remind me.'

' 'Course, I was younger then, and you were away at school and university and whatnot.' The landlord wiped his hands on the towel around his waist and smoothed it out as if this put the matter to rest. 'Happy days they were.'

'Yes, yes,' agreed Douglas amiably. He was aware that the other patrons were watching them, and actually relieved now that the place was not more crowded. 'Happy times, indeed.'

'Pardon my asking, sir,' said Cumberbatch, leaning nearer the table. He lowered his voice. 'If you don't mind, there's something that I've always wanted to know. I'd be most obliged.'

'I'd be happy to help if I can, Silas. What is it?'

'Did they ever find the man who killed your father?'

To buy himself a little space to think, Douglas took a drink of his ale, then, placing the glass carefully on the table, said, 'I am sorry to say they never did.'

'Oh dear, oh dear.' Cumberbatch shook his head. 'That's a right pity. Did they never have a suspicion, then?'

'Suspicions, yes,' replied Douglas, 'but nothing more. The coroner's verdict at the time of the inquest reads "unlawful killing by person or persons unknown". At this late date, I fear it is likely to remain a mystery.'

'Ah, dear me,' sighed Cumberbatch. 'That is a shame, that is. He was a good man, your father – a very decent chap, if you don't mind my saying. A solid and upright fellow – always treated me well, and that's a fact, that is.'

'Yes, well, as you say it was all a long time ago. Perhaps it is best forgotten.'

'No doubt, sir. I'm with you there.' Cumberbatch brightened once more. 'But it is good to see you, Mr Flinders-Petrie. Here, now, can I get you another pint?'

'Thank you, but no, I –'

'On the house, sir – for old time's sake. It would please me no end.'

'Very well, then. Thank you, Silas. I would enjoy that.'

'Coming right up, sir.'

The landlord beetled off to pull the pint. Douglas drew his pocket-watch from his waistcoat and flipped it open. It was half past nine. In another hour he would make his move. Until then, he had a warm place to wait and watch. The landlord returned with his pint and, after another brief exchange, he was left alone to finish it and his meal in peace.

It was after ten thirty when he finally rose and, promising to return for another visit next time he was in the neighbourhood, retrieved his black cape from the coat-rack and went out into the mist and drizzle. The weather was perfect for his purposes – a miserable night meant fewer folk around to notice any peculiar comings and goings. The gas lamps hissed and fluttered, pale orbs that did little to cut the all-pervading fog. Perfect.

He smiled to himself as he walked to the corner of Montague Street, turned, and proceeded along the side of the museum to where the service alley joined the street at the rear of the building. There he paused to observe the street one last time; a lone hansom cab rattled away in the opposite direction, and two men in top hats staggered along – one in the gutter, the other on the pavement – oblivious to their surroundings, singing their way home from an evening's celebration.

Satisfied, he ducked into the alleyway and hurried quickly and unerringly in the dark to the back of a town house opposite the rear of the museum. There, lying in the lane beside the house, was the wooden ladder. With swift efficiency, he placed it against the high iron railing, climbed to the top of the fence, balanced on the upper bar while he pulled over the ladder, then climbed down. Once on the ground, he hurried to a window near the corner of the enormous building where even the lowest windows were eight feet off the ground. Positioning the ladder, he climbed up and rapped on the glass, counted to ten, and then rapped again.

As he finished the second tap, the window slid open from inside and a pale face, round like a solemn little moon, appeared in the darkness of the opening.

'Well done, Snipe,' said Douglas. 'Hand me in.'

The stocky boy reached out and, with strong arms, pulled his master through the open window.

'Now then,' said Douglas, drawing a small tin from his pocket. He flipped open the lid and shook out a few congreves, selected one, and swiped the head against the roughened top of the tin. The slender stick of soft pine erupted with a pop and spluttering red flame. 'The lantern, Snipe.'

The youth held up a small paraffin lamp; Douglas raised the glass and touched the match to the wick, then lowered the glass and waved the spent stick in the air to cool it before placing it back in the tin. 'Let us be about our business.'

By lantern's glow they made their way through the darkened stacks of the Smirke Bequest – a small, shelf-lined chamber off the great cavernous hall of the Reading Room. This cosy enclave was given to certain exceptional volumes from the libraries of wealthy patrons who had donated or bequeathed their collections to the national archive for the general benefit of their fellow men. This ever-growing collection housed a particular volume that had long eluded Douglas Flinders-Petrie. It was this book he had come to acquire.

The Rare Books Room, as it was more commonly known, was strictly forbidden to all but the most eminent scholars, and then entry was granted only in the company of the Keeper of Antiquities or one of his assistants, who would unlock the chain at the doorway – there was no door, so that the books could be viewed from a distance even if they could not be perused – and usher the chosen one into the inner sanctum. White cotton gloves were to be worn at all times in the room, and no one was permitted to remain alone in the stacks at any time whatsoever. Douglas, having observed this exacting protocol on his survey trips to the museum, decided to forego the formalities and visit the room outside of public hours.

It had then been a matter of finding a place for Snipe to hide until well after closing: a storage cupboard in Room 55 on the upper floor was adequate to the purpose, and so, during a late-afternoon viewing of the Nineveh alabasters, Douglas had deposited his able servant in the closet with a cold pie and an apple to wait until the clock in Saint Bartholomew's chimed eleven. At the appointed hour, Snipe had crawled out and made his way down to the Rare Books Room to let Douglas in through the window.

So far so good.

'Go to the door and keep watch,' Douglas commanded, directing the glow of the lantern towards the nearer stacks. As the servant moved to the doorway, Douglas began scanning the shelves. The books, he quickly discovered, were arranged in a loose chronological order – no doubt owing to their primary interest as artefacts rather than for the value of their contents. He found the proper historical period and started working down the line book by book. What should have been a task of moments, however, dragged on far longer than he planned, owing to the fact that many of the older books had no titles on their spines or covers and had to be drawn out, opened, and thumbed to their title pages before being placed back on the shelf.

He was only partway through the 1500s when he heard a sibilant hiss – like that of gas escaping from a leaky pipe. He stopped, held his breath… waited. The sound came again and was repeated. He quickly turned down the lantern wick and put the lamp on the floor, then hurried to the doorway, where Snipe stood behind the doorpost, peering out into the great hall of the main reading room.

'Someone coming?' Douglas whispered.

Snipe nodded and held up two fingers.

'Two of them. Right.' Douglas turned and retreated into the stacks. 'Follow me.'

They crept off to the furthest corner of the room, placing the main body of stacks between themselves and the door.

'Get down,' whispered Douglas.

The two pressed themselves flat to the floor and waited. Voices drifted into the room, and then footsteps could be heard as the watchmen made their rounds of the Reading Room. Shadows leapt from the stacks as one of the guards paused and shone his lantern into the room with a practised sweep. Then the footsteps receded and the voices resumed. The watchmen were moving off.

'That's better,' sighed Douglas. 'Back to work.'

The two returned to their respective places and began again. Midway through the 1500s, Douglas found the book he was looking for – exactly as he had pictured it from his researches. One glimpse of the strange cipher writing and he knew he had it.

'Come to me, my pretty,' he whispered, carefully placing the light on the shelf beside him. With trembling fingers, Douglas opened the book to reveal page after page of tightly ordered script in the most fanciful-looking letters he had ever seen. 'You little beauty,' he mused, brushing his fingertips lightly over the script. He might have spent a happy hour or so paging through the old curiosity – and he would – but now was not the time. He slipped the slim volume into an inner pocket of his cape, retrieved the lantern, and hurried to fetch Snipe.

'I've got it. Come away – time to make good our escape.'

They climbed out the window, closing it carefully behind them, and retraced their inward journey, replacing the ladder at the rear of the town house opposite before walking back down the alley to Montague Street. Douglas's mind was so filled with the book and the treasures it was certain to yield that he failed to see the policeman standing in the pool of light under the streetlamp. Emerging from the darkness of the alley like the guilty thieves they were, the pair naturally drew the interest of the policeman, who, raising his truncheon, called out, 'Well, well, what have we here?'

'Oh!' gasped Douglas, spinning around to face the officer. 'Good evening, constable. You quite gave me a start.'

'Did I now!' He looked the pair up and down, his expression suggesting he did not care for what he saw. 'Might I ask why you were lurking in that alley at this time of night?'

Douglas's hand went to the gun in his pocket. 'Is it that late?' he asked affably. 'I hadn't realized. Yes, I suppose it is.' He glanced at Snipe beside him. The boy's lip was curled in a ferocious scowl. 'It's the lad here,' he offered. 'He ran away earlier this evening, and I've been looking for him ever since – only just found him a few minutes ago.'

The constable, frowning now, stepped closer. 'That your son, then?'

'Good heavens, no,' replied Douglas. 'He's a servant. I'm taking him home with me.' As if to underscore this fact, he put his hand to Snipe's collar.

The policeman's brow furrowed as he caught a glare of almost pure hatred playing over the boy's pallid features. Certainly, there was something odd about the youth that meant he could never have been mistaken for anyone's beloved son. 'I see,' concluded the police officer. 'Does he run away often, then?'

'No, no, never before,' Douglas hastily assured him. 'There was a bit of a kerfuffle with the housekeeper, you see, and the lad took umbrage. A simple misunderstanding. I think I've straightened it out.'

'Well,' said the policeman, 'these things happen, I suppose.' He returned the truncheon to the hook on his belt. 'You best get yourselves home. It's high time all respectable folk were abed.'

'Just what I was thinking, constable. A pot of cocoa and a biscuit wouldn't go amiss either, I daresay.' Douglas released his hold on the pistol, but maintained his grip on the boy's collar. 'I will wish you good night.' Douglas started away, pulling the glaring Snipe with him.

'G'night, sir.' The policeman watched them as they moved away. 'Mind how you go,' he called. 'There are thieves and such about. It's weather like this brings 'em out.'

'You're not wrong there, matey,' murmured Douglas under his breath. 'Come away, Snipe. Tonight we let him live.'